**Praise for *New York Times* bestseller Grace Burrowes's
rule-breaking, unforgettable Regency romance**

Darius

"Delightfully different… Burrowes brings to life a deeply
moving romance that's sure to be remembered and treasured."

—*RT Book Reviews* Top Pick, 4.5 Stars

"This rising author handles powerful romance and complicated family life with skill in romances with great appeal."

—*Booklist*

"Page-turning, breathtaking reading… Once I started reading this tale of redemption, I didn't want to put it down…
Grace Burrowes enchants."

—*Long and Short Reviews*

"Steamy… very compelling… a scorching tale of seduction
and intrigue."

—*Night Owl Reviews* Top Pick, 4.5 Stars

"Brilliant… The plot was unlike any romance novel that
I have previously read and yet the romance arc was both
realistic and believable."

—*The Royal Reviews*

"[Burrowes's] writing is sublime and even more importantly, so is her characterization."

—*All About Romance*

Nicholas

"Exquisite... breathtaking and heartwarming."

—*Long and Short Reviews*

"Infused with secrets, humor, betrayal, tender romance, sexual tension, and love, this story will have readers eagerly turning the pages amid tears and laughter."

—*Romance Junkies*

"Red-hot chemistry that's sexy as heck, yet sweetly romantic."

—*Drey's Library*

"Grace Burrowes creates characters that are emotionally damaged but still manage to be the most forgiving and caring and courageous individuals you could possibly imagine... I always find myself wanting to step into the pages of the book, so I can simply hug the dickens out of these characters, and I'm betting you will, too."

—*Novels Alive TV*

"Another beautifully written story. The characters are wonderful, and the story definitely holds your interest... Highly recommended."

—*Romantic Historical Lovers*

"Ms. Burrowes continually presses the bar and goes above and beyond the normal to give her readers phenomenal love stories that keep us manic for more."

—*Romantic Crush Junkies EZine*

LORD *of* REGRETS

GABRIEL

GRACE BURROWES

sourcebooks
casablanca

Published by Sourcebooks Casablanca, an imprint of Sourcebooks,
Inc.
P.O. Box 4410, Naperville, Illinois 60567-4410
(630) 961-3900
Fax: (630) 961-2168
sourcebooks.com

Printed and bound in Canada.
MBP 10 9 8 7 6 5 4 3 2

To the farmers and the artists,
without whom, we would all surely starve

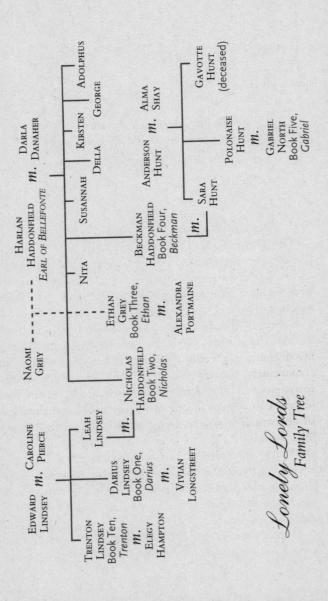

Lonely Lords
Family Tree

One

"IT'S TIME I ROSE FROM THE DEAD."

The Dowager Marchioness of Warne eyed her guest placidly over her teacup, despite the impact of his words.

Oh, to be thirty years younger—even twenty. "Is that wise, Gabriel? You never did get to the bottom of all that mischief in Spain."

Gabriel Wendover rose to his considerable height and paced to the window overlooking the back gardens. "Here's my dilemma: my younger brother is one of few who can convincingly identify me. If I don't emerge from my convalescence now, Aaron could well drink himself into oblivion, or engage in one too many duels, and then I'm an opportunistic poseur, trying to do battle with Prinny's legal weasels."

"Surely your former fiancée could identify you." Lady Warne enjoyed the view of her guest from the back almost as much as she did from the front. He was all lean, elegant muscle now, though two years ago he'd been at death's door.

"I'm not sure I'd trust Marjorie that far." Gabriel turned away from his study of the flowers. "As Aaron's wife, and the Marchioness of Hesketh, she now commands significant wealth and respect. If she's simply the wife of a younger son, she gets a great deal less."

"But an adequate portion to survive on?"

"Of course." His features shuttered, and an idea popped into her ladyship's mind.

"Does this sudden urge to come out of the shadows have to do with a woman, Gabriel?"

Not by the flicker of a dark eyelash did he betray any reaction to the question, and in his stillness, Lady Warne found a hint of confirmation that she'd guessed correctly.

"Why would you suggest that?"

She went to stand beside him, close enough that the afternoon sun revealed fatigue around his eyes and mouth. "Two years ago, you were done searching for justice, done trying to figure out who wished you dead. You took over stewarding Three Springs for me, and despite all odds to the contrary, you made it prosper. I thought you were content there and would finish out your days as plain Gabriel North, humble, if taciturn, land steward."

"Taciturn?"

"Reserved." And because he was less than half her age, she allowed herself a smidgen of fun at his expense. "Brooding."

"I was recovering from a mortal wound. This does not incline a man to a sanguine demeanor." He fell silent. He was too dear a man, and she was too old not to wait him out. "My decision doesn't have to do with a woman, but rather, with the absence of a woman."

He was lonely, and he'd been lonely when they'd met two years ago, though it appeared he was now becoming *aware* of this sorry state of affairs. And when Gabriel Wendover saw a problem, he must needs address it.

"Surely, with your looks, you don't lack for female company?"

"And all my wit and charm?" He raised an eyebrow, and Lady Warne was put in mind of those ancient, rousing days when a man took by conquest and held by main strength. Gabriel would have prospered then, too—handily—and likely had his version of fun, bashing heads and bellowing war cries.

"You're as charming as you need to be," she observed, "though you don't prevaricate any better than my grandsons do."

His brilliant green eyes showed some emotion, humor perhaps, but so briefly that Lady Warne couldn't be sure of what she'd seen.

"As long as I turn my back on my birthright," he said, "I am unable to marry, unable to even dally, really, because I'm living a lie."

Clearly, Gabriel had never moved about much in society. "Dallying men are supposed to lie. It's part of the consideration due the ladies."

"Then I've lost the knack of dallying, if I ever had it." He crossed his arms over his chest, a gesture that to her ladyship looked more defensive than stubborn. "I can't risk that a woman close to me could become a victim of the same kind of violence that befell me, or see her used somehow as leverage against me."

"You've been brooding on this."

"Considering," he allowed. "I cannot resign myself to watching Aaron fritter away the family fortune, much less fritter away his life, so Prinny can snatch up the rewards when escheat befalls the title. If I'm going to be dead, I'd rather die battling my enemies than of mortification at my younger brother's moral collapse."

"He is young," Lady Warne pointed out. Everybody was young to her these days. "Maybe he'll come right if you give him a few more years."

"The longer I wait, the less credible any story of protracted delirium or lost memory becomes."

Gabriel was not merely lonely; he had fallen in love. The notion was startling and gratifying, and the only possible explanation for a radical departure from his well-laid, ridiculous plans of two years ago. "Maybe you were captured by gypsies and held as a prisoner until the gypsy princess fell in love with you and set you free."

His answering scowl was ferocious.

"What have I said?"

"Sara Hunt was known as the Gypsy Princess when she toured the Continent."

"She's Sara Haddonfield now." May God and a handsome grandson be thanked. "Married to my dear Beckman, and no longer a traveling musician playing for coin, or the lowly housekeeper raising her daughter at Three Springs. Beckman is arse over teakettle for his lady wife."

Gabriel flashed her a rare, precious smile. "My virgin ears. Such language."

"Your ears are no more virgin than your... the rest of you. What can I do to help?" Because she *would* help, will he, nil he.

"Ask your spies what they know about the goings-on at Hesketh," Gabriel said. "I know of three duels Aaron's been involved in over the past twelve months. I hear of particularly wicked house parties with his army cronies when his wife is up to Town, and Marjorie's bills would finance a cavalry unit and their mounts. This makes no sense to me. Aaron was fun loving, not reckless, and he was raised as the spare. He should know how to go on better than this now that he's Hesketh."

"Your papa's death was unexpected, as was your so-called demise," Lady Warne reminded him. "Men can misbehave badly when a title befalls them on short notice."

"So one hears."

"I'll listen to the gossip, but you're going to need allies if you intend to march off smartly to Hesketh and declare yourself alive and well."

"I can't ask others to put their lives in jeopardy merely because I'm feeling possessive of my title."

"Not possessive, protective."

"Both. I have one other favor to ask of you."

"Anything."

He looked momentarily nonplussed by the immediacy of her answer, and that gave her satisfaction. The man had been alone too long, probably since before his injury in Spain.

"I need a place to stay, somewhere nobody will think to look for me over the next week or so." He was gazing out over the asters and chrysanthemums again, his expression distant. "I must dress the part if I'm to make a grand reentrance at Hesketh, and I want to do some loitering in low places before I go home."

"You want to make the rounds." She looked him over, seeing the dusty boots, the threadbare morning coat, the cravat that sported not a hint of lace. "Gather intelligence. You are more than welcome to stay here, young man, but you'll tell me what news you come across, and I'll do likewise."

"My thanks, and my lady?"

"Hmm?"

"Be careful. Beckman, Nicholas, and the rest of your

tribe of grandchildren would flay me where I stood did I bring harm to you."

"Having a little project is more likely to keep a woman of my age *out* of trouble, I'll have you know. Now, if you want to restore your wardrobe, you will take my advice, for the tailors gossip as freely as the modistes."

"I'm listening."

Having made his request of her, he visibly relaxed, lounging back against the windowsill as they plotted and planned.

Oh, to be thirty years younger. Even twenty.

⁓

"You've eight commissions."

"Eight!?"

How it gratified Tremaine to see the incredulity on Polonaise Hunt's lovely face. "I accepted only eight, but I could have come away with twice that number."

The smile trying to break across Polly's face dimmed. "Do they know the artist is female?"

"They don't care." Which was the God's honest truth, not that Tremaine would attempt to dissemble. "They don't care that you may take three years to execute their various portraits; they don't care that you're going to bankrupt them for the privilege of waiting for you. All they care about is being able to crow that P. Hunt is under contract to them."

"Eight commissions." Polly sank down on a red velvet settee and wrapped her arms around her trim middle. "Heavens."

"And, my dear"—though she wasn't his dear; she was his late brother Reynard's sister-by-marriage, nothing more— "your show sold out." He appropriated the spot beside her on the sofa, contenting himself with physical proximity.

"Sold…" Polly stared hard at the carpet, as if a pattern

woven in red, gold, and cream wool required study. "People bought my paintings, just like that?"

"They tried to bid on them. Next time, we're having an auction."

"Next time." Polly hunched forward, the look on her face suggesting she'd forgotten Tremaine and her eight commissions, and was instead seeing paintings and arranging her subjects.

He touched her hand. "Does this call for a drink?"

"Just a tot. Years in service at Three Springs leaves a woman with little head for spirits."

"I had a letter from Beckman today." Tremaine brought her a balloon glass with the merest slosh of amber liquid in the bowl. Polly Hunt said what she meant and meant what she said. If she'd wanted a larger portion, she would have told him.

"How fares my sister's present spouse?" Polly took the drink and brought the glass to her nose, a facial feature that might be said to have character. Tremaine liked that nose, and liked her, more's the pity. He'd liked her the first time he'd encountered her nearly six years ago, wearing a paint-spattered smock and an impatient expression.

Dear Reynard had stashed both his wife and her younger sister in a rented flat in Vienna. The air had been frigid, the scent of boiled cabbage gaggingly thick, but all Tremaine had noticed was the dab of blue paint on Polly's nose and the ferocious concentration she'd turned on her canvas within two minutes of meeting him.

He resumed his place beside her. "Your sister is thriving in Beck's care, the harvest was excellent, that peculiar wheat of Beck's is coming along, and they've a crop of fall lambs from the Dorset rams."

"Lambs? Sara married a country squire, it seems."

"Who will tell anyone he meets that his wife's sister is the renowned—and wealthy—portrait artist Polonaise Hunt."

"Wealthy." Polly smiled softly, and Tremaine took a fortifying swallow of his drink. "How wealthy, Tremaine?"

He named a figure that had Polly's jaw dropping, then snapping shut.

"I'll need a solicitor," she said, "and I want to set up a trust, for Allie."

He had not anticipated this, but he should have. "Sara and Beck provide for her very well, and the first person you should be looking after is yourself."

"I am Allie's only aunt, the person with whom she shares artistic talent. The wealthy, famous, and all-that-other-nonsense-you-said P. Hunt can dote on her niece." Polly wasn't a tall woman, but when she rose, she had an imposing presence. Whereas her sister, Sara, was tall with flame-red hair and lithe curves, Polly was a smaller package, her hair a dark auburn and her curves—like her nose—more pronounced.

"Allie is part of the reason I've scheduled your first commission down by Portsmouth," Tremaine said, dodging the issue. Polly was Allemande's aunt, and Tremaine was her uncle—he knew well the urge to spoil the girl.

Polly leveled a stare at him that did not bode well for prevaricating males of any species. "A solicitor, Tremaine. The most shrewd, accomplished, expensive one you can find me."

He poured himself more brandy. Since he'd undertaken to act as agent for Polly's art, Tremaine's consumption of spirits had risen while his quotient of restful sleep had diminished. "Worth Kettering is your man, if he'll have you."

She ceased her pacing near a small framed portrait of a dark-haired, dark-eyed young mother with a laughing infant on her lap. "Why wouldn't he have me?"

"He's selective about his clients, and his firm is much in demand. I use him, but I have for years, and it suited him at the time to have an errant French *comte* wandering his offices."

"Half-French, half-Scottish," Polly muttered. "This truly is a delightful painting, Tremaine. The brushwork is lovingly rendered, and the light wonderfully delicate. Will Mr. Kettering not take me on because I'm female, or because I'm an artist? Or will it be because I lack a title?"

"I'll write him. I think he will take you on."

She adjusted the angle of the frame minutely. "Why?"

"Because you need him." And Kettering had not a chivalrous streak, but a chivalrous quirk, such that Polly's circumstances would appeal to him.

"Because I'm wealthy," she concluded, stepping away from the portrait. "I need him because I'm wealthy. Tell me about my first commission."

Safer ground, and he hadn't even had to maneuver her onto it. "It's at Hesketh, which is only about a day's ride from Three Springs, and thus close to Allie."

Polly turned velvety brown eyes on him, and Tremaine couldn't help reaching out to tuck a lock of hair behind her ear. "For letting me start out near Allie, Sara, and Beck, thank you."

"I put Hesketh at the front of the line for another reason." Besides the need to put some distance between himself and his talented client. "Aaron Wendover is a damned good-looking devil. You won't have to flatter or artistically interpret his features to create something of significant aesthetic appeal."

Polly resumed studying the picture of mother and child. "And his lady?"

"Also lovely, to the eye."

She shot him a peevish look. "Tell me the rest. An artist must capture more than a pretty face and a pretty gown."

Tremaine wished, not for the first time, that he had artistic talent himself, though it wasn't some titled ninny-hammer he'd try to render on canvas.

"You're a scandalmonger, Polly Hunt. As bad as Beck's grandmother, who sent all her wealthy friends to your showing, by the way."

"Then we must call on her when you take me up to Town to meet that solicitor," Polly said. "I'll write her a note as soon as I've choked down the miserable fare your cook inflicts on you. I swear, Tremaine, how you keep meat on those enormous bones of yours defies science."

"I am sated on the beauty of my female relations."

Polly smiled at that twaddle, clearly not at all impressed with supercilious flattery, and no doubt telling herself Tremaine was, after all, half-French.

❧

"It's as if God took Reynard St. Michael," Polly mused to her sister, "and formed his brother, Tremaine, into his opposite."

"Half brother." Sara went about the Three Springs kitchen, collecting the detritus of one of Polly Hunt's baking sprees. "And being Reynard's opposite isn't entirely a bad thing. I know Reynard was Allie's papa, and we must always be grateful for her, but what, exactly, were my late husband's good qualities?"

Polly paused while stirring a bowl of chocolate icing.

"He was canny as hell," she decided, "and Tremaine does share that feature."

"Which makes him a good manager for your painting, provided he's honest."

"He's honest, and too quick by half."

"Too quick?"

"He proposed to me, Sara." Polly recommended whipping the daylights out of her frosting. "We had just come from the solicitor's office. Tremaine put it in the most polite, bored, business terms—to allow me to sport a ring, to fend off the wandering hands of clients and their younger sons, to quiet talk about our business association—but he allowed me to understand, should it suit me at some point, we might discuss actually marrying."

"You were tempted." Sara paused, her hands full of dirty crockery. "Oh, Polly."

Polly went at the frosting with a vengeance. "Yes, oh, Polly. He can see I'm pining for a man, and he's thinking to take advantage."

"Maybe he can see you're pretty, talented, lonely, and in need of some roots," Sara said. "I wish you'd stay here, Polly. You can paint anywhere. You don't need to become a gypsy for your art."

"One gypsy princess in the family was plenty?"

"Shame on you," Sara chided, but without heat. "Allie misses you."

"And I miss her, which is a good thing, Sara. If we hadn't struck out on separate paths, I might never have realized I do miss her."

"How could you not?"

"I miss North almost as much," Polly said, her frosting fork going still again.

"Beck thought maybe that's why you needed a change of scene." Sara set the dirty dishes in the sink. "You have a lot of memories of Gabriel here at Three Springs."

"Right." Polly used a butter knife to dab frosting on a pale yellow cake. "Memories of Gabriel getting up while I mixed the bread dough, Gabriel heading out without a proper breakfast unless I forced it on him, and Gabriel coming in exhausted right as dinner was put on the table. Memories of Gabriel avoiding me."

"I thought you two had reached some sort of accord before he left here." Sara turned her attention to wiping down the counters, which were spotless. "For the last few months, that is, but then, I was preoccupied with Lady Warne's handsome grandson and Tremaine's looming presence."

"We reached…" Polly dabbed the pattern of a flower into the frosting: a rose. "We reached an agreement to disagree. I think he left in part because he couldn't stand to see my disappointment."

"Or because," Sara said gently, "he couldn't trust himself not to take advantage. Gabriel is a gentleman."

"Titled." Polly surveyed her work, then smoothed the flower away. "He told me that much, but he also told me his family, or somebody, did not want him to survive to perpetuate the line, and Gabriel could not endanger a lady closely associated with him. Not for anything."

"He wouldn't let Hildegard suffer a sniffle on his behalf, could he avoid it. Allie considers him honorary godparent to all of Hildy's piglets." Sara scrubbed the counter with particular force. "So he's gone."

"To parts unknown." Polly glowered at her cake. "Dratted man."

Sara glanced at the door as if expecting menfolk to appear

now that the cleaning up was done. "Beck had a note from Gabriel today, and it seems he's a guest of Lady Warne for the present, but he made no mention of his next destination."

"He said he wouldn't." Polly drew the confectionery rose into the frosting again and added a few thorns. "And he made no mention of me, either, did he?"

Sara crossed the few steps to hug her sister. "You're not going to accept Tremaine's silly proposal, are you? He means well, but guilt and a broken heart are no way to start a marriage."

"You said you'd be decent to our guest," Marjorie accused. "You're not even going to be here to greet her."

"I'll see her at dinner," Aaron replied, his patience fraying the longer he stood in the foyer and argued with his wife before the servants. "George says we've a problem with one of the hay barns, and it won't keep. Unless you want all your pretty carriage horses to live on good intentions this winter, you'll make my excuses to this artist."

"Miss Polonaise Hunt," Marjorie said tightly. "Go then, but if George can't solve the problems with the estate farms, then why are you paying him to serve as steward?"

"Good day, Marjorie." Aaron gave her a curt bow. "I'll see you at dinner, along with Miss *Hunt*."

He stalked down the front steps, glad for any excuse to leave the house, but he had to concede that Marjorie, as usual, had a valid point. George Wendover had been the steward for years, for pity's sake, and with his fat salary and cozy house came the job of running the tens of thousands of acres held both through the Hesketh title and privately by the Wendover family.

But everything, *everything*, seemed to require Aaron's personal attention, because dear Cousin George never wanted to overstep or make a controversial decision. He was loyal, was George, but something of a ditherer in Aaron's opinion. George was also a distant cousin, though, and Aaron's father had trusted the man, as had Gabriel, so Aaron gave him his due.

"It's the last of the hay put up," George explained. He stood in the hay barn, an enormous structure set into the side of a hill, with room for beasts below, and three high mows in the upper part of the building. "Mold got to it, but we're only finding it now, as we're beginning to feed some of the fodder on the colder nights."

"Mold?" The hay barn was well ventilated, of that Aaron was certain. "We had good haying weather this year. I know we did. None of that hay should have been put up wet."

George was intent on studying the barn's roof beams, though they'd likely occupied their present positions for more than a century. "Must have been wetter than we thought, or it got wet, but the roof is tight, so that makes no sense."

"How much is ruined?"

George nodded at the nearest third of the barn. "That mow seems to have got the worst of it, but you're right. Haying was good this year, so there should be hay to purchase."

"Buy what we need, and sell some of the straw. This lot can be used as bedding hay, at least the parts not completely rotted."

"Bedding hay."

George had a way of repeating what had been said that made Aaron want to throttle him. "Lousy hay, not fit for eating, isn't that what you call it?"

"Mostly, we call it kindling."

"If it's not moldy, it has some value," Aaron argued, "so use it as bedding. If there's decent fodder to be had, the animals won't eat the sorrier alternative."

"If you say so." George's features remained impassive as he resumed his study of the beams, and curses learned in the cavalry flitted through Aaron's head. George never disagreed with Aaron, but he never quite agreed with him either.

"George," Aaron kept his tone patient, "what would my father have done?"

"He'd not have put up wet hay."

Do not curse at a man who's trying his best, and is a relation as well.

"Not on purpose, but say a tree fell on the barn roof and a rainstorm got to some of his hay, what would he have done with it?"

"He wouldn't have allowed trees of such a size near his barn."

Aaron gave up on parables. "Sell some of the barley and oat straw, and get us more hay. Was there anything else you wanted to discuss?"

He knew better, *knew better,* than to leave George such an opening, because there was always, always, something else. This cow had a bad foot, that mare hadn't caught, and the chickens weren't laying as well as they had last fall.

None of which, in Aaron's opinion, merited the attention of the Marquess of Hesketh. Such trivialities took all afternoon, meaning correspondence would have to be dealt with far into the night, and damn and blast if he hadn't promised Marjorie he'd appear in proper attire at dinner.

Damn Marjorie for her insistence on having portraits done.

Damn the hay for turning moldy.

And most of all, damn Gabriel for dying.

❧

Gabriel had spent months envisioning this day, months plotting exactly what dramatic, pithy, unforgettable line he would recite when his brother beheld him risen from his supposed grave. In hindsight, he saw his months of rehearsal were merely the mental posturing of one victimized by violence, seeking reassurance from his imagination when it wasn't available elsewhere.

So he handed his horse off to a groom he didn't recognize and took himself into the stables to use the mirror hanging in the saddle room, a vanity their grandfather had insisted on fifty years ago.

As Gabriel was inspecting his tired, dusty, and frankly unappealing reflection, Aaron came into the saddle room, muttering about it being impossible to find a damned jumping bat when a man needed one and owned at least ten, and where in the hell—

In the mirror, Gabriel saw the moment his brother spied him, the moment recognition tried to force its way past disbelief.

"Gabriel?" Incredulity, but also hope, relief, and genuine, unmistakable joy colored that one word. Gabriel turned, the same emotions crowding into his throat and chest as his brother hurtled into his arms.

"Damn you, damn you," Aaron whispered fervently. "Just damn you to hell, damn you to goddamned, bloody, benighted, stinking, perishing hell. You're alive." He fell silent, hugging Gabriel in a crushing embrace, until he stepped back, balled up a fist, and flashed a lightning quick right to his older brother's chin.

Then wrapped him in another suffocating hug.

Gabriel had anticipated the blow, but it still stung, leaving a reassurance as the pain dulled to a throb, but reassurance of what, Gabriel didn't know. That he was loved, maybe? That his brother wouldn't have connived at the title to the point of having Gabriel murdered—maybe?

Aaron held him at arm's length, looking Gabriel over with a scowl reminiscent of their late father.

"I am happier to see you than you can possible know, but, Brother, you are in a bloody lot of trouble."

"One suspected this would be the case. You look like hell yourself."

"Married life does not agree with me," Aaron shot back. "Nor does wearing your idiot title, nor does sitting on my arse in the library hour after hour and bickering in writing with doddering lords trying to cadge my vote on every worthless bit of self-enrichment they can legislate."

Aaron had always had a temper, a quick tongue, and an equally generous and forgiving heart. In the two years since Gabriel had last seen him, though, Aaron had laid claim to the essential darkness of demeanor previously reserved for every other male member of the Wendover clan.

In short, Aaron had grown up, and this left Gabriel feeling both sad and guilty. They were five years apart in age, though sometimes, it had felt closer to fifteen.

No more.

"Let's get you up to the house," Aaron said. "Will you have luggage coming along soon?"

"I have only what my horse could carry, though there will be more coming down from London eventually."

"Is that where you've been hiding?" Aaron's tone held a hint of that hard blow to the chin.

"Walk with me." Gabriel took charge of their progress toward the house, and led his brother around to the side gardens, where plane maples provided shade, beauty, and more importantly, privacy.

Aaron had also apparently learned some patience, or some strategy, because he kept his peace until Gabriel found them a bench under the trees, out of sight of the house or stables.

"We never did get to the bottom of my mishap in Spain." Gabriel sat slowly, the damned English roads having wreaked havoc with his back for the last ten miles. Aaron tossed himself onto the bench with casual grace.

"Mishap?" He snorted. "You were set upon by brigands, as often happens to men traveling alone in war zones after dark."

"It wasn't a war zone, Aaron. We were well behind the lines, and I was traveling between the church and the infirmary where you were recuperating. I traversed the middle of the village under a full moon."

"I was dying," Aaron said tiredly. He crossed his legs at the ankles and leaned back to turn his face up to the sun. "You were set upon while I lay helpless, and if you'd stayed in England, you'd still be... well, you are, alive... Christ."

"You weren't dying." Though in the bright sunlight, Aaron now looked to be at least exhausted. "You'd given up, and because the army knows nothing of medicine save cutting, burning, stitching, and praying, you needed better care. You were too stubborn to trade on the family name, so you weren't getting that care, hence the necessity of my travel."

And hence, indirectly, two years of backbreaking labor and heart-wrenching uncertainty as well, for them both— and for Marjorie?

Aaron swung at a bed of yellow pansies with his riding crop, missing—fortunately. "What's your point?"

"I had no money on me," Gabriel said. "I was on a humble borrowed army mount, and yet, I am larger and meaner and fitter than most—or I was. I do not think brigands set upon me."

"The men and I asked around everywhere, Gabriel," Aaron countered. "Nobody had heard the least rumor that you were ambushed as anything other than a casual crime."

"You asked around *in English*. Even if I allow that the first attack was pure bad luck, what about the second and the third?"

Aaron hunched forward, resting his forearms on his thighs and sending Gabriel a puzzled glance over his shoulder. "The second being whoever tried holding a pillow to your ugly face when I was finally recovered enough to leave you to the sisters. I know nothing of a third."

"The fire," Gabriel said. "The one that supposedly took my life. I was given laudanum for the pain in my back, but I'd mostly weaned myself rather than let it become a dependency. I wasn't fast asleep as intended when somebody torched the infirmary—I wasn't even in my bed."

"You were off trysting?"

Had *Aaron* developed a penchant for trysting despite being married to Marjorie? Was that what all her shopping and his dueling were about?

"I was taking a damned piss," Gabriel shot back. "And there but for the grace of God, I'd be sporting that halo."

"So you went into hiding," Aaron surmised.

"I am willing to be convinced that my death was not planned, but who among the Spanish, English, Portuguese, or French would torch a convent's infirmary? Too many wounded and ill depended on the kindness of the sisters, and they took in their patients regardless of nationality."

Aaron swatted at nothing with his crop, while Gabriel felt his brother putting together puzzle pieces. "By the time you were well enough to come home, I'd had you declared dead, and you suspected I was behind all the attempts."

Gabriel rose carefully—now was no time for his damned back to seize up—and paced off a few feet. They were surrounded by pansies and chrysanthemums, though a few precocious maples were parting with their leaves. The garden in all its autumn glory was easier to look upon than Aaron's face.

"I didn't want to think you guilty, Aaron. You were the only one with anything to gain, and then too, I lay in that damned bed for months, thinking myself into a stew, and your guilt was the logical conclusion."

"Is it still?"

And there, in a nutshell, was why Gabriel loved, and despaired of, his brother. Aaron was brave, unflinchingly courageous. He'd toss out a question like that, knowing it opened an unbearably painful wound for them both. And he'd do it without batting an eye. Such a man might easily believe himself to be—and might be—the better choice to hold the title.

"No, it is not the logical conclusion," Gabriel said, turning in time to see his brother's shoulders drop, the only sign Aaron had given a damn about the answer, one way or another. "It's no longer the only possible conclusion."

"Oh, famous." This time, Aaron decapitated a few pansies with his crop, and the steward in Gabriel winced. "A Scottish verdict? Insufficient evidence?"

"*No* evidence," Gabriel said, eyeing the pansy parts

scattered on the ground. "My own fevered reasoning, but no evidence and plenty of reasonable doubts."

"Such as?"

"You didn't know I was coming to fetch you home." Gabriel resumed his seat beside Aaron, though the hard bench was murder on an aching back. "It's easy enough to have a man killed if you've coin and cunning. If you'd wanted me dead, it would have made more sense for you to see the thing done while you were in Spain and I was in England."

Aaron left the bench, reminding Gabriel that his brother had never enjoyed inactivity. "If I'd wanted you dead, I would have managed it myself on a field of honor, regardless of country."

"May I assume that isn't a challenge?"

Aaron scrubbed a hand over his face. "Don't be ridiculous, but if I were you, I wouldn't turn my back on Marjorie anytime soon." The smile accompanying this advice was complicated: humorous, rueful, self-mocking. Boys did not smile like that, though married men did.

"I assume Marjorie is well?" Gabriel shifted on the infernal bench and missed the padding Polly had kept on his chair at the Three Springs kitchen table.

Missed Polly too, though that was hardly news.

"Marjorie's not breeding, if that's what you're asking. She's utterly miserable married to me, and lest there be any doubt, long lost brother, I am miserable married to her. It's the English way. She's hired a portrait artist to memorialize our misery."

Perhaps Aaron wanted to call him out after all? "You didn't have to marry her."

"Yes, Gabriel, I did. Her dear mama was crying breach of

promise and damages if I hadn't, and your Mr. Kettering was very reluctant to hand over the details of the agreement to a mere wastrel younger brother when you were yet alive."

Damn Worth Kettering and his lawyerly scruples. "You had me declared dead just to get a look at the contract?"

"No." Aaron slapped his crop against his boot, and a leaf went twirling by, as if the crop were a magic wand that might bring the heavens crashing down with the right incantation. "I had you declared dead so that, having no other plan in hand, I could try getting on with your life."

❦

Gabriel wandered every wing and corridor of his former home—his *home*—saving the portrait gallery for last, because to him it was the heart of the Wendover family seat. Of the barons, three in number, there were no paintings, not even sketches, but when a grateful crown had created the Earldom of Northbridge, that good fellow's countess had taken matters in hand and set the Wendovers on the tradition of portraiture.

Gabriel studied the portrait of him and Aaron for a long time, seeing the hubris of a wealthy heir in his younger self. God in heaven, he'd had a lot to learn.

Something made him turn, to watch the afternoon light cascading through the spotless windows. Polly had loved the fall light, calling it frisky.

He put that thought aside. A man was not entitled to dwell on a woman he'd loved and lost, much less one he'd disappointed in the process, and this gave the ache of missing her a particular resonance. He thought to bide a few minutes among the ancestors and guiltily savor his memories of his few intimate moments with Polly Hunt when movement caught his eye.

His gaze fell on a maid, catnapping, but when he crossed the room to rouse the slacker, he stopped cold, the hairs on the back of his neck and his arms prickling with anticipation.

Her lashes fluttered up just as he knelt to assure himself his eyes were not deceiving him, and then the lady did the most extraordinary thing. She rested a hand on his shoulder, leaned up on her elbow, and gently kissed his cheek.

"Polonaise Hunt, what in God's name are you doing here?"

He hadn't meant the question to sound so... panicked, so angry, but she couldn't be here, *could not*.

"Hullo to you too, Mr. North," Polly muttered, her smile fading to a frown. "I fell asleep. Did Beck tell you I was here?"

Gabriel rose lest she kiss him again and scatter his wits from Land's End to Nova Scotia. "He most assuredly did not, and if he knew this was your destination, I'm going to make him regret his reticence. You must leave."

"The room?"

"The property."

She tucked a lock of auburn hair behind her ear, the gesture conveying a significant lack of concern. "I'm hungry."

"Then take something from the kitchen when you go."

She treated him to a mulish glance, and Gabriel swiveled to sit beside her before his knees gave out.

"I'm not going." She rolled her shoulders and yawned delicately. "I have portraits to paint."

"Go paint them somewhere else." He was not going to tell her his own house wasn't a safe place, especially for her, the first woman he could honestly say he'd cared for. More than cared for.

Polly eyed him curiously. "Hesketh has contracted for my services. Who are you to be countermanding a peer of the realm?"

Her hair was tousled, and she had a crease across her cheek from the pillow seam. He crossed his arms to thwart the compulsion to touch her. "I'm Hesketh's older brother."

The words were out, blunt, unpretty, and honest, and the effect on Polly was devastating. She didn't move, she didn't speak, but she silently withdrew to a faraway, untouchable place, where men could lie to the women they kissed and the women were too smart and tough to let it matter.

"Are you a bastard?" A trickle of hope escaped into her careful tone, and he winced to hear it, because this possibility would explain much and let her forgive nearly as much.

"Not in the manner you mean."

"I see."

Silence grew, and Gabriel had the sense Polly was drifting away on an unstoppable tide of hurt feelings and female ire. He wanted to explain, to excuse, to argue on his own behalf in mitigation, but more words would only give her more reasons not to go.

"You really do have to leave, Polonaise." He said it as gently as he could. "I'm not asking."

She studied him as she might peruse an anatomical drawing exercise. "Because you are the Marquess of Hesketh, and I am a lowly hired artisan. Your word here is law, and I am banished."

She rose, not waiting for his reply, and when Gabriel came to his feet, he was reminded how wonderfully her body measured against his. If he took her in his arms, her crown would fit right under his chin. Her expression said he'd never again have that privilege, and though it cut deeply, that was for the best.

"As Marquess of Hesketh, you are bound by the contract that brought me here," she said, stepping back and gazing across the room at a portrait of two handsome, dark-haired, green-eyed youths. "It is my first commission on English soil, *my lord*, and it will set the tone for the rest of my career. Aaron and Marjorie Wendover were chosen with care, for their pulchritude and for their social prominence. I will not step back from this assignment, not for any amount of damages, and certainly not because you've waved a lordly hand and willed it so. I'll see you at dinner."

She turned to go but stopped when he shot out a hand to encircle her wrist.

"At dinner," he said, "we will be strangers."

"Will we?"

"It has to be, Polonaise. For the well-being of all involved, we cannot have met prior to today."

"Your family might not appreciate your larking away a couple of years in their backyard before assuming the title? Or did you already hold the title when you presented yourself to us at Three Springs as a poor land steward?"

"It's... complicated, and delicate," he said, not wanting to give her even that much.

"And you can explain these complications?" Her tone was imperious, but he saw the veiled plea in her brown eyes.

"I cannot. Not now."

She glanced down at where he still held her wrist. "You can let me go, Gabriel. I'll not betray your secrets over the fish course. Nor will I leave."

He did let her go, appreciating the view of her retreat, even as he knew he'd just been poleaxed, blackmailed, and kicked into a ditch in the space of five minutes. This was what he deserved, in the peculiar coincidence of circumstances he found himself.

But then a rare smile lit his features, for he recalled that in those same five minutes he'd also, however fleetingly, been kissed.

Two

POLLY STALKED AWAY FROM HIS LORDSHIP GABRIEL North Wendover Hesketh Whoever He Was, and then rounded on him and marched right back. Afternoon light gilded him from above, as if he were a saintly apparition and not a damnably dear and dark man. She went up on her toes and kissed his mouth this time, a deliberate, angry laying of her lips on his, a battle kiss, without tenderness or artifice.

"That," she informed him, "is a kiss of parting, as in I'm parting from you, not from your household."

She whirled off again, feeling better for allowing herself a small display of temper, but by the time she'd gotten to her room, the anger had burned off, leaving hurt and bewilderment.

And shame.

Shame because of course the Marquess of Hesketh would not have a romantic interest in an itinerant artist, or in the former cook from Three Springs. In his way, Gabriel had been honorable, for he'd refused to enjoy the full measure of the liberties Polly had offered him.

Flung at him, more like.

Just as she'd flung herself at her sister's husband all those years ago, a stupid girl, flattered by Reynard's Gallic flirta-tion and a mature man's manipulative interest. Dear God, would she never learn discernment when it came to men?

She'd been dreaming of Egyptian treasures on display in the Louvre one moment, opened her eyes in the next, and told herself she was still dreaming. Right before her knelt Gabriel North, whom she hadn't seen or heard from for weeks, looking concerned and dear, but rested for once. She had kissed him without thinking, without doing any-thing but giving in to the welling joy of seeing him again, apparition or flesh-and-blood man, and that kiss had been so sweet.

And it hadn't been a dream, but rather, a nightmare.

For God help her, what of Allie? Polly cringed to think what North—no, Hesketh—would think of a woman who could bear a bastard child, then allow family to step in and raise the child for her. He wouldn't understand, and he'd be particularly judgmental, because the child was dear to him.

A more reasonable voice told her a man who'd pose for two years as a lowly steward might understand some subterfuge and misdirection, but that voice was drowned out by indignation that Gabriel had never really trusted her, and worry that he could make good on his insistence she abandon her first commission.

Which she would not do.

She'd plead a headache at dinner, write to her sister, Sara, and pray for inspiration to strike. It wasn't much of a plan, but it would do for now—because it was all she had.

～

"Margie!" Aaron called to his wife over the tattoo of her gelding's hooves, while he took a moment to admire the picture she made. The woman could sit a horse, any horse, and the beasts seemed to wait for her cues and commands. Unwittingly, his mind took off in a spree of lusty associations involving him naked on his back under her. When he called her name again, it was with greater impatience.

"My lord?" She brought her mount down to the walk, looking elegant, composed, and a trifle flushed. Aaron shifted his gelding alongside hers, and peered at her more closely.

"If I forbid you to visit that miserable old besom who claims to have whelped you," he asked, "would you cry less?"

"I haven't been crying." She drew herself up in her sidesaddle as she emotionally somehow drew herself away. "And you should not refer to your mama-in-law in such terms. For shame."

"What did she say this time, Margie?"

"She is concerned for her daughter." Marjorie tossed a glance over her shoulder at her groom.

"Will you walk with me?" Aaron posed the question quietly, because the groom had ears, and Marjorie must have caught the urgency in his tone, because she nodded and waited for Aaron to get down and help her dismount. He handed the reins to the groom and considered how one broached the topic at hand.

First, one waited for the groom to lead the horses away. "We're married, right?"

"For two years now." Marjorie regarded him with patient curiosity, while something flickered in her eyes. Something a proper husband would have been able to interpret.

"Is that what her mama-ship was beating you with? There's no heir on the way, and this must be your fault? If she doesn't leave you in peace, I swear I'm going to have to do something."

"She means well."

"Right, good intentions make every cruelty forgivable." Aaron silently vowed to have a talk with dear Mama-In-Law. "I've some astoundingly good news, Margie."

She fell in step beside him, and Aaron wanted to take her hand, which was silly really, when Marjorie Wendover would never be so indecorous as to *physically* flee his presence without being excused.

"Nobody calls me Margie except you."

Aaron's lips quirked. "I'm sure if we were honest, there are names only you have applied to my own person."

She looked puzzled, then caught the humor in his eye. She was young. Not stupid, merely... inexperienced.

"What is your good news, my lord, because you don't look like a man with good news." She turned from him as they walked along, pretending to study the undergrowth dying back with winter's approach.

"Let's find somewhere to sit, but first tell me, was your mother harping on the need for an heir?"

Marjorie strolled beside him past some purple chrysanthemums. "She was. Again."

"Do we need to have that argument again as well?"

"No." She said it quietly, resignedly. "I understand you grieve for your brother, and haranguing you on this topic is not productive. Your decision still hurts me."

"I know," he said, wishing this quiet, steady honesty had remained beyond her. "But what I have to tell you should come as a relief in this regard, Margie. It really is good news, at least for us."

"Us?" She imbued that one syllable with such a wistful longing Aaron felt it in his gut.

"Let's take the bench." He nodded to a low-backed

wooden bench sitting among pots of asters. "We need privacy for this."

She held her peace, but when she'd arranged the skirts of her habit, Aaron took the place immediately beside her, wishing there was some way to spare her this. He had the strangest urge to tuck her against him, to put his arms around her when she learned she wasn't the Marchioness of Hesketh, and all her effort over the past two years had been for nothing.

What he ought to feel, what he was *entitled* to feel, was resentment.

He took her hand. "Gabriel did not die in Spain as we thought. He's alive and well, and probably at his bath up at the manor."

Her eyebrows—she had the most perfect eyebrows God ever gave a woman—knitted, as if he'd merely told her rain was likely later in the day. "Your brother, Gabriel, is alive?"

"Very much so. Upright, walking, breathing, and making grouchy remarks to all and sundry. He's alive, Margie."

"This is… good news." She nodded, as if she'd reached for the words blindly and was relieved to have seized the right ones. "This is very good news. I'm happy for you, my lord, and for your… for his lordship."

"You're taking this well." *Too well?*

"I can hardly fathom it." Marjorie made to rise, but Aaron kept hold of her hand. "Has he some explanation for allowing us to believe him dead?"

Aaron laced his fingers through hers. "As usual, you ask a good question, Wife."

"You think I ask good questions?"

"Yes, I do. You use your head, except with your damned idiot mother."

"Language, my lord."

They fell silent on that little normalizing exchange, until Marjorie looked down at their joined hands.

"Yes." Aaron divined the direction of her thoughts. "You might be free of me. Is that what you want?"

"What are you talking about?"

"Margie, you have to realize that with Gabriel reappearing, you have leverage to put this farce of a marriage behind you and snag the prize you've waited your entire life to marry."

She shook her hand free of his grasp. "Your brother is not my idea of a prize, unless he's much changed."

"Then what does that make me?"

"You are my husband." She said this with rare heat, and Aaron had to admit to some relief. She wouldn't toss him over without a show of loyalty, though he hardly deserved even that much.

"I may not be," he countered nonetheless, "because you were betrothed to Northbridge, and that was Gabriel, not my humble self."

"We are *married*." Her voice broke on the word, and Aaron did put his arms around her. "Aaron, we are. To the world, we are the Marchioness and Marquess of Hesketh. It's who we're expected to be." She bundled into him, her emotions obviously provoking an uncharacteristic display of... something. Husband and wife didn't often touch, except for the barest civilities and in public, so Aaron let himself enjoy her fragrant, female curves in his embrace.

God knew, it might be the last time.

"What do you want, Margie?" He propped his chin on her temple and rubbed a slow hand over her back. It was a beautiful back, slender, strong, and graceful, and he'd never really appreciated that before.

"I want to hear what Gabriel has to say for himself," she said, her words muffled against Aaron's cravat. "I want some time to put our situation in some kind of order, I want…"

"Yes?" He let her sit up and passed her his handkerchief. "What do you want?"

"This is confusing." Marjorie blotted her eyes. "Who is the marquess now, when your brother is legally dead? Who votes the seat in the Lords; who has title to the properties? Whose portrait is Miss Hunt to paint?"

Aaron tucked a lock of silky blond hair back over her ear. "That is the least of our worries. I'm more concerned with what we tell your mother."

"Mama." The word was a despairing oath. "Oh, God, Mama."

"Mama and the entire world. You are my wife, for all legal purposes, Marjorie. I'll not leave you to the vultures, but if Gabriel wants to put things right and have you for his marchioness, you're going to have to tell me what you want—tell me honestly."

"You're saying you'd fight for me?" She smiled, and Aaron wondered why he'd so seldom seen her smile.

But then, he knew why.

"I'm saying, I'm your husband," he reiterated, "and I will act in that capacity until you tell me you'd rather I didn't."

Marjorie sat a little straighter, and damn him, because he missed the feel of her in his arms. "We don't know what Gabriel intends, your lordship. This whole discussion might be moot. He could have married some Spanish beauty and be waiting to shock us with that surprise as well. Where was he for two years while we were getting married and mourning and trying to get Hesketh set to rights?"

"I honestly haven't asked him that, though in truth, Margie, I don't think Gabriel will be your most challenging issue."

She folded his handkerchief in her lap so the lace edges matched exactly. "If Gabriel intends to have me for some kind of wife, his wishes will carry great weight in the courts, won't they? He's used to getting what and whom he wants."

Aaron drew her to her feet. "Maybe he was, but he seems different. Every bit as irascible, but not as arrogant."

"That should be the subject of a notice in the *Times*," Marjorie said, tucking her arm around Aaron's. "Not that he's miraculously restored to us, for Lazarus at least set a precedent in that regard, but that he might have learned some humility."

"Now, now." Aaron jostled her affectionately. "People will be saying you're your mother's daughter."

"And your wife. At least for the present."

❦

"So there you are." George rose, his hand extended toward Gabriel as he welcomed him into the cozy manor house that served as the steward's quarters. "In the flesh, just as your note said."

His handshake was solid, welcoming, and in two years, George had barely changed. He was aging well, typical of the Wendover men. He wasn't quite as tall as Gabriel or Aaron, but he was quietly handsome, with brown eyes instead of green, and a patient humor with the things that set younger men to cursing and stomping around.

"It's good to be home, George." Gabriel mouthed the

platitude as they took their seats in the library, though it was the truth, too. "How fare you?"

George lapsed into the predictable soothing patter of a man stewarding a huge agricultural enterprise. The estate held dozens of tenant farms, spread over tens of thousands of acres, and after twenty years in his position, George knew every acre of the property. Gabriel let his cousin roll on, about this pond silting up, that field needing to fallow, and the other tenant having yet another strapping daughter.

"You might try barley straw in the pond," Gabriel suggested, "if the problem is scum as well as silt."

George's eyebrows rose. "Barley straw, you say? Is that something you picked up in Spain?"

"I did." Gabriel lied easily, though this was one of Beck Haddonfield's tricks. As much as Beck had traveled, *he* might have picked up the notion in Spain. Or the Americas, or the Antipodes.

"Were you so long ill, then, that you couldn't come back to us for two years?"

"It's a long story, George, best told over a long winter night with a decent bottle or two at hand. Why are you emptying one of the hay mows?"

"Mold." George spat the word, as only a farmer facing winter would. "Damned rain or some such. Hay goes bad, but this was a damned pretty crop. We're fortunate not much was damaged."

"Is the roof leaking?"

"Mayhap. We've had some bad storms this fall, and rain can get in under the eaves when the wind blows just right. I tried to suggest to his lordship, your brother, we might be caulking the eaves, but he says the hay needs to breathe. Has a lot of answers, that one."

"You educated me when I thought I had all the answers."

"That I did." George produced an unlit pipe from his pocket. "Or tried to. So who has the title now, Gabriel? And which title?"

What did that matter when hay was getting wet? "One of us is Hesketh, the other is a courtesy lord. I care not which is which, but the solicitors, judges, and the College of Arms will likely have an opinion. In either case, the land needs tending, and you're the man to do it."

"You might want to see if your brother agrees. He's full of notions and has us marching off in this direction, only to charge off another day in that direction."

"Which sounds just like him." Gabriel watched as George went through a familiar ritual of cleaning, filling, and lighting his pipe. "I trust you to interpret his orders accordingly, but until we sort out the legalities, you will continue to honor his directives."

"While the hay molds," George muttered. "I'll do as you say. Harvest is in, and the sheep are getting fat and woolly. The stock is in good shape for winter, and most of the cottages are in good repair. There shouldn't be all that much to do, in truth, not until spring."

"When there's too much to do. Will you join us for dinner some night this week?"

"Of course." George winked. "You need all the reinforcements you can get, and I've got your back."

"I'm grateful for that." Gabriel rose and offered his hand. "All the time I was gone, George, I worried a little less because I knew you were here, and you'd prevent the worst disasters and clean up after the ones that couldn't be avoided."

"A steward's job in a nutshell." George grinned, then

became more sober. "You're going to have to let the world know what you were about, though, Gabriel, gone for two years without so much as a letter."

"Had I been able to communicate, I would have, and likely with you. My man of business in Town knew what was afoot at all times, but things grew complicated."

George shot a look in the direction of the manor house. "With you lot, they usually do. Me, I tend the sheep, and life is not complicated at all. You work, and then you work some more, and then you work yet still more, with eating and sleeping tucked in somewhere between sheep, goats, cows, horses, crops, and cottages."

"It's not a bad life, though, is it, George?"

"For some it's not. For others, well… Let's just say I'm not sure you or your brother would find being a steward entirely agreeable."

Gabriel took his leave on that note, but wondered what George would think did he know that for two years, Gabriel had been the one to tend the sheep, the cows, the crops, and so forth.

And he'd never been happier.

❧

Gabriel's reunion with his former fiancée had been an awkward, uncomfortable moment when they'd gathered in the family parlor before the evening meal. She'd curtsied, he'd bowed, and then he'd taken a step toward her, only to see her cringe and back closer to Aaron. Gabriel had followed through nonetheless, and offered her a careful, fraternal hug, even as he wondered how this tall, slender girl—no, woman—was managing the burden of being the Hesketh marchioness.

And she was a woman, a pretty, though very young woman upon whom Gabriel had made duty calls between terms at school. He'd ridden out with her in pleasant weather on holidays—properly chaperoned, of course—and danced her first waltz with her. She'd been a quiet, inevitable presence in the back of his mind, and as she'd reached adulthood, her calm blue eyes had asked if he were going to set a date.

He hadn't, being far too enamored with the pleasures of being an heir, then gradually, as his father had aged, with the burdens thereof. And through all this, when they might have become friends, they'd remained strangers—awkward, proper strangers.

How had he let that happen?

"Welcome home." Marjorie's smile seemed genuine, if shy, and Gabriel tried a smile in response.

"It's more wonderful to be home than you can imagine, my lady. I must compliment you on the house, for I've never seen it looking better."

"Are your rooms comfortable?"

The polite question of a conscientious hostess caused her to blush, and Gabriel saw endless evenings like this, conversation stilted, more unsaid than said.

And that was his fault too.

"They are exactly as I'd wish," he replied, and the response caused Aaron's eyebrows to twitch with what looked like consternation. "My surrounds have been humble the past two years, and I've developed a taste for simpler living. The day starts more easily when one doesn't have to await a valet to dress, a maid to dine, and a groom to fetch one's horse."

"And you'll enlighten us about those two years?" Aaron

posed the question, taking his wife's arm—protectively?—as he did.

Marjorie spoke up. "My lord, can I not enjoy your brother's company for a single meal before you men must talk of serious things? I noted his lordship is riding a splendid fellow of mature years with a story emblazoned on his quarters."

Aaron slid his arm around Marjorie's waist, his expression bemused. "The girl is horse mad. One of her many fine qualities."

Another blush, but softer, and directed at Aaron by his own wife. Gabriel was reassured by the exchange, because surely a woman didn't blush at a husband she resented?

"Soldier was at the knacker's when I found him," Gabriel said, "stoically awaiting his fate with a great gash on his backside from one too many skirmishes with the French or the local bandits or heaven knows whom. He was all I could afford, but he has excellent conformation, and all the sense and bottom of a seasoned campaigner, provided I make allowances for his injury."

"He looks like he'd be a keen jumper," Marjorie said, and the topic of horses and the current population in the Hesketh stables served to get them through dinner. Marjorie excused herself thereafter, leaving the gentlemen to their drinks.

"Shall we remove to the library, so the kitchen can clean up?" Aaron suggested.

"We shall." Gabriel rose and moved across the hall with his brother. "And so these old bones can rest by a roaring fire, because the night is getting damned chilly."

"Your back bothers you when it's cold?" The question was posed casually, because even a brother trod lightly in certain areas, and Aaron was careful to be busy poking up the fire as he spoke.

"My back bothers me constantly," Gabriel admitted. "I'm like my horse. I manage well enough, but if I overdo, I pay dearly. And sometimes, when I don't overdo, I pay just as dearly."

"Laudanum?"

"Not on a bet."

"This might help." Aaron passed him a glass of brandy. "These past two years, you were close by?"

"For most of it."

"You came by, didn't you?" Aaron poured his own drink and studied the decanter upon which, Gabriel knew, he would see the Hesketh wheat sheaves etched—the heraldic symbol for hopes realized. "At times, I felt as if you were watching, but I'd turn around, and no Gabriel. Gabriel was dead. I was almost sure of it."

Gabriel said nothing, because admitting he'd spied on his brother wasn't going to help their situation.

"I know what you're about, Gabriel." Aaron set the decanter aside. "You've been trying to decide whether I attempted to have you killed. And you couldn't come to a conclusion from a safe distance, so you're bearding the lion, so to speak."

Gabriel lowered himself into a well-padded chair— though the seat still wasn't as comfortable as his chair in Polly Hunt's kitchen. "If I ask the question directly, you'll have to call me out."

"Suppose I will." Aaron took the other chair while Gabriel envied him his ease of movement. "You're suffering more than a twinge in your back now, aren't you?"

"Not really. It knocks me on my arse from time to time, but mostly it's stiff without being painful. I meant it when I said the place is prospering. You've done well, Aaron."

"I'm not sure if I should resent that comment or appreciate it, coming from you. I've made some changes, but it's all right there in the estate log."

"What's the estate log?" Gabriel didn't make the effort to rise. The day had been long, the ride down from Town grueling, and the estate book wasn't going anywhere.

"I've found dear George doesn't have perfect recall," Aaron said. "He isn't one for noting exactly which herd dropped the first lambs, or which farm the scours started on, and so forth, so I started keeping a log. It's useful."

"Useful?" The heat from the fire was the most useful thing Gabriel had encountered since finding Polonaise Hunt lurking in his portrait gallery.

Aaron's portrait gallery.

"George was going to let three hundred acres fallow three years in a row," Aaron said. "We damned near came to blows about it. He was sure it had been planted the year before. I showed him the harvest entries, but even then, he tried to tell me I'd forgotten to enter three hundred acres of yield, rather than admit he'd forgotten the land had sat idle. The tenant didn't want to get into the middle of the argument, but eventually his was the deciding vote."

"Stewarding is a much more difficult and interesting job than I'd thought. Exhausting, too."

"Is that what you were doing? Serving as somebody's land steward?"

"Yes." When he wasn't falling in love.

"I'll bet that was an adjustment."

The comment was neutral, not angry, not resentful, not even jeering, but Gabriel wasn't sure what to say in response.

Aaron rose and set his glass on the mantel. "I know you're still trying to make up your mind. Am I your brother or your enemy or both? You've been through an ordeal, and though I ought to treat you to some bare-knuckle oratory for thinking as you have about me, you've had your reasons. Still, your reappearance has cast a great deal into confusion, and for Marjorie's sake more than my own, we need to know what you're about."

"What I'm about?"

"She was your fiancée, not mine. I married her for reasons you may discuss with her, but I'm wondering if the marriage is valid, given that it was effected under false pretenses."

In all his wildest imaginings—and some of them had been wild indeed—Gabriel had not envisaged that Aaron's marriage would become a bone of contention. "You're accusing me of fraud, when I lay on my stomach for months—?"

Aaron held up a hand. "Part of the reason I find myself with your wife, so to speak, is because Lady Hartle started rallying her solicitors for a breach of promise suit. Her daughter was to be the Marchioness of Hesketh. Your arrival means some other lady will hold that title."

"Unless I never marry." He'd been almost resigned to such a fate, in fact.

"I won't ask that of you, because it would put the burden of the succession on my humble shoulders, exactly where it is now. Moreover, it won't spike Lady Hartle's guns if you remain a bachelor. The simple fact that you're alive takes the title from Marjorie and me."

"Blessed Infant Jesus."

"Marjorie asked me, when I told her you lived, who votes your seat when you're legally dead. Who directs the solicitors? To whom do the Hesketh holdings belong? Whose portrait is Miss Hunt going to paint?"

"Your artist." The artist who'd dodged dinner in a show of either pique or great good sense. "That one is easy. Send the lady packing, given the confusion you allude to."

Aaron picked up his glass from where he'd set it on the mantel, and appeared to study the contents. "And thereby notify the entire polite world you kept your existence secret from your own brother for two years, that you made a joke of the Lords, or you've gone half lunatic on us, seeing plots where they don't exist?"

"I take your point." Gabriel felt weariness pressing down on him. Getting Polly the devil away from Hesketh had become his most immediate concern among *many* immediate concerns. "She can start with a portrait of Marjorie. That should be safe enough if we keep the footmen close at hand and insist on an indoor sitting. Your wife is very pretty, by the way."

"Ah, but is she my wife?"

"Do you want her to be?"

"It matters naught what I want. The resolution of Marjorie's status will lie with what she wants, and let me be clear on this, Brother. As far as I'm concerned, it matters not what you want, either, not one bit, not to me."

"That's as it should be." Gabriel tossed back brandy that should have been sipped and set his empty glass aside. "But I'm loath to suggest I could be marrying her."

"Why?" Aaron regarded him steadily. "If she's used goods, it's not her fault."

"Used... Aaron, don't be vulgar. I'd hardly hold it against Marjorie that she did her duty by her lawful husband as she knew him to be, though it would be decidedly awkward. I get the impression she's fond of you."

Aaron's fingers tightened on his glass. "She's too decent

to give any other impression, but we're not close. That would hardly be fashionable."

"Hang fashion. My hesitance stems not only from reluctance to displease the lady, but also from a desire not to see her dragged into whatever ill will has been directed to me."

The last swallow of Aaron's drink disappeared. "You are absolutely convinced somebody tried to kill you?"

"Repeatedly," Gabriel said. "Even as I prepared to take ship from Spain, I was set upon on the docks, twice. Both times, my attackers knew my back was weak. Were it not for the Spanish sailor's inherent championing of the underdog, I'd be gone in truth."

"And you were supposedly dead by then," Aaron murmured. "A tragic victim of the convent fire."

Gabriel stared at the crackling blaze his brother had obligingly built up for him. At this rate, the reading balcony immediately above would be a cozy place to hide, except stairs lay between it and Gabriel's present location. "All of which means I am still a target."

"Unless your detractor was content to have you out of Spain, but who in that country could wish you ill?"

"And who even knew I was there, except my family?"

"Complicated," Aaron agreed. "The sooner you make your intentions known in terms of the legalities and practicalities, the sooner Marjorie can get on with her life, or her mother with a scandalous lawsuit."

"There will be no lawsuit."

"You'll marry Marjorie then, if Lady Hartle insists?"

"I can't promise that. Make sure Marjorie knows I can't promise to wed her."

"You make sure she knows," Aaron said as he headed for

the door. "It should be an interesting conversation, and I'm sure one of you will let me know how it goes."

"Good night, then." Gabriel was too tired to heed the requirement of manners and rise. "You won't mind if I have a look at that estate book?"

Aaron waved a hand. "Do your worst, and please God, don't neglect the ledgers. For my part, I really am glad you're back, Gabriel. The less time I have to spend with the paperwork, the correspondence, and the damned bills, the better. You argue with George, and meet with Kettering, and dance the damned pretty at all the mandatory social events."

"While you do what?"

"Admire my brother." Aaron bowed, and came up smiling not quite innocently. "One other thing, Gabriel?"

"Hmm?"

"The girl, Melinda? She's thriving."

"I know." Two words, but even keeping that much steady had been an effort. "Kettering told you?"

"Your will has that codicil, and he had to show it to me because I'm your executor, nominally, and then too, I think Kettering has a care for children."

"He does. My thanks. I've kept an eye on her as best I could, but that hardly served."

"Thought you'd want to know."

Gabriel let him go, knowing Aaron hadn't owed him that last exchange and hadn't owed the child anything. And this was the brother Gabriel had been convinced was intent on fratricide. Increasingly, that notion seemed ludicrous.

But this business with Marjorie… A visit to Kettering was definitely in order, and soon, because even now Aaron could be getting the Hesketh heir with Marjorie, and then where would they be?

Three

Taking dinner on a tray was not an act of cowardice. Polly assured herself of this as she studied yet another botched sketch of a certain breeding sow who had been dear to the land steward at Three Springs—the former steward. To allow the Wendover family to dine in privacy the first time they sat down together since North's return was *courtesy*.

Not North. He was Hesketh, the marquess himself. Had been, the whole time he'd been feeding slops to Hildegard and wrestling sheep from the pond muck at Three Springs.

Polly tore off the sketch of Hildy—the pig's expression had been uncharacteristically downcast—and instead drew a careful, aquiline curve near the middle of the page. The curve grew into Gabriel's nose, then his mouth, and his beautiful, serious eyes.

Not Gabriel, not North. Hesketh. *Lord* Hesketh.

The entire time he'd been permitting Polly the occasional liberty—a kiss, an embrace, a cuddle—he'd been Hesketh.

With a huff of self-disgust, Polly set her sketchbook aside. The Wendover family Bible would be in the library. Knowing Gabriel's antecedents would appease the curiosity she had about him—had always had about him.

From the first time he'd showed up at her kitchen door—tall, gaunt, and bearing a letter from Lady Warne—Polly had been interested in Gabriel North.

Gabriel Wendover, she corrected herself, finding a flannel wrapper and belting it tightly. The corridors were lit by only the occasional sconce, but it was enough, because the moon was full and Polly knew her way.

Someday I am going to have my own house. Nothing so grand as this, but something as light and elegant and comfortable. *I'll have a library and a studio, and my family will be welcome.*

My daughter will be welcome.

She opened the library door, a comforting warmth enveloping her as she stepped into the room.

And stopped.

Somebody had pushed the long sofa right up close to the hearth, using it as a sort of fire screen, though the spark catcher was still in place as well. Moving silently, Polly stepped closer, peering over the back of the sofa.

Gabriel was stretched out on his stomach, a fat ledger open for his perusal.

"Brandy is on the sideboard, if that's what you're looking for."

He didn't glance up, but Polly knew he could identify her scent—he'd confessed as much once on a dark, lovely night.

"Would you like some?"

"I've already indulged, but help yourself." He stirred, setting the book aside and shifting to sit.

"Your back is hurting?"

"Of course. You're having trouble sleeping?"

"Of course."

"Come sit, then, Polonaise, and you can tell me how our dear Allemande fares."

He would ask that, damn him.

She helped herself to brandy and poured him a glass despite his demurral. By the time she'd brought both to the sofa, he'd pushed the furniture back to a more usual distance from the fire.

"Should you be shoving furniture around if your back hurts?"

"Should you be offering brandy to me when you're in such fetching dishabille?"

"Don't be churlish." She handed him his drink and sat a small distance from him. He rose and tossed a log on the fire, while Polly watched his movements. She'd seen him move much more slowly, and manage in surrounds far less commodious than these.

"Allie is well enough," Polly said. "She's angry at me for leaving Three Springs, but Beck and Sara are patient with her, and her Uncle Tremaine is a nice distraction."

"The Sheep Count. His *nom de guerre* among the merchants. Every girl can use a wealthy uncle."

"He doesn't use the title." They fell silent, but when he resumed his seat, Gabriel settled right beside her, hip to hip, as he often had at Three Springs. When he'd first developed the habit, she had thought he'd done it as a simple, animal way to garner some human warmth for himself, but when he'd taken no more advantage than that over weeks and weeks of opportunity, she'd realized he was doing it for her, to alleviate her loneliness in the small ways that wouldn't cause talk or stir feelings.

And she'd been grateful.

She was still grateful, which would not do.

"So tell me why you did it, Polonaise." His voice was the same rasping baritone she'd heard many times before, but here before the fire, it carried a kind of fatigue she'd not sensed previously.

He wanted to send her away, and they might not cross paths again. The thought inspired honesty, of a sort, and sadness.

"Why I did what?"

"Why did you leave your family at Three Springs to make wealthy, spoiled people look pretty for all eternity?"

"Why did you leave?" Polly had never been intimidated by him, not by his size, his intellect, his brooding silences, or his irascible demeanor. "You told Allie your family was in trouble, but this"—she waved a hand—"looks as untroubled as can be."

"I lied."

"You don't lie." She took a sip of very smooth spirits, such as a true lady would not admit she drank. "Well, perhaps you do."

"Not willingly or often," he countered. "I don't care for it."

She glanced at the saturnine planes of his face as the firelight cast them in flickering shadows. He did not care for *himself* when he dissembled.

"Which was the truth, then? That you desired me, or you were only humoring my… attraction to you?"

He helped himself to a sip of her drink though she'd brought him one of his own. "Polonaise, will you never learn a little indirection? The day has been long and fraught, and either answer leaves me looking like a bounder."

"So which bounder will you be?" She sipped her drink from the exact same place on the glass he had, and let the brandy burn down to her center before going on. "Will you be the man who didn't want to tell me my importuning was pathetic to one of his stature, or the man who took small liberties for the sheer hell of it, without thought to the consequences?"

"Not pathetic," he ground out. "You've gotten your nightcap. Hadn't you best be off to bed?"

She tidied her skirts as if to rise, but rather than heed him, she scooted her feet up under herself on the sofa.

"I'd like an answer," she said. "Any answer, Gabriel, because you owe me that much. I don't have to like it, but if it's the truth, I'll live with it. You mean to send me away, after all, so grant me this boon: What were you doing with me, Gabriel? Why mess about with the lowly cook when you could have entertained yourself in any style you chose in Town?"

"You're not asking what I was doing at Three Springs in the general case, I note."

"That is your business. I'm not going up those stairs until you tell me what you were doing with me, in the specific case." She had no way of enforcing her threat. Sore back or not, he could easily toss her over his shoulder and eject her from the room bodily.

And she would like to see him try, because it would give her an excuse to be in some form of his embrace.

"I'm not sending you off immediately," he replied, and they both knew he was dodging her question yet again. "Aaron wants Marjorie's portrait done now, and I will respect his wishes, but there are rules."

Polly took another sip. "With you as the Marquess of Hesketh, one expects rules regarding a great deal."

"You will pose her indoors, and there will be footmen in attendance," Gabriel said. "You will keep me or Aaron informed of your whereabouts at all times, and when

Marjorie's portrait is done, you depart without a word of the goings-on here."

She gave him a peevish look for the insult implied at that last condition.

"Whatever is going on here, the news has already reached every estate within a five-mile radius, Gabriel."

"You don't need to add fuel to the flames of gossip. For your own safety, you do not."

"Is that a threat?"

"Jesus save me." He hunched forward and scrubbed a hand over his face. "You'd call me out were it intended as such."

"And my weapon of choice would be the muffin pan," Polly replied. This provoked a tired smile from the man beside her, and she let herself smile back. "Gabriel, I really would like to hear that you weren't trifling with me. A woman feels foolish when the first man she's taken an interest in for years turns out to be so far above her touch."

His expression was genuinely—reassuringly—baffled. "What did you ever see in me, Polonaise? I am no more above your touch than Soldier is fit for the Derby."

"You are telling me the truth, now." She wished she had her sketch pad, so she might catch that bemusement on his features. "I treasured that, you know? When our entire household was at sixes and sevens, you always told us women the truth. Allie noticed it first, that you never prevaricated with her, even when Sara and I were trying to spare her."

"You like that I have no tact?"

"I like that you have courage," she said softly, "and you are more affectionate than you want people to know."

"*Affectionate?*"

With her finger, she traced on her thigh the curve of his

upper lip. "Don't say it like it's an insult. You carried Allie around on that bad back of yours, you were always scratching and petting the beasts, and I know about those nights you spent arguing over cards with Beck. You left your brandy glasses about like the lordly fellows you truly are."

"Until you scolded us for our sloth," he replied, his slight smile flashing in the dim light. "And one can't help Beckman's nature. His whole family is that way, like wolves that spend the night in the same cave, all draped over each other with no dignity at all."

"You held me."

"Is that an accusation?"

"It's a blessed fact." Polly drew the curve of his smile next. He was self-conscious about this topic but not bolting from the discussion entirely. "I was the irascible, cranky cook, and you were the irascible, cranky steward, and you spiked my guns simply by putting your arms around me one night and telling me to hush."

She lapsed into silence, letting the memory have a space of respect in their dialogue. She'd been so wroth when the lazy twins bearing the title of footmen had helped themselves to the dessert intended for the next night's meal. Allie had been a brat, Sara was upset with Allie, and Polly's courses had been tormenting her for two straight days. She'd picked up a tin cup, intent on hurling it at the fire, when Gabriel had come in too late for supper and asked what a man might find for sustenance.

And midway through her harangue about a grown man being able to tell time, he'd simply slipped his arms around her, gently pushed her head to his shoulder, and told her to hush. She'd made a token protest, more surprise than indignation, and then let him soothe her with the simple comfort of his body next to hers. Then he'd sat her down, fixed her a cup of tea, and set out bread, cheese, apples, and butter, and made her eat with him.

That encounter had marked a turning point in their dealings, one punctuated with shared looks, shared cups of tea, and occasional embraces.

"You weren't afraid of me," Polly said.

"Nor you of me," he replied, and he might have leaned toward her a hair or two on those words. "I wasn't trifling, Polonaise. If I were trifling, you'd hate me now."

"How do you know I don't?"

"You have a temper, but you don't hate me. You only needed someone to be with you. You deserved a great deal more than I had to offer."

"That was for me to judge." Polly had a terrible urge to ask him for another of those embraces, so comforting and dear. She had missed him, missed him until her guts had ached with it, until she had no more tears to mark the sentiment.

"You think everything is for you to judge," Gabriel rejoined, affection in his voice. "When I say it's time for you to leave here, Polonaise, you'll go. That is for me to judge."

She gave him another glare, though his infernal conditions suggested he might genuinely be worried for her safety. He'd do that and let her think it was his concern over her ability to hold his confidences troubling him.

Idiot man.

"You're going to have to tell your brother what you were about for the past two years, Gabriel. He loves you, and you do owe him."

"Him and Marjorie both, though he tells me their marriage may be invalid as a result of my resurrection."

The logical consequences of such a notion had Polly

tracing a vintage Gabriel North scowl. "Is that why you were so careful with our dealings? You knew you had a fiancée?"

"She was married to my brother. It never occurred to me their union might not be valid, but Aaron has warned me Lady Hartle threatened breach of promise did he not marry Marjorie. In my case, the scandal would revolve around fraud in the inducement."

Polly had never heard such a term in spoken English, suggesting Gabriel's acquaintance with law far exceeded hers. "She'd do that to her own daughter?"

"She'd do it *for* her daughter. So you see, Polonaise, this place will soon be rife with unpleasantness and intrigue. You must not remain here too much longer, lest it taint you by association."

He was concerned for her, at least some. "Bother that. I'm associated with the Gypsy Princess, who played her violin for coin, and I've been to most of the courts of Europe, some of which were little better than orgies in progress."

Gabriel touched her cheek. "I would not see you burdened by my difficulties."

"So you'll really send me away?"

"I will."

She believed him, because he slipped an arm around her shoulders, tugged her against him, and held her just as he had that night in the Three Springs kitchen more than a year ago. She went into his embrace and cuddled up without a whimper of protest, because there was such strength and comfort to be had in his arms.

For her. As she breathed in the scent of soap, cedar, and tired adult male, Polly hoped their embrace held comfort for him too.

❦

Gabriel waited until the lady had fallen asleep, a warm, soft feminine bundle of heat, temper, and talent, and then let his lips cruise her temple. She smelled good—of spices, rose water, lavender, and Polonaise Hunt.

Even her name gave him pleasure—artistic, unique, and bold like her.

He should have told her the truth. When he'd gotten to Three Springs, he should have told her who he was and why he dissembled, but the idea that he could trust two women and a little girl to protect his interests had seemed laughable at the time.

He was the man; he did the protecting.

He'd learned differently.

As a steward, it hadn't been lost on him that the mamas among the beasts did the protecting. The mares, ewes, nannies, heifers, and she-cats all defended their young, while the stallions, rams, billy goats, bulls, and toms enjoyed reckless liberty until the mating urge struck yet again.

Sara and Polly had done what needed to be done to protect Allie and each other, and gradually, their care had extended to Gabriel as well. He had been awed and grateful, particularly when he'd suspected even his own brother of trying to kill him.

Those women, and looking after an old woman's estate with them, had changed Gabriel in ways he was only now coming to understand. He looked at Hesketh with new eyes, at the whole business of the marquessate differently.

And Polonaise Hunt appeared in the middle of this awkward adjustment as if Gabriel's chronic longing for her conjured the lady at his side.

He should have shooed her up to her room, but he couldn't stand to have her thinking their affections for each other had meant so little. She'd been a lifeline for him, pragmatic but kind, forcing food and rest and dry clothing on him when he'd been more inclined to work and work, and go back out in the rain, wind, cold, and mud, and work some more. She'd made him appreciate the small comforts—a cup of tea, a touch, a fresh, hot muffin slathered with butter, a smile—and made him realize that somewhere along the path to becoming the marquess, he'd missed the need to become Gabriel.

To her, he was simply Gabriel, and that had been precious. He feared it still was.

He carefully extricated himself from her warmth, secured the fire screen, and blew out the candles. By the light of the hearth, he scooped her up and carried her to her room. His back protested, but the warmth of the fire, and quite possibly Polly's company, had eased some of the grinding ache.

When he laid her down on her bed, he tugged off her slippers, drew the covers up over her, and permitted himself to kiss her cheek.

"Sleep well, my love."

She stirred but didn't waken, so he forced himself to leave her and take himself to the cold comfort of his solitary bed. Why it should be harder this time than any other, he really couldn't say.

<hr>

Gabriel rose before dawn, as had become his habit when at Three Springs. He was surprised to find Aaron in the breakfast parlor, a mountain of eggs, bacon, and toast on his plate.

"You're up early." Gabriel looked over the selections and wondered if there'd be cheese in the scrambled eggs, a dash of salt, a pinch of oregano.

"Habit from the cavalry," Aaron remarked between bites. "I've helped myself to most of the chocolate."

"Tea will do for me." Gabriel passed on the bacon, which wasn't as crisp as he preferred, but took ham, eggs, and toast. "Where in the hell is the butter?"

"Here." Aaron gestured with his elbow. "With a nice sprinkling of toast crumbs in it already."

Gabriel took a seat on his brother's right. "Marjorie doesn't have you trained yet?"

"She takes a tray in the morning. Saves a lot of bother first thing in the day. I trust you slept well?"

"Well enough." Gabriel tucked into his eggs. No cheese, not even a hint of salt or cream or chives greeted his palate. "You?"

"Not that well," Aaron said, eyeing his brother fleetingly. "Your reappearance has sparked a few old nightmares, but they'll fade. They always do."

"I'm sorry." Why hadn't it occurred to Gabriel that a veteran cavalry officer would have nightmares? Aaron had participated in nearly the entire Peninsular Campaign, for God's sake. "Is a wife an antidote to troubled slumber?"

Aaron paused, a forkful of eggs halfway to his mouth. "Little you know. Have you seen that wife's millinery bills?"

"Not yet." Gabriel took another dutiful bite of the most boring eggs he'd attempted in years. "Has she an allowance?"

"Nominally." Aaron poured himself the last of the chocolate. "But she has a she-dragon mother telling her that being marchioness means always dressing to the teeth, never uttering an unkind word, and generally behaving like a beautiful saint with a number of useless flirtatious devils always at her side."

"I was under the impression mothers were prone to

such nonsense. The good ones, in any case. Haven't we any jam?"

"I don't care for it. Shall we send a footman?"

"I'll manage," Gabriel replied, though having servants about while he ate was one of the things he'd not missed in the past two years. "I did look at your estate book, however briefly. You've our father's handwriting."

"As long as it's legible," Aaron said, cramming a piece of bacon into his mouth. "Any questions?"

"If you're game, I'd like to have a look at the mow where the hay went bad." The ham was too salty—suggesting it hadn't been allowed to soak—which was probably why there wasn't any salt in the eggs. Gabriel managed by taking half a bite of each simultaneously.

"I haven't looked at it yet," Aaron said. "George claims rain gets in under the eaves when we get the right type of Channel storm."

"You dispute the theory?"

"We've had storms all summer and fall, from every direction. That's the only load of hay gone bad, and we have three hay barns, Gabriel. George's theory simply doesn't fit with the facts, but far be it from me to argue sense when he has tradition and stubbornness on his side."

"He said you two butted heads from time to time." Gabriel pushed his plate aside, deciding the meal was not worth the effort. His hunger was appeased, but the fare was pedestrian, at best. "Father went rounds with George, and with George's predecessor all the time."

"One forgets this, but it's probably a good reason to have family in the steward position. You won't get quite as much deference as you would from some lackey."

"Valid point." Gabriel settled for another dainty cup of

tea, though he missed the sturdy, plain mugs Polly's kitchen had boasted. "I'll look over your estate book more carefully when I've more time. For today, I wanted to ride out, if you can join me?"

"I can." Aaron smiled, the first such offering of the day. "You're sure your delicate backside is up to it?"

"The worst thing for my delicate backside is inactivity," Gabriel said, rising. "I'll fetch my horse—"

Aaron gave him a vaguely concerned look.

"You don't fetch your horse, Gabriel. You send word to the stables you want the beast, and he appears, groomed and under saddle, shortly thereafter. You can't have forgotten that much."

Gabriel sat back down. Yes, he could forget that much. Easily. A pang of homesickness went through him for the many fine discussions he'd had with his horse as they'd prepared for their morning ride.

"You were a cavalry officer," Gabriel said. "How can you bear to let someone else groom your mount?"

"Now that you ask, it's damned difficult, but it gets easier when I recall the uproar it caused when I first sold out and didn't let the lads do their jobs. Then things went absolutely to hell when I learned you wouldn't be following me home from Spain, and Papa refused to let me go investigate. I was too busy after that to even manage grooming and saddling a horse, much less idling around the property on one's back."

"So we won't idle." Gabriel pushed to his feet. "We'll get our own damned horses because we please to, and then we'll inspect the property."

Aaron rose as well. "The harvest is in. What is there to inspect?"

"The livestock, the ditches and ponds, the lanes, the

pastures, turnip fields and winter gardens, the sheep pens... there's everything to inspect," Gabriel said as they left the parlor. "I picked up some ideas you might be interested in."

"I might," Aaron allowed, "if I were the marquess, but as that's not the case, why should I be filling my head with such things?"

"Because you're legally the marquess for now and this is your home and you're my heir should the title ever befall me again and because it's a pretty day for a ride with one's brother, perhaps the last of same for weeks."

"You have a point." Then Aaron stopped short and muttered, "Enemy approaching dead ahead."

Lady Hartle, looking tall, handsome, and hell-bent on a mission, swept into the foyer, a nervous footman taking her bonnet from her hand.

"So it's true." She advanced toward Gabriel, smiling brilliantly, both hands extended. "The Lord has granted us a miracle, and you are returned to us hale and sound." She kept on coming, so Gabriel took her hands and tried not to roll his eyes at his brother while the woman kissed the air on both sides of Gabriel's face. "This is splendid, just splendid." Lady Hartle retreated to arm's length, but didn't let go of Gabriel's hands. "We must plan a celebration."

"Greetings, Lady Hartle, and my thanks for your felicitations, but a celebration would be premature." Also damned inconvenient. "Protocol requires we consult with the solicitors first and follow their direction regarding the title, the vote, succession, and so forth."

"But what direction can they offer?" She smiled that smile again, conveying a world of tension. "You are Hesketh now. You must take your place accordingly."

"We will parse through that soon enough. For now, may we offer you tea?"

"I'm afraid I'll have to pass," Aaron said. "Press of business, you know. George was expecting me at the stables."

Lady Hartle tolerated him bowing over her hand then waved him away.

"Perhaps you'd like us to summon your daughter, my lady?" Gabriel posed the question as he offered his arm, though he shot Aaron an I'll-deal-with-you-later glower as well.

"Good heavens, no. She needs her beauty sleep, but with regard to this other, have no fear. She'll do as I say, or I'll know why."

Gabriel heard the sound of a cannonball whistling over the bow of his figurative ship. "I own I am puzzled. I was under the impression you were instrumental in assuring Marjorie married my brother with great dispatch and no little ceremony. One would think she'd take her direction from her husband now."

"Of course, of course. But in matters domestic, she receives guidance from her trusted mama. And this is quite the domestic matter, my lord."

"This?"

"Why, your miraculous return," she said. "I'm sure it will take some time, because you must take your seat, and we must figure out something for your brother, but Marjorie will honor her obligations under the betrothal contracts without a murmur of protest. You may depend upon it."

Gabriel's homesickness spread to encompass the nightly sessions philosophizing with the fair Hildegard as she and her piglets went at their scraps. "You expect your daughter to *switch husbands*, my lady?"

Lady Hartle... tittered. God spare him, the woman was better than a decade his senior, and she was tittering. "Not switch husbands. Rather, become wife to the man she has long been promised to. Surely, you don't intend to deny your obligation under the contracts drafted all those years ago, my lord?"

"Surely," Gabriel countered, "what God has joined together should not be put asunder for the sake of mere legalities, but this is not the time or place for such a discussion, my lady." Lest he himself be reduced to tittering. "Tell me how your property fares, and please accept my condolences on the passing of your late husband."

She drew herself up, no doubt to insist that this *was* the time and the place, but Gabriel kept his expression somewhere between frigid and forbidding, and she apparently rethought her strategy.

"It's been nearly two years," she replied, and as if she were falling into a dramatic role, Lady Hartle's visage went from Doting Mama-In-Law to Tragically Bereaved Widow Still Bearing Up Heroically.

Hildegard knew a thing or two about bearing up. She'd had litters spring and fall, and never once complained or tried to shirk her maternal duty—or tittered.

Gabriel bore up for a polite half hour of neighborhood gossip over the teapot, then saw his guest to the door and breathed a sigh of relief as he lit out for the stables. If his worthless deserter of a brother had ridden off without him, he'd...

Not do a damned thing.

"You're going to berate me because I scarpered?" Aaron led out a big black gelding with a white star on its forehead, while a groom held Soldier over by the mounting block.

GABRIEL 63

"I scarpered for two years." Gabriel swung up into the saddle. "I left you with a great deal besides the mother of the bride to contend with. Let's have a look at the hay barn."

Aaron gave him a measuring look, then mounted and fell in at the trot beside Gabriel's horse. "He's a little unprepossessing, isn't he?"

"Soldier?" Gabriel petted what was likely going to serve as his best friend for the duration. "He's got sense and bottom and he was left for dead much as I was."

"What did Lady Hartle want?"

"To ensure her daughter will continue to be the Marchioness of Hesketh, regardless of which insignificant fribble holds the title or beds down with her."

"What did you tell her?"

"That protocol will have to be observed, and solicitors consulted, but I'm telling *you* I'll be damned if I'll let the girl be passed from one of us to the other like some doxy." The woman. Marjorie was a grown woman.

"What if she wants to be passed?"

The world would run mad before Gabriel could accommodate that foolishness. "Talk her out of it, Aaron. She's been your wife for two years. I can't think she'd prefer me over you."

"Can't you?" Aaron fell silent, as if choosing his words while his black gelding picked its way around a muddy patch of the lane. "I can think she'll choose the title over me. Her mother has raised Marjorie to believe she has no value without it."

"Marjorie didn't want me to go to Spain," Gabriel recalled. "Nobody did, but his lordship wasn't going to forbid it, either."

"I want to say I'm glad you came for me." Aaron drew

his horse down to the walk as they approached the big building housing some of their stored hay. "The situation isn't so simple anymore."

"It isn't so complicated, either. If you want the title, Aaron, I won't fight you for it."

"I most assuredly do *not* want it. I will fight you to get out from under it, but not if it leaves Marjorie as the butt of gossip. She did only what she was told was her duty."

"In all likelihood, your marriage is valid, I have the title, and Marjorie is going to have to tell her mother to take a tisane." Or whatever a lady did instead of getting half seas over.

"You and I are going to have to tell Lady Hartle to take a tisane," Aaron said, swinging to the ground. "And we're going to have to tell her solicitors to take a tisane as well, probably all over the newspapers."

"A good scandal or two will liven things up."

"I beg your pardon?"

Gabriel swung off his horse. He couldn't reproduce the lithe maneuver Aaron executed, but he got himself safely to the ground.

"So we have a little scandal," Gabriel said. "That won't affect how I go through my day one bit, nor likely you or Marjorie. As long as the woman is married to someone, she'll be received. Was it only the one mow?"

"Beg pardon? Oh, yes, only the hay on the west end of the barn was affected, thank God."

They climbed up onto the huge beams separating one mow from the next, and peered at the eaves, soffit, supports, and the walls as the morning sun rose higher.

"The one wall shows signs of damp," Gabriel said, "while nothing else does. What do you make of it?"

"The water sure as hell didn't sneak in under the eaves,"

Aaron muttered. "Somebody dumped a barrel or two right down the wall and let it do its magic. The worst of the summer sun hits that wall on the outside, creating heat on the dampness."

"Ergo, mold. It wouldn't be too hard to use the pulley on the crossbeam to get a barrel of water up over the hay. Do you suppose we're going to have to guard the damned hay?"

"You put it to George," Aaron said, beginning his descent from the mow. "Seems to me it would be easier to put a lock on the barn."

"Suppose it would. Would a lock be an invitation to fire the entire lot?"

"The entire lot could have been fired already. What else would you like to see?"

Sound reasoning, and delivered without a lot of dancing about. "Everything, though not all at once. What do you want to show me?"

Aaron led him off over the countryside, down bridle paths, through the home wood, over some of the tenant farms, and into the village. They stopped for a pint, where Gabriel was gaped at and slapped on the back at length and stood to a few rounds of ale. Aaron took it all in with surprisingly good grace.

"One would think I was the one who survived the entire Peninsular Campaign," Gabriel groused. "Did they at least fuss over you when you came home?"

"Some." Aaron tightened his gelding's girth as they prepared to leave the pub for home. "You were still in Spain, and Father taken shortly thereafter, so it was a restrained greeting all around."

"From one war to another." Gabriel grimaced as he hoisted himself to the saddle. "Do you ever miss it?"

"The war? God in heaven, how could you ask such a thing? I saw more good men of many nations cut down, and for what? So the Russian winter and the Corsican's own hubris could do in a few months what we barely accomplished in a decade."

"The Russians might expect honorable mention in that story too. If it isn't the excitement and violence you crave, how does one explain all the duels, Aaron?"

Aaron's boot barely touched the stirrup as he mounted his horse. "You heard about those?"

"The betting books hold wagers regarding how many duels you can survive before your marchioness is widowed and the title forfeit. This disturbs me, Brother."

Aaron kept his eyes front as they trotted away from the village green. "You tell me where you've been for the past two years, and I'll tell you what compels me to the field of honor."

A silence went by, broken only by the rhythm of hooves on cold, hard earth.

"Give me a week," Gabriel said. "I want to set up our meeting with Kettering and give you time to make Marjorie see reason."

"Our meeting?"

"How many times must I say it? You are legally the marquess; *you*, not me. A succession is delicate. I'm sure there are formalities involved with shifting that burden onto my shoulders."

"We'll do this your way," Aaron said, "though as for talking to Marjorie, I've already told her I'd abide by her wishes."

Gabriel shot his brother a puzzled look. "After two years of bedding the woman, seeing her across the breakfast table, paying her bills, and leading her out? I can't believe you resent her so much you don't have any affection for her."

"You talk to her," Aaron said. "I have feelings for her, of course, more protective than I'd guessed, but the rest is private, Gabriel. You'll have to hear it from her, and if you don't change the subject now, my fourth duel will soon be scheduled."

"Right. I go to all the trouble to provide a perfect imitation of Lazarus, and all you can do is call me out."

"Treat Marjorie with anything less than perfect consideration," Aaron replied evenly, "and I'll do just that."

"Of course you will, putting an end to all this academic discussion about the succession. Now, is that fidgety bag of bones you're sporting about on capable of some speed and stamina, or is he merely for show?"

"To the bottom of the lane." Aaron grinned and stood in his stirrups, bending low over the gelding's neck. "Go!"

Four

"DID I LEAVE YOU TO BREAK YOUR FAST ALONE?" Marjorie, Lady Hesketh, looked truly distressed to have discommoded her guest.

"I like the occasional solitary meal," Polly said, rising from the sofa in her makeshift studio. "Though you're going to have to say something to your kitchen."

"I beg your pardon?"

"Let's sit you here, by the window," Polly suggested, indicating a bench upholstered in blue velvet. Morning sun streamed in the window, giving way to a view of the extensive back gardens.

"Your kitchen has stopped trying," Polly said, "at least for breakfast. They know you don't come down, and hungry men will eat most anything. Turn your shoulders two inches." Polly demonstrated, turning her own shoulders to the left. "Chin up one inch."

"What should I tell my cook?"

"You should probably take a meal or two in the breakfast parlor." Polly pulled up a stool and opened her sketch pad. "Then they'll know you check on them and be motivated to please them accordingly. Otherwise, they'll think his lordship, or perhaps his brother, peached on them."

"Peached?"

"The eggs are merely scrambled, not a dash of salt or a sliver of cheese to enhance their palatability. The toast is yesterday's bread, I'm thinking, and the tea wasn't exactly kept hot. Wrapping a towel over the pot is a simple thing, something you'd notice and the footmen wouldn't."

Marjorie's spine straightened. "I'll see to this, but did you run your own household, Miss Hunt, that such oversights are apparent to you?"

"Chin," Polly reminded her. "I ran the kitchen of a modest manor, though I'm told that's not to be repeated among my betters, which most assuredly includes you. You have the loveliest hair."

"Blond." Marjorie put a wealth of despair in one word. "Mama laments that I should have been anything more remarkable than merely blond."

"My sister has flaming red hair." Polly's pencil flew over the page as she tried to capture Lady Marjorie on her dignity. "Appreciate your blond hair, my lady. Hair color alone can brand a woman a strumpet."

"A strumpet?" Lady Marjorie's pretty blue eyes went wide, then she caught Polly's mischievous smile. "Shall I dye mine?"

"A little henna might bring out the red highlights, but first threaten to do it, and see what Hesketh's reaction would be."

"One threatens to use cosmetics?"

"Married to a handsome fellow like that, one does."

"It won't do any good," Marjorie replied, and her chin did not dip, but her expression wilted. "He hates me."

"Most spouses think they hate each other at some point. It's part of the charm of marriage, and then a baby comes along and there's no time for that nonsense. Look out the window, my lady, off into the distance, as if your knight in shining armor were due back from the pub at any minute."

"You think I'm being silly." Marjorie said it quietly. "Everybody thinks I'm silly, because I'm young. I think I'm silly too, but one doesn't quite know what to do about it."

Rather than mindlessly reassure an insecure young aristocrat, Polly recalled all the times she and Sara had traded ideas, gripes, insecurities, and fears with each other.

"Silly, how?"

"Unless I'm on a horse, I'm uncomfortable. I take a tray in my room to avoid my husband in the morning. I ride about all day so I won't be home when Mama calls, but can time my calls on her for when I know she's busy. I dread going over the menus with Cook, and the evenings when my husband dines with me nearly give me hives. I spend hours dressing for him, and he never even glances at me once he's held my chair and poured my wine."

"You want him to notice you?"

"Of course I want him to notice me!" The despair was back, more evident than ever. "He married me because Mama said it must be so, not because he chose me, and the least I can do is try to be a good wife to him."

Polly inspected her sketch, as if scratching lines on a page were a complicated undertaking. "There's been talk that the betrothal contracts may be revisited because your mama dearly wants to see you remain Lady Hesketh."

Marjorie's eyebrows rose. "Already?" She had perfectly symmetrical eyebrows, which was rare. "That didn't take long. And I can't tell if Aaron wants me to toss him over or leave Gabriel free to choose elsewhere. Aaron is being the perfect gentleman about the whole business. It makes me bilious to think of it."

"Bilious?" Polly's subject had become *animated*, so Polly kept her ladyship talking and kept the pencil moving.

"I feel like a broodmare—put her to this stud; if she won't catch, put her to another," Marjorie spat. "But I won't catch with Aaron, not ever."

"I can't believe he's lacking the equipment. Shoulders back a hair."

"He has the equipment, or so the gossip suggests, but I've never had the pleasure, so to speak." A hot, very visible blush followed those words. "You won't tell anybody?"

"Of course not." Polly's pencil went still as she beheld a bewildered young wife, not a marchioness, and certainly not a subject. "Men can be idiots, on this we may agree, regardless of station. Why do you suppose Aaron is being so shy?"

"Shy? That man couldn't spell the word if you told him all three letters," Marjorie huffed. "I can't think what he's about, not now. Two years ago, I would have said he resented his bride bitterly, but if he's dutiful enough to marry me, then why isn't he dutiful enough to see to the rest of it?"

"Because he's an idiot." Polly made a few more lines on the page, because symmetric eyebrows were not the only lovely feature on the lady's face. "I have a suggestion, though."

"He can't be made jealous," Marjorie said. "Mama suggested that, and it has been a crashing failure. He can't be made angry—another of Mama's brilliant ideas. I've spent eons with the modistes to run up the bills, and he merely lectures and pays them anyway."

Polly grinned, flipping to a new page. "Well done."

"Well done, Miss Hunt?"

"You're assessing strategy. One has to sort through one's choices of weapon before any battle, to see which is most appropriate to the instant challenge. Please stop wringing your hands, my lady."

"What strategy would you propose?"

"You could always show up naked in his bed. Probably give him apoplexy if you did."

"In his *bed*?" For all her consternation, Lady Marjorie was fascinated with the suggestion.

"Or in the saddle room. Hands, my lady. Or the still room, or wherever he's likely to have some time and privacy."

"In the light of *day*?"

"Men are particularly frisky in the early morning, so I'm told. But all of this assumes you want to woo him. Do you?"

Marjorie bit her lip in thought, and Polly let her, as a thoughtful Lady Marjorie was as interesting as a bewildered Lady Marjorie.

"I do," she said. "I most assuredly do want to woo him."

"For his sake?" Polly asked. "Because the poor beleaguered man has been stuck with such a harridan for his wife?"

Marjorie's shoulders slumped. "He has been stuck with me. Any spouse chosen for one's brother has to be a bitter pill, but I also want to do this for me."

Marjorie was pretty; she was by no means stupid, but she was young and lonely. On the strength of those observations, Polly presumed to ask another question. "You love him?"

"That is a... sensitive question. I'd take Aaron over his brother any day." She shuddered at the thought, and Polly knew it was time to change the subject—or it should be.

A woman with scruples would change the subject.

Such a woman wouldn't swill brandy in the dead of night, pretending to fall asleep rather than be forced back to the solitude of her bed.

"You don't care for your former intended, my lady?"

"I hardly know him." Marjorie's eyes did focus on the distant gardens, as if she could see the past. "Gabriel has changed, that's obvious, and he wouldn't be a terrible husband, but he's so... fierce. He's dark, inside and out, and while Aaron is also older than I, Gabriel has always seemed remote in ways that do not inspire easy affection."

"So you were relieved to marry Aaron?" Polly asked gently. "Aaron is a fine man, from what I've seen, and I do think he has feelings for you."

Marjorie gave a wan smile. "Exasperation, mostly."

"Take him riding. If that's where you're at your best, then show him that."

"It's less intimidating than your other suggestion." Marjorie's smile became more pronounced, and Polly's pencil moved more quickly.

"Keep thinking what you're thinking now," Polly ordered, "about how surprised your husband would be if you beat him in a race on horseback, how he looks when he's had a good gallop, how you look when you've beaten somebody over a half-mile course. Think about your mama, vacationing for months in Portugal, think about... those few, discreet comments you can make to the cook, and watching the respect grow in her eyes when she sees you do notice her work and appreciate when she does it well. Think about—" Polly put her pencil down. "Think about this woman."

She showed Marjorie the sketch, one of a lovely young woman whose smile sparkled and whose eyes held warmth, wit, and intelligence.

"That cannot be me."

"That is one image of you. An accurate one, because I do not believe in taking license with my subjects. You can make Aaron Wendover see that this is the woman he married, not..." She flipped the page, to the first image. "Her."

Marjorie studied the sketch. "She's young and scared and uncertain and... dull."

"All of which"—Polly flipped back to the other sketch—"is something this woman can take in stride. Think about it, Lady Marjorie. If you don't stake your claim now, you might lose your only remaining opportunity to do so. If Aaron will marry you out of duty, he'll likely also let the solicitors set the marriage aside out of the same motivation. You have to *show* him what you want, if he can't hear you when you tell him."

"Men." Marjorie's formerly guileless eyes began to dance. "Can be..." She lowered her voice and looked around. "Idiots."

"They can be." Polly stuck her pencil into the bun at her nape. "Women can be too. Now let's do this study from the other angle, which means you shift to let the sun hit the other side of your face. And keep thinking wicked thoughts, my lady. They bring out the sparkle in your eye."

❧

"I need to talk to you."

Gabriel nodded, because Polly had murmured nearly in his ear as he'd seated her at dinner, and he knew better than to make a fuss. Of course, he'd been sneaking a whiff of her scent by leaning in so close, which was a pathetic comment on the state of his self-discipline.

Dinner was surprisingly pleasant, with both ladies carrying the conversation into all sorts of interesting topics.

Marjorie interrogated Aaron about cavalry mounts, and if anybody thought it odd that husband and wife had never discussed such a mutually agreeable topic before, it wasn't remarked. Polly volunteered some details of her plans for Marjorie's portrait, and Aaron tossed in the occasional observation about the tenants they'd visited.

"Mr. Danner's back is acting up." Aaron turned his claret by the stem of his wineglass. "The man's eighty if he's a day. One wonders what he can be thinking."

"He's not supposed to be eighty?" Polly asked.

"He's not supposed to stand up with every young girl at the local assemblies," Aaron countered. "The last one was this past weekend, and Danner is still hobbling around."

"And likely grinning," Gabriel chimed in. "I want to be just like him when I grow up. If a man's going to have a bad back, he should at least put it to the test flirting with the fillies, don't you think?"

"When he's eighty?" Marjorie looked puzzled at such a notion. "One fears for his daughter's nerves. Miss Hunt, shall we leave the men to their port?"

"We shall." Polly rose, and again Gabriel assisted. "Or we could repair to your wardrobe and start choosing outfits to pose you in."

"It makes a difference?"

Aaron answered Marjorie's question. "Of course it would. That blue-and-cream habit makes your eyes positively snap, and pink makes you look like a schoolgirl. And despite what your mother claims, she puts you in yellow only so you don't outshine your younger sisters."

"Forgive him," Gabriel said. "My brother is tired and not thinking clearly. I'm sure you'd look lovely attired in sack cloth and ashes."

Polly linked her arm through Marjorie's. "My lord, you might convince the lady that's a compliment if you tried smiling as you said it. Come along, my lady. They've drinking to do."

"In the library?" Aaron asked when the ladies had departed.

Bless a younger brother with common sense. "Where there's a big, roaring fire."

"I like her," Aaron offered as they ambled across the corridor. "Miss Hunt. Marjorie is lonely, though I hadn't noticed it before."

"And consorting with other women of her station can be trying," Gabriel added. "They can be such cats. Cribbage or something else?"

"I can beat you easily at cribbage, but it will at least take up the time while we drink."

The casual jibes and insults took them through about a third of the decanter, until they'd won two games each. Aaron excused himself, pausing at the library door.

"That week you mentioned earlier?"

"Hmm?" Gabriel stoked the fire then shoved the sofa closer to it.

"You'd best talk to Marjorie before we go see the solicitors," Aaron said. "Talk to her privately."

"You talk to her," Gabriel shot back. "She's your wife and likely will remain so."

"I don't talk with her about our marriage, Gabriel." Aaron's tone was simply weary.

"Why not?"

This seemed to give him pause, for he leaned back against the closed door. "At first, because I was so angry, and then because I didn't know what to say. Maybe you can get the truth from her. I'm not sure I ever did."

On those words, he slipped away, leaving Gabriel to arrange himself gratefully before the fire. He'd dozed off, his head pillowed on the estate book, when the library door opened on a barely audible creak.

"Close the door, Polonaise. You're letting in a draft."

"I passed Aaron on the stair." She moved into the room on silent feet. "He said your back was hurting."

"My brother has aspirations toward the medical profession, then." Gabriel rolled to his back. "The fire helps. What have you been about, though, Miss Polonaise Hunt, wandering the house alone after dark?"

"Thinking," Polly said, dropping down on a hassock.

"About?"

She gave him a basilisk, Polonaise stare. "What do you make of your brother's marriage?"

"They seem cordial." Gabriel lay where he was and passed her the estate book, which was rude of him, when a lady was present. He'd told the truth, though: his back had just started to ease, and movement did not appeal.

"They seem awkward to me," Polly said. "Cordially awkward."

"Typical marriage among the English quality." The firelight turned her nightgown and wrapper to gossamer as she put the estate book back on the desk, then stood before the hearth, warming her hands. Gabriel did not close his eyes.

"Beck and Sara will never be cordially awkward," Polly rejoined. "Nicholas and Leah won't be either, and that other brother of Beck's... Mr. Grey, he has a way to go before he even merits cordial among strangers."

"Beckman's brothers came to Beckman and Sara's wedding, I take it?"

Polly resumed her seat, which was a mercy. "I half expected you to attend."

"Beckman would not have known where to send the invitation." Gabriel arranged a pillow under his head. "I was scouting the territory here before I went up to Town. It was lovely?"

He saw too late the question was unkind, considering Polly had resigned herself to the life of a spinster artist.

"Shall I hold you again, Polonaise?" He made the offer quietly, as much of a bracing taunt as a genuine overture. She stiffened, and he thought maybe he'd achieved his objective, but then she nodded once. He shouldn't have asked this either, especially not this, but he held out his arms to her anyway.

She surveyed his recumbent length. "You're just going to lie there?"

"I'm getting quite good at it. Come, don't be silly. You've lain in my arms before."

She muttered something, then straddled him gingerly and folded down onto his chest.

"Budge up." He petted her derriere. "Warmth makes me biddable. Now what were you thinking about, Polonaise, that dreams of me elude you tonight?"

"I'm going to violate a confidence."

"Then it must be serious." He'd known her two years, and she'd never once betrayed a secret or indulged in gossip.

"If there were a legal argument making it easier to invalidate your brother's marriage, would you want to know about it?"

"Serious, indeed." He rested his chin on her crown and traced her spine with his fingers, a serious pleasure. "What do you think you know, Polonaise?"

"Is nonconsummation a ground for annulment?"

"I couldn't honestly say," Gabriel answered slowly,

"though I doubt it. You claim Aaron hasn't consummated his union with Marjorie? Aaron, who can't take his eyes off his wife, and Marjorie, who resembles a well-bred version of every mistress the man has ever had?"

"I didn't need to know that. But yes, that Aaron and that Marjorie."

"She told you this?"

Silence, which said enough.

"Interesting."

Polly rubbed her cheek against his chest, and warmth began to make Gabriel something besides biddable. "I've thought maybe the Wendover men are all shy and sexually reticent."

She used such bold, naughty words to hide her hurt feelings.

"Because I didn't swive you?" Gabriel let his hand travel to the very base of her spine, then retrieved his errant appendage before it could perpetrate true mischief. "I regret that, you know."

"Oh, of course." And without moving, Polly communicated to him that her feelings had been more than hurt. Damn him, he'd become not just a marquess, but a heartbreaker.

"You think I regret missing a mere moment of pleasure, don't you?"

"Don't you?" She shifted to peer at him. "Or possibly several moments?"

What he regretted was missing a lifetime of moments with her, for every one would have been a pleasure.

"Had there been a child," he reminded her, "I would have insisted on marrying you, my dear, and you weren't willing to take that step; hence, I allowed no opportunity for consummation."

Allowed was a grand term for having barely hung on to his scruples.

"I understood your conditions, and you apparently understood mine." She fell silent, but she was prostrate upon him, his arms around her, and Gabriel could feel her gathering her courage. "I can't have children, Gabriel, or so I've been told."

His hand went still, but then he said the first thing that popped into his tired brain.

"I am so sorry." He gathered her closer, and again, she resisted at first but then capitulated with a weary sigh.

"I haven't had much occasion to test the diagnosis," she said. "You would have been the first in a long, long time."

"For me as well," he said, the need to protect her from this hurt so great, he would have taken her into his very body had there been a way. "I couldn't risk leaving a child to fend without a father, and you won't agree to marry on any terms, so there we were."

"And now we're here."

Fatigue, brandy, and Polly's latest revelations made it easier to hold sexual arousal at bay. Gabriel let longing simmer in his vitals, while Polly fell asleep on his chest. To hold her thus was a privilege he'd been granted on only a few occasions, and they burned in his memory as moments of profound ambiguity.

Polly had trusted him, and all the while, he'd been lying to her. He'd savored the forbidden pleasure of limited intimacy with her, even as he'd been tormented by his dishonesty toward her and toward every member of the Three Springs household.

He hadn't been lying, though, when he'd told her he'd marry her. If she'd conceived his child, he'd have had a special license in hand before sundown the same day, and no argument in the world would have stayed him.

No argument from her, no argument from anybody.

Which meant Aaron had best fall in love with his damned wife and put period to Lady Hartle's damned maneuvering. But what on earth could the man have been thinking, to leave his lovely young wife untouched after two years?

And why had Polly chosen now to confide that she couldn't have children?

❧

"So, lad." Old Mr. Danner settled into his padded rocker. "What was you doing, being dead these two years past?"

Gabriel eyed his tenant, a man who'd always been ancient to him. What he noticed now was that Danner also appeared enviably contented. "I was farming, and growing up."

Danner grinned around his pipe stem. "Done a bit of both myself. Of necessity only."

"Your fields and stock suggest otherwise, but was it necessary to stand up with every last one of the pretty girls, sir?"

"Somebody has to give George Wendover a run for his money." Danner's smile faded. "That one thinks he knows everything, and thinks the ladies should be grateful for his attentions."

"And you don't think the same thing about your own attentions?"

Danner wheezed merrily at this reply then sobered. "It's well you're back. Young master Aaron was giving it a good try, but he's distracted by that little wife of his."

"She tops you by several inches, and that's before she puts on her riding boots."

Danner waved his pipe. "She's just a girl. How that she-beast Lady Hartle raised up such a one is beyond me. But her pa doted on Lady Margie, and that will tell."

"Margie?"

Danner jammed his pipe back into his mouth. "Her husband calls her Margie."

"How can you know these things?"

"You ever take to napping, lad, you'll overhear plenty, and when the women think you're harmless, you'll overhear plenty more."

As if old men invented eavesdropping? And Gabriel had taken to napping, and not so he could eavesdrop in the library of an evening. "I've given your daughter a recipe for a salve that I've found helpful when my back troubles me."

"And isn't it a grand thing a man can't put salve on his own back? You were smart to take that knife in your backside."

Oh, yes, brilliant of him. "It was in my back, not my *backside*."

"More fool you. When you getting married?"

"Not anytime soon." Gabriel scowled at him, but either the old man didn't see well enough to know he trod on thin ice, or he didn't care—and why should he?

Danner sat forward, a deliberate scoot that involved using his hands on the rocker arms to pull himself about. "Have you taken marriage into dislike at your tender age? Your pa had both you bull calves on the ground only late in life, and you and your brother are past your quarter century. Lady Hartle makes poor Lady Marjorie's life a hell, ranting about the heir and the title and all. Best get your own wife, my lord, and find an easy breeder while you're at it."

"And one can tell this by looking at their teeth?"

Danner smirked. "It's a place to start. Mostly, you look at their willingness for the task."

"You have the one daughter," Gabriel pointed out bluntly. "Aren't you out of your depth on this issue?"

"I had the one daughter," Danner said softly, "because I was willing to have only the one wife. Joan's mama was the love of me life, and there was no other for me when she passed."

"How long have you been alone?" The question wasn't one Gabriel would have asked had they any company, but Joan was bustling in the kitchen, the grandchildren were off at their chores, and a great-grandbaby slept soundly in a basket by the hearth.

"I have been a widower for nigh fifty years, but I am never alone. We had eight good years together, and they've lasted me the entire eighty. It's like that, you see, when you can marry where your heart lies. But you lot wouldn't know anything about such, which, if you ask me, is why your womenfolk are so peaked and wan."

"Fifty years?"

"Fifty-one this spring. Losing her was hard, but I'd not choose else, not for a moment." His expression turned mischievous. "And the ladies do dote on a young widower, offering him all manner of comfort."

"Bother you." Gabriel rose and peered at the baby in her cradle as a means of avoiding the old man's gaze.

Danner gestured at the infant, who'd begun to make wakeful-baby noises. "You can bring that one here. We're of a mind to rock for a bit, aren't we, lambkin?"

Two years ago, Gabriel would have summoned Joan to pick up the child. Hell, two years ago, he wouldn't have been here, offering the recipe for Sara's salve to a mere tenant, and two years ago, he wouldn't have admitted to needing the damned salve himself.

But he'd spent that two years tending the land and bringing forth every kind of young the farmyard boasted, so it was no great feat of courage to pick up the baby and cradle her against his shoulder.

Only a little feat of courage. "What's her name?"

"Edith, best I can recall. They're all of a piece at that age."

Gabriel took the other rocker and settled with the child, an odd feeling starting up in his chest. "How many do you have?"

"Seven grands, living, and eight great-grands," Danner replied. "That child looks mighty comfortable on your shoulder, lad. I'm thinking you were telling the truth about those two years of farming."

"I was down by Portsmouth," Gabriel said, which was vague enough.

"Didn't know Hesketh held land down that way, though God knows you own every parish for fifty miles."

"Hardly." Gabriel began to rock the baby, who stirred quietly against his shoulder. "I ended up working for a man who'd traveled extensively. He'd seen agriculture on at least four continents and had learned some neat tricks."

"Good luck showing your neat tricks to old George."

"George Wendover is old? What does that make you?"

"I'm merely eightyish. That boy is old, in here." He tapped his bald skull. "He hasn't had a new idea since he were thirty, and when an old idea will do, that's fine; but times change, and the land needs our best ideas, new or old, as strange as they may seem."

"There's a place for tradition," Gabriel temporized, because any steward would have his detractors, and any old man would find things to criticize.

"Tradition is fine for Yuletide," Danner spat. "You think my acres prosper? They do, and not only because they're well situated. I do as I damned please here, and so does Joan's Tom and their boys, because George learned long ago that my yields will outperform his."

"Give me an example." Gabriel wasn't really interested in hearing Danner's rantings about a steward who'd served loyally and without complaint for two decades, but neither was he in a hurry to leave the fireside and the company he'd found there.

Joan sang softly in the kitchen, Danner's rocker creaked gently, and the scent of fresh bread stirred precious memories few titled lords could claim.

"George understands that land must fallow, and he understands you run the stock over the land after harvest, to give them a little start on winter," Danner said. "But he lets the sheep have first go, half the time, and then you spend the fallow year recovering from the sheep."

"The sheep are as hungry as the cattle or horses." Gabriel shifted, because the baby was raising her head to peer around the room. "Hello, sweetheart."

"Damned flirt, that one. Takes after me handsome self."

"The sheep?"

"The sheep eat right down to the roots," Danner said. "The cows not so much, and it's the cows that need the fodder more than the sheep."

"Why do you say that?" Gabriel knew these arguments as well as he knew the particular ache a man suffered when breaking sod with a tired team, but he'd never before held a baby to his shoulder.

"Sheep is growing only wool, lad," Danner said patiently. "Cows is growing hair too, but also putting milk in the bucket, and half the time growing a calf while they're about it. But it's still the sheep that are harder on the land."

"But penning the sheep on the fallow ground over

winter fertilizes it." Gabriel got up to make an inspection of the room with the baby on his shoulder.

"Horses do the best job of fertilizing." Danner sat back, no doubt ready to start in on a rousing difference of opinion over the merits of various types of manure. "Anybody knows horse shite works a treat compared to the others."

The baby grabbed Gabriel's ear. "You believe this?"

"I know it. I've the yields to prove it."

"If I sent Aaron here to discuss this with you, could you make the time?"

Danner cracked another smile. "You don't be sending that one anywhere. You be asking him to look in on me, and that'll do. There isn't a man standing can resist Joan's sweet rolls."

"Get her to make you up some of that salve." Gabriel bent to hand off his burden. "And you'll be dancing with Edith when her turn comes."

"I plan to." Danner took the baby and cradled her in his arms. "You've a way with a babe, my lord. You should be finding yourself a bride."

"What has one to do with the other?"

"Ah, now," Danner chided, "you've been farming and growing up, you say. A man who can handle a wee child is ready to handle a wife as well." He shouted for Joan, which caused the baby to giggle. "Send his lordship along with some sweet rolls, and make up another batch. Looks like we might be having more company."

Gabriel waited for Joan to wrap up the rolls, though as a younger man, he would have made his excuses rather than been seen stealing off with treats like a schoolboy.

A younger, stupider man. The thought made him smile as he thanked Joan for the rolls, complimented her on her grandchild, and urged her to give the salve a try. The first bun was gone before he'd gotten within a mile of the manor; then he spied Marjorie out with her groom and changed direction to intercept her.

Marjorie offered him a tentative smile. "Good morning, my lord. You called on the Danners?"

Gabriel returned her smile, though this seemed to alarm her. "I did, including the fair Miss Edith. Is that the half Turk you mentioned at dinner last night?"

She petted her horse, her whole demeanor relaxing as she went into a rhapsody about the horse's stamina and sense.

"Could I trouble you to sit with me for a few minutes?" Gabriel asked when she was done with her panegyric, and immediately her guard went back up. "I've sweet rolls, you see, and wouldn't want to eat them all myself. Or I would, but you will preserve me from such gluttony."

"It's clouding up, my lord." The clouds were lowering, true enough, but clouds lowered over most locations in England several times a day.

"It's been clouding up all morning." Gabriel dismounted and handed Soldier's reins to the groom. "My horse asks you to spare him from the additional weight of all these sweets, on me or my person." He reached up to lift her out of the saddle and saw something like panic flare in her eyes. But she got to the ground in a lithe movement, and he found she was not quite as insubstantial as her appearance suggested.

"I don't bite, my lady," he murmured quietly so the groom wouldn't overhear. "Not without an invitation anyway. Shall we stroll?"

"Let's sit, if we're to see to your sweets."

"Come." He winged an elbow, and she wrapped a hand

around his forearm, though he could feel the tension in her and wondered if she'd always been so high-strung. "Will that bench do?" The very same bench upon which he'd first spoken with his brother.

"Of course."

When they were seated, Gabriel passed along a sweet roll and laid his handkerchief between them. "Danner claims they're irresistible. I have to agree. But, Marjorie?" She risked a glance at him when he paused. "I'm going to gobble up my treat, not my sister-in-law."

❦

Marjorie set the roll down untouched, and Gabriel couldn't read her reaction. He munched in silence, wondering how one broached the topic he had in mind. The groom was patiently walking the horses a good distance away, and there were only so many rolls to stall with.

A yellow leaf came twirling down and landed beside his handkerchief.

"You don't want to be married to me, do you?" Gabriel figured that was a fine place to start, while Marjorie found it worthy of a blush. "You won't hurt my feelings, Marjorie, if you tell me you've developed an attachment to my brother. I rather like him myself."

"It's difficult, my lord." Her voice was low, and she hunched forward as if to hide her face.

Gabriel munched on his roll, though all he could taste was guilt that Marjorie was to be subjected to awkwardness. More awkwardness. "Eat your sweet, my dear. It isn't difficult. I was more than willing to marry you previously. You're pretty, intelligent, pleasant company, and familiar with the Hesketh seat and holdings. The match would have been appropriate." Which was an awful word for an intimate, lifelong relationship.

She stripped off her gloves and dutifully picked up a roll. "But now?"

"Now I think your affections have been engaged elsewhere, and I do not give one good goddamn—pardon my language—for what your mother wants. Neither should you."

"She isn't your mother, my lord."

Gabriel dusted off his fingers on the handkerchief. "I think we might address each other informally, don't you?"

"I don't know what to call you." Marjorie tore a bite off her roll but did not eat it. "And you don't know my mother when she's determined on something. Ask Aaron, for he's borne the brunt of her maneuvering."

Twenty yards away, the groom walked the horses, their hooves sloshing through the carpet of fallen leaves with a sussurating rhythm that put Gabriel in mind of the springs at his former post.

"I do ask Aaron. My brother tells me I'm to get the truth out of you, and he'll abide by whatever your wishes are regarding the disposition of your marriage. But it isn't that simple, you see."

"I don't see." Marjorie hunched farther forward, looking young and put upon, which she was. "Mama claims there are legalities upon legalities, and good solicitors could make a great batch of scandal broth out of the lot."

"And why would she do this to her oldest daughter? You and Aaron seem not exactly content, but suited."

"He doesn't think so," Marjorie muttered around a mouthful of pastry. "He's merely dutiful, my lord, and so am I. So here we are."

Here we are, on a pretty fall day threatening to turn damp and miserable.

"So where are my heirs, Marjorie?" Gabriel put the question quietly, his conversation with Polly ringing in his ears. "I know my brother, and in two years, he hasn't become a monk."

She was silent, brushing the dead leaf off their bench, which told him Polly had likely been right.

Gabriel scrubbed a hand over the back of his neck and longed for the days when a simple steward might have a pleasant chat with his friend and confidante, the fair Hildegard. "A man doesn't threaten to call out his own brother over a woman he regards as a mere duty."

"Aaron threatened to meet you?"

"Which could leave him with the title anyway, something he says he does not want," Gabriel pointed out. "This suggests he's not thinking rationally. He cares for you."

"He's a gentleman," Marjorie said, staring at her half-eaten roll. "He hates the business, though. All that correspondence, hours in the library with a pen in his hand, when what he wants is to be out, seeing to the land."

"So he criticizes George at every turn and finds many excuses to leave his desk and get into the fresh air."

"George finds many excuses to bother him," Marjorie countered. "The man is afraid to make a decision, or so Aaron has said."

"My father did not suffer fools," Gabriel rejoined, though Papa had had a sweet tooth. "He took the management of the land most seriously. George learned diplomacy and deference as a result. But we stray from my topic, Marjorie: Will you fight for your marriage, or must I do it for you?"

"You?" She shot him such an incredulous look that Gabriel was assailed by... not simply guilt, but shame.

A coolish sort of breeze fluttered the edges of his handkerchief and sent more leaves cascading toward the earth.

"I wasn't a very good fiancé, was I?"

"You're a dozen years my senior. Were you supposed to play dolls with me?"

"Yes," Gabriel said, "if that's what it took to become your friend."

He was friends with Polly. The realization caused a trickle of warmth to well up through his insides.

"*Now* you want to be friends?"

"You could use a friend," Gabriel said. "God knows, I can use a few more."

Marjorie's expression became thoughtful. "Miss Hunt said the same thing. About me. She said…"

"What did she say?"

"A good friend is the best defense against any adversity."

"Eat your roll." Gabriel passed the remaining half to her. "We need to talk again, my lady, but know this: even if you let your mother set aside your marriage to Aaron, I will not be eager to wed you."

"Plain speaking," Marjorie allowed as she nibbled on her roll. She did not seem overset by plain speaking.

"You don't care about the title, do you?"

"Honestly?" Eating her pastry, she looked very pretty and very alone. "I hate it. Aaron hates it, but it's what brought us together."

"Hate is a strong word." Particularly strong coming from Marjorie.

"The title cost me my mother," Marjorie said, popping the last bite into her mouth. "Your title did. She's a good mother to my brothers and sisters, but in my case, she stopped seeing *me* long ago. I'm not a daughter to her; I'm a marchioness on the hoof."

"One comprehends your point." Gabriel smiled at her bluntness and at the way the roll had disappeared now that her nerves had settled. "Do you also hate the idea of providing the Hesketh heir?"

Marjorie dusted her hands together and made a production out of folding her gloves over and tucking them into a pocket. "You were blunt before, but not... not like this."

"I've been away from society," Gabriel replied, "but I ask, not out of vulgar curiosity, but because it's the duty of a spare to provide the offspring if the title holder can't. As Aaron's wife, that duty could well befall you."

Marjorie waved a second roll in the direction of the Hartle holdings. "Tell that to Mama. She craves the title, not the right to crow that her grandson is the heir."

"Are you sure?" Gabriel thought back to little Edith and the magic of her gummy smile.

"I am certain." Marjorie made short work of her second sweet. "It's as if Mama gets the title by having it hung around my neck."

"I suppose I could die again," Gabriel mused, shifting about to ease the ache in his back. "That would serve her ends."

"Don't even jest about it." Marjorie's tone was uncharacteristically sharp. "You didn't see your brother upon the occasion of your death. He wanted to go to Spain, because the reports did not satisfy him you were truly gone. But then your father took ill and Mama started her nonsense and the estate was without leadership. You put much on him, and it's not a joking matter."

The female of the species apparently did the protecting at Hesketh too. "Believe me, Marjorie, I was unable to come home at the time, not unwilling."

"Aaron says your back still pains you."

"Sometimes." When had Aaron passed that along? "He's decent to you?"

"Always. He's better since you've come back, though. He's not so beset, not so terribly worried every minute."

"We were never exactly close, not like some brothers," Gabriel reflected. "I think we each assumed the other would always be there. I didn't want him to buy his colors, but he was horse mad and going quietly crazy here."

"I tried to talk him out of signing up, but he's as stubborn as Mama."

"Stubborn is not necessarily a bad thing." Gabriel bumped her shoulder gently with his. "You might try it yourself."

"No, thank you." Marjorie passed him his handkerchief, which allowed him to capture her hand and hold it. "There's enough stubbornness hereabouts to suffice."

"You love him, don't you?" Gabriel said it quietly, but she heard him because she held his gaze long enough for him to see her eyes filling with tears.

"It doesn't signify."

Gabriel prevented her from rising by his grip on her hand, because he had the sense her next words would be the most important they'd exchanged.

"Mama says..."

"Hang Mama." Gabriel pulled her to him and looped an arm across her shoulders. "Would you treat your daughter the way your mama treats you?"

"N-no." She shook her head, her forehead resting on his shoulder. "Never."

"That should tell you something, Marjorie the Reluctant Marchioness." He tucked his handkerchief into her hand. "You and Aaron need to talk about your marriage. I know he's stubborn and he's hardheaded, but you love this about him too. Find a way to use it to your advantage."

"There isn't a way." She shifted, and he let her go. "You'll see. Mama will get that dreadful Mr. Erskine to threaten all manner of legal warfare, and you'll fall into line, and Aaron will allow it."

"Talk to him," Gabriel urged, patting her hand. "I'm satisfied you don't want to be my bride, and you must understand I won't want you for my wife."

"I understand, and ought to thank you for it, but it's Mama who must understand," Marjorie said as she rose and smoothed out her habit. "If Aaron lets me be set aside and you won't have me, then I can't think what my life will be like under my mother's roof."

"You'll have the dower house, if you wish it," Gabriel said, the decision made as the words left his lips. "If it comes to that, which I doubt, you'll have support for life from Hesketh. Aaron will insist on it, at least."

"You mean this?"

"I'm not in the habit of jesting over such matters."

She regarded him, looking not quite so young. "That is more like the man I was engaged to. Not in the habit of jesting about much of anything. You're different now. Aaron says it's as if you've been to war."

"I've the injury to support the analogy. Shall we walk back, or would you prefer to ride?"

"Walk," Marjorie decided, letting Gabriel signal the groom to return the horses to the stables. "So what were you doing all those months we feared you were dead?"

"Learning to jest," Gabriel replied. "I'm not a quick study, but there is hope."

Five

GABRIEL WASN'T LOOKING FOR POLONAISE AS HE MADE his way to the library—or so he told himself—but rather, he was intent on examining further the fascinating details Aaron had catalogued in the estate book. The book was a first-rate idea to Gabriel's mind, one of those why-didn't-I-think-of-it notions smart landowners likely stumbled on independently. Aaron's record filled in gaps and went a long way toward reassuring Gabriel that Hesketh had been in good hands during his absence. But God above, the parade of petty and not so petty annoyances Aaron had documented beggared description.

Entire herds of cows stuck in the ponds, sheep tearing through huge sections of fence, drainage dikes breaking so newly planted fields flooded—the list went on and got Gabriel to thinking of a similar run of bad luck they'd had at Three Springs.

His thoughts were interrupted by the prickling sense he wasn't alone as he gained the library.

"Polonaise?" He spied her dark auburn bun over the back of his favorite couch. The sofa was long enough that he could stretch out on it full length and bake his carcass before the fire.

She waved a hand but didn't rise or turn, and he saw a handkerchief in her hand. A sinking sensation gathered in his guts, for if he'd made Polly Hunt cry, he was a dastardly specimen indeed.

Cautiously, he moved around the couch, spying letters scattered over the cushions. He gathered those up and set them aside, staring down at her bent head. For want of other inspiration, he settled beside her and took her in his arms.

"As bad as all that?"

She burrowed against him, a gratifying shift from her usual token resistance.

"Tell me."

She shuddered through a fresh bout of tears while he stroked her back and poached lungfuls of her scent and generally wondered why he thought he could ever leave her for long.

"Allie."

Well, of course. "You have a letter from her?"

"Finally." She tried to pull away, a belated version of her token effort.

"Do you really want me to see your face when you explain this heartache to me, Polonaise?"

She pressed her nose to his neck. "You are so mean."

"I'm awful. A disgrace and a miserable excuse for a gentleman. What did Allemande say?"

"She is angry with me for leaving, when Sara has a baby on the way." Gabriel let her shift in his arms so her head was on his shoulder. "She's scared, Gabriel, and I'm not there."

"She's afraid Sara won't fare well in childbed?"

"That, yes." Polly blotted her eyes with her handkerchief. "But she's also... She's scared Sara and Beck won't l-love her once the baby comes along. She doesn't say it outright. She goes about it by indirection and points out that Hildy doesn't have to push one piglet aside to have another. She loves them all at the same time."

"God spare us from the logic of children and breeding hogs," Gabriel muttered, though he could understand Allie's reasoning and her insecurities better than Polly knew.

"She's alone, Gabriel, and Sara will love that baby, and just when Allie's trying so hard to grow up, and I've left her, left them both, to do what?"

"To establish yourself as an artist. To give them room to be a family without you." Though Gabriel had left his own family behind at Hesketh, and hadn't that become a marvelous disaster?

"I can't do this..." She leaned into him, her grip on him becoming fierce. "What difference does it make if I paint, when Allie feels so lost?"

"Hush, and let me hold you." Gabriel tucked her against him more closely, wishing he'd locked the door, because Polly wouldn't want anyone, not a chambermaid, a footman, or God himself, to catch her at her tears.

Not over this.

"Allie is growing up," he said, searching for words. "This lost feeling you allude to is part of it, Polonaise. She is loved dearly, and Sara and Beck won't push her aside for the baby. Beck especially will take her under his wing, because she's his princess."

"He'll have another princess," Polly wailed quietly. "Or worse, a fat, squalling little prince, all blond and charming like his papa. Allie will hate her own sibling, and me too, for leaving her there."

"She will resent having to share, but she's one of the

most loving, tenderhearted creatures on God's earth, my dear." *As was Polonaise.* "When she sees that Beck and Sara trust her to be the older sister, and this baby isn't the end of the world, she'll have more confidence and one more person to love." Though it might take a decade or so.

"It isn't like that." Polly heaved a shuddery sigh. "You're the oldest, and you can't know. I was the youngest, the one without much music, and it's an endless exercise in not being paid attention to."

"You needed an Aunt Polly. Someone to balance the family's focus on the two older children."

"An army of Aunt Pollys. Rich ones, who understood the difference between painting and music." So fierce, and so heartsore.

"What about a single rich, famous aunt, in demand for her portraits in England and on the Continent?"

She rested against him more pliantly, and he could feel the tension in her easing. "I hate you, Gabriel Wendover."

"You can visit her anytime, you know."

"I have a portrait to paint, after which time, I will be escorted off the property by Hesketh himself, a very intractable exponent of spoiled nobility if ever I met one."

"I'm not Hesketh yet." *God be thanked.* "You might consider putting Marjorie's picture aside and going on to your next commission." His back twinged at that suggestion, and his heart.

"Are you really so anxious to see the last of me, Gabriel?" She craned her neck to peer at him, and he was struck by the hurt lurking in her eyes. Of course, she'd sympathize with Allie's feelings of rejection and bewilderment.

Of course, she'd doubt herself and her chosen path.

"Don't think that." He brushed a kiss to her cheek. "I

have my reasons for wishing you well away from here, love, and they've nothing to do with a distaste for your company."

She laid her cheek against his. "I'm an idiot."

"A man of sense hesitates to agree." He didn't pull away, because certain varieties of idiocy were contagious. "Might he inquire of your reasons?"

"I'm going to kiss you if you don't hare away, Gabriel. Really kiss you."

"You are an idiot, then." Her other cheek also received a kiss. "As am I, for I can't just now consider haring anywhere, for any reason. Thunderbolts from heaven couldn't—"

She shut him up by gently sealing her lips to his, and for Gabriel, the sensation was one of coming home. Coming truly home, not merely returning to the family seat, but returning to *himself*, to where he should be. Like having the heart put right back in his chest after looking for it for ages and ages.

He held off as long as he could, letting her tease at his lips then graze her tongue along them. When her hand slid down his chest to wrap around his waist and anchor her more firmly to him, he took over. Gently, he kissed her onto her back, until he was sprawled over her, caging her with his body but holding her with only his mouth. Crouched above her, he started the kiss over, so he was the one doing the teasing and tasting, and then the invading.

She made a moue of relief as she opened to him and spread her knees. While Gabriel delicately explored the warmth of her mouth, she got her skirts tugged out of the way and brought her legs up around his flanks.

"Polonaise." He ran his tongue down the line of her throat. "We have to—"

"No." She clasped him with her legs and arched up

against him, right up against the erection roaring to life in his breeches. Her mouth went from beseeching to demanding, and heat began to pour off her body, into his veins and organs.

"My dear, the door—"

"Kiss me."

She gave an upward push below the waist, and he couldn't *not* kiss her. Kiss her, and give her his weight, and start a slow, rolling rhythm with his hips. She arched up to him with surprising power and slid her hand down the length of his spine.

"Gabriel." His name was a curse on her lips, an imprecation directed toward men who moved too slowly and left their women frustrated with desire.

"Easy," he murmured, but had to smile when she worked a hand under his waistband and over his buttocks, and dug in with her nails.

"More, Gabriel. Now, please God, more."

He felt the possessive sting of her nails, and through his clothes, felt the sheer, perfect pleasure of being cradled against her. She was living flame in his arms, writhing, clutching, and demanding he relieve her need.

He got a hand untangled from their bodies enough to slide it up her side, then eased a breast free of her bodice. He rested his cheek against the ripe, plump fullness and breathed in her scent, the way a hungry man took a moment to give thanks for a meal before devouring it.

She went momentarily still before she resumed her slow rocking against him. He took her nipple in his mouth then paused.

"Clove?"

"Mmm." She arched her back and offered herself to him like a feast, then winnowed her fingers through his hair.

"Gabriel…" Not so insistent, a little breathless, a little bewildered, and he was going to spend in his breeches like a randy lad if he didn't exercise some—

She'd taken over the rhythm of their meshed bodies, rocking herself tightly against him with a greater sense of urgency. He drew on her, and through the haze of his own building lust, it occurred to him *she could find pleasure like this*. He shifted his hips, giving her more of his weight as she began to breathe more harshly.

"Gabriel, I can't… It's too much…"

"Not enough," he managed, freeing the second breast and teething her lightly. "Come for me, Polonaise. It's the least you deserve."

"I don't… Oh, *holy saints, Gabriel*…" He felt the spasms rock her, felt her buck up against him desperately, and rode her hard when she would have shied back at the first searing bolt of pleasure. By divine providence, he held off his own climax, easing away from her only when she was spent and panting beneath him.

"What in God's name…?" she whispered, while he sat back on his heels and undid his falls with shaking hands. He dug frantically for his handkerchief with one hand while he took hold of himself with the other and finished in a few quick, short strokes. His pleasure came upon him fast and hard, and then harder, leaving him breathing like a bellows, eyes closed as he tried to steady himself in the aftermath.

Cool fingers brushed over the head of his cock, making him flinch back.

"Not yet," he cautioned. "Too sensitive."

"So that's what you feel when you spend?"

He opened his eyes and focused on the way firelight danced through her hair—because letting his gaze linger on her rucked-up skirts, her abundant breasts, or even her lush, reddened lips was purest folly. He managed... a nod.

She hadn't known? Hadn't she been knocked witless by erotic pleasure before? Holy saints, indeed.

His Polonaise looked puzzled as she started to tuck herself up, but he stilled her with a hand and crouched forward over her, his cheek against her chest.

"Christ, Polonaise." It was barely a whisper, but provoked her to stroking her hands over his hair, a slow, sweet caress that helped ease his racing heart. "Sweet, ever loving Christ."

And cloves, which would forevermore be an aphrodisiac to him.

Perceptive woman that she was, she let him gather his wits and his wind for long, quiet moments, and he had to hope she needed the time as well.

"You are dangerous." He sat back and surveyed her, then climbed off the couch. "Don't you do that." He stilled her hands again, but gently. "I will put to rights what I disturbed." Carefully, he eased her breasts back into her bodice, and to his relief, she let him.

"You needed to do that?"

"You're full of questions. Come here." He lay down beside her without righting his clothing and dragged her over him. "I don't hold with the notion that every good swiving requires endless verbal recounting. You stole my wits, love. I haven't spent like that since I was a mere boy, and you will leave me a little dignity by not gloating."

She turned her face into his chest, and he felt her smiling at his expense. Her smile warmed his heart and made him want to start up again, which was a very bad idea indeed, and not simply because the door was yet unlocked.

"I'm not sorry." He could hear the humor and pride in her tone.

"You are sorry indeed"—Gabriel tucked his chin against her temple—"to accost a man in his own library, leaving him no modesty and less control. For shame, Polonaise. Now go to sleep and dream of me."

"You'll sleep too?"

"With one eye open, lest you have your wicked way with me again."

She cuddled up, while he wrestled with consternation. What was wrong with those imbeciles on the Continent, that they'd failed to see to Polly's pleasure? She was a Congreve rocket, as volatile in her passions as she was about her cooking or her art.

Jesus, to have her in his bed would be—

He yanked hard on the reins of his unruly desire, and nuzzled her hair as it occurred to him that in some ways, he was her first. The notion pleased him profoundly, and he was still savoring it when he fell asleep and dreamed of clove-scented sheets and huge mugs of chocolate topped with whipped cream and cinnamon.

Voices in the corridor awakened him. Gabriel put a finger to Polly's lips, and as the voices passed, she went limp against him.

"Time to make our escape," Gabriel whispered, shoving to a sitting position. When Polly would have climbed off the couch, he caught her with a hand behind the head and kissed her again, a right smacker, a kiss of dominion and gratitude. Polly smiled at him, a soft, radiant, devastatingly lovely smile, and he had to look away.

Only to notice his breeches were still undone. "Lock the goddamned door, Polonaise, or you'll see the banns being cried."

She smiled more broadly and rose to do his bidding—for once. He ran a hand through his hair and knew he should be buttoning his falls as fast as human hands could manage. He let his hands fall to his side and left his clothing in disarray as Polly advanced on him.

"I'll tend to that."

"Woman, you are unnatural, and I am perfectly capable—"

She knelt right between his legs. "And you are shy." She gently extricated his softening length from his clothes and surveyed him. "Shy," she murmured, "and… well proportioned."

He watched as the artist in her measured, assessed, and turned him this way and that.

"Love, you keep that up, and I won't be the only one set upon in this library. Best put away your toy."

"Toys," she corrected him, lifting his cock to run her fingers over his balls. "You got to see my bubbies, so hush. With models, one isn't allowed to touch, and this is frustrating, because seeing the poor thing just hang there…"

"Polonaise." His voice was hoarse to his own ears. "Might we have the anatomy lesson some other time?" Many other times?

She gave him a look from between his thighs, a look conveying hunger, artistic and erotic hunger, and he had to gaze past her head at the portrait of the third earl over the fireplace. The blighter seemed to be silently laughing.

"Right." She tucked him away. "Your dignity won't stand for it, and in your own library and all."

"Just so." She finished buttoning his falls, then ruined her display of sense by stroking him through his breeches a few times before she rested her cheek squarely on his genitals. "Gabriel, what have we done?"

"I don't know." Though he knew damned good and

well what they had not—quite—done. He trailed his hand over the softness of her hair, the weight of her head an odd comfort. "I should be sending you away, Polonaise, not trifling with you."

"And I should have enough pride to flounce off and not stay where I'm not wanted."

"You're wanted." She was far more than wanted, which announcement would only make it that much harder to send her safely on her way. "You can't doubt that now. You're wanted until I'm coming like a hopeless stripling at the simple sight of you, wench."

"You did, didn't you?"

And he'd pleased her all over again, which hadn't strictly been his intent.

"I said you could stay until the portrait is done," Gabriel reminded her. "You haven't even put paint to canvas yet."

"The next sunny day, I will, and I can be very fast, Gabriel. Marjorie is a wonderful subject."

Polonaise had accepted that she must leave, which should have been a relief. The notion was, in fact, intolerable, as intolerable as the idea that Gabriel's situation might put her welfare at risk.

Which meant his best hope was to make her time at Hesketh memorable, and perhaps someday…

"Marjorie will be wonderful to work with," he said. "I am a wonderful lover, however, and you must allow me to prove that. It's only fair." He was just another horny sod, soon to be reduced to a begging horny sod.

"So romantic." She sighed against his thigh. "You could be a terrible lover, and I wouldn't know the difference."

"But I'm not," he said, feeling both sad for her and pleased for himself that Polonaise Hunt did not have the sophistication to know good lovemaking from the common variety. "You'll indulge my need to establish this beyond doubt?"

"You know I will." She sounded bleak, and that had his good humor fading. "But it can't come to anything, Gabriel. Promise me right now, you won't start getting notions."

"I already have," he countered, meaning it. "I'll promise you nothing but pleasure, Polonaise."

"And the loan of a coach at the end of my stay here."

He stroked his thumb over the sweet, stubborn curve of her jaw. "So mean," he chided. "But hear me: I know I was dishonest with you at Three Springs, Polonaise. I had my reasons, though they seem less worthy now. I understand you want to decamp to higher ground when your work here is done—"

"You've ordered me to."

He gently put a palm over her mouth, only to feel her tongue tasting his skin.

"I'm sending you away for your safety, not because I want to. If I had my way—"

She covered his mouth with her hand in a reciprocal gesture.

"No, Gabriel." She peered up at him solemnly. "You need heirs and I am not the stuff a marchioness is made of and we won't discuss this again. I'll paint, and then I'll leave, and if we dally a little betimes, that is simply for our own fleeting, private pleasure."

"Those are your terms?"

"And discretion," she added. "No one can know. Not Aaron or Marjorie or even the staff."

"I accept your terms." *For now.* He also silently assured her they wouldn't be dallying a little. They'd be dallying one goddamn hell of a *lot*, and her pleasure would be far from fleeting.

"Mr. Erskine, you will devote your utmost efforts to this case."

Erskine kept his expression deferentially bland. "My lady, I do so with all of my clients' concerns."

"You mistake me." Lady Hartle drew herself up. She was a tallish woman and wearing boots, which put her a tad below eye level with her solicitor. "You will devote *all* of your efforts to this case, until Gabriel Wendover and his younger brother see reason."

Erskine wished, not for the first time, that he'd followed his mother's advice and gone for the church instead of the law, though rising early on Sundays would be a pain. "Reason and the law are only nodding acquaintances. I am powerless to change the one, regardless of how compelling the other."

"My daughter is the Marchioness of Hesketh." She rapped the point of her parasol on the floor, like a judge might strike his gavel to demand order of an unruly courtroom. "I'm not asking you to change anything, but rather, to inspire the Wendover menfolk to abide by contracts that have stood for almost fifteen years."

Erskine knew better than to back down. "As you've explained it, the only possible argument for invalidating the marriage is fraud in the inducement, but because the older brother was declared legally dead, it's hard to know who was responsible for the fraud."

"The bridegroom, of course." Lady Hartle nearly shook with her determination. "Aaron had his brother declared dead. Gabriel didn't rise up from the grave and see it done himself."

Gabriel Wendover, who was never *in* the grave.

"So your theory is Aaron deceived his way into your daughter's hand in marriage. A novel outlook, I'm sure, and the judges are not particularly fond of novelty. I don't suppose there's any chance of nonconsummation?" Not that this made the legal turf much easier to spade.

"Don't be ridiculous," Lady Hartle snapped. "My daughter is a beautiful young woman who knows her duty, and Aaron Wendover is a former cavalry officer in fine health with no younger cousins or sons to inherit."

"So you've said." Erskine's tone begged leave to doubt Lady Hartle's assessment. "Who are their solicitors?"

"The old marquess used Hamish and Hamish. You will contact them immediately and threaten suit."

Which was absolutely the least prudent course. "Of course, my lady."

"Be delicate about it." She put her gloves on, which to Erskine bore a bit of symbolism. "Be firm, though. If I have to threaten scandal, I will. This is Marjorie's birthright, and I will see it protected."

"I understand." Erskine bowed formally and hoped that would be sufficient cue for his client to make her farewells. She swept out, leaving the door open behind her, and Erskine's partner, a dapper young blond chap by the name of Hay, came sauntering in.

"Hell hath no fury?" Hay asked.

"Hell hath all kinds of furies, but a mama-in-law scorned has to top the list." Erskine kicked the door shut, lest all the heat leave along with her ladyship. "Join me for a pint?"

"That bad?"

"She schemed and maneuvered and threatened to get the younger brother's foot in parson's mousetrap, now the older brother has reappeared, and we must jettison brother-the-younger and get our marital hooks into brother-the-elder."

"This is Hesketh, right?"

"How could you possibly know?"

Hay shrugged. Though young, he had an impressive network of informants and was smart enough not to brag about it. "Word travels. So can you do it?"

Erskine sighed mightily and thought of his daughter's millinery bills. "Possibly."

Hay slapped him on the back. "Or possibly not, but you can definitely spend a great deal of coin in the trying?"

Erskine grabbed his coat and hat, for it had become a suitably miserable, wet day. "Sometimes, my lad, even the coin doesn't make the aggravation worth the effort."

～

"It's time we went up to Town." Gabriel made that decision after dinner, when he wasn't watching the candlelight bring out red highlights in Polonaise's hair, or contemplating the late evening he intended to spend lying in wait for her in the library.

Resting his back.

Aaron glanced around at the footmen tidying up after dinner. "How about a game of billiards?"

Privacy was always the better alternative, so they were soon behind a closed door, with another fire roaring, the balls racked on the green felt.

"You want to meet with the solicitors?" Aaron broke and stepped back for his brother to take his shot.

"It seems the next thing to do." Gabriel bent over the table—carefully, always carefully when the weather was turning—and sank a ball, but missed his next shot.

"There's the matter of my being declared dead, of course, and your having been invested, but also the looming threat to your marriage."

"Marjorie's happiness isn't a threat."

"You try my sanity, little brother."

Aaron sank two balls quickly—easy shots—then blew the third easy shot.

"If you think I'm going to take her to wife, you're mistaken. The notion is barbaric."

"You wouldn't abuse her."

"I would *swive* her, were we married," Gabriel said patiently, "and she is my brother's wife, not some broodmare coming into season as she approaches the breeding shed."

"I know that."

"So what are you going to do about it?"

"Beat you at billiards," Aaron ground out.

"I have no legitimate children, Aaron." Gabriel studied the cherubs frolicking on the ceiling among oaken strawberry leaves.

"One comprehends this."

Gabriel finished the oldest syllogism in aristocratic memory for him. "Ergo, *one's* duty is to produce my heirs. Why the hell else would you take the title if not out of a profound appreciation for your role in securing the succession?"

"Leave it, Gabriel." Aaron's tone was relaxed, though he gripped his cue stick so tightly his knuckles gleamed white.

Gabriel bent low over the table and sank three balls in rapid succession. "We go up to Town and meet with Kettering, but we discuss only my death and the title. Your marriage can wait until Lady Hartle actually rattles her sword."

"Is your back bothering you?"

"My brother is bothering me, but yes, stretching out like this is something I attempt cautiously."

Aaron twirled his cue stick, a cavalier, graceful show of disrespect. "One might think you'd attempt it regularly, so as to accustom the body to it again. You were abed for how many months?"

"Too many. I used to spend a great deal of time soaking in hot springs, and that helped significantly." As had Polly's padded chairs, and her cooking.

"Why not have a bathing chamber put in here? We can afford it, and there aren't any hot springs to be had."

"That is a capital idea." And offered with studied casualness.

"My quota for the year."

Gabriel put aside his cue stick. "In truth, you have them fairly often. Whose idea was it to set up a schedule for swapping around the various rams on the tenant farms?"

"Mine." Aaron appeared to study the balls arrayed on the table. "A young fellow likes variety."

"And inbreeding is never a good idea," Gabriel responded primly, though the British monarchy was comfortable enough with the notion. "I understand you favor bullocks over horses for the smallholders, too."

Aaron sent the cue ball careening off various bumpers. "The heavy horses take more fodder and bedding, and aren't as palatably put into the stew pot when their days are over; nor are they as strong for their size as the bullocks."

"So now you're getting rid of our draft teams?"

"Not ours." Aaron lowered himself into a chair before the fire—the very chair Gabriel had been considering. "I'm former cavalry, recall, and George would call me out did I advocate getting rid of all the farm horses, but for the yeoman, the bullocks are the better bargain. Where are you off to?"

"The library," Gabriel said. "There to consult further with your Domesday Book. Design us a bathing chamber, why don't you? You were always good at such things."

Aaron waved a hand. "Your wish, et cetera. When are we going up to Town?"

"Tuesday suits, and our week will be up then too."

"Famous."

"Aaron?"

"That would be me."

"I want to help, you know." Gabriel's hand was on the door, but his back was to his brother. "Whatever is turning you so damned grouchy, I want to help."

"You can't. I'm just growing into the Wendover legacy, you know. Bad dispositions, the lot of us."

Seeing his brother wasn't in the mood for confidences, Gabriel went prowling in the direction of the library, there to... rest his back.

Six

"AARON?" MARJORIE'S VOICE FLOATED FORTH FROM the doorway to the game room. She was in shadow, because Aaron had blown out all the candles, leaving only the hearth light to think by.

"Here." He held up a hand so she could see where he was over the back of his chair.

"I thought Gabriel was with you."

"Sorry." Aaron knew he should get to his feet, but instead he held out a hand to her. "Just me. Was there something on your mind?"

She advanced into the room, peering around as if to make sure Gabriel wasn't lurking, though mentally, Aaron considered his brother nigh haunted him, and had for two years. His musings were cut short when he saw his wife was in her nightgown and wrapper. He'd seen her thus only for a very few moments on their wedding night, two years ago, and the image had haunted him right beside that of his brother's pain-wracked face.

"You don't normally seek me out at such an hour, Margie. Did you need me for something?" Did she need him for *anything*?

"I needed to talk to you," she said, still darting nervous glances into the shadows.

"Come then." He patted his knee, and when she approached, tugged her onto his lap. He settled his arms around her. "It grows chilly. We can talk like this."

She nearly levitated at first, like a broody hen whose dignity had been slighted, so badly had he startled her. Then she settled, her arm tentatively sliding around his neck.

"I have always liked your scent," she said.

"You came here to discuss my scent?"

She gave a tired sigh, and Aaron felt a stab of remorse. He was forever tossing barbs at her, because it was the only way he knew to keep his emotional distance.

And here he'd gone and pulled her into his lap.

"Mama is going to try to set our marriage aside."

"We can assume that much," Aaron replied, and in order that he didn't clutch her to him in an obvious display of need, he stroked his hand down over her unbound hair. "Your hair has more red in it than I suspected."

"Firelight does that. I don't want to marry your brother, Aaron."

"You're sure of this?"

"He's a good man, and he's different from when he left two years ago, more human, but still…"

"You can't stomach the thought of bedding him now?"

"Do we have to be specific?"

"Maybe it's the scandal you can't stomach," Aaron suggested. "Gabriel doesn't seem to mind the thought of scandal."

Marjorie shuddered, and perhaps, just perhaps, her hand tightened its grip on his waistcoat. "He'd marry me then? He said he wouldn't want to, and I might have the dower house and a stipend."

"At least," Aaron said, but because he'd discouraged Gabriel from bringing up this topic, the plan was news to him. "Would you like that, Marjorie, to be free of the Wendover men altogether?"

She shook her head.

"Still want your title, do you? I'd be the heir, at least until Gabriel took a wife and got down to business. We'd have the courtesy titles."

"It isn't the blasted title." She muttered the words against his chest.

"So what is it you want, Wife?" He bent low, his lips near her ear, and inhaled a tormenting whiff of flowers, soap, and female warmth.

"You," she whispered. "Aaron, I want *you*."

❧

Gabriel headed directly for the library, and realized for once his back did not hurt; nor did it ache or twinge or throb. His muscles weren't even particularly tight, which was odd, because bad weather usually wreaked havoc.

Anticipation was a wonderful salve, he concluded as he reached the library, only to find his quarry… nowhere to be seen.

His first inclination was to spread himself out on the sofa and lie in wait, because Polonaise was no doubt up in her room, shedding clothes and lingering over her ablutions in preparation for their evening encounter.

His second inclination was to see to himself, because waiting for her was going to make him ache in places other than his back, and he wanted to have as much patience as she needed.

He set those two thoughts firmly aside and went up to

the guest wing on the second floor. The light under Polly's door confirmed her whereabouts, because she'd neither waste candles nor risk fire by leaving them unattended.

"Come in."

She looked startled when Gabriel stepped into the room and closed—and locked—the door behind him.

"I thought you were the maid, bringing extra wood."

Gabriel eyed the wood box and the lady sitting in her nightgown and robe on the hearth rug before the fire. "You have plenty of wood, though maybe you were building up the fire for me?"

"Hardly. Tonight isn't a good time, Gabriel. If you'd please leave?" She rose to turn down the covers and run the warmer over the sheets, a brittleness to her movements.

"You're tired," he suggested, "and those letters put you out of sorts."

"I *am* tired." She even ran the warmer over the pillows, something Gabriel had never thought to do. "And the letters did put me out of sorts, but it isn't only that. You'll have to come back some other time."

"And give you days to man your battlements?" Gabriel advanced into the room, which at least qualified as cozy. "I think not, Polonaise."

"I'm not manning anything." She put the warmer back on the hearth. "It's just..." She didn't back away as he moved toward her, but he thought she might have muttered an oath as his arms came around her.

"Your menses, right?" He rested his chin on her crown and held her gently. At Three Springs, he'd known her biological schedule, and not because she'd ever discuss such a thing with him.

"Not my... not that. I am tired, and flirting with a

headache. It happens when I paint for too long or sketch too much. I suspect I need spectacles, and I know I need you to leave." She tried to slip free a moment later, but he held her fast. "Gabriel?"

"I am not accustomed to taking orders," Gabriel said, "even though we are in your bedroom, and if I were to take orders anywhere, it would be here."

"Idle promises."

"Word of a Wendover," he intoned solemnly; then he patted her backside. "Pain makes everybody cross." How the nuns would laugh, to know he was quoting them.

"I wish suffering for my art didn't mean a throbbing at the base of my skull."

"I never did understand why suffering was a prerequisite for making something pretty." Gabriel fished carefully through her hair for pins—there were a deuced lot of them— then sank his fingers onto her scalp and massaged gently.

"That feels... divine."

"Hmm." He kept at it a few more minutes then left off in self-defense. She was all but purring in his arms, and the feel of her silky, fragrant hair sliding through his fingers brought to mind images of it down around her hips while they—

"I'll be going up to Town next week," Gabriel heard himself say. "With Aaron, and you ladies are to stick close to the house when we leave." This was what he'd come to her room to tell her—among other things.

"Right now, I would promise you nigh anything if you'd just keep doing what you're doing." Her voice sounded wonderfully sleepy.

"Lowering, that." Gabriel resisted the urge to sweep all her hair aside and kiss her nape—strictly in the interests of making her feel better. "One prefers such sentiments from beautiful women under other circumstances."

"Bother, you."

"Right." He did steal the kiss then. "Cross. I almost forgot. Shall I braid you up?"

"One braid. Over my left shoulder tonight."

"You alternate?"

"It's like riding sidesaddle. If she can afford the extra equipment, and the extra habits, a lady alternates sides to prevent herself from getting uneven."

"God forbid a lady's fundament should be anything other than perfectly symmetrical. Not that I'd remark such a thing, ever."

"You'd notice. You men."

"And enjoy the noticing." Though he hadn't noticed any lady's fundament since he'd noticed hers. He steered her over to the vanity stool and kept his lips to himself long enough to do her braid, as ordered, but then he rested his hands on her shoulders and had a minor orgy of kissing over her neck, shoulders, nape, and jaw.

When his lady was sighing softly, her head cradled on her arms, Gabriel desisted. "Time for bed, Polonaise."

"You are bossy, Gabriel Wendover." She rose and untied her wrapper as she scolded him.

He brushed her hands aside. "Allow me."

"I'm not a child." She spoiled the effect of that pronouncement by yawning as widely as any child, and standing docilely while he divested her of her robe. Perhaps she truly was tired, but Gabriel suspected she also sought to draw out the pursuit phase of their dallying, and in this… she was wise.

Damnably wise, given the magnitude of the issues unresolved between them.

"Into bed."

She complied, sending him only one half-hearted peevish look over her shoulder as she did. "Good night."

"Hardly." He sat on the edge of the bed and tugged off his boots and stockings, then started on his cravat.

"Sir, what are you about?"

"You've never seen a man undress before? Suppose that reflects badly on me."

"I've watched you undress," Polly said, settling back against her pillows. "At the springs and the pond. I was shameless."

"Note the erroneous use of the past tense. Did you spy on Beck as well?"

Polly smiled sweetly. "Sara caught him once, by the cistern. I wasn't so fortunate, but what could he possibly have to interest me?"

"You are a naughty woman." Gabriel pulled his shirt over his head, grateful for the low light. Polly had seen his scar on occasion, but he didn't have to force the issue.

"You like that I'm naughty."

"Adore you for it." His hands went to his falls, and he paused when he saw Polly was watching those hands.

"Your scar continues to fade," she said. "Or maybe it's that you're not in the sun of late, and your skin is not as dark."

"I've a Portuguese grandmother, hence the Mediterranean cast to my skin. Move over, my love."

He shucked out of his breeches and drawers in one motion while Polly remained right where she was, frankly eyeing his half-aroused cock.

"You wanted to look earlier, but the circumstances didn't allow me to indulge you."

Her brows flew up, and she bit her lip, suggesting he'd found one way to silence her, at least temporarily.

"You know you want to, naughty lady, and I live to serve you." When he wasn't sending her away or leaving her side without explanations.

"Right." She bounced off the other side of the bed, all traces of fatigue gone, and lit a branch of no less than six candles.

"Will that be enough?"

"Broad light of day would be better," she muttered, not catching his sarcasm.

He scooted back to lie against her pillows. "Touch gently, particularly my stones."

"You didn't touch yourself gently." Polly hopped back onto the bed. "Yesterday in the library, you were quite brisk with yourself."

Gabriel steeled himself to be inspected. "Sometimes, gentle touches arouse, not so gentle touches sustain the arousal, and ungentle touches can consummate the pleasure."

Polly put the candles on the night table, while Gabriel considered the erotic potential of hot wax.

"Touch my bubbies the way you were going at your self yesterday, and I'll ungently deter you."

"So you say." His arousal was fading at Polly's matter-of-fact demeanor, but then she drew her fingers over him, standing him up, and lust came roaring back on a big, fast horse. "Do your worst."

Her worst was considerable.

Gabriel hadn't been tortured in Spain, but his wound had been fierce and his recuperation painful. He'd learned to set his mind apart from his body, to separate his awareness of pain from his awareness of all else. All his mental discipline was useless when Polly leaned close to his cock and wrapped her fingers around him.

"You're larger than the models I worked with in Italy. Quite a bit larger."

"I'm taller too." Gabriel tried to sound nonchalant. She fiddled with his foreskin, which was retracting the longer she touched him and the harder he grew.

"What does this feel like?"

"Polonaise, will you leave me no dignity?"

"You left me none. You are fastidious, but you must miss your hot springs."

"I do. Do you miss spying on me as I stripped to the skin?"

"Oh, very much." She leaned in, and because Gabriel had once more closed his eyes, he wasn't prepared for the sensation of her tongue sliding up the length of him.

"There will be no more of that." He sank a hand into her hair to ensure it.

"Coward." She nuzzled the base of his shaft, and Gabriel's hold relaxed because he'd made his point—hadn't he? "I won't bite, unless you ask it of me."

The words sounded familiar, though he could barely comprehend them. "I forget you came of age on the Continent. What was I thinking?"

She fondled his sac in reply. "I like these. They are so soft and strange."

"So vulnerable, you mean. Are you quite finished? I intended this to be a visual inspection."

"I am not finished." She stroked him with her tongue again. "I like the taste of you."

"No doubt you're comparing me to cardamom, and zest of orange, concocting some fricassee with my name on it."

"Hush." She licked him all over, leisurely, and finished with a little suck on the end. "You'd be a dessert."

"God in heaven." His hand in her hair became... guiding. "I'm aspiring to be drizzled with chocolate glaze."

It didn't take her long, not long at all, to learn the coordination of her hand around his shaft and her mouth on the head of his cock. He forced himself to move his hips only minutely and slowly, so she could properly torment him for a quiet eternity. When she was drawing firmly on that spot just under the tip, and fire was boiling out from the base of Gabriel's spine, he tried to tug her away.

"Love, I want to finish," he rasped. "Need to."

"Hnn." She got her mouth back on him, and God help him, he arched his back, just once, feeling the drag of her lips and the tight glove of her fingers and the sheer, pounding bliss of all she was doing to him, and it was too much.

"Goddamn it, Polonaise..." His whisper was harsh, guttural, and drenched in erotic pleasure. He might have said her name again, more than once, as he gave in to the sensations swamping him. This wasn't intercourse, but it was still his Polonaise, and it was more intense pleasure than one man could sanely bear.

"You... are... a... menace." Fraught moments later, he was still whispering, trying to catch his breath in the aftermath of a bodily cataclysm, his hand in her hair, her head pillowed low on his stomach, and her fingers still wrapped around him. "You can let go."

"Hush." She swiped her tongue over the head of his cock, and he felt it from his toes to the ends of his *hair*. "I won't hurt you."

"No more," he managed. "I mean it."

She subsided onto his stomach and nuzzled him, a sense of smugness radiating from her.

"You're pleased with yourself," he accused, stroking his hand over her hair.

"Are you complaining?"

"Yes." He tried to sit up, but Polly stayed where she was, her head against his belly. "You aren't supposed to be so... accommodating, Polonaise. Not in such intimate particulars."

"I'm supposed to tease and withhold and play stupid games?"

"You're supposed to leave me a little something to work for," he suggested. "And as to that..."

"Yes?" She turned loose of him and rolled over to stare up at him, her gaze trying to hide a hint of uncertainty.

"I loved it," he said simply. "I adore you, and I love that you're so generous and curious and bold. I don't deserve it. I came here thinking to dally, yes, but when you're tired and uncertain, I'm the one who's supposed to be spoiling you."

"You aren't truly upset?"

"Yes, I'm truly upset." What the hell was he saying? He grabbed a handkerchief from the night table and shoved it at her to use on her fingers. "No, I'm not, but I will be if you don't let me hold you."

"We can't..." She pushed up, frowning right back at him.

Gabriel snatched the linen from her, swabbed at his belly, then pitched the handkerchief to the floor. "Hang we can't." He pulled her to him and settled down on his side, so he was spooned around her. "We won't, though, because you deserve perfection, and I can't offer it tonight."

"Because you've used up your powder and shot."

"Because you're tired and not inclined to dispense any further favors, which is likely the only reason I will live to see the morning. You are not, however, supposed to know about making a naughty dessert of my intimate person."

"I have ever been fond of sweets." She rubbed her cheek against his biceps. "Perhaps I'll have seconds. This naughtiness is the only thing I've seen render you speechless."

"Witless," he corrected her. "I recall babbling the entire time."

"Details."

"Cross, despite being capable of great generosity," he concluded when she tucked his hand against her middle. "Onto your belly, that I might be generous too."

He stroked his hand over the elegant architecture of her back, let it wander into her hair, and down over the lush curve of her derriere, paying special attention to the base of her skull.

"I hate that you hurt." And he didn't refer to only an inchoate headache. "How long ago were you told you were barren?"

"I was young. It was most of a decade ago."

"And were you examined by a physician or just a midwife?"

"Midwife, and she knew what she was about. You don't have to do that, you know."

Yes, he did. He had to cherish her every way she would allow it. "You like it, and I'm on reconnaissance for when I have my revenge on you."

"I'm aquiver with fear."

"One senses your abject terror." He kissed her again, a glancing buss to her cheek. "Go to sleep, love."

"You too," she murmured, scooting closer.

"You want me to stay, Polonaise?"

"Hmm."

"Beg pardon?"

She said something more, which sounded like the single word "forever," though Gabriel knew that couldn't possibly have been what she'd meant.

❧

"What does that mean, Margie? You want me?" Aaron's voice didn't shake but his hand nearly did as it swept slowly down her hair.

"Mama will try to see me wed to your brother." She shuddered beneath his hand. "I can't bear it, and you mustn't allow it."

"If she succeeds in invalidating our marriage," Aaron surmised, "you will be forced back into Gabriel's arms, so to speak. You'd have me spare you that?"

"Of course I want to be spared that," she wailed softly. "He's a stranger to me, and you're... you're my husband."

"A stranger to you? You were engaged to him for fifteen years, weren't you? And from the circumstances apparent when you wed me, you and Gabriel were cordial enough."

He was being mean, and it wasn't well done of him. He stroked his hand over her hair, more slowly, more gently.

"Of course we were cordial." Marjorie rubbed her cheek against his lapel, like a cat getting comfortable. "When he recalled he had a fiancée. But he isn't... he isn't you."

Three words, but they gave Aaron an odd, reluctant sort of hope.

"You don't need me to spike your mama's guns. Gabriel has all but promised me he won't have you. He wants us to have children, in fact."

"He does?" She tilted her head back to study him. "He told you that?"

"Cheeky of him, if you ask me." Aaron shifted her closer on his lap. "Gabriel has never lacked for audacity when it gains him his own ends."

"Sometimes, Aaron, you sound as if you don't like your brother very much."

"Sometimes I hate him, though it's easier to like the man when he hasn't given his life to see me safely sent back home."

"You blamed yourself for his death," Marjorie said. "One sensed this, in the grim way you went about the estate business. Often, I used to think were it not for Gabriel's death, or the way he died—"

"What?" Aaron gathered up her long blond hair and brought a rose-scented strand to his nose. "What did you used to think, Margie Wendover?"

"You like the estate work. The part where you solve problems and spend hours on horseback and listen to all the tenants."

"They mostly want to gripe about the weather, or the price of corn, or about George. Simply listening isn't difficult." So why had he spent so little time listening to his wife?

"But you didn't let yourself enjoy it, because of the guilt."

She fell silent, though her words had the ring of insight to them, and he had to allow she was right. He'd punished himself for months, thinking Gabriel was dead because of him, hoping he was wrong, but not knowing.

"I still resent him." A man should be able to safely admit such a thing to his wife.

"Which makes two of us."

Aaron twined her hair around his finger, pleased with her response.

"Mama was content to carp at me over the need for an heir. I could have stood years of that more easily than her latest queer start. Why do you resent Gabriel now? Is it you who wants the title?"

"Hardly. I resent him for not trusting me. He saved my worthless hide in Spain, bullying the doctors, hiring decent nurses, and keeping the damned surgeons from bleeding me nigh to death, and after all of that, he thought I'd repay him by snatching his title, his bride, and his wealth." He tickled his nose with her hair, and wished he might tickle her too.

"He was very ill, Aaron. Maybe he didn't know what to think, and you did benefit from his death, at least in the eyes of the world."

"Do you think I plotted and schemed to be where I am?"

"For God's sake, Aaron." She sat up in his lap, and he missed the feel of her like… like the calves missed their mamas the first night after weaning. "I was there when you had to be all but hauled up the church aisle by a press gang. I was there when my father all but called you out for not honoring the betrothal in place of your brother. You didn't want this, and you would never scheme to hurt your brother. Never."

He was silent for a long time, playing with her hair and wondering why it should mean something that she trusted him when his own brother hadn't. Aaron had been in Spain with Gabriel; he'd had both motive and opportunity.

But the wife he'd ignored for two years believed in his innocence.

"Let me light you up to bed." He patted her hip, and she blushed.

"You'll fight Mama?"

"If it comes to that, I will, and it won't be pretty, Margie. You've chosen your side, you know, and she can keep your brothers and sisters from you, poison the well of gossip, and make your life hell."

"No, she can't." Marjorie slid off his lap. "Hell would be spending the rest of my life married to Gabriel when he's not who or what I want."

"If you say so." He bent to light a single candle and

winged his arm at her, then walked with her to her door, which was right down the corridor from his.

"Thank you." She glanced up at him uncertainly as he reached past her to open her door.

"Let's make sure your candles are lit," he said, because her sitting room was in shadows. Her fire was blazing, though, so he lit a few candles and offered her a bow. "Pleasant dreams."

"To you as well, and... thank you."

"You're welcome." He ran one finger down the golden wealth of her hair, curled his hand around a gleaming skein, and tugged her one step closer. "Maybe, when this whole issue of our vows is behind us..."

He stopped, unwilling to say more. But she must have read his mind, because she went up on her toes and kissed his cheek, then disappeared into her bedroom without another word.

❧

Gabriel bounced into the breakfast parlor, his mood blessedly at variance with the sullen chill of the day. "Are the women still abed?"

"They've come and gone," Aaron said, setting his paper aside. "Try the eggs. I think Marjorie had a word with Cook."

"I thought your marchioness took a tray in the morning." Gabriel scooped up a large serving of eggs, added toast, bacon, and an orange, then sat at his brother's elbow.

"She's sometimes up early to ride." Aaron shifted his chair a few inches away.

"Not on a morning like this." Gabriel gestured toward the window with a toast point then started on his breakfast.

"Ah, cheese in the eggs, and perhaps a touch of oregano, or… something."

"You approve?"

"Of course," Gabriel said between bites of what he was sure was Polly's omelet recipe. "And the toast isn't simply day-old bread, it's got… onions or chives, and sesame things on it."

"Sesame things?"

"Seeds. Are you going to stare that teapot into submission or pour a cup for your dear older brother?"

Aaron poured, a grin quirking his lips. He added cream and sugar, and pushed the cup toward Gabriel's plate. "Marjorie has made up her mind."

Gabriel paused, his fork halfway to his mouth. "Send a notice to the *Times*. Regarding?"

"She wants to remain married to my humble self."

"A woman of sense and discernment. Pass the salt, would you?"

"A woman of sense would marry the titleholder." Aaron pushed the saltcellar toward his brother.

"Not if she's Marjorie," Gabriel retorted. "She'd no more enjoy going up to Town for the opening of Parliament or for the Season than you would. She's choosing to be your wife over my marchioness, and I'd say that's the better choice."

"I like Town well enough." Aaron was back to staring at the teapot. "Or I used to."

"We grow up." Gabriel sprinkled a mere touch of salt on his eggs. "Or we do if we're lucky."

"It's not that." Aaron looked like he meant to leave it at that, but his mouth kept forming words. "I can't very well be paying coin for what my wife would offer for free, not when I know how offended she'd be."

Gabriel's eyebrows rose over a mouthful of eggs—ambrosial eggs. He set down his fork and patted his lips with his napkin.

"They aren't just offended," Gabriel said. "They're *hurt* when we do stupid, selfish things, like visit the whorehouse though we love our wives."

Aaron turned his stare on his brother. "You have a wife now, to be handing down such serious pronouncements?"

"I do not. I'd best not have aspirations in that direction until I figure out who wanted me dead—or wants me dead."

"Because it wasn't me, and I benefited. Who else benefited?"

"I don't know." Gabriel swirled his teacup, which, if he wasn't mistaken, held a particularly delicate gunpowder he was quite fond of. "I wish to hell I did, and it's not for lack of thinking it through. Are you free this morning?"

"I am."

"Then I want to go over your estate book and make sure I understand all you've written."

"What a penance on a dreary damned day." Aaron rose and went to the window. "I never meant that book to be a public record. I just started writing things down."

"It's useful," Gabriel said, attending to the food on his plate. "I don't doubt you wish his late lordship had kept something similar when you took over the reins two years ago, but Papa wasn't much of one for bookkeeping."

"He wasn't?"

"God, no." Gabriel poured himself another cup of tea. "He'd far rather be out mucking around in some drainage ditch or walking a colicky yearling than at his desk."

"You're sure of this?"

"I'm the one he dragged around for entire summers

to every clogged drain, silted-up pond, flooded field, and sagging cow byre on the property." And why did Gabriel now consider them some of his best memories of his father?

"You two were in each other's company a lot." Aaron appropriated the orange from Gabriel's plate. "You three— George was usually in attendance."

"For which, God be thanked." Gabriel downed his entire cup of tea in less than two swallows. "George could talk Papa into stopping in for a pint, or at least hopping some stiles on the way home."

"Were they close?"

"As close as a titled, distant cousin can be to his steward," Gabriel decided. "I don't really know what their relationship was. I was usually interested in flirting with the barmaids or being first to gallop up the drive."

Aaron was tearing the skin from the orange at a great rate. "Were you serious yesterday when you asked me to design a bathing chamber?"

Gabriel set down his teacup and wondered silently what about barmaids and racing home would necessitate a change of subject.

"I was," he said. "Rustic doesn't have to mean primitive, and even the Romans figured out how to get hot water most anywhere they pleased. Can you do it?"

"I thought about it last night, after you left me, and yes, there are two fairly easy options."

He was still describing the merits of each, his hands sketching in the air, when Gabriel ushered him into the library. Gabriel left the final decision to Aaron, but put in his vote for the simpler and thus more quickly constructed option, which would locate the bathing chamber on the first floor in a little-used guest parlor above the kitchens.

An hour later, Aaron was pacing before the hearth, while Gabriel lay full length on his favorite sofa, the estate book propped on his chest.

"What about this?" Gabriel ran a finger down the outside margin of a page. "Twenty damned cows went swimming at once and got stuck in the pond mud?"

"What about it? We'd had rain, and the banks were soft."

"Was it beastly hot?"

"Not particularly."

"Did something spook them into the pond, or were our cows turning to the fashionable pastime of pond bathing because Lyme Regis no longer appeals?"

Aaron paused in his pacing. "I doubt they were spooked. That pasture lies close to the Hattery's cottage, and the cows would be accustomed to the comings and goings."

"Were the cows all preparing to go courting, such that a yearly bath was in order?"

"Hardly." Aaron took off on another circuit of the library.

Gabriel considered building up the fire yet again, and discarded the notion because his back wasn't even twinging, despite the weather. "We'll attribute it to a sudden penchant for fastidiousness among socially aspiring bovines. What about your broken drain on the north pond?"

"Drains break, especially after large storms."

"Yes, they do, though two months earlier, you recorded a sizable expense for replacing drains. Was this one of them?"

"It was." Aaron's scowl was a copy of their late father's. "I suppose it could have been faulty or improperly installed."

"Fine." Gabriel flipped a page. "Passing incompetence, though how one improperly installs a quarter-ton grate over an open ditch is a mystery."

Aaron shoved his brother's boots aside and sat. "What are you getting at?"

Gabriel set the book on a hassock and struggled to a sitting position. "At the risk of finding your fist in my face, I can tell you I worked a very badly neglected estate over near the South Downs—"

"You were less than a day's ride away?" Aaron shot back to his feet. "The whole bloody time, Gabriel?"

"Not the whole time," Gabriel replied, keeping his seat, because it was the warmer—and safer—location. "Most of it. In any case, the place hadn't had a decent steward for years, or any resident owner. Every roof was sagging, every field was tired, every beast was inbred save for the market sow."

"So it was easy to see what was needed." Aaron closed the ledger and put it on the mantel.

"At first. Though in a place that had suffered a quarter-century of neglect, Aaron, we didn't have the kinds of mishaps and bad luck you did in two years at Hesketh."

"You didn't have the kind of acreage we have here, either. If you record the mishaps and bad luck of a very large patch of ground, then you get a very large list of mishaps."

"Perhaps." Gabriel rose as well, because his brother was becoming defensive, and that was not the purpose of the exercise. "When things did start to go seriously wrong—equipment breaking dangerously, a starving mongrel turning up in the chicken yard, and so forth—it wasn't bad luck."

"Sabotage?"

"You always were a bright lad."

"You think somebody's trying to make my estate management look bad? Gabriel, is it possible you've grown excessively suspicious?"

"It is." Gabriel paced to the window, where rain and something colder slapped against the panes. "It's even likely, but then I started hearing about your duels, baby brother, and I wondered if some ill luck might not have been planned for you as well."

"The duels... well." Aaron scrubbed a hand over his face. "They were nothing, really."

"So there won't be any more?" Gabriel ambled across the room to stand near his brother, the temperature being considerably more comfortable near the fire.

"There will not." Aaron said it so fervently, Gabriel had to believe him. He studied his brother's profile as they stood side by side, then settled a hand on Aaron's shoulder.

"Good."

Aaron looked over at him, a cautious, assessing glance, though Gabriel said no more. His brother was a grown man, and matters of honor were private.

Aaron moved away, out from under Gabriel's hand. "Tell me about your last two years, sir, and don't think I'm pleased to learn you were lurking right in my backyard the whole time."

Gabriel heard the sound of Aaron taking the stopper out of the decanter—before noon, for God's sake.

"I'll have a tot myself," he said. "It's a long and thirsty tale."

But for reasons Gabriel did not examine too closely, it was not going to be a tale that disclosed his previous acquaintance with Polonaise Hunt. Time enough for that later, if he survived the moral beating Aaron was going to deliver before the first installment of the story was reported.

Seven

"ARE YOU DONE WITH ME, THEN?" MARJORIE FOLDED up a pale blue riding habit with cream trim and sank into a chair.

"I am, for now," Polly replied. "Is that habit comfortable?"

"It is. It's at least three years old, and I've hunted in it many times."

"I'm surprised your mother allowed that." Polly started putting away the other wardrobe possibilities, wondering why she'd bothered considering them. Lord Aaron's eye had been accurate, and the blue habit was quite flattering. "Foxhunting can be dangerous."

Marjorie's smile suggested dangerous was good. "For the fox, and he's dangerous to the chickens, so it's not exactly unfair. Mama didn't like it, but I was always careful, and Papa loved to ride out. I used to go with him a lot when I was a girl, and Mama used to ride out sometimes too."

"But you don't ride with Aaron?"

"I haven't felt welcome, though we occasionally meet up when we're both out. We often do, now that I think about it."

Well done, my lord. "And you'd rather be on your horse

now, wouldn't you?" Polly glanced out at the bleak, damp day and sent up a prayer for Gabriel's back. She thought of such days as charcoal days, days when no color would be necessary to sketch the out of doors.

"I would rather be on a horse most all the time."

"I'd rather be in the kitchen, making something delicious, hot, and sweet." And what that description brought to Polly's mind would have shocked the marchioness.

"A cup of chocolate?" Marjorie looked puzzled, because no doubt kitchens were terra incognita to her.

"An apple, walnut, and sour cream pie." Polly felt a craving start up. "Sweet buns with lots of walnuts and a thick rummy glaze, maybe a big pot of chicken and vegetable stew with plenty of spices to it. Some toasted baguettes and butter melted with crushed garlic and a pinch of oregano…"

Marjorie's perfect brows rose. "Good heavens. You can prepare these things?"

"One has to eat, my lady." And if those were some of Gabriel's favorite dishes, what of it? "It might as well be pleasurable."

"Those buns you mentioned." Marjorie rose with more purpose than grace. "Are they the type that might appeal to, say, men?"

"Come with me." Polly took her by the hand. "The enemy is ours, or he will be by teatime."

They baked right through lunch, until the entire house smelled of cinnamon and goodness, and then they baked some more, while a thick, savory stew cooked down on the big black stove in the main kitchen. An hour before teatime, Marjorie excused herself to take some buns to George when she invited him to share dinner, and Polly set about cleaning up, the kitchen staff having abandoned ship entirely rather than hover while the lady of the house played cook.

"I thought I'd find you here." Gabriel sauntered into the kitchen, sniffing at the air.

Polly bent to wipe down the long counter under the window, though she could tell from his gait that his back wasn't hurting. "The kitchen is forbidden to anybody with a title."

"Did your cross moods always provoke you to baking?" In the manner of men who have more curiosity than common sense, he leaned over the cooling racks of sweet buns, peered at the pie, and unwrapped a long loaf of bread.

"Rainy days," Polly said, not bothering to correct him for his forward question. It was personal, that question, a small intimacy, and whether he was entitled to it or not, a part of her liked that he'd ask. "It heats up the house, chases the chill away. If you're going to purloin sweets…" She rewrapped the loaf. "Just do it."

"I'm going to purloin sweets." He came up behind her, and his arms fastened around her waist while his lips settled on the side of her neck.

"A sweet bun, you oaf." But she tilted her head, and her hands settled over his muscular forearms.

"I prefer a more rare and precious delicacy."

"Bother, you." She closed her eyes, letting herself lean back against him.

"How are you feeling?" He rocked her against him, something his height and sheer muscular bulk made easy.

"I need to get off my feet, but I'm almost done cleaning up."

"You hungry?"

"I am. A little." And not only for sweets fresh from the oven.

He switched to the other side of her neck then petted her hip when he let her go.

"You finish wiping the counters. I'll join you in a bowl of stew and a mug of tea."

A shared meal, like so many they'd had at Three Springs, just the two of them, right in the kitchen and not at any particular hour. Gabriel would come in for a clean shirt or after spending a long night with a colicky beast, and Polly would feed him, mostly to make him sit down and catch his breath.

And simply to spend time with him.

She watched from the corner of her eye as he arranged two place settings at the worktable then sliced up a few pieces of fresh bread. He added a crock of butter to the offerings and poured them each a cup of tea. To hers, he added cream and sugar, and then he stood by her chair until Polly joined him at the table.

He pulled back her chair. "Get off your feet, Miss Hunt."

"Yes, your lordship." She let him seat her and paused to inhale the fragrance of the stew.

"Was Marjorie in here with you?" Gabriel asked as he took his seat.

Polly let him lead the conversation, because she was too busy taking in the sight of him dipping his bread into his stew like the peasant he'd impersonated for two years.

"Gabriel?"

He glanced up from buttering yet another slice of bread.

"Why were you at Three Springs?"

He set the bread down and directed his gaze to the blackened beams overhead, seeming to come to some decision. "The scar on my back?"

"I know it."

"The blow was intended to be mortal, and was the first of several attempts on my life. I feared my brother was behind the attacks, and I needed a safe place to heal before I confronted him."

Such a simple recitation for what was no doubt complicated. "Do you still think Aaron wanted you dead?" The question was put as evenly as she could manage, but God above, she liked Aaron Wendover. Liked him a lot.

"I do not."

"What changed your mind?"

"Time." Gabriel resumed dipping his bread. "His behaviors. He's been increasingly reckless, and the gossip coming back to me was not about a man relishing his fortunate acquisition of a title; it was about a man dutifully bearing up under a burden he'd never seek. To hear how miserable Aaron was brought me a backhanded relief."

And for two years, Polly had thought the worst of his troubles was a sore back or an empty belly. "You didn't think you could tell us? We would have protected you, Gabriel."

"I know that now, but it's hard to convey how... rattled an injury like that, and the subsequent events, left me. I had much to learn about how most people go on in life."

"In what fashion?" While he was willing to talk, Polly would press her advantage, because God knew he wasn't willing to talk very often.

"I was... innocent, in some ways, Polonaise. I rarely paid coin for anything before I was hurt. I waved my beringed hand and directed the bills be sent here. I'd seldom saddled my own horse, never washed the dishes I'd eaten off of, never missed a meal unless I was sleeping off a drunk, never had to wash out my own linen because I hadn't any spares. I'd never taken care of myself, so to speak, and hadn't a clue how to go on."

And more amazing than that recitation—for such as he were the people ruling the land—he could smile at the man he had been. "You were uneducated about life. When I departed for the Continent with Sara and Reynard, I was fifteen, an age at which many girls are engaged to be married. I knew nothing of life either."

"You got a swift and difficult education."

Polly wished she had the nerve to tell him how swift and how difficult her transition to adulthood had been.

"I did." She squeezed his hand, though she wasn't nearly finished with him. "Tell me why you couldn't confide in us, Gabriel."

"I was ashamed, my dear." He'd put rueful humor into the observation, though Polly knew it had cost him.

"Of?"

"Of not being able to ensure my own survival." He tore off a bite of his bread and held it poised over his bowl of stew. "Of having many drinking companions and cronies, but not even one friend whom I would trust to keep me safe against my brother's supposed schemes. I was ashamed of not knowing how to go about proving Aaron's guilt. I was stunningly helpless, and for the first time in my life, unsure of all I'd taken so easily for granted. Without belaboring the point, I was... afraid. That realization was as novel as it was unwelcome."

"Knocked on your arse." Polly snatched his uneaten bread away and tore off a bite. "It isn't much fun."

"It isn't," he agreed unsmilingly. "Then I began to enjoy my work at Three Springs and to enjoy being part of the household."

"We were teetering on the brink of disaster before you arrived. Sara started including your back in her prayers, and then Allie did too. I could not help but follow suit."

"And my back got better," Gabriel said. "I should have told you, should have warned you ladies somebody might come calling to put period to my existence, except I'd been declared dead, so I should have been safe."

"You were safe. I hope you told Beckman."

"I told him." Gabriel rose and ladled them both more hot stew. "I told him enough to explain why I had to leave. He would have thrashed me silly had I not."

"I would have liked to have seen that." Polly picked up her spoon. "This needs a pinch more tarragon."

"You miss cooking?"

"Painting helps." She took a cautious spoonful. "But yes, I miss cooking, and I miss meals around the kitchen table and Allie chattering about her day and you standing her on a chair at the sink so you could wash your hands together."

"You miss her a great deal, don't you?"

"Terribly."

She stared at her food lest he catch her blinking, but there was a telling silence before she heard, "Eat your stew, Polonaise my love, and it lacks for nothing, save a little more of your delicious bread to enjoy with it."

She bent her head and for once did as he told her without protest.

❧

My love?

My love?

Aaron backed down the hallway connecting the kitchen to the front stairs and let out a silent breath.

My love. Obviously, Gabriel and Miss Hunt had a past, one that related to Gabriel's tenure as a steward for the previous two years. All thoughts of how to pipe the bathing chamber flew from Aaron's head as he considered what he'd overheard.

Gabriel cared for the woman, perhaps even more than he himself knew. Aaron had been on the occasional carouse with his older brother. Gabriel was capable of flirtation, and the women, damn them, seemed to love his brand of imperious banter.

This wasn't banter, for all it was tinged with high-handedness. Gabriel's voice had held a *caressing* quality, a humility Aaron hadn't heard previously.

Gabriel Felicitos Baptiste Wendover had admitted he was ashamed and afraid.

And he was still lying to his brother.

Aaron silently made his way to the library, sat at the large estate desk, and stared at the fire in the hearth for long, gloomy moments. When Gabriel had explained his whereabouts for the past two years, he'd been vague—an estate on the South Downs, a cook, a housekeeper, some laborers, their families, and then the owner's grandson, but no names had been mentioned, save for that of Hildegard, an immense market sow of whom Gabriel had become inordinately fond.

Sara, Allie, Beck… and Miss Hunt, whose name was not the prosaic Polly, but the more lovely and musical Polonaise.

And for two years, Gabriel had lied to them as well.

Out of fear and shame, he could admit to the woman, but not to his brother.

Which was consistent with the pattern between surviving Wendover menfolk, truth be told. Gabriel's dalliance with the artist was not the most significant secret the brothers had hanging in plain sight between them.

❧

The first Wendover male to turn Marjorie's head had not
been her fiancé. Gabriel had been a looming presence on
the edge of her life since her childhood, and Marjorie had
tried to like him, tried to find things to approve of about
him for as long as she'd understood they'd be married.

But all she'd succeeded in doing was finding more
reasons to wonder how on earth they'd go on together.
Gabriel had been impressive to her girlish eyes, but not
particularly easy to spend time with. He was impatient by
nature and gruff, and so… forbidding. She had dreaded
their duty encounters and was no end of relieved to see him
trotting off back down the driveway to return to school or
university, or whatever young men got up to when their
fiancées and families weren't looking.

And it hadn't been Aaron who was the first to charm
her, though she'd developed a serious *tendresse* for him by
the time she was thirteen and hadn't felt the sentiment abate
yet. Aaron had been good-humored, reassuring, and not at
all cowed by his larger, darker older brother.

Even before her affection for Aaron became entrenched,
however, she'd lost a part of her heart to George Wendover.

He'd been a handsome, robust man in his twenties when
she'd taken a tumble off her pony, and George had been
there to pluck her off the ground and toss her right back
into the saddle.

George had *winked* at her. "Show the little blighter who's
boss, my girl. You can't be allowing any fellow to treat you
like that."

Often, riding out with her groom, her path would cross
George's as he saw to the vast Hesketh acreage. Her own
father was horse mad, as she'd been, but Papa had eight children and his own estate to see to. George had no children,

and the vast majority of the estate he managed would never be his. He'd always had time to listen to Marjorie's little woes and joys, and now that her papa was gone and her mama was determined to ruin Marjorie's life, George's friendly ear seemed the only one to be had.

"I've brought contraband," Marjorie said when George ushered her into his study. He kept the door partly open, of course, but Marjorie closed it behind her.

"You'll let out all the heat," she scolded, "and you're family, George."

"I'm in the presence of a pretty girl bearing gifts." George set his pipe aside, because pretty girls were supposedly unable to breathe around pipe smoke. "Whatever's under that linen smells as sweet as the lady bringing it. Have a seat, and we'll have the teapot up here forthwith."

They chatted about the wet weather and the coming winter, and demolished two sweet buns apiece before Marjorie got down to business.

"Mama's going to ruin everything."

"She's only one woman. What can she do to ruin anything?"

"She's going to turn her solicitors loose on the task of setting my marriage to Aaron aside and getting me married to Gabriel."

George took up his pipe and fussed with it in some ritual known only to men. Marjorie understood this to be a delaying tactic but did not ruin her dinner with a third sweet bun.

"You'd keep the title," George said. "And Gabriel's a good man. A better man for having been out from under the title a while."

"Gabriel is… Gabriel. I am married to Aaron."

"So tell your mama to desist."

"You tell her. She doesn't listen very well."

"She doesn't," George agreed pensively. "Have you put this to your menfolk?"

"I put it to Aaron. He'll stand up to Mama, as will Gabriel."

"Puts Gabriel in a bit of a pickle." George got up to rummage in a drawer. "He'll have to repudiate the contracts he signed upon your betrothal."

"And Mama can have him put in jail for that?"

"Mama can go after damages and create scandal like you've never seen, my girl. Have a spot more tea. It's chilly out."

George was not being much help. "A cup of tea will hold back all evils." Except Mama.

"A good marriage can make them all seem surmountable." George held up a square nail and resumed his seat.

"You've been married, then, George, to speak so highly of the institution?"

"It might interest you to know, young lady, I was not discovered among the dinosaur eggs. I had a mama and a papa, and because we are the distaff side of the family, they were a love match. I have hoped for the same for you." He used the nail to clean out the bowl of his pipe.

"You're not that old, George." Marjorie poured them both more tea. "Why haven't you married?"

"A man in service usually doesn't."

"You're not in service like some footman." Marjorie added cream and sugar to his tea and passed it over as he tapped his pipe out into his palm.

"I'm bound hand and foot to thousands of acres of crops, cows, and cottages. You mind?" He gestured with the pipe.

"Stop asking." She stirred her tea. "It's a comforting smell, after all these years."

"So you're sure you want young Master Aaron?"

"Lord Aaron. I've never been more sure of anything in my life. I only wish he were taking Mama on out of similar sentiments, not out of devotion to duty."

"What a man says and what he feels are usually two different things. Particularly a young man, particularly regarding his young lady."

He was barely twenty years her senior, and talking like some crony of Mr. Danner's. "You weren't found among the dinosaur eggs, George. You really could marry and have children."

"Oh, right." George smiled ruefully and looked very like Aaron. "I could if I ever gave up my post. As busy as the land keeps me, my wife would see little of me."

"I see little of Aaron." Which George should have realized, because Aaron spent much of his time out with George inspecting piglets or ditches or heaven knew what.

"And where are those babies Lord Aaron's supposed to give you?"

Marjorie nearly threw her tea at him. "That's in God's hands. Will you come to dinner tonight?"

George lit a taper from the candle on the tea tray, then drew on his pipe to light it. "It's nasty as Hades out, and you summon me to the manor."

An invitation was not a summons. For the first time, Marjorie understood Aaron's exasperation with dear George. "It's a good night to be with family, and you know you can always stay up there if you don't feel like braving the elements. I keep a guest room ready for you."

"I'll be happy to join you, though if it starts sleeting again, I might take you up on that guest room. When do you think your mother will fire off her guns?"

Marjorie rose as the scent of pipe smoke filled the room. "She's already gone up to Town. That doesn't bode well."

"She's forever going up to Town, which means she leaves Tamarack to the tender mercies of old Pillington far too much."

"You say that like Pillington won't do his job in Mama's absence. He wouldn't dare slack when she might catch him out."

"It's cold out, Pillington is as old as dirt, and he would dare," George countered. "Somebody ought to put him out to pasture before he truly wrecks your brother's birthright."

"Dantry will soon be old enough to take over the duties of the title," Marjorie said as George escorted her to the foyer. "Pillington can step down as steward then."

George passed her a pair of black leather gloves, his expression particularly serious. "A few more years, you mean." He kept speaking as he helped Marjorie get her cape fastened. "Tamarack hasn't got a few more years, Marjorie. Pillington follows no schedule for fallowing and rotating his crops, he lets the herds get inbred, he marls when the shells are cheap, not when the land needs it. He doesn't even set the stone walls to rights come spring unless the sheep are running loose on a neighbor's land. And the tenants have ceased to stand up to him provided he leaves them in peace."

Marjorie lifted her chin while he wound a scarf about her neck. "You're angry about this. Have I ever seen you angry, George?"

"When your papa was alive, it wasn't so bad. For a steward to neglect his duties because he's serving an earl's widow and children rather than the earl himself is inexcusable. Now, especially, Pillington should be taking his duties more seriously than his grog."

"Mama won't listen to anybody about this," Marjorie predicted. "Maybe Aaron can say something to Pillington." Provided Marjorie found a way to say something to Aaron.

"Have Gabriel do it. Aaron will try to do Pillington's job for him to keep the peace. Gabriel will put the fear of Eternity in the man."

"You know them well." Marjorie paused with a hand on the door latch. "Has it been very upsetting, having Gabriel come home?"

"Upsetting?" George handed her a large umbrella. "What was upsetting was not knowing for two years if he lived or died, and if he lived, whether he was bedridden, crippled, or mad with pain."

"You didn't assume he was dead?" Marjorie took the umbrella, surprised at George's disclosure. "I don't think Aaron was sure either, at first. He kept looking down the driveway at odd hours, and he sent post after post to his fellow officers in Spain, and then he just stopped."

"What's important is that Gabriel is with us again, relatively whole and happy. We'll get your mama sorted out, and then you can be about providing the Hesketh heir, hmm?"

Marjorie resolved to ask Polly Hunt to teach her some curses a lady might use in the privacy of her thoughts.

"Talk to Aaron, or the Lord Almighty." Marjorie kissed his cheek, patted his lapel, and went back out into the rain, feeling somewhat better for having been able to share her concerns with George.

She didn't see her friend's eyes narrow shrewdly on her departing person, or hear the quiet, heartfelt oath he muttered in her absence.

~

Polly scooted over, making room for Gabriel in her bed. "You shouldn't be here."

"I shouldn't be anywhere else. It's storming miserably tonight, and you need me to allay your fears."

"I fear you'll hog the covers." Though when he stretched out beside her and wrapped an arm around her shoulders, she bundled into his warmth gratefully. "It is a wicked storm."

"Could be worse." Gabriel commenced tracing patterns on her back, and immediately Polly felt her eyes getting heavy. "Could be snow."

"I like snow," she said, determined not to slip off as easily as she had the past three nights.

"I nearly cried at my first sight of snow after leaving Spain. I'd thought never to see it again."

Snow had nearly made him cry? "What was it like in Spain, Gabriel?" She hadn't asked him this, because it had clearly been a time of suffering for him, and the moment to ask hadn't been right. But here, cuddled up with no immediate thought of mischief between them, the fire crackling softly, and the wind howling outside, she wanted to know.

"It's very different. Exotic, more Eastern than I'd thought it would be, and pretty, in its way."

"In its way." Polly snorted. "You nearly died there. How pretty can it be?"

"I didn't die there. The nuns wouldn't allow it."

"Tell me."

"They were all Sister Maria Something," he said, "and they were the silliest bunch of women I've ever met, always teasing and laughing, and enjoining one another to ridiculous prayers. 'We must pray for Señor Wendover's sense of gratitude, because he fails to appreciate this fine, rich broth we bring him five times a day…' and so forth, but God, they were fierce."

Who else would he describe as *fierce* in such admiring tones? "Fierce, how?"

"Like you, Sara, and Allie. They ran off the English surgeon when it was clear all the man wanted to do was bleed me, and they pestered the Arab physician until he was visiting me daily. A chaplain or two was commandeered for my spiritual comfort, and they taught me Spanish whether I wanted to learn it or not. They also cheated at cards, the lot of 'em."

Nuns played cards? "They didn't remind you of your mother?"

"She cheated too," Gabriel said, his lips brushing Polly's temple, "but no. She was a lady, for the most part, as best I recall."

"How old were you when she died?"

"Eight."

A cold pang of guilt pierced the haze of well-being Polly felt in Gabriel's arms. "So you had some sympathy for Allie, who also lost a parent very young." Both parents, in fact.

"She lost a wretched excuse for a father, but to her, he was as dear, I'm sure, as her mother is."

Gracious heavens. Polly leaned up and ran her tongue over his nipple, because talking about Allie was the last thing she wanted to be doing when Gabriel was in her bed.

"Cease tormenting me, Polonaise."

"You're always telling me what to do." She swiped wetly at the second one.

"And you're always ignoring my generous guidance."

"I'll give you some guidance." She glided a hand down his torso to rest her palm over his half-erect cock. "Take you in hand, I will."

"You'll go to sleep." He removed her hand but kept it tucked in his own and folded it against his chest. "Roll over, and I'll rub your back."

"You drive a hard bargain, Mr. North."

He didn't comment, though Polly suspected he liked her reference to his former alias. She flopped over to her side and presented him with her back, thinking he had the absolute best touch with her aches and pains.

Her physical aches and pains.

"We leave for Town tomorrow." He fell silent while his fingers spun pleasure up and down her spine then made the most wonderful slow circles on the muscles of her buttocks. "I suppose we could put the trip off."

He was offering to delay this trip, and she loved him for that. "You're meeting with your men of business, though, aren't you?"

"We are." He squeezed firmly and held his grip until Polly let out a sigh of pleasure.

"Did the nuns teach you this?"

"Naughty, Polonaise." He added a kiss to her shoulder. "If I said yes, you'd be taking holy orders. The solicitors will be as happy to spend our coin if we wait a day or two."

His grip on her backside was heavenly, his voice in the darkness lovely, and yet, Polly would send him on his way. "Marjorie is on pins and needles as it is, so be off with you both and have done with it."

"It might not be that easy. What is this?" His finger traced a thin, puckered line from her nape out to one shoulder.

"An excuse for you to stop what you were doing. I fell out of a tree and landed awkwardly when I was very young."

"I'll kiss it better, when I can see what I'm aiming for."

If only he could kiss all of her hurts better. "You're a candles-blazing type, aren't you?"

"I'm whatever you need me to be," Gabriel rumbled, his hand going still.

"Such a tease."

"I offer you heartfelt declarations, and you mock me." He pinched her behind, affectionately, if such a thing could be done affectionately. "Go to sleep, Polonaise, and dream of me."

"Believe I might." She reached around and linked her fingers with his, then brought his hand up to cradle her breast through her nightclothes. He allowed it, as she'd known he would.

She wasn't a stranger to the way men got when intent on gratifying their base urges, so she knew Gabriel was showing a monumental patience with her. He seemed genuinely content to cuddle and talk and tease in these dark, private hours in her bed.

Soon, she knew, he'd take what they both wanted him to take, and likely be on his way, as would she.

So why was she hugging these moments of uncomplicated proximity to her heart as if they were something more than simple bodily comfort between consenting adults?

◆◆◆

Cold rain dripped down the back of Gabriel's neck, because unlike Aaron, he'd eschewed a hat for the journey into Town.

"We could stop," Aaron volunteered. "Hole up somewhere with a toddy or two, wait for this to pass."

"This pissing weather will pass in about five months, for the fifteen minutes or so known as spring."

"You sure that gelding of yours won't suffer for this?"

Gabriel glanced at his sodden brother. "Soldier campaigned in Spain, just like you. He's tough."

"You don't get tough; you get resigned. You bargain with God for no more mud, no more flies, no more puking recruits so scared they're shitting their pants. No more drinking with a fellow one night only to be burying him in parts the next. You don't get tough."

"What about the glory?"

"The *glory*?" Aaron snorted as desultory thunder rumbled off in the west. "There was mud, and flies, and death, and more of same. I was never so glad to see a man's face as I was yours when you walked into the hospital tent."

"Nor I, yours." This particular exchange was one they hadn't had yet, and Gabriel was left to wonder why.

"How did you conclude I was trying to kill you?" Aaron's gaze was on his gelding's wet mane.

"Had I truly concluded that, I would not be here, or perhaps you wouldn't."

"You'd kill me on a whim?"

The thunder sounded again, closer. "Not on a whim. The day I left Spain, still sporting a deal of stitches, I had convinced myself you were the only logical source of my troubles, and still I couldn't confront you, much less kill you."

"Why the bloody hell not? It would have saved me a marriage, you know."

"Not by then."

"How long were you there?"

Eternities. "Four months."

"By choice?"

Soldier stopped and shook all over, like a dog, then resumed plodding down the sloppy track. The effect on Gabriel's back was exquisitely painful.

"The wound was infected, Aaron. There are pieces of my life I can't recall, save for the pain and humiliation of lying on that cot, too weak to do more than retch and moan. Had the nuns not kept the surgeons from my bed, you would have been faced with my death in truth."

"The nuns are enough to make a man consider papism." Aaron smiled soggily while Gabriel watched him mentally calculating what all had gone on in those first four months.

"I couldn't take all the piety," Gabriel said, though he hadn't minded at all that Polonaise had prayed for his recovery. "I vote we change into dry clothing before descending on Kettering. How about you?"

"Likewise. If I catch a cold, Marjorie will hold you responsible."

"Is your mother-in-law still in Town?"

"She is, and I hope she tarries longer, because Marjorie asked me to have a word with Pillington when we get back."

"Lady Hartle still has the same land steward?"

"The very same, though I'm sure he's seen his three score and ten."

"From what I've seen, he's falling asleep on the box." Gabriel stood in his stirrups to ease his aching back and thought of Aaron, campaigning for years in weather at least this miserable. "Where Tamarack land marches with ours, the fences are in disrepair, the flocks look small, there's a spring going to bog near the deer park, and it would make a perfectly suitable location for a cistern."

"I'm to make him a list," Aaron said. "I can't credit why I'm to do this, when Pillington works for the very woman on the verge of suing us."

Gabriel did not tell him that men in love were prone to contradictory behaviors. "Marjorie sees only that her brother's birthright is going to ruin. You might consider having a word with young Dantry."

Aaron's brows knitted, and a blink of lightning provided an instant's bright illumination of the dreary landscape. "That is likely the better approach. He has a couple of years of university left, but should be home for the holidays."

"You could write to him, let him know what's afoot here. As the current title holder, it likely falls to him to put his imprimatur on any lawsuit Lady Hartle seeks to bring." Unless his mother's scheming included a willingness to commit forgery.

"Hadn't thought of that either. We should discuss it with Kettering."

"When we're warm and dry." They rode along in silence for the last few cold, wet plodding miles into Town, but as the grooms were leading their mounts into the mews, Gabriel mustered a final question for his brother.

"Aaron, if you hated the military, why stay? You could have sold out at a considerable profit at any point."

"And done exactly what, Brother? Younger sons are for the church, the military, letters, or occasionally, diplomacy. I'm a horseman, so the choice was obvious."

"To Papa, but what is the choice now?" And why did Gabriel presume to press his brother this way?

"God knows." Aaron's boot sent a loose stone skittering down the damp, deserted alley. "I've never thought beyond the day you might come back."

"You had me declared dead. Why would you have been looking toward the day of my return?"

Aaron turned his face to the miserable sky for a moment, then started walking toward the back gardens of the Hesketh town house. "A good question, but I haven't an answer. Are we going to eat before we take on the men of law, or just change?"

"Kettering will feed us. He's sly like that."

"A fine quality in one's solicitor."

Yes, but what about in one's brother?

~❧~

"You might want me to discuss these matters with you separately," Kettering said.

"Because?" The question came from Aaron, who was sprawled in a chair, having demolished the substantial tea tray offered initially.

Kettering sat at his desk and twiddled a pencil over, under, and between his fingers. He was a big, dark, curiously elegant fellow, and yet, that nimble twiddling spoke volumes about the way his mind worked. "I'm going to ask things like who has had carnal knowledge of Lady Marjorie, for starts, and what exactly you knew regarding the state of her chastity before you married her."

"Holy Infant Jesus," Gabriel expostulated from where he'd propped himself against the mantel, back turned to the fire. "Is that necessary? I thought we were going to deal with the title and succession today."

"We're facing two suits, which ought to take precedence over your return from the dead," Kettering said, "at least as far as I can figure. If you are undisputedly restored to your title, Lady Hartle will be that much more motivated to wed her daughter to you."

"Two suits?" Aaron muttered from deep in his chair.

"At least. The first will be for fraud in the inducement, suggesting you, Lord Aaron, knew or should have known your brother yet lived, and used the false report of his death to gain the title and the advantageous match to Lady Marjorie."

"And the second?" Gabriel hated to ask, but forewarned was forearmed.

"For specific performance," Kettering said. "To enforce the original betrothal contract and get Gabriel Wendover to the altar with Lady Marjorie."

Aaron shot to his feet. "Is there any chance we can reason with Lady Hartle?"

Kettering flipped the pencil to his left hand without missing a beat. "Reason, how?"

"Offer her damned money, Marjorie's dower lands back, our firstborn, I don't know, but I cannot countenance violating Marjorie's privacy like this."

"Her mother apparently can," Gabriel said. "Kettering?"

"We will expect negotiations, but from what Erskine has said, we're not likely to get far."

"Said to you?"

"Said to Hamish," Kettering replied, "to whom his initial correspondence was directed. He delivered it himself to Hamish the elder, and as much as confessed Lady Hartle has the bit between her teeth."

"He's lost control of his client," Aaron said, popping the last tea cake into his mouth. "Gentlemen, it seems we are to have a scandal."

"Scandal is of little moment, Aaron," Gabriel said, "as long as I don't end up having to marry your wife."

Kettering's infernal pencil came to a halt. "That outcome, at least, isn't likely."

"And why should we be shown that bit of mercy by the gods of legalities?" Gabriel asked, his eye on his brother, who had never looked more miserable.

"I've done the research. I can't find a single case where an English court has ordered two people to marry who were both unwilling, not in the past hundred years or so. It shades over into church law, and even the church hasn't a recent precedent for such a thing."

"Marjorie might not be *un*willing, despite declarations to the contrary," Aaron said, tossing himself back into his chair. "With her mother holding a figurative gun to her back, and knowing Gabriel would treat her decently, Marjorie might eventually accommodate the notion. She has younger siblings to think of. Many younger siblings."

"Have you considered getting her with child?" Kettering posed the question casually and resumed flipping his pencil.

"Getting her...?" Aaron bent forward, face in his hands. "So Gabriel can raise my son, who will disinherit Gabriel's son? I thought you were clever, Kettering, not perverse."

"If she's carrying your child," Kettering said, "Lady Hartle might back down, because the offspring could be become illegitimate if the fraud suit succeeds. She has to know we're years away from any judicial decisions."

"Clever," Gabriel allowed, "and perverse, also damned risky to the child." More to the point, he could not confess to Polonaise that he'd endorse such a scheme, and thus it became untenable.

"Risky to Marjorie as well," Aaron said. "Let's not pin our hopes on that strategy."

"It's just a thought." Kettering put down his damned pencil an instant before Gabriel would have grabbed for it. "Suit has not been formally joined, so we have time to gather more information. As a starting point, I want you both to make a calendar for me."

"Of?" Gabriel asked, because lists of sobriquets for Lady Hartle would likely not aid the situation.

"A list of events," Kettering said. "From the day each of you left England, to the day you showed up in my office. I want you to post anything that could bear on this situation, but your calendar, Lord Aaron, is the more noteworthy."

"There'll be a deuced lot of 'got drunk and cursed my fate' on my calendar. It hasn't been a jolly two years, Kettering."

Kettering reached for his pencil, but Gabriel snatched it up first.

"I want to know when you first feared your brother dead, what steps you took to confirm or deny the rumors, how long you waited before taking legal action. You'll need to note when Lady Hartle approached you about marrying her daughter, what your response was, who witnessed it, and so forth. Then I'll need to know who planned the wedding itself."

"You're trying to make Lady Hartle look like the hypocrite she is," Aaron said. "Will that work?"

"Lady Hartle wants what is called equitable relief, not damages, and those who come before the courts of equity are admonished to do so with 'clean hands.' Her dainty white hands are not legally any cleaner than my head groom's, if she was the one to force the issue of marriage over protestations from the principles."

"Marjorie didn't protest," Aaron said, studying the muddy toes of his boots. "She went like a lamb to slaughter, and I protested only behind closed doors, because one wouldn't want to imply the lady was in any way lacking."

"So how worried should we be?" Gabriel raised the question Aaron would not voice.

"About scandal, plenty worried, because the very

drafting of a complaint starts the gossip rolling, and once it's filed, you have no privacy whatsoever. About having to marry Lady Marjorie, not very worried."

Delightful. This was why the Bard recommending killing all the lawyers. "Not very worried is not the same thing as not worried at all."

"I'm a solicitor," Kettering said. "Anybody who promises you they can deliver a given outcome in any legal case is lying or preparing to commit a crime. More tea?"

"Hang the damned tea." Aaron got to his feet. "My thanks, Kettering. This has been enlightening, and depressing as hell. Maybe the cavalry wasn't the worst place I could have ended up."

"Right." Kettering smiled genially. "You might have become a barrister and had to deal with the likes of me regularly, and not simply to pull you through a little scrape."

"Gabriel, I'm off to fetch the horses, I'll see you out back."

He left a thoughtful silence in his wake.

"He's hiding something," Gabriel said, pitching Kettering's pencil into the fire. "I don't know what, but it's eating at him."

"What are you hiding?"

"I'm not sure." Though he had a strong hunch. "Possibly that I'm trying to woo a female, and I don't want Aaron getting wind of it yet."

"Why not?"

"Because I think there's a part of my brother that wants to see me married to his wife. Aaron and Marjorie aren't quite cordial, though he's never rude to her, never upbraids her in public, never shows her the slightest discourtesy."

Kettering lifted the lid of the teapot—a delicate, flowery bit of antique Sevres that somehow suited him—then bellowed for a clerk to bring a fresh pot. "Maybe Aaron and Marjorie are reserved. They've had a couple of years to burn through their initial lust."

"Even reserved couples have a private vocabulary of looks and glances, muttered asides, veiled references, that sort of thing. Aaron and Marjorie don't seem to be a real couple in the married sense."

Kettering opened his fussy French desk and withdrew another pencil. "Who is this woman you're interested in?"

Gabriel smiled, because denying any lawyer any answer was that much fun. "She isn't likely to have me, not at first, so I must wage a stealthy and determined campaign."

"God help her. You can't think to offer marriage while suit is pending?"

"I suppose not." Trust a lawyer to leave a trail of blighted hopes. "What of that other matter, the question of who tried to have me killed, Kettering? Have you learned anything further?"

"I have the names of the men your brother met over pistols." Kettering opened another drawer, rummaged briefly, and read three names.

"Those names are familiar. Fellow officers?"

"Every one of them served with Lord Aaron in Spain, and was there when you were injured."

"This does not bode well." Not that much that went on in a lawyer's office ever would. "Any idea what they were attempting to murder each other over?" And where was that fresh pot of hot tea when a man faced yet more cold, rainy weather amid the reek and mud of London?

"That's peculiar." Kettering shoved the pencil behind his ear and settled his large frame onto the front of his desk, provoking a chorus of creaks from the delicate furniture.

"Nobody was hurt in any of the three duels, not a scratch, not a close call, not a near miss, and in each case, the participants were crack shots, experienced with their weapons."

"Common sense often prevails when people have had a chance to cool off."

"But cool off about what?" Kettering hunched forward, leaning his weight on his hands. "There isn't a single bet on the club books, not a rumor to be found, not a second willing to gossip."

"You're sure they met?"

"All three times, yes, and shots were fired, and seconds present, and so forth, but not one word about what the underlying challenge entailed."

"Do you suppose my brother has a mistress?"

"He doesn't," Kettering said. "I see all the money, and none of it is going to any lightskirt."

"Remind me never to cross you."

"Well, cheer up." Kettering smiled, a frighteningly chipper expression. "Just as soon as we figure out who wants you dead, what your brother is hiding, and how to keep you safe from Lady Hartle's schemes, your troubles will be over."

"You forgot the most important matter." Gabriel paused with a hand on the door latch, because Kettering had taken the pencil from behind his ear, and Gabriel did not want to murder the best solicitor in the realm.

Kettering considered that pencil, then shot Gabriel a curious look. "The title? That shouldn't be too hard."

"Tell me you're joking."

"I didn't say it would be cheap." Kettering's smile was nowhere in evidence. "Once we clear up these other matters, I'll look into it in greater depth."

"I couldn't care less how long Aaron sports the title,"

Gabriel said. "He's growing into it nicely, though he's still feuding with our steward too often."

"So if it isn't the title," Kettering said, "what's your greatest remaining challenge?"

"The lady. The greatest and most worthy challenge is the lady, and how to make her safely and permanently mine."

Eight

"YOU WERE WORRIED ABOUT SOLDIER," GABRIEL SAID, "while it's your mount who seems to be tiring."

Aaron's horse half slipped, half shied itself nigh into the ditch.

"If certain horses didn't spend the first three miles from Town dancing around and spooking at every passing bonnet, then certain horses wouldn't be so damned tired when we're still three miles from home." Aaron's testiness and fatigue showed in his tone of voice, which had the same horse tossing its head and switching its wet tail.

"We could borrow a mount from a neighbor," Gabriel suggested. "You know you want to get off and walk the silly blighter. I'd walk with you. Soldier shouldn't be abused simply because he has more sense."

"You wouldn't mind?"

"Of course not." Gabriel swung down, grateful not to have to admit his back was screaming at him to get out of the saddle. Their stay in London had been marked by cold, rain, and a house staff caught unused to having anybody to look after. He'd gone days without having a truly hot soak.

Or smelling freshly baked sweets.

"So what did we learn, Gabriel, on our sojourn up to Gomorrah?"

"We learned your horse is town-shy, much as I've become."

"I noticed you stuck close to home." Their boots squishing in the mud made a wet counterpoint to the hooves doing likewise directly behind them.

"As did you, baby brother."

"And you wrote to Miss Hunt."

"While you couldn't be bothered to send along a single word to your wife," Gabriel noted airily. "She's likely worried, Aaron."

"And Kettering didn't exactly scoff at the notion one should be worried," Aaron rejoined. Gabriel let a silence take root, until, a quarter of a mile later, Aaron spoke again.

"You're right. I should have written to my wife. What did you have to say to Miss Hunt?"

"I passed along some greetings from a mutual friend."

Gabriel could tell Aaron was itching to ask how a portrait artist and an earl-turned-land-steward could have a mutual friend, but it took another quarter mile.

"You know her from before?" Aaron asked, gaze on the dripping brown hedgerows on either side of the road.

"I do. We were not involved, if that's what you're thinking." In love with a woman was not the same thing as involved with her.

"Involved." Aaron pursed his lips, petted his tired horse's neck, fiddled with the reins he was leading the animal by, and then glanced at his brother. "Is that how a land steward refers to swiving a decent young woman toward whom he has no marital aspirations?"

The silence this time lasted about eight steps of muddy boots. "Grown puritanical in my absence, Aaron?"

"Until such time as you resume the title, Miss Hunt is under my protection, isn't she? And she's the first thing like a real friend I've seen in Marjorie's life. You weren't a choirboy before you went to Spain, Gabriel, but you played by the usual rules."

"I learned to, and your unwillingness to mention the cost of my education is appreciated. Miss Hunt and I were not involved, make of that what you will, and were I to offer for her—again—she would not have me." *Yet.*

Not silence, but rather Aaron's eyebrows risen in surprise. "You *offered* for her? When you were merely a land steward?"

"Merely a land steward," Gabriel said. "She didn't hold that against me, any more than she'd be impressed with my title. Miss Hunt has seen most of the capitals and courts of Europe, as well as many works of the great masters in the original."

"She's different," Aaron concluded. "Sophisticated in some regards, unassuming in others. Also very competent in the kitchen."

And the bedroom, and the library. "Well put, and she's stubborn. I tried to tell her it wasn't safe to be at Hesketh until we'd figured out who tried to kill me, and she pretty much read me the Riot Act."

"Did she raise her voice?"

"Not in the least." Gabriel sloshed along. "She politely gave me leave to consider that if I were so concerned about the safety of my loved ones, perhaps I ought to be taking myself off to distant parts, rather than ordering others from my presence."

"But you did that," Aaron said. "For two years you were on the South Downs, herding sheep or bullocks or something."

Gabriel endured a wave of cold, muddy homesickness—for the sheep, the bullocks, and that padded chair in Polly's kitchen. "We raised a little of everything, because it was an old-fashioned estate and intended to be self-supporting."

"And was it?"

It had certainly supported Gabriel. "When I left, it was on its way to thriving, though by then it had acquired a competent owner who was both knowledgeable and committed to the land."

"You're right; it takes both." Aaron's horse took a slippery step but righted itself easily enough. "I was committed but knew exactly bugger all about the land."

"You've managed well, better than I would have."

"George plays games with me," Aaron said. "He wants me to fall on my own sword, as if I'm a little boy and can learn only by his silent, disapproving example."

"George is more tired of his job than he knows. He's been doing it so long he no longer brings fresh ideas to it."

"But one can't approach it thus," Aaron rejoined. And for the next two miles, Gabriel was treated to a surprisingly impassioned diatribe on stewardship of the land and modern agriculture and the necessity of innovation if one was to go on profitably.

All from a man who professed to know little about the subject.

They were halfway up the drive, the elegant and imposing facade of the manor before them, when Soldier's back foot slipped in the mud. The horse threw up his head in a bid for balance, and Gabriel's arm was jerked out and up, because his fingers were nigh frozen around the reins. Aaron plodded a few steps farther before pausing and eyeing

Soldier, who had come to a rock-steady halt. "The old boy isn't turning up balky now, is he?"

"No." Not the four-legged old boy.

"Well, are we to stand out here until the heavens open up again? I'm for a hot bath, myself, and some of that baking one can hope Miss Hunt has gotten up to, and perhaps even a... Gabriel?"

"Bloody, benighted fuck."

"Your back?"

Gabriel managed a nod. A careful nod. Aaron blew out a breath, tied up the reins on the horses, then sent both beasts trotting the last distance toward their long-awaited stables.

"Can you get an arm around my shoulders?"

"The left one," Gabriel said, because even long words would hurt unnecessarily. It took slow, cautious movement on both their parts, but Aaron soon had Gabriel hobbling toward the house.

"Marjorie is going to blame me for this," Aaron muttered. "And she'll be half-right. Could we stop at an inn and warm up? Why no, of course not, because Gabriel Wendover was on campaign, anxious to tell my dear wife we've learned exactly nothing, for all we've spent a delightful week in the stinking, filthy hog wallow of Town. But will he listen to me when I suggest we might wait for more salubrious weather to make this journey?"

"Aaron." Gabriel's voice was little more than a whisper. "It's all right. I won't fall into a swoon, and I won't die from this."

"You might," Aaron said darkly. "When I get done scolding you for your pigheadedness, and Marjorie gets done scolding *me* for your pigheadedness."

Gabriel's lips quirked, despite the pain and the mud and

the cold and the fact that he'd scared his little brother badly. "We're in for it now. It's fortunate that my back will come to rights with some heat and rest."

"You're sure?"

"It always has before."

"Marjorie will still kill me."

❧

"Any grouchy old cripples hereabouts?" Aaron asked as he waltzed into Gabriel's room, a tray balanced on his hip.

Polly snatched a pillow from Gabriel's hand. "Don't throw that. Aaron's carrying hot soup and hot tea on that tray, of which you will partake, sir."

Aaron appeared vastly entertained by Polly's high-handedness. Well, so was Gabriel, or he would be, if the murderous pain in his back weren't making humor impossible.

"You will leave us, Miss Hunt," Gabriel said. "My thanks for your kind wishes, but my brother can be trusted to make sure I eat my pudding."

Polly shot a dismissive look at Aaron. "He cannot. He's your brother, and siblings are ever willing to conspire with each other."

"I can," Aaron said, "because it's delicious, and the only stops we made coming down from Town were to rest the horses, so yonder old man will be nigh starving."

Gabriel barely got out a muttered, "Now you've done it," before Polly was off, ranting about two idiot men and it must be bred into them and this was why sensible people went traveling in the summer and why did she ever think...

"Bother the both of you." She marched toward the door. "I am going to have a soothing cup of chocolate with

Lady Marjorie, and we are going to lament the Creator's missteps with his practice model."

"The male of the species," Gabriel supplied in her absence. "The Creator, in Miss Hunt's opinion, is subject to all the trials of any other artist, requiring practice models and initial sketches and so forth. The donkey is the initial sketch of the horse, in her theology."

"Interesting." Aaron pulled a hassock over closer to the fire and put the tray on it. "Interesting that you've debated theology with the portrait artist."

"One doesn't debate with Polonaise Hunt; one listens attentively and takes notes. Is that chicken stew?"

"Marjorie said Miss Hunt was in a cooking mood today because it was too dreary to paint. It smells delicious." They consumed every single thing on the tray in the concentrated, appreciative silence of tired, hungry men, and the tub was full and steaming by the fireside by the time they were finished.

Aaron rose and frowned down at his brother. "I'm not going to ask how you managed this sort of problem when you were a mere land steward."

"Carefully." Gabriel scooted to the edge of his seat, pushed gingerly to his feet, then made himself stand, mentally beating back the pain—and the memory of Mr. Danner, effecting the same maneuver far more smoothly.

"It's bad, isn't it?"

"Uncomfortable."

Aaron walked him over to the tub. "Why in the hell can't you take a tot of the poppy?"

"And have whoever wishes me ill know I'm completely incapacitated?"

Gabriel fell silent for long, teeth-gritting moments while

they got him into the tub. "I'll be in this tub until spring," he declared. "Is there any more of that tea?"

"Of course." Aaron shifted to fix his brother a cup, then dragged the dressing stool over to the tub. "Can you manage in there, or do you need assistance?"

"I need to soak." Gabriel leaned back and closed his eyes. "It's good and hot, a little bit of heaven."

When the water began to cool, Aaron saw to the washing of his hair and did the honors with the rinse water. Getting Gabriel out of the tub was easier than getting him into it.

"You're not to get into the bed until I use the sheet warmer," Aaron cautioned.

"Don't forget to warm the pillows as well, else General Hunt will have a court-martial."

"She's worried for you. It's sweet."

Also improper as hell for Polonaise to be in his bedroom at any hour, much as it pleased him that she'd fuss over him. "You like seeing me scolded like a puppy who's made a puddle in the front hallway."

"I truly do." Aaron eased him onto the bed. "You said Miss Hunt refused you. She's not acting like a woman indifferent to your situation now."

Gabriel went still in the act of pulling the comforter up over his lap. "She isn't, is she? Ah, well, she has a big heart, does Polonaise. She feels for creatures too stupid to stay out of the rain, and if I'm not mistaken, I hear the footsteps of her invading army."

A knock verified the evidence of Gabriel's ears.

"I'm back," she said, striding into the room, several footmen behind her. They dipped buckets to empty the tub, quickly, silently, and were soon wheeling the thing from the room, the door left open behind them. "You're clean?"

"And fed and a good deal warmer. My thanks."

"You made him eat?" This to Aaron, whose smile disappeared when Polly swung her gun sights on him.

"I didn't have to. The repast was sufficiently enticing on its own."

Polly rewarded him with a smile. "A fine answer. I'll take the first shift here, and you can attend your lady wife, who needs more than a few comments regarding your progress in London, my lord."

"You needn't be my lording me, Miss Hunt, not on Gabriel's say so."

"Don't give her an inch," Gabriel warned softly.

Polly put her hands on her hips. "You are in enough trouble."

"Out of my room, Polonaise," Gabriel retorted. "I'm not so helpless I need witnesses to any further indignities."

"Well, I'm leaving." Aaron backed toward the door. "Miss Hunt has given me my orders, which, like the dutiful, prudent soldier I am, I will heed." He offered Polly a bow, his brother a smirk, and took his leave.

Polly advanced on the bed. "You can stop pretending now. I know it hurts like blazes, Gabriel, and I'm sorry for it."

"It isn't your fault," he said, smoothing a hand over the comforter. "You really need not hover, Polonaise. Only Aaron knows you're closeted in here with me, and myself undressed down to my nappies, but the footmen will squawk."

"Like geese. It's complicated, having help underfoot. Where did you say that salve was?"

"I'm not telling." Though he longed for the feel of her strong, competent hands on his person, and for once, not in any sexual sense.

"Aha." Polly closed the drawer to the night table. "This helps, Gabriel, you know it does."

"Peace and quiet help," he grumbled as he shifted onto his stomach.

"So you accomplished little in Town?" Polly sat on the edge of the bed and waited for him to get settled, clearly knowing better than to try to assist him.

"A lawsuit is like a military campaign, I gather." Gabriel did let her deal with his pillows until he was flat on the mattress, like a day-old filleted herring. "There is endless strategizing and gathering intelligence and planning supply lines and moving cannon into position and so forth. You prepare thoroughly, in hopes you'll have to skirmish only briefly, with all the casualties on the opposing side." He fell silent, then couldn't help an oath of combined pain and relief as Polly's hands smoothed the salve into his skin.

"This is bad," she observed some minutes later, her fingers kneading gently. "That hurts, doesn't it?"

"I should say, rather, it agonizes. Promise me something, Polonaise."

"What?"

"No laudanum. Not to get me to sleep, not to ease the pain, not for the sheer pleasure of disobeying me."

"Disobey…?" She fell silent while Gabriel struggled to shift to his back. "You fear to be insensate."

"That's my girl. Bad things have happened to me often enough that I need not compound incapacity with insensibility."

"We'll post a footman." Polly rose off the bed. "Two footmen, and someone can stay with you."

"Polonaise." He pushed the covers back as if to get out of bed, and she stopped halfway across the room.

"Back under those covers, Gabriel, *now*."

"And you," he said. "Quit haring off to post guards and advertise to the entire world that I'm sitting here like a trussed goose."

"All right, but I'll stay with you."

"You cannot," Gabriel insisted, letting some of his irritation show in his voice. "It would be unseemly, and you know it. Those commissions you value so highly would evaporate overnight, Polonaise."

It was a low, telling blow, and he delivered it with the right hint of condescension. In the moment when Polly stood there, hurt, angry, and framing her reply around a gathering scowl, Aaron knocked and sauntered in, leading Marjorie by the wrist.

"We're visiting the sick," Aaron said, "or is it the halt and the lame?"

"How conveniently Christian of you," Gabriel drawled. "Lady Marjorie, my apologies for remaining abed, but certain people relieved me of nearly every blasted stitch of my clothing. One wouldn't want to offend the innocent."

"Don't mind me," Marjorie said with a sly grin.

"Gone over to the enemy, have you?" Gabriel closed his eyes. "Wait until we're married, my girl, and see how I seek my revenge."

"You said we wouldn't be marrying."

"I'm incoherent with pain and unwilling to die alone," Gabriel threatened. "You've visited, Aaron. Now take your cruel wife and gloat elsewhere."

"Marjorie has a point you ought to hear." Aaron's hand was still wrapped around his wife's wrist, and Gabriel considered that anything causing the two of them to touch was likely worth taking an interest in.

"Seeing as my sickroom has become the local equivalent of Piccadilly"—Gabriel waved a hand—"say on."

Aaron took a moment to bring the chairs to the side of the bed and get the women seated before he took up a position lounging at Gabriel's feet.

"Go ahead, Margie. Tell Gabriel what you said in the kitchen."

"I asked Aaron, if somebody is trying to kill you, wouldn't now be the best time to finish the job?"

"Yes," Gabriel said. "It would, which is why I will not be swilling any damned nostrums or patent remedies."

"So why not advertise your helpless condition?" Marjorie went on. "When your attacker stalks closer, we can snatch them up."

"Bait," Polly said, looking grim. "You're suggesting Gabriel use himself as bait."

"He's incapacitated," Aaron pointed out. "We let him recover a bit, then put the word out he's taken a turn for the worse and developed a lung fever and so on."

"I should be substantially improved by morning." Gabriel dearly hoped so anyway. "I like this plan." He sought his brother's gaze, willing Aaron to understand that not knowing who wished Gabriel harm, not knowing when they'd try again, not knowing *why*, was eating at him.

"We could move you into the lord's chambers," Aaron suggested. "There's no way to get to the bedroom except from the sitting room, and it's easy to stand watch from Marjorie's sitting room."

"I don't want to discommode you," Gabriel said, but he was considering the logistics, and Aaron had a point.

"Aaron and I can vacate that apartment by tomorrow night," Marjorie offered. "There are plenty of connected guest rooms, and you're expected to take over the main chambers at some point."

"Polonaise?"

That he would ask her, and before others, was a risk, but she didn't let him down, didn't toss back some witty, cutting retort, though she would have been within her rights to do so.

"You are haunted by this," Polly said slowly, "not knowing whom to trust and whom to watch. This is a sound plan, provided we can guard you closely enough."

"Well, there you have it," Gabriel said. "General Hunt is willing to give it a try, but then, she will be moving on soon, won't she?"

"Soon enough," Polly murmured, when Gabriel would rather have heard a rousing argument. "I'd like to know you're safe when I go."

A telling shot. "Very well. Give me a day or possibly two to recover, and then I will make a tragic turn for the worse. Now, if you ladies would excuse me, I require my brother's company for a few minutes."

"It's all right," Aaron said to Polly. "I won't leave him until you return."

"Now I'm a third person," Gabriel groused. "Not even a 'his lordship' third person, just a 'him' third person."

Marjorie held out her hand. "Come, Miss Hunt. You no doubt forgot your own supper, and men need their privacy."

The door closed behind the women, leaving a relieved silence in its wake.

"Did you have to get catty like that?" Aaron asked, putting the furniture to rights. "That woman you're not involved with has feelings for you, Gabriel, and reminding her of her departure wasn't especially kind."

"What's unkind is her deciding to leave me so easily," Gabriel rejoined. "Get me to the damned privacy screen, if you please."

"You don't want to merely tumble her, do you? She's the one you want to woo."

"On three." Gabriel got his arms around his brother's shoulders, and Aaron lifted gently on the count of three. "Oh, holy, suffering Christ…"

"I'll stay with you this evening."

"My thanks." Gabriel tottered over to the screen and dropped his brother's arm. "If you don't, Polonaise likely will, sitting upright at the foot of the bed like some loyal beast. She has a wide protective streak, too wide sometimes."

"You know her that well?"

"We were part of the same household for almost two years," Gabriel said, tending to his errand as he spoke. "She was the cook, I was the steward, and there was more work for either of us than you could imagine. You can't help but develop some familiarity in such proximity."

He emerged from behind the screen, trying to test his balance without courting disaster.

"Miss Hunt was in service?"

"In a manner of speaking." Gabriel waved his brother off and made the long journey back to the bed on his own two feet. "Her sister was the housekeeper, and Polly took the post of cook when the person holding the position abruptly retired. It was a decided improvement, because Polly's palate is as well educated as her palette.

"Don't watch," Gabriel said, lowering himself to the bed. "This is a tedious business and utterly without dignity." He elbow-crawled back onto the mattress, pausing frequently and moving with all the grace of a jug-bitten tortoise.

When he was once again under his covers, Gabriel let out a disgusted sigh. "Growing old is not for the faint of heart."

"You aren't old; you're just… a little worn."

"Such a diplomat. Now, tell me whether you've been considering Kettering's very sly suggestion that you and Marjorie start a family."

"That is hardly your affair." Aaron's words were the verbal equivalent of the sleet now pinging against the windows.

Gabriel moved lower on the pillows, carefully, like an exhausted plow horse sinking onto a bed of straw after a day in the traces. "The hell it isn't my affair, particularly when I'm facing another installment of my own attempted murder. I'd say one of us should be reproducing some legitimate offspring posthaste, and you're the only one with a willing accomplice."

Which frustration was almost enough to eclipse the pain and indignity of Gabriel's blighted, benighted damned back.

⁓

Gabriel wakened from a drowse, not quite a sleep, because he couldn't let his guard down enough to relax into slumber when he was completely alone with a bad back. Polly was silently padding across his bedchamber, a candle in her hand.

"You've come to check on the baby?"

"I've come to take you to my tower," Polly said, setting the candle down by his bedside. "Aaron said you can walk if you move slowly."

"Aaron knows precious bloody little of what he speaks." Gabriel pushed to a sitting position rather than pull Polly into bed with him. "Do you promise to enslave me for eternity once we arrive to your tower?"

"I haven't already?" She gathered up his dressing gown

and reading spectacles, politely giving him time to dock at the edge of the bed like some ungainly human coal barge, steered by the primitive expedients of pushing and hoping.

Gabriel slid on his slippers while seated, in the manner of a man twice his age. "If you aren't convinced of my adoration yet, Polonaise, then I've been too subtle. Or perhaps, you are too hardheaded."

"That must be it." She sat beside him on the bed. "I could not imagine you'd sleep well by yourself in here with your back paining you."

"One does get to fretting, though at least four footmen and two chambermaids have been privy to my infirmity."

"No one will think to look for you in my room. Up you go." She slid an arm around his waist and waited for him to initiate the effort.

The woman was an optimist, for Gabriel went nowhere. "If I didn't agree with you, you know, I'd be ordering you from the room."

"You'll likely order me from my own room," Polly predicted. "You're stalling, sir."

"It's always hardest when I've been inactive. Getting moving is uncomfortable, but it gets better once I'm under way. The footman is not yet on duty?"

"Not yet, but if you sit here prevaricating much longer, he'll be right down the hall to witness your kidnapping."

He rose, slowly, but not as painfully as he would have even a couple of hours earlier, and gave Polly a moment to get his dressing gown onto him.

"Prepare to give chase," he warned before shuffling toward the door, leaning on Polly mostly for show. He might have moved more quickly, but tottering along at her side was a pleasure, and there really wasn't any hurry.

In fact, now that he was heading for her room, there to spend the entire night with her in her bed, Gabriel had to wonder if he hadn't exchanged one kind of misery for another of far worse variety.

⁓

Polly watched her patient teeter over to her bed and wondered if he'd move like that when he was elderly.

Probably not, unless he'd been foolish enough to forget his limitations and aggravate his back. In all likelihood, he'd be one of those men who was vigorous and attractive even to his threescore-and-ten years.

She'd like to do his portrait then, too.

"You coming to bed, Polonaise, or will you guard the door to my prison?"

"I'm coming." She wedged a fringed rug under the door, then positioned a chair under the door latch, and finished with a string of bells over the chair back.

She expected to find him smirking at her for these ineffectual measures, but his expression was oddly grave, or perhaps puzzled. He ended the moment by shrugging out of his dressing gown and climbing onto the bed in all his scarred, naked glory.

Her slave, indeed.

"I'll get you back to your bed before the maids are about," she said. "Marjorie gave orders you weren't to be disturbed in the morning."

"Our Lady Marjorie is proving to have a brain in her head. One hopes my brother can appreciate it."

"She wants me to paint him, you know." Polly watched as Gabriel settled back against her pillows. How was it he could look so... alluring, when he was debilitated, tired, and he'd just deliberately treated her to an unfettered view of his horrendous scar?

"She wants any semblance of a normal marriage she can create with Aaron," Gabriel said. "They are as nervous with each other as a pair of sixteen-year-old virgins. It's an abysmal reflection on the prowess of the Wendover male."

"Hush, you." Polly blew out the candles, banked the fire, and only then folded her dressing gown across the foot of the bed. "There'll be no talk of prowess from the man who turned me down flat only a few months ago."

"I didn't turn you down, Polonaise." Gabriel's voice had acquired a darkness all its own. Smoky and sweet, like the scent of a wood fire on a frigid, starry night. "I stated the conditions any gentleman would insist on, and you rejected me."

"I rejected—?" Her mouth dropped open and her hands went to her hips, but she was backlit by the hearth—any artist had a sense for the light sources in a room—and caught the gleam in Gabriel's green eyes.

"Come to bed, love." Gabriel gestured with a hand. "We can argue in close quarters, and perhaps in my weakened state, you'll have your way with me yet."

"You're ailing," she said, advancing on the bed. "Helpless, and depending on me to keep you safe."

"You've summarized the situation well enough, Polonaise, now *come to bed*."

She took another step toward the bed, then whisked her nightgown, a voluminous business of thick cotton that covered her from neck to toes, right over her head.

"Sweet Infant Jesus *and* the singing angels."

"You rejected me," Polly said as she sauntered toward him. "Not well done of you, Gabriel."

The look on his face expressed admiration for her pluck

and her audacity, male hunger for her feminine charms, and something else she couldn't fathom.

He lowered his hand. "I've changed my mind. Don't come to bed just yet."

Her courage faltered as she stood a few steps from the bed, naked, hands at her sides, eyes searching his for... another rejection, or reassurance?

"You are so lovely," Gabriel said. "But you'll be safe enough with me tonight, Polonaise, and not because I'm rejecting you. When we make love—and it will be love-making, my dear, regardless that your fevered brain tries to rationalize otherwise—I will not have our first encounter hampered by my feeble back." His expression promised Polly it would be *perfect*. She tried to ignore that promise and seized on the lifeline he'd tossed her pride.

"Empty boasts," she rejoined. "Move over. I won't have you hogging the middle."

"A slave driver." Gabriel sighed, obliging her. "And me so meek and obliging."

"You haven't a meek bone in your body." Polly bounced onto the bed and saw him wince at the movement of the mattress. "Roll over."

He accommodated her, giving her the vast, muscled expanse of his back. She went to work with her hands, knowing by the quality of his silence he was enjoying it.

"Heat helps, doesn't it?"

"It does. You have strong hands."

"From kneading more bread than you'd care to know." She left off her massage and pressed herself against his back, spooning her body snugly around his, so her legs were drawn up under his thighs and buttocks, and her breasts were pressed against his back.

Gabriel's hand settled over hers where it cradled his waist. "While I applaud the selfless generosity of your nursing, this might not be wise, Polonaise."

"Hush." She kissed his shoulder blade and laid her forehead on his nape. "You're my slave, and I'm telling you to hush, Gabriel. For once, let me keep you safe."

❧

Gabriel woke some hours later, surprised he'd been able to sleep so deeply. Polly was still spooned around him, her fingers still closed over his wrist. Even in slumber, she protected what was hers.

What she wouldn't admit was hers, the silly widgeon.

Well, he'd been silly too, trying to put distance between them in the name of keeping her safe, and here fate, or a mischievous Deity, had tossed her right back into his lap. Gabriel would keep her safe, and he wouldn't do it by stuffing a rug under her door.

Carefully, he got up and poked some life into the fire. His back was greatly improved, and he had to wonder why that should be so. The first time the damned thing had seized up, he'd been laid flat in a rooming house in Portsmouth for a week, nerves snapping at the sound of every footstep on the stair, knife under his pillow at all times.

At Three Springs, he'd had the frequent hot soak to speed his recovery, and Polly and Sara's fussing and scolding.

And then Beckman Haddonfield had come along and added his two pence of clucking and finger-shaking, and thank God, the man had enough brawn himself that when Gabriel had been laid low, Beck had kept up with the chores and the farming while Gabriel healed.

But hot springs, friendship, and some extra muscle were

not the same thing as *protection*. Aaron and Polly between them, abetted by Marjorie, would see to Gabriel's safety if he asked it of them.

God willing, it wouldn't come to that, but to know they were offering...

"Gabriel, you'll catch your death." Polly flipped back the covers and thumped the mattress once. "Now, if you please."

He complied, curling his body around hers.

"I can't keep your back warm this way," Polly protested sleepily.

"You keep my heart warm this way," he replied, kissing her ear. "Go to sleep. We've a long, boring day ahead of us tomorrow, and you'll need your strength if you're to endure my company without being moved to violence."

"Idle threats." She seemed willing to subside into sleep, but then Gabriel felt her hand sliding over his hip and around to his shaft. "What's this poking me?"

"A token of my proximity to a certain intemperate, very warm female. I suggest you desist."

She desisted from carefully shaping him, and closed her fingers around him instead.

"Polonaise... Please."

"Ah." Polly's fingers drifted over the sensitive head of his cock. "You're on your manners. I must be truly aggravating you."

"Aggravating my lust." He let her play for a few more minutes, until that lust was a seething heat in his vitals, and the urge to mate was stealing a march on reason and determined intentions.

"Consider yourself warned, Miss Hunt." He counted to five silently, but she merely detoured to his ballocks, which were threatening to draw up, even under the heat of the bedcovers.

He drew his hips back, but this only provoked the infernal woman to scoot around so she faced him and presented him with the very temptation he'd been trying to avoid.

Gabriel traced his palm up Polly's ribs, slowly, slowly, as consideringly as he'd run his hand over a fine fabric he was thinking of purchasing. Her fingers went still on his cock as he closed his grip gently over her nipple.

"I thought you said I was safe."

"When did your safety equate with my complete abdication of instincts of self-preservation? You started this, and I never promised not to pleasure you."

"You said we'd make love."

"And so we shall, as soon as I can properly manage." He gave her nipple the most gentle pressure, because the time for talking was past. "For now, pleasure will have to suffice. Your pleasure."

"Again?"

Her tone was part incredulity and part longing, and he had to smile in the darkness.

Under his hands, Polly began to smolder. Her fingers coursed over his chest, to his nipples, to his shoulders and the side of his neck, to his face, his hair.

She's painting me by touch, learning me as she would a subject, memorizing the feel and contour of my body.

The thought was lamp oil on a bonfire of determination, and Gabriel let his hand slip lower, one rib, one sigh, at a time.

Polly's eyes opened, her hand closed around his wrist. "Gabriel?"

"Let me," he said softly. "I need to give you this."

She closed her eyes and turned loose of his wrist, only to tuck herself more closely against him. He lay on his side so his touch could range over her body. Rather than immediately go a-plundering, he stilled his hand, cupped her mons, and leaned in to kiss her.

He was owed this much, and if she sighed into his mouth like she'd missed his kisses for half her life, well, he owed it to her too. He'd meant to keep their oral joining leisurely, to slow the headlong sprint toward fulfillment Polly seemed willing to accept.

She was owed more. His heart broke for her that she didn't know enough to demand more. From him, from life, from fate.

As his tongue gently seamed her lips then stole inside, her fingers tangled in his hair.

"I want..." She could get that much out, but she sounded winded and bewildered. He let her feel the press of his hard cock against her hip, and she pressed back as her mouth opened under his and her hands tightened in his hair. "Gabriel, please..."

She arched into him, hiking a leg up over his hip as if to drag him closer, but that he would not allow. While his tongue twined delicately around hers, his fingers explored slick, soft folds with an equally careful touch.

"What are you about?" She drew back, but he followed her with his mouth.

"Kiss me, Polonaise." He sealed his mouth over hers and gave her a hint of penetration with one thick, blunt finger. She broke off the kiss and pressed her face to his chest.

She made no sound of protest; if anything, she lifted herself to his hand then went still, her body listening to his touch on her most secret flesh. He took long, quiet minutes to learn her, tracing her sex in slow strokes, spreading heat and dampness while Polly held on to him. When he felt her breath soughing against his chest, he circled that spot at the apex of her folds and became minutely attentive to her reactions.

Tension coiled in her body; the pulse at her throat kicked up, and the leg she'd kept over his hip pulled her more closely to him, and to his hand. An altogether lovely moment of enslavement all around.

He detoured to penetrate her heat again with the same finger, a slow, shallow foray that provoked her to a soft groan and an undulation of her hips. So he plied her with that finger, slowly, until he was sinking deep and she had a rhythm.

"More, Polonaise?"

"Everything, please."

He wasn't going to give her everything, not tonight, at least, though it was killing him to show such restraint. He added a second finger, and she wiggled on his hand as if in pleasure and relief.

"You behave," he whispered. "All you have to do is trust me. Trust me to give you pleasure."

She nodded jerkily, closed her eyes, and circled his neck with her arm.

He let his thumb drift over the swollen, damp glory of her sex, though he longed to take her in his mouth, to taste her passion and feel her pleasure on his tongue. She wasn't ready for that kind of torment—that intimacy. Not yet.

"Gabriel." His name caught in her throat, and he stroked her again, and a third time with a hint of pressure. She clutched at him hard and began to move on his fingers in helpless pursuit of pleasure.

He gave it to her in lavish, unstintingly generous abundance. When she fisted around his fingers, he plied her with unrelenting tenderness, until she was keening against his chest and bucking on his hand in complete abandon.

"Gabriel... Gabriel..." She panted against his chest. "What have you done to me?"

Nine

GABRIEL ANSWERED POLLY'S BEWILDERED QUESTION BY shifting himself closer to her, pressing his hard cock to her wet sex, and gliding along it with firm pressure. He managed to wrap one of her legs over his waist, so she was opened to him and at just the right angle.

She understood and tucked into him.

"Polonaise... you..."

She kissed him, and he was lost, swearing gutturally as his body thrust against hers. She clung to him with arms and legs and mouth, and met his rhythm so seamlessly he was soon spending against her, his seed spreading a thick heat between their bodies.

"I am undone." He rolled to his back, separating their bodies and cursing himself for creating such untidy awkwardness. Certain intimacies should be shared only between familiars, and humping her like a university boy was one of them.

"Your back..." Polly kissed his cheek then flopped to the mattress. "I can't move."

"At least I got that much right," Gabriel muttered. "You are not to budge. Just catch your breath." He lay there, humoring his back as best he could, but really his back wasn't suffering as much as his pride.

To come on her belly like that... he hadn't planned it, and it had been... awful and wonderful and not well done of him, and he couldn't wait to do it again, if that's all she'd permit.

Though it wasn't. He knew that with the certainty of a man in bed with the woman he was put on earth to pleasure. Polly had years and years of sexual neglect to make up for, and Gabriel would see to it personally she caught up as quickly and thoroughly as she wanted to.

For now, he contented himself with retrieving a handkerchief from the night table and passing it to his lady.

She dabbed at herself and returned his linen to him. "Your back is all right?"

"You've caught your breath," Gabriel concluded, scrubbing at his belly. "If you dare to scold me for asking too much of my back, I will turn you over my knee and paddle you soundly."

She lay naked among the tossed-back covers, firelight flickering over her curves and hollows, and damned if she didn't look intrigued at his suggestion.

"You like to be spanked," Gabriel lamented. "I'm told this is characteristic of prim, strong-willed women. All I ask is that you indulge only me in this regard. I've earned the privilege."

"You are scandalous, Gabriel Wendover. Your back..."

"What back?" He tossed the cloth away and kissed her, mostly to keep her quiet.

"You think you can use kisses to keep me from scolding you," she began, and while her words were tart, the way she traced his eyebrows with one finger was tender.

"You're complaining about my kisses, Polonaise? Will you resort to begging?" He flopped down beside her, pleased all this thrashing about had not afflicted his back—yet.

She pursed her lips, her expression an adorable blend of satiety and frustration. "I do believe I might beg. This cannot be good."

"It's wonderful." Gabriel reached over, felt his way down her belly, and tugged gently at her curls. "This is a lighter red than the rest of your hair."

"I'm apparently living down to the narrow-minded implications of having red hair. I cannot believe what just happened in this bed."

"Neither can I." Gabriel heaved a disgusted sigh and ruffled her curls. "To spend like that, without your permission… it's your fault, you know."

"My fault?" He heard the uncertainty in her voice, saw it carefully hidden in her eyes. He wanted to kill someone slowly and painfully for putting it there, maybe several someones.

He scowled thunderously at the ceiling, where firelight cast dancing shadows. "If you weren't so gloriously, beautifully passionate in your pleasures, a man might be able to hold on to a little restraint."

Polly's smile bloomed, sweet and smug. "You're right. It's all my fault. So what do we do now?"

"We rest." Gabriel linked his fingers with hers, lest his petting escalate to more wonderful folly. "And we do *not* quiz me at length about why I was so ungallant as to spend my seed all over you, or why I have so little dignity where you're concerned. Really, Polonaise, you should show some consideration."

She rose up and straddled him, then cuddled down

exactly where he'd wanted her but had been too cowardly to arrange her.

"When we get to the spanking part, I'll spank you first."

"Who could ask for more than that?" Gabriel tucked her hair over her ear, then kept up a slow, repetitive caress over her back. "Would you like to use your bare hand, a leather riding crop, or perhaps a birch cane?"

"We'll have to try them all and see which one I like best."

"Methodical. There is much to admire about you, Polonaise."

"Now you try to butter me up." She bit his collarbone, so gently. "It won't work. You're still my slave."

"Go to sleep, love. You've worn your slave out."

She drifted off, mouth eventually going slack, while Gabriel stayed awake for some moments longer.

He hadn't lied. She really had worn him out, in every sense. He hadn't felt this good since... since... forever.

❧

God and a conscientious older brother be thanked, Gabriel used several days of his fictitious indisposition to catch up on the reams of correspondence generated by the seat in the House of Lords. Aaron had cheerfully agreed that until the matter of the title was resolved, he'd abstain from voting his seat.

Abstaining from relations with his wife, however, was becoming far less palatable. Their rooms were smaller and adjoined directly now, not by virtue of dressing closets and sitting rooms. Marjorie had asked again about having his portrait done, but Aaron hadn't found a way to put her request to Gabriel.

Mostly because Gabriel was the one whose likeness

ought to be hanging in the gallery where Aaron strolled with Marjorie.

"I will ask him today," Aaron told his wife. "What are you ladies up to?"

"It's too cloudy for Polly to paint. She's going to teach me how to make an apple walnut pie."

"You enjoy cooking, Margie?"

"I find I do, and she told me it's your favorite dessert."

"I like a lot of sweets," Aaron admitted. And he liked his sweet wife, which was not as irksome as it had been even a month ago. "That recipe of hers would bring tears to the Regent's eyes."

"I have to do something with my time." Marjorie paced to the window, her back to him. "You haven't heard anything else from Kettering?"

"Such correspondence would be directed to Gabriel," he said gently, "but there hasn't been anything in the post from him, no." He came to stand beside her, and the banked misery he saw in his wife's eyes gave him the resolve to broach a delicate topic. "I've been meaning to raise something with you, Marjorie, an idea Kettering came up with."

She studied him in a sidelong glance, one that emphasized her classic profile. "Marjorie? This is serious. Shall we walk?"

Because she'd crossed paths with him in the frigid expanse of the long portrait gallery, and it was too miserable out to walk elsewhere, Aaron offered his arm.

"This *is* serious," he said. "Or it's ridiculous, depending on how you look at it."

"I comprehend the ridiculous part," Marjorie said, pausing before the first marquess and his lady. "My mother is entirely ridiculous."

"He looks like my grandfather. They both looked perpetually dyspeptic."

"Rather like my mother."

"Margie?"

"Hmm?"

"May I kiss you?"

She gave him a puzzled glance, as if she were expecting one of his rare, perfunctory pecks to the cheek. "Of course."

"I mean a real kiss. Humor me."

"If you like." She put her hands on his biceps tentatively. When he tugged her closer, his hands on her hips, her expression turned wary. "What is this about, Aaron?"

"I'll explain in a minute." His voice had dropped to a coaxing whisper, and as his head dipped, he closed his eyes and settled his lips over hers.

He was fairly certain he desired her, which had been variously a disgrace, an amusement, an irritation, and a growing intrigue. But Aaron was old enough to have had the experience of pursuing something madly, only to find when he'd acquired it, his desire for it—or her—had fled completely. The title had been like that, something every younger son dreams about acquiring, thinking he'd make such a prime go of it, and then the having of it had been full of resentment, weariness, and a willingness to bargain with the devil if it might spare him the prize he'd dreamed of for so long.

Aaron didn't want his brother's fiancée to fall into the same category, or to make the discovery too late to preserve them from folly.

He eased his tongue over Marjorie's lips, and she opened to him generously, sighing into his mouth and arching her warmth closer to his body. She made a sound in her throat, of… longing? It certainly wasn't protest, and as Aaron felt her sweet, generous curves pressing against him, he got an answer to his question.

Even with various stern-faced ancestors looking on, in the chilly expanse of the gallery, he *truly* desired his wife.

She parted his wit from his volition when ₁she took one of his hands and planted it right over the lush velvet-covered abundance of her breast, then made that sound again, a yearning sound, yearning for him, or at least for what he could give her.

Still, he didn't end the kiss. He let his hand explore the contour and weight of that gorgeous breast, then tactilely inspected its twin, even as his tongue dipped and tasted and dueled with Marjorie's.

She was plastered against him, his arousal rising between them, but still he didn't let her go. He broke the kiss and tried to recall what this experiment was to have been in aid of.

He'd needed to know if they could desire each other.

"Sit with me." He led her the few steps to the window bench and sat, trying to ignore the cold at their backs—and the way his breeches were fitting too snugly over his parts.

"I'm sorry." Marjorie settled nervously on the bench. "I wasn't expecting that, and you've never… we've never…"

He hated that she was so nervous. "What are you apologizing for, Marjorie?"

"I didn't kiss you decently."

"Nor I, you. Let's say it was more a married kiss. Did you enjoy it?"

"What kind of question is that, Aaron Wendover? You rob me of my wits and then ask if I enjoy it?"

"A woman's interest in a man isn't as obvious as his in her," Aaron said, trying for patience, and resisting the urge to arrange himself in his clothes. He instead reached past Marjorie to free the heavy window drape from its tie, which only plunged the room into greater gloom. "I need to know if you can desire me as you have my brother."

"Your... what?" She looked thoroughly distraught now, confused, angry, aroused, and not at all in charity with him. "You want to know if I can desire your brother?"

"No," Aaron said, his voice cool in the face of her rising ire. "I want to know if you can desire me, as you've desired him, at least on occasion."

"I have never *desired* Gabriel Wendover. I respected him and felt a proper affection for him as the man my parents chose for me to wed. Aaron, are you trying to be cruel? Gabriel and I are agreed we will not marry, regardless of what my mother tries to do legally."

"I'm not exploring your desire to marry him," Aaron said. "I'm wondering if perhaps you might want to have a baby with me, because he's no longer able to oblige."

She scooted to the edge of the bench, as if she'd leave him alone with the scowling ancestors in the frosty gloom. "You're accusing me of something, Aaron, though I can't think straight enough to fathom what it is. You're making an accusation, and I think, an... an offer."

"I am making an offer." How had the discussion gone from their first real kiss to *this*, and in less than two minutes? "I'm offering to try to get a child with you, something Kettering suggested."

"A child?" She looked at him with glittering, heart-broken eyes. "Now, two years from our wedding, you're willing to offer me intimacies? Why, Aaron? You've kept yourself at arm's length until now, and I cannot say it has made sense to me. We've a duty to the title, or we did."

"Duty." Aaron spat the word. "Not you too, Marjorie."

"What is this about then, if not duty?"

As usual, Marjorie asked a pertinent, difficult question, and also as usual, Aaron's answer was not precisely on point.

"It's about producing a child, so if your mother succeeds in her suit, she'll make her own grandchild illegitimate. It's a tactic, Marjorie, one I felt I should inform you of."

Marjorie looked puzzled as she worked out the legalities. Her expression became sad, then sadder. "You don't want to be a father, do you?"

"A father?" What was she asking, and why couldn't she ask it in plain English? "I generally assumed at some point I would be, because children happen along in the normal course, but a burning desire to reproduce isn't where the topic sprang from in this instance."

God help him, he sounded like his pompous, dyspeptic grandfather.

"I'll take that as a no." Marjorie's smile might have been described as tragic. "Well, I do want to be a mother, Aaron. A mother to your children, and I comprehend what conception entails. I am unwilling to conceive a child, one possibly destined for bastardy, simply to hedge a legal bet. It wouldn't... Mother would think I was bluffing, and God help the child born under such a star. I don't think you want that for your firstborn."

He did not want that for his *wife*, now. He reached for her hand, and she let him have it.

"I honestly hadn't thought beyond the idea of it," Aaron said, "and it might work, whereas I'm not sure what else we've got to throw at her."

"It might not work," Marjorie countered. "And if Gabriel isn't blessed with sons when he marries, there I'd be, your former mistress, raising your child in the dower house, while you what? Married a woman who could produce the legal heir?"

"I'd marry you. I know my duty, Marjorie."

"But you haven't done it, have you? Not with me, not for the past two years, when your brother was presumed dead and you have no heir of your body?"

He said nothing, because Marjorie had *again* put her delicate finger on an obvious, if uncomfortable truth.

"And I've never understood *why*, Aaron." She looked at their joined hands, misery in her eyes, her voice, and her hunched posture. "I realize I'm not dainty, or sophisticated, or well traveled. I realize I wasn't your choice, and you might not find me particularly inspiring as a… woman, but I'm not… I'm not awful."

"Margie, stop." He put an arm around her shoulders and pulled her against him. "Just stop. You're lovely, you're desirable, and sometimes, when we're out riding on a pretty day, it's all I can do not to tackle you in the deep grass of the far pastures and consummate this marriage once and for all. The difficulty lies not in my desire for you, of which I think I just assured us both, but in your lack of desire for me."

"You're being particularly biddable," Polly observed. She sketched Gabriel as he sat on his grand bed, glasses perched on his Iberian beak, correspondence spread all over the comforter.

"I'm practicing for your next enslavement of me." He glanced at her over his glasses, looking professorially stern.

"What are you scribbling over there, Polonaise? Have you given me horns and a tail?"

"Hold still." She moved her pencil faster, trying not to smile at him. He went back to his documents, muttering about stubborn wenches watching him sit on his backside and disrespecting him in broad daylight when he was being so docile and meek.

"Here." Polly settled at his side, careful not to move the mattress suddenly, because even now, three days into his convalescence, his back might be tender. "This is you."

"Oh, for the love of Christ." He took the sketch pad, scowling mightily. "You can always take up a career as a satirist, once your disrespect has cost you all your portrait commissions."

"You don't like the wings?"

"I thought those were the bed hangings." Gabriel studied the drawing, as if he'd glower the image right off the page. "They're supposed to be the bed hangings."

Polly leaned close enough to catch a warm whiff of cedar. "They looked like a suggestion of wings to me. I'm an artist, and when inspiration strikes, I don't question it." Even when she should.

"Strikes." Gabriel took his glasses off. "Is that why you're off to choose a riding crop with Marjorie? You've decided to indulge me tonight after all?"

Polly closed her sketch pad, lest he start turning its pages. "I can't tell if you're serious. Sorry to disappoint. I'm not choosing a toy for your enjoyment. I'm choosing a prop for Marjorie to hold in her painting."

"I thought you said you were quick, Polonaise." Gabriel tidied up the documents spread across the covers. "I don't see this portrait progressing much."

"We need the light, and the weather hasn't cooperated. Are you trying to get rid of me?"

"Maybe I'm tired of waiting for you to enslave me." Gabriel set the stack aside then patted the mattress. "Come here."

She went, because they were alone and she'd not been close to him since the night they'd spent in her bed, which seemed an unholy age ago.

"Cuddle up." He delivered his order with a pat to her bottom, so she straddled his lap and curled up obligingly. "Now listen to me, Polonaise, all teasing aside. I have never found it titillating to strike a woman, nor do I find it enhances my ardor to be struck." He stroked his hands down her back in a caress that had become wonderfully familiar to her in a short time.

"You're serious?"

"Absolutely serious," he said, kissing the side of her neck. "It has always seemed to me as if those antics are for people who lack imagination and must inundate the body with gross sensations simply to recall where the damned thing is. You do not lack imagination. Now if you want to strike me, I will, of course, enjoy granting your every intimate wish."

Polly buried her face against his neck, where the scent of cedar blended with his shaving soap to create a fragrance unique to him. "I couldn't hit you."

"Not even on my handsomely muscled and adorably scarred derriere?"

"Especially not there."

"So, my love, why not tell me you find the topic insipid and put me in my place?"

Cedar symbolized strength, of which she had none where he was concerned. "One doesn't want to appear ignorant."

"Pride." He kissed her temple. "Your besetting sin, Polonaise."

"Or yours. Along with arrogance and a questionable sense of humor."

"At least I have an adorable derriere. You didn't argue with me over that."

"You're ridiculous." Polly burrowed closer and said something else. Her besetting sin was an inability to keep her mouth shut when Gabriel scolded her.

"Beg pardon?" His hand did not beg her pardon but went questing over the curve of her adorable parts.

"I've missed you."

"Polonaise?"

"No more lectures, please. I find them insipid."

"Feel this?" He arched up against her sex, and through the covers and the clothes, Polly felt the magnificent, engorged length of him.

"I feel it."

"Do you know what I'd like to be doing with it right now?" He kissed the spot where her shoulder met her neck, the place that made her reason depart with all haste, and Polly let out a sigh as Gabriel murmured softly against her neck.

"I want to bury myself, bury my whole being and my passion inside your body, and pleasure you and pleasure you and pleasure you until you're screaming out your satisfaction to the heavens and calling forth my own from the depths of my soul. I want to possess every particle, thought, and sense you own, and give it back to you, drunk with pleasure from our shared bodies. I want to have you until you own me, heart, mind, body, and soul. And then I want you again and again and again."

Men spoke like this to the women they'd never marry. This was the language of dalliance, and Gabriel was exceedingly fluent. "That all sounds very naughty."

Gabriel lifted his face from her neck. "My heritage is Portuguese, in part. The Iberian temperament is not tepid. Perhaps you've noticed."

Marjorie's voice sounded in the corridor, directing a footman to fetch Aaron because Miss Hunt needed relief from her visit to the indisposed.

Polly scooted off the bed and picked up her sketch pad. She hovered until Marjorie appeared, and then they both hovered until Aaron came in, still dressed in riding attire, slapping a crop against his boot.

Polly took one look at the crop, started laughing, and pulled Marjorie from the room.

❧

"What on earth have you said to our dear Miss Hunt?" Aaron sat on the edge of the bed and craned his neck to look at the letters Gabriel had written. "And how is it you are more productive when supposedly ill than I am when hale?"

"I didn't put pen to paper for days at a time when I was stewarding," Gabriel said. "It's appalling what a man can miss when it's denied him." Whom he could miss.

"George has been very worried for you," Aaron replied. "They're praying for your recovery below stairs."

"I don't think this is going to work, Aaron." Gabriel waited until Aaron closed the door to the sitting room to swing his legs off the bed. Now that Polly had gone giggling on her way, restlessness plagued him.

"How long will you give this strategem?" Aaron went to

a window and stood gazing out at something below. Gabriel shifted to stand beside him.

"Thick as thieves, those two." Across the gardens, Polly and Marjorie disappeared into the stables, arm in arm, two muscular footmen trailing them. "We'd best make use of their absence while we have it."

Aaron did not take his gaze from the direction of his wife's departure. "How much longer will I be sleeping in that sitting room?"

"Good question." Particularly for a man who might be campaigning for a place in his wife's bed. "What is my supposed condition?"

"You're very weak, you need assistance with everything, and can barely manage beef tea. You refuse to see the doctors but think this is some fever you picked up in Spain, one that's often fatal. We despair of your recovery."

"And I've been in this condition how long?"

"This is your fourth agonizing day, but you're tough, and we put our faith in God."

"Keep the Deity out of this, if you please. You're tired of your cot?"

"It's not that." Aaron cleared his throat, glanced away, and Gabriel set himself to hear a spate of babbling, for Aaron—bless the boy—babbled when he was nervous.

Aaron cleared his throat again.

"Aaron? If you need a night's sleep, just say so. I can steal off to a guest room, and no one will be the wiser." One guest room in particular held significant appeal.

"Marjorie may be amenable to having a child," Aaron said, letting out a pent-up breath. "I say may be, because we're in negotiations and it's delicate and difficult, and every damned thing I say seems to annoy her, and I can't

read her bloody, infernal silences, and when she says something, I can't even comprehend *that*, and suffice it to say…
well, we might make more progress were I actually sleeping,
that is to say…"

Babbling at a great rate, indeed. "Cease saying, if you
please. If Marjorie did not expect to bear your heirs, why
marry her?"

"Because her mama insisted rather pointedly, legally,
and expensively?"

The entire family's miseries all seem to lead back to Lady
Hartle. "Marjorie's dam has much to answer for," Gabriel
retorted. "If you're asking me for fraternal advice, I'd say
don't, for God's sake, have a child out of duty."

Aaron studied the empty stable yard below, dark brows
knitted. "I'm your only heir, or, as Marjorie puts it, you
have no heirs of your body."

"And I might not ever," Gabriel said, particularly if
Polly were barren. He appropriated a dressing gown from
the bedpost, because the window gave off a chill, as did the
topic under discussion. "We're wealthy, personally wealthy,
Aaron. If the title lapses, it lapses, and we're left with a paltry
twenty-six thousand acres, and pots of money between us.
I think we'll muddle along somehow."

"Twenty-six thousand seven hundred sixty-three. You
honestly don't care?"

Not the way he'd cared about Three Springs. Not the
way he cared about Polonaise Hunt's happiness and safety.
"I honestly don't care about the title one whit, compared to
how I care about your domestic contentment. That you had
to marry on my behalf bothers me exceedingly."

"It didn't bother Lady Hartle. Not at the time."

Gabriel eyed his baby brother, wondering why the

Wendover coloring looked so much more handsome on Aaron. "I've figured something out."

"This sounds ominous."

"What's ominous is how badly I've misjudged my brother." The ladies had apparently found something to occupy them in the stables, for the gardens below showed not a sign of life, and yet, Aaron lingered at the window. "I think I've figured out why you were so hasty in having me declared dead."

"I wasn't hasty. I was prudent. Papa was gone and matters were in an uproar, and nobody could sign anything, or move money, or even pay wages when your status was undetermined, and there was that awful fire, and some-damned-body needed to marry Marjorie rather summarily, and what?"

"You figured out," Gabriel said slowly, lest he be interrupted by more babbling, "the safest place for me to be if someone wanted me dead was in the grave."

The words lay there, very much alive, between them. Alive and squirming with innuendo, overtones, and implications—not all of them unflattering.

"There was a fire," Aaron said again, his voice pitched low. "There was. And there was no body."

"How did you learn that?" Gabriel's tone was merely curious, which seemed to relieve his brother.

"I had the fellows make inquiry," Aaron said. "The fighting was over, and they had little to do, so when I wrote about the circumstances of your death, they got to poking around."

"A bunch of British officers poking around a Catholic convent." Gabriel could not keep the irony from his tone, nor could he help but wonder what those two women were getting up to. "Surely no one would remark such activity?"

"They're not stupid." Aaron's gaze was on the stables, where the ladies had disappeared a full five minutes earlier. "They got to drinking with the gardener, who of course digs the graves, and he made some comment about it being a damned big hole just for a few rose bushes, but the roses were there so nobody would disturb the plot."

"I wondered about the roses. An excessive display of sentiment, considering the ladies buried patients regularly."

"They were fond of you. Else why protect you like that?"

"Because they are fond of all God's creatures. So did you know I was alive, or merely hope?" And how long would Aaron have waited to admit he'd been guarding Gabriel's back for two years?

"Hope, only hope, and the silly notion I'd feel it if something happened to you, when all I felt was bewildered and resentful."

Gabriel's back felt better than it had in ages, but his knees had abruptly turned unreliable. "Two years is a long time to hope."

"It is."

Gabriel shifted away, toward the bed—the patient should not be seen malingering at the window—while Aaron resumed speaking.

"Then I got word last year there was an estate over on the Downs sporting a new steward. A big, quiet, dark-haired man who moved slowly but never stopped working. He was in a house full of women, though there was no hint of impropriety about him, and his horse was a nice specimen, if a little worn at the heels. I began to hope a little harder."

"You knew I was at Three Springs?"

"I knew the steward there answered to your description,

kept to himself, and was named Gabriel North. The coincidence was too great to ignore."

"So you've been keeping secrets too, eh, little brother?"

Aaron nodded, then his breath hitched. "I wanted you to be alive, but I knew what you had to be thinking, because there I was, sporting about with your title, your wealth, your woman. The implications were obvious, and I'd never done anything or been any sort of brother to make you think better of me than those implications suggested."

"You must have done something and been some sort of brother," Gabriel said, "because here I am, alive and well, and thinking better of you."

Aaron stared off into the empty gardens as if his life—or at least his dignity—depended upon what he saw.

"Aaron?" Gabriel touched his arm. "I didn't want to be alone either. Couldn't stand it. All this"—Gabriel waved a hand at the fields spreading to the horizon beyond the window—"it's too much to bear alone. Yet you did it for two years. I am in your debt."

"If you hadn't come to fetch me home from Spain, you wouldn't be flat on your back every time you take a bad step! You wouldn't have been denied your birthright for two years, much less your fiancée's affections. You would have been at Papa's funeral, for God's sake, not holed up in some sweltering infirmary, the flies so thick... I can't... I have nightmares about leaving you there."

He wept silently, tears coursing down his cheeks, leaving his brother without one helpful thing to say. Gabriel pulled Aaron into his arms, and held him, stroking his hair while Aaron grappled with two years of guilt, secrecy, and overwhelming uncertainty about how to keep his only brother safe.

Aaron rested his forehead on Gabriel's shoulder. "This is unbecoming."

Gabriel blinked hard while he still had the privacy to do so. "This is what brothers are for. Nobody cried at my funeral, you know, and I was too bloody furious to cry myself."

"I cried," Aaron said. "When Papa died, I cried for you both, mostly because you couldn't be there, and it was…"

"Yes." Gabriel turned him and walked him to the couch. "It was your fault. Because you so carelessly got yourself injured while at war with the utterly blameless Corsican, and then were subject to the inept treatment of the blameless surgeons, and we mustn't forget our blameless Papa, who dispatched me to the same region to retrieve his spare, or the blameless individuals whose blades found their way to my back."

Aaron sat, apparently felled by an onslaught of reason, though Gabriel wasn't finished.

"And we can't forget my blameless self, who was stupid enough to travel alone after dark in a town full of Spanish refugees and cutthroats, and then even more unthinkably stupid to conclude his brother, out of his mind with fever and pain, somehow concocted a plan to kill me so he could have all the jolly fun of keeping Hesketh from the crown's greedy paws with a woman he'd never thought to marry."

"You're babbling, Gabriel."

"It's contagious," Gabriel said, crossing to the sideboard. "But curable by decent brandy. Here." He poured two fingers for them each then sat beside his brother. "Are we done with this topic?"

"You're saying I've been an ass."

"I'm saying perhaps the Deity created in you an unfair propensity for guilt, but you don't have to let it ruin your happiness, any more than your love of horses dooms you to mucking stalls for the rest of your life."

"Profound." Aaron lifted his glass in salute. "Also probably true." He took a thoughtful sip. "So, brotherly affection aside, how long will you be sick?"

Gabriel eyed his liquor, when he wanted to toss it all back at one go. "I understand the question, and you want to be about swiving your wife. What's amiss, Aaron? Are you so far beyond the newlywed stage you can't swive her in the saddle room or on the balcony in the library? That was ever a favorite hiding place when we were boys. You must enjoy each other in silence under cover of darkness only?"

"I liked you better when you were blamelessly babbling. Conceiving a child is serious business."

Gabriel took a sip that drained half the contents of his glass. "One should hope it's enjoyable business, wherever one conducts it. But to answer your question, I've been sitting on my arse for four nights and four days, and there hasn't been a single footman suspiciously straightening pillows in the sitting room, or a maid wielding an enthusiastic poker. I don't think this is going to draw out my detractor."

"No laudanum or rat poison has gone missing, either," Aaron said. "So how much longer?"

"I'll take a turn for the better this afternoon," Gabriel decided. "Then I'll make slow progress back to my former glory."

"You're not going crazy with the inactivity?"

He was, when Polonaise abandoned him to his paperwork. "A little, but I'm also napping, Aaron. Grown men aren't supposed to nap." Not alone, anyway.

"I do recall that from my reading of the law." Aaron peered into the bottom of his glass. "Nor cry."

"Cut line." Gabriel shoved his shoulder, but not hard enough to even slosh his drink. "Grown men aren't supposed to nap, but I left Spain far sooner than I should have attempted any travel, then found the position at Three Springs, and the work there was endless."

"You're short of rest. Marjorie said you looked like you'd been to war. I had to agree. There's a kind of weariness the infantry get when they've been on too many forced marches in bad weather on foul rations. They become indifferent to their own suffering, and one wonders where they find the strength to fight."

Was that what the marquessate had felt like to him? Was that how his marriage to Marjorie felt?

"I'm not indifferent to my own suffering, but I'd forgotten what it feels likes to have more energy than the immediate task demands. I'm enjoying the first real rest I've had in years."

Particularly when Polonaise was on hand to enforce his inactivity.

"So nap a few more days, sleep in, and enjoy the company."

"Yes, well." Gabriel took a slow sip of his remaining drink and wondered how long two women could fuss over a choice of horsewhip.

"What are you going to do with her, Gabriel?"

"She thinks I'm going to tumble her witless while she's here at Hesketh, then stuff her into our newest traveling coach and wish her all the best when she goes on to her next commission."

"And the flaw in that plan?"

"She's tumbling me witless, for starters." Gabriel rose to set his empty glass on the sideboard. "And there will be none of this getting into traveling coaches, not unless I'm in there with her."

"Tumbling about."

"Precisely."

Aaron fetched the bottle and returned Gabriel's glass to him. "This should be entertaining. I'm going to try to woo my wife, and you're going to convince your artist to become your wife, or am I mistaken?"

"You are not."

"That's the second thing I wanted to bring up with you."

"Hmm?" Gabriel held up his glass for a refill, the spirits and the company both being fine, though the topic was daunting.

"Marjorie has asked that I sit for the second portrait, and I've told her I'll leave it up to you."

Bless Lady Marjorie, for many reasons. "Do you want to do this for your wife?"

"I find I do."

"Well, then I have only two requests, if you're determined to have the painting done."

"I'm not posing out-of-doors as winter comes upon us. Not even for my long-lost, blameless brother." Whom Aaron silently toasted with a bumper of brandy.

"Him," Gabriel snorted. "No, you are doing this for Mr. North, who spent two years worshipping the object of his affection—"

"Lust."

"That too, from afar, only to have to nobly part from the ungrateful little baggage so she could pursue wealth and fame while avoiding her true fate as my beloved marchioness."

"Perilously close to babbling, Brother."

"Two requests," Gabriel said. "First, choose a brilliantly sunlit pose, because winter's gloom will soon descend in earnest, and second, fidget ceaselessly."

Ten

"MY HUSBAND IS ACTING MOST PECULIARLY." As Marjorie spoke, she appeared to study the assortment of sidesaddle whips hung in order from longest to shortest on the saddle-room wall.

"One hardly knows what constitutes peculiar behavior in a husband," Polly replied.

Marjorie paused before a particularly sturdy whip. "You don't have a very good opinion of men, do you?"

"Not of some men. My sister's husband is a prince." Gabriel Wendover was something beyond even that.

"He treats her well?"

"He adores her, enough not to show his affections in any way uncomfortable for her," Polly said, selecting a long, delicate whip. "He also adores her daughter, and that, more than anything, probably won Sara's affection."

It had certainly won Polly's. And her respect.

"I like this one." Marjorie held out an elegant black leather whip. "I use it a lot."

"I'm not keen on the hue of the leather," Polly said, flexing it then smacking it against her skirt. "Can we find a brown one with some brass on the handle?"

"Here." Marjorie passed her another. "It's short for the horses I ride."

Polly tried the shorter one and held it up to the light. "How is Lord Aaron behaving?"

"The perfect gentleman, as always." Marjorie fingered a short, stout jumping bat. "Except he did kiss me."

"Kisses can be nice." Kisses could be so much more than nice, too. Polly tried smacking the second whip, which was stiffer than the previous candidate. "This one isn't used as much, but I like the handle better."

Marjorie tried the whip then examined the handle. "This wasn't a nice kiss. It was a naughty kiss."

Well done, Lord Aaron. "He's your husband. From him, the naughty kisses can be the best. Let's take this outside to see how daylight strikes the fittings on the handle."

Marjorie put the longer whip back on the rack and followed Polly down the shed row. "So a husband's kiss can be naughty, and it doesn't... imply anything?"

Polly considered the question and considered how young the marchioness was and how few people the lady had to confide in. Her mother certainly wasn't an option, which left... Polly.

"Such a kiss implies he desires his wife," Polly said as they emerged from the shadows of the barn. "That is a wonderful thing, to be honestly desired by one's mate. I think, with a good polishing, this whip will do nicely."

"What color gloves should I wear, then?"

Polly passed her the whip. "Let's see what some of the choices are. Hasn't Lord Aaron made lusty overtures in the past?"

Marjorie's stride put a particular swish to her skirts. "He has not. He was trying to imply I..." She stopped walking, glared at the house, then glanced behind them at the two brawny footmen Gabriel insisted they take everywhere.

The footmen fell back a good dozen yards.

"What did Lord Aaron imply?"

"That I'd given my heart and perhaps a bit more to Gabriel."

"A bit more wouldn't be unusual if a couple had a long-standing engagement. Particularly when the gentleman is handsome and... capable." And the lady's mother was shoving her into his arms. Polly shot a longing glance at Marjorie's whip.

"Handsome, maybe," Marjorie said, resuming a more dignified pace. "But Gabriel was so... forbidding, I suppose. He's different now, though I was little more than a pesky future obligation to him, Polly. He'd no more dishonor me by anticipating the vows than I'd run naked through the village on May Day."

"Maybe Aaron thinks otherwise. Men get odd notions." Particularly where their dignity was concerned.

"They do." Marjorie's expression became thoughtful. "Then they're stubborn about them. Aaron suggested we have a child, for example."

"A child?" Polly sensed they'd come to the heart of the discussion, and took Marjorie's arm. "Shall we admire the winter gardens?"

Marjorie fell in step, though the winter gardens were nothing more than bracken and bare plots.

"Tell me about this sudden desire for a child," Polly said. "One notices the absence of an heir." And somebody ought to be producing children here, after the past two years' doings.

"I suppose that could be part of it. As Aaron explained it, if I'm carrying, Mama might desist in her attempts to set our marriage aside. Should she succeed, any child I bore could be illegitimate." She used the whip to whack at a dangling maple leaf, and missed.

"And should your mother's suit fail, you're on your way to producing the Hesketh heir, which might be some consolation to your mother."

"I hadn't thought of that. Nonetheless, I don't want Aaron coming to my bed as some convoluted legal maneuver to confound my mother."

Polly drew her down onto a cold stone bench. Of the fall flowers, only some damp, droopy pansies remained near the bench, though they were the exact blue of Gabriel's eyes.

"Except once Lord Aaron's in your bed, the marriage is harder to attack. He's not stupid, Marjorie."

"Far from it."

They were quiet for a moment, each likely considering the ramifications of Aaron's keen intelligence. Pansies symbolized thoughts, after all.

"You're suggesting," Marjorie said, "he might truly want to consummate our union, not only to get a child, but also to… keep me."

"That would be the logical result, even if a child isn't conceived. But, Marjorie? A child changes things. A child changes *you*, and can strengthen your marriage as well."

Marjorie used the lash of the whip to stir the dead leaves at their feet. "Changes things how?"

"I'm not speaking from firsthand experience of marriage," Polly said, "but consider my sister, Sara, and her husband. Beckman loves Sara, but he loves Allie as well, both of them, fiercely, and loving the child is what makes their bond not simply marital, but familial."

And far too painful for Polly to behold with any regularity.

"A child makes a larger circle of love," Marjorie said, the whip going still. "My father loved each of us, and even when my mother was being her most exasperating, he loved her for giving him children."

"When two people both love the same child, they can love each other a little more too." Polly thought not of Sara and Beckman, but of herself and Sara. She'd been not yet sixteen when she'd conceived, and as cursed with temper and moodiness as a human can be, but she and Sara had put aside their terrible differences to protect Allie.

Sitting on that cold, hard bench, Polly saw those tense, exhausted months of early motherhood not as a forced march but—for the first time—as a healing time for her and her sister.

More than anything, Sara's silences had comforted. She'd tossed aside one recrimination after another, and instead showered Polly with kindness.

"Let me hold that baby so you can get some sleep."

"You're so patient with her, Polly, and she has your eyes."

"You're doing so well, and she's growing like a weed."

"She has your spirit, and that will serve her well in this life. Never doubt it."

Tears rose, and Polly held the backs of her gloves against her eyes. How could she not have seen all the ways Sara had tried to support her as a mother?

"Miss Hunt? Polly? Have I upset you?"

"Of course not." She was far beyond merely upset and had been for years. "You have the chance to have a child with a man you regard highly, a man who will find a way to stay at your side, Marjorie."

Marjorie stood the whip straight up against her palm, catching it before it toppled. "He said he'd remarry me if he had to. I didn't find that very romantic."

"Loyalty is romantic. Try finding romance with its opposite, and you'll agree."

"And Aaron will be a wonderful father," Marjorie said earnestly. "He's already like an older brother to my younger siblings. It comes naturally to him."

"He's kind," Polly said, her gaze on the tearstains of the backs of her gloves. "That's the main thing. Kind, sensible, and honorable. Moreover, he can provide well."

Marjorie sighted down the handle of the whip, a rare, chilly shaft of sunlight glinting on the brass fittings. "So why am I hesitating?"

Excellent question. "Because you want to be sure he cares for you as well."

"Very sure."

"So ask him. He might give you some blather about duty and respect, but if he's giving you naughty kisses, Marjorie, he might give you his heart as well."

Marjorie gently patted her lips with the handle of the whip, once, twice, in a gesture her husband would probably find provocative. "I thought men were happy to kiss nigh anybody like that. Mama says base instincts plague men far worse than they do ladies."

"Perhaps ladies are immune from base instincts." Though Marjorie was one of eight children, suggesting Lady Hartle's theory was questionable. "But I've met *women* of every nationality and social stripe, Marjorie Wendover, and I can tell you, women are not immune."

"Women." Marjorie rose and swatted the dead leaves with her whip, sending several twirling into the air. "Can one be both lady and woman?"

Gabriel certainly thought so. On that cheering notion, Polly got to her feet. "If one's husband is both gentleman and man, I think it becomes second nature. But let's continue this discussion over a cup of tea, shall we? It's getting nippy out, and we can't have two people falling ill at once."

They made their way back to the house arm in arm, footmen trailing at a discreet distance.

"I don't mean to pry," Marjorie said as they approached a back entrance. "Somebody betrayed you, didn't they? Some man."

"My lack of common sense betrayed me. It was a long time ago, and there were few lasting consequences. Do you think we're in for some snow?"

Polly told her polite lie and changed the topic to the weather, but inside, where those lasting consequences threatened another bout of tears, she had to wonder at herself. What was wrong with her, that she could live for years as her daughter's beloved aunt, but now, separated from Allie for the first time, she felt like a raging fraud?

❧

"You're awake!" George strode into the room, sporting the false cheer of one compelled to visit the sick.

"Barely." Gabriel dragged himself up to a sitting position, and because he'd been enjoying one of his frequent, shamelessly lovely naps, it wasn't hard to feign the mental fog and heavy-limbed movement of the indisposed. "Good of you to come."

"Spot of tea?" George gestured to the service sitting on the raised hearth.

"Help yourself. Maybe half a cup for me."

"Voluminous intake of fluids is at variance with the need for bed rest," George observed. "I had a lung fever last winter, which allowed me to appreciate this truth." He busied himself with the tea service and brought Gabriel's cup to the bed. "Drink up. A little scandal broth is good for the soul."

Gabriel took a parsimonious sip because George had added neither cream nor sugar. "I gather Aaron deserted his post in the sitting room, leaving you to take a turn with the invalid?"

"I chased him off." George fixed himself a cup with the dispatch of a bachelor who knew his way around a tea tray. "He was in a lather to talk to the ladies about something."

"No doubt trying to cadge another pie out of Miss Hunt, or perhaps Lady Marjorie." Gabriel again put his lips to the delicate rim of the teacup, but as if he were truly ill, the brew tasted off. He set the cup aside, wondering how long the leaves had been left to steep.

"I think Marjorie is in better spirits for having another lady on the premises." George flicked out his coattails and took the chair next to the bed. "Aaron might consider hiring a companion for her."

"Miss Hunt gives Marjorie someone besides her agitating mama for moral support, and evens up the numbers a bit." Gabriel tagged on a small, raggedy cough lest George overstay his welcome.

"What of you?" George's smile became sly. "Any new friends of the female persuasion on the horizon?"

Gabriel held up a hand. "Wait until the title has been properly hung around my neck, and then I'll be swarmed with bleating little debutantes."

"Assuming the courts don't march you up the aisle with Marjorie." George slurped his tea enthusiastically, suggesting the flavor agreed with him well enough. "There are worse fates than ending up with Marjorie for a wife."

Gabriel produced a semi-genuine yawn. "You've been breeding livestock too long. I am not going to marry Marjorie, regardless of what the courts suggest. She is my brother's wife, and that's an end to it."

George peered into his teacup. "Courts don't suggest. They order, with rather nasty consequences for those who disobey their orders."

"If I commit a crime, I'll be tried in the Lords. They won't hang me for nearly getting killed in Spain, then doing what I thought proper to keep body and soul together. Aaron has forgiven me, and as far as I can see, he's the most wronged party."

"You don't consider Marjorie is wronged?"

"She got the better man." Gabriel yawned again, because George in the role of Marjorie's knight errant was tiresome, if novel. "And she's as besotted with him as he is with her. If you ask me, their marriage is one good thing to come of this mess." Among several very good things, among which acquaintance with Polonaise Hunt figured prominently.

George set his cup down. "I do believe you have the right of it, at least in Marjorie's eyes, and Lady Hartle never was one to see what was in front of her face. But I've tired you, so I'll take my leave."

"You can't." Gabriel let his eyelids lower. "Not until you have Aaron fetched from his skirt chasing. I'm not to be alone. Lady Marjorie has declared it a requirement of good care that I have no privacy whatsoever."

"And we mustn't disappoint our marchioness, right?" George left on a wink and a smile, dutifully lingering in the sitting room until not Aaron but Polly appeared in Gabriel's bedroom.

George stuck his head in the door to deliver his parting

quip. "She's easier on the eyes than your brother, and likely to make you recover faster, because you'll listen to her. Good day, Miss Hunt, and pleasant dreams, Gabriel."

Gabriel slumped back on the pillows, oddly disquieted by George's visit. When he let his gaze fall on Polly, his disquiet found a different focus.

"Polonaise, come here."

"I'm here." She settled into a cushioned chair. "You're there, and that's fine with me."

"Ah, we're cranky." Which in that special lexicon of terms he used to refer to her, meant he needed to hold her.

"Marjorie and Aaron are considering having a child," Polly said, the way somebody might mention an impending spate of decent weather to a neighbor in the churchyard. "This should relieve your mind."

"Do not make me spring from my sickbed to chase you around this room, Polonaise. You only think you want to provoke me into a row, but what you really want is comforting."

"In broad daylight, Gabriel? You really must be feeling better."

"I'm positively frisky, though that's no threat to you, I assure you, because my self-restraint is legendary. Now, my dear, quit spooking and shying at imaginary rabbits, and join me on this bed."

She looked wary and disgruntled as she minced over to the bed and perched at his side. "I'm here."

"Bodily," he allowed, studying her face. "You've been crying, my love." He dragged her to his chest and settled his arms around her. "This is not permitted, unless I'm to know the reason why."

"Damn you." She sighed against his shoulder. "I have no privacy with you."

"You deserve none, if all you're using it for is to hide your heartaches," he chided. "Talk to me, Polonaise, and if it's within my earthly power, I'll make it right."

"You can't," she murmured against his neck. He felt the first hot trickle of a tear slip over his collarbone. "Gabriel, I wish you could, but you can't help. Nobody can."

❧

"Gabriel has given his permission for my portrait to be done," Aaron said, his gaze on the embroidery Marjorie was stabbing away at. "I wasn't aware you embroidered."

Nor had he known her favorite flower, her favorite dessert, or that she had been as lonely in their marriage as he'd been.

"Only out of sheer desperation." Marjorie tucked the needle into a corner of the piece. "And not well. You don't seem pleased about this project, Aaron."

Aaron, not my lord. He had to hear that as progress, but toward what?

"The prospect of sitting on my backside, looking elegant or noble or mysteriously impressed with myself for hours on end strikes me as a protracted attempt at fraud, though I refuse to be immortalized dragging dead bunnies about by the ears or breathing in the scent of some hound slobbering at my booted feet."

"Fraud?" Marjorie brushed her fingers across the fabric in her hoop, upon which had been stitched two creamy-white birds—doves, if Aaron wasn't mistaken—and some green twiggish things. "Have you seen my portrait yet?"

"I wasn't aware we were allowed to peek." He'd wanted to, because if Miss Hunt thought to make his wife look silly, vapid, immature, or anything unflattering, he'd hang the thing in the attic.

"Polly isn't particular." Marjorie's gaze followed him as he paced the sitting room. "I've seen it since the day she started, and the whole business is fascinating."

"Do you like it?"

"Love it."

Aaron paused in his peregrinations to stare at her, because for a moment, his wife's lashes had lowered, and her voice had turned smoky. For that instant, she hadn't been the rather-too-young marchioness, but a pretty woman bent on enticing her husband.

"What do you like—love—about it?"

"That's hard to say." Marjorie set her doves back in a sewing basket. "Polly did a number of preliminary studies of me, and she showed me those too. She showed me that I can be different people."

"As we all can, I suppose." Aaron was not agreeing merely to be polite, but because Marjorie certainly had many interesting facets.

"She'll show you some of those people you are but didn't know you had lurking inside."

"And what if I don't like what she shows me?"

"You will," Marjorie said. "Because even a part of you that doesn't have much appeal deserves to be acknowledged, and when you allow it's a part of you, it loses some of its... disenchantment. I am too easily swayed by my mother's opinion, but when I see an image of myself as a bewildered little girl whose gowns look too big for her—"

"They aren't too big for you. They fit... exceedingly well."

His cravat was fitting exceedingly well too, and the air in Aaron's lungs had gone somewhere unavailable, while Marjorie continued to study him in a considering, very female way.

"You like my gowns?"

"I do."

"That was the easy version," Marjorie said. "Do you like me?"

"I always have." He'd gotten it out without a hint of hesitation, for it was the truth, and idiot that he was, he'd forgotten it himself. "I have always thought you were the pick of Hartle's litter, the one with the most sense, joie de vivre, and beauty besides. I envied my brother, not his title, not his wealth, not his impressive Town friends, or his first in Latin, but you."

"Me?"

"Just you." He stepped closer, because words like this, too long unspoken between them, were not for overhearing or mistaking. "Will we be trying for that baby, Margie?"

She regarded him with a slight frown, then went up on her toes and pressed her lips to his.

He froze, trying to recall when, if ever, in the two long, lonely years of their marriage, she'd initiated a kiss on the mouth; and then he couldn't recall what day it was, because Marjorie Wendover was running her tongue over the seam of his lips and sliding her hand right over his chest to encircle his neck.

"I'm thinking about it," she murmured before seizing his mouth again.

He wrapped his arms around her, cradled her head for a better angle, and thought about it right along with her for a good five minutes. When she sighed and subsided against him, she tucked her cheek against his chest, kept one arm around his neck, and one hand laced with his where he'd folded it against her heart.

"Was that an affirmative decision?"

"Perhaps." She fell silent for the space of an inhale and a slow exhale, while Aaron knew his heart must be hammering under her ear. He could feel his pulse in his privy parts, for God's sake, and she wasn't being shy about the consequences where his erection pressed against her belly.

And she was saying "perhaps." Perhaps was not "no," but it left a great distance to "yes."

"What can I do to assist with an affirmative decision?"

She nuzzled him, and he knew a compulsion to sweep her off her feet and abandon this duel of words to the saner arguments of the body. He wanted her, had always wanted her, and she seemed to want him.

And they were married with a duty to the title, and he had a cock-stand this bloody, panting minute.

"Do you care for me, Aaron?"

"Of course." He couldn't help holding her more tightly as the words made it past his lips. Then, more deliberately, "I care for you and your happiness a great deal, Marjorie, and I'm sorry if I've given you leave to doubt. This marriage is not your fault. I've never believed it was."

She regarded him, some of the haze leaving her eyes.

Was that the wrong thing to say or the right thing? He watched her with an intensity he couldn't mask.

"Then to assist me in coming to an affirmative decision"—she kissed the side of his neck—"you must tell me these things, Aaron. Husband."

"Husband." He'd always thought the word prosaic, perhaps a little negative, implying as it did a man answerable under the law for the care and well-being of at least one female, and possibly a brood of hatchlings as well. Not a very free person, the husband.

But on her lips, "husband" sounded like the highest title in the land, carrying the greatest wealth and privilege.

"What must I tell you?"

"That you care for me, that you desire me, that you do not resent me," Marjorie said. "I will tell you the same things."

She cared for him? Desired him? "Love words? You want us to court each other?"

"We never did, and yet I don't think it beyond us if we're to expect a baby of each other."

"It's not beyond us." If she'd told him to run to London and back, he'd do it in his bare feet. "It's just... you want this?"

"I do *not* want to have a baby to placate a solicitor or to drive off my mother's wrongheaded notions, Aaron."

Damn and blast. "You don't."

"I want to have a baby, your baby, because you are my dear husband and it will make our family real."

Husband, family. Two words he'd have to reconsider—later.

"And you are my dear wife," he said, his embrace gentling. "And it will be my privilege to court you, but, Margie? We haven't a great deal of time. Your mother might join suit at any moment."

"This is true." Marjorie's smile was diabolically sweet. "So you'd better get busy, hmm?"

❧

Gabriel's hand smoothed over Polly's hair in a repetitive, soothing rhythm, and the intended comfort of it just made her cry harder. He began speaking to her, softly, so softly that in her great upset, she likely wasn't intended to hear his words.

"Hush, my love, be calm in your heart. I'm here, I'll

never leave you to face your troubles alone. Take courage, and lean on me, for my life is given meaning by the ways I can ease your burden and share your path. This is caring, too, to comfort and aid each other, and I offer it to you. Take it, take it please, and take my heart with it."

How florid his sentiments, and Polly had no idea what to make of them. Just words, likely, to pour over her weeping, like a lullaby to the ears of a distraught, weary child. She took the handkerchief he'd tucked into her hand and tried to tidy her face.

"I hate to cry."

"You need to cry more then," Gabriel said, resting his chin against her temple. "One gets better at it. It merely wants practice."

"As if you'd practice your crying." She knew what he was up to. Confounding her, tangling her in a small argument to distract her. "Don't be so sweet."

"Sweet?" He made a face; she could hear him making a face, and she wanted to see it but didn't want him to look at her, all blotchy and red and at her worst. "For you, I can tolerate being called sweet, but I know what you're about, carping at me already and my handkerchief not even dry. You won't sway me from my interrogation, Polonaise. Who has put you in such a lachrymose frame of mind, so I might call them out or simply shoot them on sight?"

"You'd never do such a thing." She bundled in closer as his hand slipped to her back, there to caress away her sorrows.

"For you, I'd challenge the French army single-handedly, provided you'd fed me properly first. Now, spill."

"I miss Allie." Saying the words out loud was hard, and good, too. Gabriel had loved that child if he'd loved anyone—admitted to himself he'd loved anyone—and Allie had loved her Mr. North.

"She is easy to miss." His voice held no teasing, no banter, no latent challenge. He missed Allie too, and that was as much a comfort as the strength of his arms around her. "She writes to you though."

"She does, though the letters are not her usual cheerful chatter. She's lonely, Gabriel, and growing up and not sure what to make of Beck, or the baby, or of all those people Beck is related to."

"Family like that would overwhelm anybody. Particularly a little girl raised almost exclusively by her womenfolk. Would you like to go visit?"

She bit her lip to stop herself from saying that what she wanted was to go *home*, to set aside this silly notion of painting portraits for coin, and reestablish herself in the Three Springs kitchen, scolding as exuberantly as she cooked.

"I've had another letter from Tremaine," Polly said. "I haven't opened it. He's no doubt asking for another progress report and crowing about more sales or commissions."

"Your commercial success doesn't warm your heart, does it, Polonaise?"

He meant this as a comfort, as an admission he'd make for her so she need not articulate it herself. "Success warms my pockets. I have a need to warm those, Gabriel. I hated, absolutely hated, being dependant on my sister for my every meal when I was younger. At least at Three Springs, I could work for a wage."

"Not much of one." He patted her bottom. "Filthy lucre won't solve your missing the child, will it?"

"Never." Polly rubbed her nose against his neck, taking in the clean, spicy scent of him and drawing comfort from that too—for his logic held no comfort at all. "I didn't think it would, and painting is proving to be an inadequate distraction."

"So go home, Polonaise," Gabriel urged. "There will always be portraits to paint, and Allie will be a little girl for only a short time. You can paint portraits when you're of a certain age. Your talent won't leave you because you turn it on different subjects for a time."

"Traitor." Dear, sane, tender traitor. "Tremaine would call you out for inciting such rebellion. He's worked hard to get my talent in the public eye, and I'll not let him down that way."

Gabriel traced a hand along the side of her jaw, his callused touch reassuring Polly in a way words could not. "The painting is important to you, and you should do it if it makes you happy, but it will never love you back."

"Damn you." She curled into him, hating him for his ruthless honesty, and loving him—a little more—for his willingness to tell her hard things in the kindest possible way.

"Is Tremaine pressuring you?"

"Of course not. Not as you think. I needed to get free of Three Springs, in any case, Gabriel. Enough of your lectures." She eased off of him, and he let her go, which was a small disappointment, but as she started to move around the room, tidying up, trying to collect her dignity, she chanced a look at him.

He was smiling at her. Not the usual sardonic quirk of his lips or the passing dry amusement she saw on his face frequently. This was an open, sweet, even tender smile, and she had to turn her back on it.

That smile… She wanted to paint that smile, to paint it on her bedroom walls, on the tops of her shoes, everywhere her gaze could chance to fall. That smile warmed the heart and encouraged, and more than anything, it offered the pure, selfless *understanding* of a close friend.

God help her, God help her. Simply for something to do, she reached for a sip of his cold tea, then set the cup down with a clatter.

"Nasty. Did somebody boil the leaves?"

"I doubt it." Gabriel got off the bed and crossed to the tea service to sniff the tea in his cup. "Why do you ask?"

"Your tea tastes awful." Polly passed him the cup. "It's off."

He sniffed again. "It wasn't as obvious when it was hot."

"This has… something in it." Polly dipped her finger in the tea, only to find Gabriel's hand closing over hers.

"No more of that. God knows what the something might be."

"Poppy syrup, I'd wager." Polly sniffed again. "Something ghastly sweet and laced with spirits."

Gabriel took a cautious whiff as well, then set the cup down. "I'd have to agree, and now we're left with who in the kitchen would disobey my direct orders?"

"You're full of direct orders. Which one was this?"

"No damned laudanum," Gabriel growled. "I've been clear enough about that."

Polly sniffed the teapot. "It wasn't the kitchen. They couldn't know which cup you'd use, nor would they have sent up a cup with poppy syrup sloshing about in the bottom."

"Suppose not." He sat on the edge of the bed and held out a hand to her. "That leaves George."

"George Wendover?" Polly sat beside him and kept her hand in his.

"What could he have been about? What's in that cup won't kill me. It probably won't even get me to sleep."

"Maybe he was trying to ease your suffering." But

George would have known better, wouldn't he? Being drugged wouldn't have eased Gabriel's suffering, not in any meaningful sense.

"I must discuss this with Aaron. George is softhearted, at least with beasts in pain, but he's also in my employ, at least for the present. This will take some explaining."

The half-full cup was pretty, delicate, and impractical as hell, like much art.

"Maybe there is no acceptable explanation. You didn't drink much of that tea, Gabriel. Perhaps George was hoping you'd down the lot of it, or even a couple of social cups with him, and then he could ease your suffering permanently."

"Something like that was tried in Spain," Gabriel said, his voice holding no emotion save resignation. "I can't like this, Polonaise."

She positively hated the notion somebody was trying to do him harm. "Hear George out and warn Aaron of your suspicions. George was alone in here with you, Gabriel, and for all he knew, you've been very sick. He could have tried something, and he didn't."

"George is not one to take a risk," Gabriel countered. "He's a good steward because he's cautious and methodical."

"I leave it to you, then." Polly brought his knuckles to her lips and planted a kiss there. "Please, for the love of God, be careful."

"You remind me of a dilemma, Polonaise."

She stayed where she was, stroking his hand with her fingers.

"I've granted permission for you to paint Aaron's portrait, because this seems to mean something to his lady wife, whom he is motivated to please, but now we have George skulking about the house, up to God knows what, and you running tame through the halls besides."

She knew what was coming. "Marjorie's painting is almost done. I can be gone by week's end."

"Is that what you want?" Again, he gave nothing away in his voice, and abruptly, Polly wanted to hear a spate of his fantastically romantic whispered blather. As lavish and foolish as it was, it lifted a weight from her soul when he spoke to her like that. Every woman should hear such pretty, impractical words, even if only in the course of the flummery of a dalliance.

"I do not want to leave."

"Then you are going to have to abide by some rules, Polonaise."

She nodded, it being all she could do to keep the words behind her teeth: *Don't send me away, please not yet. Not before...*

"You will be careful," Gabriel said. "You will not be alone, except with me, of course. You will have two footmen attending while you paint, so one might fetch and carry, and the other remain on guard. You will obey me without question if I tell you to quit a room or come to me, and you will do nothing, not one thing, to encourage George's notice."

"Not one thing. You'll let me paint Aaron?"

"I am concerned for my life now," Gabriel said. "Did I deny Marjorie this immortalizing of her swain, that life would not be worth a farthing. Either she or Aaron would see to it I suffered the torments of the damned for denying them this gift to each other. And sending you away abruptly, your commission only half-discharged, would signal to the household something was afoot."

"You were always a perceptive man. I don't suppose you'd let me paint you?"

"Some privileges should be reserved for a more

permanent association, Polonaise." He hadn't teased back: he'd spoken with a hint of remonstrance in his tone. He softened the rebuke by guiding her head to his shoulder. "But then, if you asked me to pose nude for you, my resolve might falter."

And if she begged him to pose nude? "You'd do that?"

"You'll have to ask, won't you?"

"Rotten man." Polly rose, grateful the mood had lightened. "How much longer will you be recovering?"

"Several days," he said, rising as well and shrugging into a dressing gown. "Aaron prowls the corridors in the east wing with me at night, and that's enough to keep me from qualifying for admission to Bedlam. I'm rather enjoying the respite, though it pains me to admit it."

Except he did admit it—to her. "You haven't had a respite since I've known you. Learning how to rest again takes time, or it did for me. I got up in time to bake the bread for weeks after Lolly took over the cooking. I started doing Allie's chores with her in the morning."

"She'll wake you up, that child will. Never stops chattering."

And why had she brought up Allie? "I don't think she chatters as much as she used to. I'd love to know what she's painting now."

"You must write and ask her," Gabriel suggested, going to the door to the sitting room and opening it. "Perhaps you might do that, while I reply to the latest spate of good wishes from former associates in Town?"

She complied because it was a pretext to stay near him, then abandoned her task ten minutes later and started in sketching him again, mentally trying various poses that would flatter him when he wore not a single stitch of clothing.

Eleven

GEORGE GLARED DOWN AT PILLINGTON'S RUDDY-faced, bandy-legged, pot-bellied form. "If you put adequate fodder out for your damned sheep, they'd be on their side of the wall, wouldn't they?"

"If you'd put up some decent board fence," Pillington retorted, "then they wouldn't be hopping over to trim your weeds."

"This is timothy and clover," George shot back. "Weeds, indeed, and this stone wall has served both Hesketh and Tamarack for nigh a century, because no steward worth the name is stupid enough to think stone will keep sheep from food when they have none."

"So you'll put up board fence?"

"Move your bloody, bleating, cursed sheep, man!"

"We're moving them"—Pillington's glower transformed to a grin—"as much as they'll be moved."

The sheep, rather than respect the stone wall running between two pastures, were vaulting onto the damned thing, trotting about, then hopping down on the Hesketh side, which, as George had said, boasted a lush carpet of fall grass. Several boys tried to herd the sheep back onto the

Tamarack side of the boundary, but the sheep were having more fun chasing the boys than conversely.

"You lot!" George bellowed at the boys. "Hold up." He let out a long, piercing whistle, and two black-and-white collies that had been sitting at the edge of the mayhem sprang into action. Between them, with George giving the occasional subtle cue, the sheep were soon leaping the wall and heading for home pastures.

"And that," George snapped at Pillington, "is how it's done. Tell your lady to expect a call from me."

"You tell her." Pillington sneered. "I'll be too busy having fodder put out so these sheep can fatten for winter."

"See that you do." George whistled for his dogs and stalked off.

"Of all the bloody nerve," George muttered to his companions. "Purposely setting the beasts over the fence, for the love of God. The old earl is no doubt spinning in his grave, and the present countess will answer for this."

He cooled down somewhat as he dropped the dogs off at the kennel in the back of his own small stable and walked on to Tamarack. He could call on Lady Hartle. He was not specifically required to use his hands in his employment, and was thus nominally a gentleman.

Except he liked using his hands, his back, his muscle. He wasn't meant to sit on a fine horse and give orders from a tidy distance. Working the land meant working, in George's view, and so he scythed weeds from the drainage ditches, poulticed the sore hocks on the plow horses, took his turn at foal watches and shearings, and had brawn, stamina, and a fine sense of accomplishment at the end of the day.

Still, he wasn't committing a social faux pas by calling

on Lady Hartle—merely taking his common sense in both
hands and pitching it over his left shoulder.

"My lady will see you, Wendover."

"That's *Mister* Wendover to you, Soames," George
murmured. "One would think you'd observe some courtesy
when introducing a fellow who's spent two years as the heir
to a marquess."

Soames's eyebrows rose to his shining bald pate, but
he said nothing, and George felt a stab of irritation with
himself. Aaron was the marquess only until all those legal
fellows in Town got matters straightened out.

"Mr. Wendover?" Lady Hartle's smile was gracious, if a
trifle wary. "To what do we owe the pleasure?"

"We?" George looked around her elegant pink, white,
and blue parlor. "Is the Regent lurking in your closet, that
the royal pronouns are appropriate? Has he perhaps made
you an offer, my lady?"

"Still without a hint of manners." Lady Hartle's smile
became the more familiar frown. "Really, Mr. Wendover,
was there a reason you called, or are you simply spreading
ill will and bad feeling?"

"That is your province," George countered. "But I am
remiss." He took her hand and bowed over it most cordially, then—because he'd caught her without gloves—he
kissed her knuckles.

Not the air above her knuckles, which would have been
cheeky enough, but her actual, smooth, neroli-scented flesh.

"Mr. Wendover!" She snatched back her hand, but not
before George had seen the hint of distress in her blue eyes,
and it cheered him, that hint. He'd go sometimes for years
without seeing it and forget how gratifying it was to behold.

"I am pained to recall what a lovely woman you are,"

George drawled. "Particularly when it's your legal maneuvering I behold and not your charming countenance."

"You flatter only to insult, sir." Lady Hartle inhaled
through a less-than-dainty nose, but she was a good head
shorter than George, despite being tall for a woman, so her
imperiousness lacked effect. Her children had gotten their
height from both parental antecedents, though their lovely
golden hair and fine features were her gift to them. "If
you've no business to state, then please be on your way."

"What?" George crossed the room to study a portrait of
her ladyship as a young countess. Even then, she'd carried a
subtle air of worry about her. "No tea and crumpets for a
neighbor, my lady? Your sheep were certainly helping themselves to at least that much in my home farm's south pasture."

"Take it up with Pillington. I am not a farmer, and you
waste my time with these details."

"You think it a detail?" George sauntered off on a tour
of her parlor, which might have been their parlor, had matters taken a different turn. "I would be within my rights to
butcher the lot of them, my lady. I would also be within
my rights to put up a high board fence in place of the stone
wall, and then see how all your foxhunting friends would
howl when they had to stop and go through a gate—
assuming I'd install a gate for that harebrained pack of titles
you trot around with."

"But Hesketh has never begrudged us a good run!"

Her disdain slipped, as George had known it would
when her standing among the local foxhunters was threatened. Harriette Hartle no longer rode in the first flight
herself—few woman did—but back in her day, before she'd
taken up the dubious sport of countessing, she'd been a
bruising rider.

"Hesketh is up to its elbows in stupid legal machinations, thanks to your hen-witted attempts to put wrong what's finally coming right," George said, stepping close to glare right down into her blue, blue eyes. "What are you about, my lady, to make a trollop of your daughter?"

"How dare you!" She cracked him a good one right across the cheek, but George only smiled at her, because Harry had ever been fond of her dramatics.

"You know how I dare," he replied, rubbing the sting from his jaw. "What I can't fathom, Lady Hartle, is how a mother can be so blind to her daughter's happiness. Marjorie is *happy* with Aaron, she's always preferred him, and he's showing every evidence of finally appreciating his good fortune. Then you go and ruin it in the most public fashion possible."

"My daughter is owed a title." Lady Hartle seethed as she rubbed her hand. "She'll have it if I have to beggar this estate to make it so."

"What she is owed," George said softly, "is a little happiness in this life, which Aaron Wendover will see to. She is also owed respect as an intelligent adult, one who can make her own choices. She isn't like you, Harry. No matter how you bully her, or wheedle, or threaten, or beg, she knows her own mind and knows whom she wants for her spouse."

He'd gone a bit far with that last, but she'd struck first, so to speak.

"Get out," Lady Hartle whispered, the shock in her eyes genuine. "You have no right to speak to me thus, and I'll not put up with it under my own roof."

"The roof," George said evenly, "you share with seven children, who will not understand when you beggar them for the sake of a title their sister doesn't even want."

He stepped back, unable to stand the hurt in Lady Hartle's eyes any longer. This made no sense, not when they'd been hurting each other for years, almost out of habit.

"I thought you, of all people, George, would understand my motivations."

She'd called him George for the first time in years, and he sensed she had not done it to cause him pain.

"Of all people," George replied, "I understand Marjorie's motivations. She loves her husband, Harry. Loves him. Can't you just leave it?"

"I'll not leave it, as you put it, while I have breath in my body."

He studied her, saw the monumental determination he'd first admired about her nearly a quarter century past, and shook his head.

"Harry, my dear, while you're on this silly quest to mate your firstborn to whomever ends up with the title, Pillington is slacking, cutting corners, wasting your coin and your resources while he wears on the nerves of all your neighbors. You need to rein him in, or you won't have much of an estate to beggar. Good day."

He showed himself out, because he'd run tame through Tamarack as a lad, having been friends of a sort with the late earl.

Only of a sort, though the man's taste in countesses was above reproach. Lady Hartle was younger than George, a couple of years past forty, but she was maturing like a good vintage, growing only more attractive with time. Her fine blue eyes had laugh lines at the corners, and her gaze held knowledge of life's up and downs, as well as patience, humor, and relentless determination.

And he hadn't seen her at such close range in months.

She was damned pretty, regardless of her age, was Harriette. Her figure was still trim and lithe as a girl's—George had noticed that too.

But she was as stubborn as a goat once her mind was fixed on a goal. Thank God Marjorie had some of her father's even temperament, else God knew how the girl had put up with Lady Harry's nonsense.

"It's in Gabriel North's handwriting," Sara Haddonfield said, "but it's franked by the Marquess of Hesketh." She handed the sealed missive to her husband.

"Hesketh?" It rang a bell, an ominous, low tolling sort of bell in the back of Beckman Haddonfield's mind.

"Marquess of. The estate is a few hours' ride to the west of us. Will you read it?"

"I haven't my spectacles," Beck said, because he'd been measuring a hallway for the addition of a dumb waiter. "You read it to me."

They sat hip to hip halfway up the main staircase while Sara carefully broke the seal.

> *Beckman (I assume you will plant me a facer do I embel-*
> *lish my salutation with honorables and endearments),*
>   *I have resumed my role at Hesketh, but whom should*
> *I find ensconced in my household but one P. Hunt, por-*
> *traitist, hell-bent on immortalizing my younger brother*
> *and his wife on canvas. To the extent that the hand of*
> *Fate was attached to the body of Beckman Haddonfield,*
> *you are warned I will someday get even with you for this*
> *little joke. Rest assured your dear Polly is thriving, in*
> *as much as she can without her family about her. She*

*pines particularly for her Allemande, and wonders what
the child is painting and how she fares. I trust you are
keeping my assistant steward locked in a garret, living on
bread and water, and allowing her only the association of
that minor planet known as Heifer for company.*

*You will give my regards to little Hildegard and
my other familiars at Three Springs, and were you
so inclined to pay a visit here, I would be inclined to
welcome you. I think.*

> *Though formerly North, I will
> end this epistle as merely, yours,
> Gabriel*

"He sounds in fine spirits," Sara remarked as she refolded
the letter. "Will you go?"

"He does sound like himself." Which implied a certain
fatigue and dissatisfaction with life, still. "Allie will be
relieved to know we've heard from him."

Sara leaned against her husband, which Beck took as
an effort to comfort him rather than any neediness on the
part of his wife. "We could hold a contest. Who is fretting
more about whom? Allie keeps staring down the driveway
as if she could will Polly to reappear, and now we learn
Polly fares no better, though she's once again sharing a
roof with Gabriel."

And Sara fretted for the lot of them. "It's hard for Allie
to understand why Polly had to go."

"It's hard for me to understand," Sara said. "I'm her
sister, and I tried to talk her into staying here, but she muttered things about life changing and married couples needing privacy, and there being some memories she needed
distance from."

Beck slipped an arm around her shoulders. "Have you ever considered Allie might rather be with Polly now?" Because *he* considered it as the child became more withdrawn with each passing day.

Sara nodded, her face pressed against Beck's shoulder.

"It's a puzzle," she said. "I thought I'd be hurting now for Polly, who left our household and essentially turned her back on Allie, but I hurt terribly for both of them. Allie was more attached to Polly than I knew, and I'm attached to them both as well."

"You hurt for them both," Beck said, kissing her temple. "What about for you?"

"Allie is not my daughter, and I have always known she was more or less on loan to me," Sara said slowly. "I love her as much as if she were mine, but now…" Her hand slipped over her womb. "It's different, now, Beckman. I'm expecting our child, and I can see all the things I missed with Allie because I am not her mother."

Beck's hand covered hers where it rested low on her abdomen. "But Polly hasn't been a mother to her either." And he was certainly too late an addition to the child's life to be a father.

"I used to tell myself that. Now I'm not so sure."

"What do you mean?"

"Polly was sixteen when she gave birth. What woman at that age, much less one who has to share a household with the man who seduced her, would be perfectly sanguine? Childbirth was hard for Polly, and she took a long time to recover, but she nursed that child without hesitation whenever Allie cried, fussed, or simply wanted comforting."

Beckman loved his wife, but the depths and twists of her

reasoning still had the ability to surprise him. "Do you think you sabotaged Polly as a mother?"

"That's an ugly word, though I might have, in small ways. I wanted a child so much, and yet I'd never consider allowing my husband into my bed, not after the way he treated Polly."

"I know you," Beck said. "I know you would not have betrayed your sister in any conscious way. Had she fought you, you would not have taken on the role of Allie's mother."

"She had nothing to fight with, Beckman," Sara said softly. "She was exhausted, heartbroken, dependent on me, and enough my sister to know how much I wanted a baby. I made a suggestion that we present me to the world as Allie's mother, and Polly couldn't very well refuse her child legitimacy, could she?"

Beck was quiet for a while, holding his wife and considering what she said, and what she did not say.

"We all want what is best for Allie," he said, "much as it pains me to think of losing her."

"We lose our children," Sara replied, smiling sadly. "If we're lucky, we lose them to a happy, meaningful adult life with families of their own. I think of Polly, who will lose her daughter without ever really having had her."

While Beck had not wanted to let that thought into his mind. "Not for a few years, at least. Can we take some time to consider this, my love? I wouldn't propose we ask Allie what she wants at this point, but North—his lordship—is amenable to a visit from family. Perhaps we can take Polly's measure and see if your intuition is accurate."

"Part of me can't believe we're even discussing this," Sara said. "Another part of me knows we need to at least discuss this. Allie hasn't painted much of anything since Polly left, and that scares me."

She hadn't painted, she hadn't named any of the fall lambs, she hadn't done much of anything but stare down the driveway. "I'd noticed, but I thought Allie stopped painting earlier, when North left and we didn't know where he'd gotten off to."

"Good lord. You're right. This is worse than I thought."

And wasn't it a fine thing, when a man heaped worries upon his gravid wife? "Not worse, maybe more complicated. Let's show Allie the letter. She'll be so pleased that she'll read the thing to that pig North doted on so."

Beck followed up his suggestion with a protracted kiss to his lovely wife's mouth. No more work was completed on the dumb waiter that afternoon, and Allie did indeed read the letter twice to that quarter-ton of porcine maternal pulchritude known as Hildegard, and to the eleven piglets who called the fair Hildy mama.

Polly had gone to bed with almost as much relief as disappointment, for Gabriel hadn't come to her. Maybe those broody looks over his wineglass at dinner had been about reconsidering his options and coming to his senses.

Yes, she was a likely candidate for a dalliance, but as a woman under the Hesketh roof, she was arguably, if temporarily, under his protection as well. Gabriel had a scrupulous sense of honor, and it might be catching up with him.

Polly had a scrupulous sense of honor too, but not so scrupulous she had to alert Gabriel she was still awake when he silently padded into her room and locked the door behind him. She remained quiet under her covers as he disrobed, methodically folding one piece of clothing after another over a chair.

He paused when he was down to only his breeches, and poked up the fire. To Polly's artistic eye, he was moving more fluidly than at any time in their previous two years' association. When he tossed his sleeve buttons into her vanity tray, there was a hint of dash about the gesture, a grace he hadn't displayed before.

He was truly coming back to life, coming back to the titled aristocrat he'd been before going to Spain, and while she rejoiced for him—who wouldn't be pleased for him, knowing how badly he'd suffered?—she was a trifle broken-hearted for herself.

Gabriel North, grouchy, tired, hardworking steward of Three Springs, had been a man she could dream about. This fellow, with the airs and graces of a title in addition to the brawn and nurturing heart of a land steward, she couldn't allow herself to build dreams around.

Except, her scruples pointed out, it was too late. The dreams were built, fully assembled in her heart and resistant to her every effort to dismantle them. Watching him shed his breeches then stand for a moment before the fire, all muscle and lean, virile male, Polly stopped trying to wrestle her heart under the control of her common sense.

She would not have much with Gabriel, a few nights, maybe, but what they shared, she would enjoy to the fullest.

"You can stop peeking." Gabriel addressed the darkened corner where the bed stood. "And why haven't you let down the bed curtains, Polonaise? The nights are getting beastly cold, and you're all by your lonesome in there."

"I wouldn't be alone if you'd cease lecturing and come to bed. Or you can stand there, scolding and catching your death."

"You've warmed up both sides of the bed?"

"Oh, of course." She gave a huge yawn.

"Then I suppose I'd best capitulate to your carping." He poured a glass of water, tossed his handkerchief on the night table, and climbed onto the bed. "If I leave the curtains back, there will be more firelight, the better to see what you're about. If I let the curtains down, we'll be warmer."

"I was warm enough by myself." Polly subsided onto her back. "Suit yourself."

"Do you know what would suit me?" Gabriel reached across her to let down the curtain on the side of the bed facing the windows.

"Spring?"

"Spring means endless work."

"For George," Polly said, "or his replacement, though my guess is you haven't confronted him yet."

"He's not acting at all like a man who tried to do me harm."

For Polly, it was impossible not to stare at the muscled expanse of chest stretched inches above her face. After a small, frustrating eternity, Gabriel got the damned curtains untied, and she could breathe again.

"George isn't about to lurk in corners and announce his guilt. Did you come to this bed to tell me your steward is innocent of wrongdoing?"

"I did not." Gabriel leaned back against the headboard. "I was all but chased out of the billiards room, where I think my little brother is teaching his wife how to play the equivalent of 'I'll show you mine if you show me yours.'"

A fine game between consenting adults, particularly if they were married. "So you've repaired here, where you needn't bother coaxing me to get my clothes off."

Gabriel peered over at her. "You're in a mood, Polonaise. Shall I leave?"

She shook her head, but as seductions went, or dalliances, this one wasn't launching properly at all, now that the moment was upon them.

"Are you having second thoughts, my love? A last-minute attack of virtue?"

"My virtue and I parted ways years ago. You know that."

"Were that not the case," Gabriel said with curious gentleness, "I could not be here. You know that."

"I do. But I wish…"

"Tell me what you wish, Polonaise." He hefted her against his side. "And stop being coy. It undermines my confidence."

"Your… right." Bless him and his insecurities. "Your confidence. Mustn't undermine that."

"What do you wish?"

She wished she could fall asleep every night for the rest of her life with a whiff of cedar and tooth powder wafting across her pillows.

"I wish that for you, tonight, I could have some of my virtue back. Enough innocence to make this new, not enough to remind you this is folly."

"This bothers you?" He stroked a hand over her shoulders even as his chin came to rest on her temple. "That you aren't a dewy-eyed, blushing virgin?"

She should keep the moment light, because theirs was going to be a brief dalliance. Brief but memorable.

"It bothers me. I am not a blushing virgin, though I hardly bring enough experience to the situation to merit a mention. I will not impress you."

"Good heavens, you'll not impress me," Gabriel murmured. "I suppose I'd be better off beating my brother at another game of billiards, then. But tell me this, you sorry excuse for a strumpet, how would I impress you, had you all this experience you lack? Hmm? Do you know how many years it's been since I allowed myself the pleasure of congress with a willing female, and how all that abstinence is weighing against my own efforts to be impressive?"

"Years?" She twisted around to assess the veracity of his statement, because she wasn't always sure when he was teasing. "Years, Gabriel?"

"Years, Polonaise," he assured her solemnly. "I cut one hell of a dash when I came down from university, as all the young idiots do. I soon learned that swanning about with a merry widow or some other fellow's straying wife is a damned lot of work and has consequences nobody really discusses."

"Consequences?" Polly knew all about consequences and the havoc they could wreak.

"Life gets complicated in a hurry." He worked himself down farther under the covers. "Between the gifts and flowers that must be sent, but discreetly, and the dance cards that must be kept straight—and then you find half the women were merely inspecting you intimately for some niece or goddaughter, to whom they want you to propose marriage… ye gods, it was scarifying to a mere lad."

"You were never a mere lad." But the idea that he, too, at one point had lacked sophistication was comforting. "So are you here to swive me?"

"Of course not." He crouched over her. "I'm here to make love with you, if you'll have me."

Thank God. "I'll have you."

He rested his forehead against hers. "Aren't you going to make me beg and plead and wheedle a bit?"

"No." She stroked a hand through his dark, silky hair. "Else you'll feel justified in making me beg, and I'm not so inclined. Begging would give you a surfeit of confidence and spoil my mood."

She realized she'd just mentally set him a challenge he wouldn't refuse, though some of her earlier melancholy had lifted. He'd called it lovemaking, and that was something. "How does lovemaking differ from swiving?"

"Were I swiving you, we'd be about done by now."

"Oh."

"There'd be no begging involved at all," he went on. "No newness whatsoever, none of this petting and cuddling you seem so fond of."

"I'm so fond of—not you?"

He kissed her cheek. "I'm a man, Polonaise. What use have I for displays of affection?"

"I'm tattling on you to Hildegard," Polly said just as Gabriel shifted to kiss the side of her neck. "I saw you scratching that pig's ears more often than Allie pet Heifer, and you got in your share of affection with that cat too, Gabriel. Discretion alone prevents me from naming the sentiment you attach to your horse."

"I'm caught out, a closet fiend for affection, exposed to the ruthless light of day—or night." He sighed, and she felt his breath against her skin. "You like that, though, don't you? That I have a high tolerance for affection in the right circumstances?"

"A tolerance?" Polly shivered as his tongue traced her ear. "You are reduced to petting a pig and her piglets, and you call it a tolerance. You are a sad, sad case, Gabriel Wendover."

"Hush, you." He settled more closely against her.

"You're trying to distract me with your insults, and while I appreciate it, the effort isn't necessary. The night will be plenty long enough to see to your pleasure."

"You aren't worried about all those lonely years undermining your impressiveness?"

"They were lonely," he said, oddly serious, "and that will inspire me, Polonaise, not undermine my resolve. Now kiss me, and we'll see about impressing you." He settled his lips onto hers, and the teasing was over, just like that. He'd coaxed her out of her self-doubt, though, and made her smile—made her shiver, in fact, and when was the last time she'd shivered with pleasure?

Twelve

"None of that." Gabriel lifted his head and brushed Polly's hair back from her brow. "You're thinking, Polonaise, and now isn't the time for it. Kiss me."

Polly levered up and kissed him, because it was an entirely worthy suggestion. When she would have sealed her mouth to his and started in with the plundering, he drew back and denied her, insisting on a slower pace.

Begging was apparently on her agenda, though she'd enjoy it, and they both knew it, too.

Gabriel's hands and mouth flowed over her, magically relieving her of her nightgown, and of her fears and insecurities. He inspected every inch of her with his kisses and caresses, until Polly couldn't lie still beneath him but had to let her hands roam his skin in retaliation.

She lingered at his back, sketching not just the muscles and bones, but also his scar. When she raked her nails lightly over the puckered flesh, he sighed his pleasure. When she sank her nails into the taut musculature of his buttocks, he started whispering to her in purring, naughty murmurs.

She counted his ribs and counted his nipples, often, coming back to explore his chest between forays down his sides, over his lean hips, and back up to his overlong, thick hair. While he waited patiently above her, she traced his features, bit his shoulder, and took his earlobe into his mouth.

Every bit as much as a cook anticipates enjoying the dishes she prepares, Polly wanted to consume *him*.

"You're deciding which spices would go best," Gabriel rumbled in her ear. "I do the same thing, you know. On the hotter days, something bracing, like lavender, peppermint, or lemon suits you. On cold, windy, wet days, you put me in mind of cinnamon and nutmeg and tropical sweetness."

"Of cloves?" Which she occasionally wore because cloves symbolized dignity.

"I have always been fond of the fragrance of cloves." He kissed her nose then lapsed into his whispering.

"You torture me with the tenderness in your touch, the innocent curiosity, and the possessiveness of your hands. You make me want to hear you claim me as your own, only and always your own, for you are mine, and mine alone."

She kissed him to stop that nonsense, because the way he touched her left her all too willing to believe his words. His caresses were deliberate, as if he were determined to monitor her response to every touch and kiss.

And Polly realized between one sigh and the next, that for them both, there *was* newness here. True, they both had experience, but this luxurious learning of each other, this leisurely exploration of what pleased her and aroused her, it was new for Polly. And precious. Gabriel's care with her provoked a wealth of tenderness toward him she hadn't felt toward another, not ever.

"Gabriel?"

He grazed his nose along the upper curve of her breast,

where Polly had indeed dabbed a drop of oil of clove. "My dear?"

"You don't need to linger over this part," she said, threading her fingers through his hair. "I know what comes next, and I'm not concerned with being impressed."

Nor was she concerned with being impressive, which was surely a symptom of a woman besotted.

"You have such confidence in me," he mused, then gathered her breast in his hand and covered her nipple with his mouth. "Is this what comes next?" He settled in to draw on her. "You must tell me, Polonaise."

"Mmm."

She felt him smile against her skin, but didn't care that her dignity had gone begging. The sensations he aroused were different from before, more intense, and both local to her breast and diffused into all the secret corners and depths of her body. This wasn't what had come next, not in her few, awkward couplings with Reynard, and not in the very few encounters she'd attempted thereafter.

What typically came next was grunting, poking, and panting for the man, and enduring for Polly, while she wondered what was wrong with her that she couldn't enjoy passion the way a sophisticated, experienced female was supposed to.

"Stop thinking, *my love*."

"I can't think. You steal my wits when you do that."

"I don't steal them." He switched breasts, dragging his nose across her sternum in a slow, teasing slide. "I put them in a safe place, where they won't do themselves an injury. You aren't begging yet, though, so I must exert myself further."

"Not much further," Polly assured him, because she

struggled to get out even three words as she arched her back and tangled her fingers in his hair. "I won't beg, Gabriel."

"Perhaps not." He left off teasing her breast. "You might be incoherent with pleasure, though you could beg me without words." He shifted off her, and she nearly commenced begging that moment. She preserved her pride by hiking a leg across his hip when he settled on his side next to her.

"You are so delectable," he murmured, running his hand down her sternum. "I could spend the entire night touching you with one hand."

She struggled to take an even breath. "You could not. Not if you value your life."

Gabriel leaned in and swiped his tongue over her breast. "A threat. That's encouraging." He made a little threat of his own, gliding his hand down to linger over her ribs and belly, then teasing his fingers through the curls over her mons.

"I believe you grow interested, Polonaise." He let her feel the press of his erection against her hip, and she wrapped her hand around him to indicate the accuracy of his surmise. He laughed quietly and cupped her sex with his hand while she ran her fingers over his cock. "I certainly grow interested."

"You mustn't encourage me." Polly ran her thumb over the velvety head of his cock, then over and over that spot right under the tip, the one that made him hiss through his teeth with pleasure.

"I'll distract you," he challenged, sliding his fingers slowly, slowly down, over curves, through curls, and into soft, damp folds of intimate flesh. He stroked gently while Polly's knees fell open and her hips rolled toward his touch. "Be still a moment, love, let me learn my way a little first."

She tried to comply but soon realized this was one of his tactics to provoke begging, and it was working wonderfully. "Let me move," she pleaded. "When you do that…"

He circled the little bud of flesh at the apex of her sex again, slowly, watching her face by the firelight.

"Not yet," he whispered, leaning in to draw on her nipple. "Soon."

"Gabriel…" Her hand landed in his hair, to hold him to her, while the urge to move against his touch was building, overwhelming pride, dignity, wit, and any remaining vestige of modesty. "Gabriel, you make me want…"

She heard the bewilderment in her own voice, because this kind of wanting was torment. It wasn't a craving for a hot cup of tea on a cold day, or for bed when exhaustion threatened. This kind of craving trumped the desire for her next breath and her next sunrise. "Oh, please, Gabriel…"

"Then yield to your pleasure," he rasped, intensifying the pressure of his touch. "Yield to me, Polonaise."

With a slow, groaning inhalation, she thrashed out her need against his hand, all pretense of thought abandoned as pleasure washed her mind clean and rendered her body his to delight and torment and delight yet more.

"Be easy," he whispered, shifting to again cage her body beneath his when she was reduced to a panting, pleasured, witless thing. "That was to raise your expectations a mite."

"Raise my expectations?" She whispered her incredulity into his neck, wrapped her legs around him, and tried to steady her breathing. He settled himself over her, not pressing her down, but giving her something solid, warm, and wonderful to anchor herself against.

"You are worth every patience and sacrifice a man can make with a woman in bed, Polonaise. Did you command it, I should willingly roll over and go to sleep, having seen to the first hint of your pleasure. Hold still."

He kissed her, and she felt his erection kissing at her sex at the same time, soft nudges with that smooth, blunt, warm tip of him, right against her sex. She turned her head, away from his mouth, so she could focus on that one splendid feeling. He seemed to sense what she needed, for he laid his cheek against hers and let her have the first hint of penetration.

"Gabriel…" His name was a prayer of thanksgiving as Polly gave a slow roll of her hips and rejoiced until her body met his, and from nowhere, her sheath was clutching at his cock in renewed paroxysms of pleasure. And this was worse, far worse than what had gone before, because he was inside her, filling her, and focusing her pleasure right *there*, until it rebounded and ricocheted through every particle of her being.

"I can't do this." She hadn't meant to speak out loud; she'd merely thought the words endless moments later as Gabriel held still above her, his hand cradling the back of her head while she pressed her face to his shoulder.

"Do you know how profoundly you please me, my heart?"

She burrowed against him, afraid to move lest her body visit more excesses of sensation upon her. "But, Gabriel, I can't bear this…"

"Shall I withdraw?"

"I couldn't bear that either. Please… let me catch my breath."

As he kissed her cheek and gathered her closer, Polly had the sense he'd wait all night, all week, or the rest of her life if she asked it of him, and that realization let her relax a little.

"You do this," she suggested. "I'll hold still."

"Do this?" He gently pushed into her, and Polly felt a lightning strike of pleasure right up her spine.

"Slowly." She fought for a breath. "I'm not usually like this. I'm never like this."

"I hope you're always like this with me, Polonaise." Though to Polly's ears, there was a slight harshness in his voice. He advanced so slowly, not a thrust at all, more a glide.

"I like that." Polly relaxed a little more. "When you move like that, it's almost soothing."

"We'll go slowly then, until you say otherwise."

"Can you pause a moment?"

He went still.

"Now try a single, slow… yes, like that. Oh no…" She was off again, unable to stop her hips from bringing their bodies closer. "Gabriel… Not again, oh, please…"

"Be still," he whispered. "Let it wash over you like a spring shower. Breathe in the pleasure, Polonaise." He inhaled slowly, and the pressure of his chest against her breasts reminded her how to breathe even as the pleasure came for her again. It wasn't so voracious this time though, not as terrifyingly intense.

"That wasn't as overwhelming. Can you be still for a time again?"

He became her slave in truth, giving her one-half a slow thrust, then one-quarter, as she experimented with her own limits and pleasures. When she'd relaxed enough to let him rock her from one slow, sizzling peak to another, she brushed his hair off his forehead and wrapped her legs around him more securely.

"You've impressed me," she assured him. "Much more of an impression, and I doubt I'll be able to walk tomorrow."

"You might be sore." He kissed her brow. "You should

start the day with a hot bath." He made as if to withdraw, but Polly stopped him by locking her ankles at his back.

"I'm not going to be that sore," she said, though in truth, she had no way to gauge such things. They'd been joined far longer than her previous experience indicated was possible. "You are worth every patience and sacrifice a woman can make in bed with a man, Gabriel. This woman at least." Also out of bed, which was why she'd soon be leaving him.

"You're sure?" He braced above her. "If you give me leave to seek my own pleasure, I'm not certain I can be a gentleman about this, Polonaise."

"You mean, you're not sure you can minutely manage your behaviors at my every whim?"

"Not now. Not very impressive of me, but I'm ready to go off like a primed cannon."

She smiled, and he saw that smile and must have taken courage from it.

"You're on your own then, my girl. Try not to scream the house down."

It was a short march off a very high precipice, but as Gabriel set up a slow, relentless rhythm, Polly gained insight into how much restraint he'd shown her. By the third deep, hard stroke, she was coming again, but this time, she didn't tell him to stop, nor did she go still herself.

She tried to ride out the pleasure, but he kept driving into her, until her sense of her own skin dissolved and she was wrapped around him in a desperate embrace, and still she clutched at him, internally, externally, mentally, emotionally. She was wrapped so tightly in his embrace, she heard a roaring in her ears, then a hot, screaming pleasure seized her, more intense than before. Her vision went dark, and Gabriel was all around her, inside her, and *with her*, even as Polly's sense of her physical limits evaporated into pleasure upon pleasure upon pleasure.

"Ye heavenly hosts." Gabriel tried to raise himself off her several lifetimes later, but Polly held him close.

"Not yet."

He complied, but didn't let her have half the feel of him she needed.

"Closer. Need your weight, or I'll fly to pieces."

He snugged his body back down over hers. "Better?"

She nodded, having used up her spare breath through at least the next week. They breathed in counterpoint with each other, a novel intimacy, with Polly's body hitching as aftershocks shivered through her.

"Did I hurt you?" Gabriel's lips slipped over her eyes some moments later, and Polly realized there were tears on her cheeks.

"Not hurt. The opposite of hurt."

"My love"—Gabriel's voice was bewildered—"you are in tears. What is the opposite of hurt in this situation?"

Polly wrapped her arms around him out of sheer excess of emotion. "You've made some hurts better. Hurts that can't be seen."

He kissed her eyes and took some of his weight from her, and she let him. They lay like that for a long, long time amid clean linen and the scent of cloves, the only sounds the fire crackling in the hearth and their gradually steadying breathing.

"Will I set you off if I withdraw?"

"Likely, you will, but, Gabriel, having done this with you, you'll likely set me off if you look at me."

"You do it then. I might start up again myself if you permit me to linger, and I've tried your body and your patience enough for one night."

"You want me to touch you?"

"Gently. I'm a little sensitive too, but yes. Untangle us, as it were." He raised up enough to allow Polly to reach between their bodies.

"I don't want to hurt you." Not ever, which nearly provoked fresh tears.

"Understood."

He wasn't going to give her any more guidance than that, so Polly took her courage in one hand and her lover in the other, and eased him from her body. "Like that?"

"Just like that." He climbed off her, leaving the covers flipped back. "Don't run off. Would you like cool water or warm?"

"Warm." She didn't mistake his meaning. She liked it, liked the intimacy of it and the consideration. He came back to the bed with a basin of hot water poured out from the kettle on the hearth swing and mixed it with a little of the cold drinking water from the nightstand.

"Spread your legs, love."

She eased her knees apart and watched as he regarded her intimate flesh.

"I want to go at you all night," he said, wringing out the cloth.

"I want to go at you all night, too." Polly closed her eyes as he gently held the cloth over her swollen parts. "That feels good."

"But if I moved just so"—he applied a touch of pressure—"you'd likely be galloping off again, wouldn't you?"

"I don't know…" She opened her eyes to visually offer him permission. He moved his fingers on her, and sure enough, her body drew up in one tight, sweet little contraction.

"Amazing," he said, pressing a damp cloth to her very

gently. "Do you know what you've done for my confidence, Polonaise?"

"This has to be an aberration." Polly stared at the shadows dancing above them rather than meet his gaze. "I'm not usually like this." Though she was usually a lowly cook, and trying to convince all and sundry she was a spinster cook at that.

"Oh, right." Gabriel wet the cloth, wrung it out again, and tucked it against her. "Call it an aberration when you share such passions with me, will you? It's what you're owed, Polonaise. Every damned time."

"I couldn't survive such owing. Gabriel, I don't think this was normal."

"It isn't," he replied, using the cloth on himself as he sat on the edge of the bed. "It's so far beyond normal there's something of the transcendent about it, Polonaise."

On that peculiar remark, he put the basin back near the hearth, leaving Polly puzzled and longing for him.

He was only halfway across the room, he'd just pleasured her witless, and she longed for him. God help her.

"Now I see what you're about." Gabriel put his hands on his hips, and naked as God made him, frowned down at her in the bed. "You're on my side of this bed. You thought I wouldn't notice your poaching. Back to your own territory and give a fellow some room to cuddle up after his exertions."

Polly obligingly scooted at least six inches closer to the middle of the bed. "Can you cuddle on top of me?"

"Briefly," he groused. "Only briefly." He climbed over her, situated himself above her, and rested his cheek on her crown. "Tell me about the tears, Polonaise."

"Must I?"

"Yes, else your precocious little mouth will get to exploring my sensitive parts, and you'll be suing me for return of the use of your privy parts by noon tomorrow."

"I don't know why I cried," she said, nuzzling his chest. "I didn't realize I was crying. I think it was in relief."

"Of?"

She bit her lip, trying to think of a credible dodge.

"Polonaise?" God himself couldn't have put more imperiousness into the simple utterance of her name.

"Loneliness."

"Ah." That was all he gave her as he wrapped a hand around the back of her head and cradled her face to his throat. "Just so."

She took comfort from that embrace, so close and cherishing, and felt her body give up the last of its passion-induced tensions. She was safe with him; he wouldn't trespass or presume on the strength of their physical intimacies.

But then, he was so perceptive and she was so transparent, he wouldn't have to.

❧

Holy, ever-loving, squalling infant Jesus.

Gabriel tried to slow his whirling thoughts, taking comfort from the way Polly wrapped herself around him in sleep. No wonder she'd dropped off so easily; Gabriel had never seen such passion in another person. Her body was virtuosic in its erotic tendencies, taking pleasure from every smallest taste of sexual congress.

She'd come on his hand; she'd come at the first hint of penetration. She'd come when he'd done little more than attend her breasts. She'd come when he moved, come when she'd moved.

And when he'd come… her pleasure had plowed over his gentlemanly intentions like a tidal wave wipes out all in its path. The sense of union… of meshing souls… not even in Latin could he have fashioned words to articulate such sentiments.

And while he could attribute some of her sensitivity to years of abstinence, for the most part Gabriel knew Polly had simply found a man who showed her some consideration. All over again, he wanted to take his fists to whoever had been so cavalier with Polly's virtue, with her pleasure, and with her confidence.

But that violent satisfaction was not to be Gabriel's.

If Polly had her way, this sexual interlude would be kept carefully discreet, superficial, and temporary. Her precious, damned painting was enough for her.

Not so, for Gabriel.

He wasn't going to wait two years to make love with her, only to let her go merrily painting on her way. As soon as he had his own safety sorted out, he'd be down on his knees, making her blush and stammer, and God willing, come, while she accepted his ring.

She'd fight him, of course, and argue and elude, but she'd not given herself to another the way she'd given herself to him in the past hour, and even Polly had to acknowledge the significance of that. It was a small tragedy that their loving would not likely result in a child, but Gabriel would offer her every consolation time, money, and caring could afford.

Let somebody else see to the succession—Aaron, even George, or the damned Regent, for that matter. Polly was meant to be his wife, his for all time, and he was meant to be hers.

Next time, he would have to remember to tell her these things.

Provided, of course, she permitted him a next time.

Gabriel awoke to hear a pencil scratching over expensive paper. More than a week after he and Polly had become lovers in truth, this sound was familiar to him. She was working diligently on Aaron's portrait by day, and Gabriel was working diligently on her resistance by night, but she, artist to her toes, was sketching him as much as she was making love with him.

"Get back in this bed, woman."

"Hush, and don't move."

"Five minutes then," he ordered. "My backside is half-exposed to the chilly night air, and I'll catch a lung fever."

"You like modeling for me," Polly murmured, pencil flying.

"I like your gaze on me," Gabriel countered, but in truth, he did like modeling for her, because it allowed him to study her even as she studied him. Her sketching him served as a kind of sexual teasing, with each too absorbed to care where the other's eyes were fastened.

"Of course," Gabriel went on, "I like your hands and your mouth and your body on mine too." And her scent. He loved knowing he left her bed smelling slightly of cloves and passion.

"I said hush."

He'd yet to do it, but Gabriel suspected that with enough practice, he could make her come with mere words. As her menses approached, her sexual fuse had lengthened, or perhaps she was simply gaining her balance with increased experience.

He certainly wasn't. He was gaining a nigh constant erection, and were it not for the need to tend to estate, legal, and personal business, he'd tie her to the bed and tie himself to her.

"Three minutes, beloved, and you're waking up parts of me that need their rest."

"Do not move."

He waited half a minute before his next attempt at shifting her focus. "A fellow with a delicate back is taking a chill here."

"I built up the fire," she shot back, and the room was cozily warm accordingly. They both liked it that way, because it left them with more light to see by and allowed them to make love on top of the covers, gloriously exposed to each other's eyes and hands and mouths.

Gabriel lay partway between his side and his chest, the covers wrapped around only one leg and hip, leaving him more exposed than not. He was curled around a pillow, facing his artist, though he knew she'd caught him in about every pose a man could occupy in bed.

"You need to keep two notebooks, love. One for leaving around the house, that includes all your subjects, studies, and the decent parts of me, and one exclusively for our bedroom."

He used the first person plural as much as he could: our, ours, we, us. She'd stopped flinching visibly when he did it, but he still felt her resistance.

"All of you should go in one notebook," Polly said, frowning at her work. "Your hands are as erotic as your mouth or your manly parts."

"How is a fellow supposed to mind his manners when you offer him such naughty talk, Polonaise? One minute."

"You mind your manners as you steal my wits. God above, you are beautiful."

"Could you experience sexual satisfaction merely by sketching me?"

"Gabriel Felicitos Baptiste Wendover, shut up."

He smiled, his best wicked, arousing smile, and knew she'd be closing that sketchbook in a minute, possibly two.

"Are you growing damp for me, beloved? Do you anticipate our pleasures as much as I do? I had to tend to myself while dressing for dinner tonight. It was all I could do not to come, thinking of you at your bath."

"Please, Gabriel."

He fell silent, because he'd never outright refuse her request, unless she were begging him to deny her pleasure. She rewarded him a few moments later by closing her sketch pad and setting it aside. Or perhaps it was a defensive maneuver, for he'd assisted at her bath a couple days ago and had the sense the experience had left her leery of bathtubs, bath sheets, soap, and her own body.

But not his. She remained fascinated with his body, and that offered him badly needed encouragement.

"You aren't going to show me your work?"

"Oh, very well." She fetched the sketchbook and leafed through it. When she brought it to the bed, he levered up to sit on the edge of the mattress, tugging her down to sit beside him.

He considered her most recent sketch. "You wanted more time?"

"Always." Usually, Polly had no vanity about her work and no insecurity. That her likenesses would be accurate was a foregone conclusion. What she puzzled over and spent time on was the emotional content of the image, the subjective impact.

"You make me look like a weary, naked angel. A fellow who has put his wings aside at the end of a lovely day and has awakened from dreams of another lovely day."

He sensed she saw his body, scar and all, as that perfect. Silly woman. When she touched him, the same intense regard was there in her hands, so he didn't tease her about it, didn't question his great good fortune.

He instead kissed her cheek. "When you marry me, you can order me to strut about all day without clothes. We'll bankrupt ourselves keeping the fires going all winter, and expire regularly of bliss."

"Gabriel, not tonight, please?"

"No expiring tonight?"

"None of your nonsense about marriage." Polly put the sketch aside. "It makes me want to avoid you."

A cold draft wedged its way into their cozy boudoir. "Avoid?"

"We can't marry," she said, staring at her hands where they were linked in her lap. Her talented hands held no tension, but Gabriel sensed her growing desperation anyway. "You have the title, I have my art. I am too attached to you as it is, and your talk of marriage is not… entertaining."

"A proposal is not usually considered mere talk of marriage," Gabriel countered, though he knew he wasn't going to grouse and bluster his way past her resistance. "We care for each other, Polonaise, and we are famous good friends in bed. Give me a reason other than the bloody title why we shouldn't be wed?"

There was a reason. Her silence, the despair in her eyes, confirmed it.

"Perhaps," she said slowly, "I am too passionate to confine my amours to one man."

"Well, all right then." He wrapped an arm around her shoulders. "When you've tired of me, you are free to have your amusements, and I shall do likewise if I can still walk and have any higher functions left to go on with."

He'd called her bluff, and Polly dropped her forehead to his shoulder. "This isn't a joke, Gabriel."

"It isn't funny," he agreed. "Come to bed, Polonaise, and we'll argue later."

"No, we won't." She let him help her out of her nightclothes, and snuggled up to his side under the sheets. "You'll bully and tease and make love to me, and the arguments will grow without another single word from either of us."

"You think I can't be married to an artist?" He settled his arms around her. "This is arrogance on your part, Polonaise. I am capable of flexibility and tolerance, and I can be happy with one pair of boots and one old horse." All he needed to be happy was her, and the ability to provide for her.

"I know that."

"Let me rub your back." He rolled her over, as easily as if she were a tired puppy, and rearranged himself behind her. She was soon breathing the steady, relaxed cadence of sleep, while Gabriel was, as she'd predicted, silently growing his arguments.

They belonged together, or so he'd decided, but doubt fractured his resolve with a thousand tiny fissures.

She was suffering. As much as she delighted in his sexual attentions, as much as she allowed herself to be comforted by his affection and regard, Polonaise Hunt was also tormented by the weight of the succession, or by some burden known only to her. For this reason—because she suffered— he'd eventually lose the heart to press his suit upon her.

Forcing confidences from her would break something of the trust they already had, and that he would not do.

⚜

"Bring a book," Polly suggested in exasperation.

"A book?" Marjorie blinked at her. "To read to him?"

"Your husband is as difficult a subject as a trio of little boys," Polly said, naming one of her most challenging projects from years past. "He cannot hold still, can't remain silent, can't abide inactivity."

"You think he'll abide it if I'm underfoot?"

"You can't make him any worse. He can barely hold still for five minutes."

They detoured to the library, where Polly selected some of Byron's verse, and then hied themselves to Polly's studio on the third floor. Lord Aaron paced a slow pattern from window to window. Wintery sunlight gilded him as he passed each one, making the highlights in his hair wink everything from sunset red to molten gold.

"I've brought a distraction," Polly announced.

Lord Aaron smiled at the ladies. "Sorry. I'm not used to maintaining immobility."

"One senses this," Polly said. "My lady, you must sit where his lordship can see you and hear you easily."

"Here?" Marjorie took up a hassock not far from where her husband was to stand. The sunlight hit her hair and came over her right shoulder, just as it had in the portrait Polly had done of her. The angle was the most flattering Polly had found for a lady who was quietly stunning to begin with.

"That will do," Polly said, tying a full-length apron on. "You, sir, assume your pose, and we will make progress today if it's the last thing we do."

His lordship fixed his gaze upon his wife, and Polly realized she should have tried this approach a week ago, when she'd first started work on the man's portrait. As Lady Marjorie read the poetry in the cool, ironic tones the poet intended, Aaron's mouth relaxed into a sort of half smile, one Marjorie, with her eyes on the book, could not see.

Polly saw it. Polly had been watching for it for days, and there it was. She painted with an intensity that had previously eluded her with this subject, and knew some relief, and reassurance, to be lost in her work.

She tried to ignore the impending despair Gabriel's nights in her bed had provoked, but it crowded in on her, compressing her art, her joy, even her very breath.

She was going to leave the man she'd come to love, because she couldn't bear to confess to him that for two years, she'd been living a lie, as had both Sara and Allie at Three Springs. Gabriel was piercingly intelligent. He'd see soon enough that even Beckman had been allowed in on the secret, but not Gabriel.

Not Gabriel North, overworked steward, and certainly not Gabriel, Lord Hesketh.

She could not bear the contempt she'd see in his eyes when he realized how far from marchioness material she was.

Or worse, the pity.

So she ignored despair, ignored the tearing guilt she felt with every cheerful, stupid letter she wrote to her daughter and sister, and ignored all the epistles Tremaine sent, no doubt filled with requests for progress reports and threats of more artistic success.

Artistic success, alas, mattered little. An artist could have a youthful indiscretion, at least on the Continent, provided she was repentant and very careful thereafter.

A marchioness could not. And if Polly had to choose at that moment between the child she'd passed into her sister's keeping and the man she'd come to care for too much, well… she'd have to choose neither. For the sake of both of them, she'd have to choose neither.

Thirteen

"HOW'S THE PORTRAIT COMING?" GABRIEL PASSED HIS brother a glass of brandy and poured a second one for himself. A cold wind soughing around the corner of the house and gusting atop the chimney announced that this would be not an autumn night, but a winter night.

"She won't let us see the painting." Aaron took a sip of his drink and sighed out his pleasure. "Marjorie says that's unusual for Miss Hunt."

"It is. Our artist looks tired to me." And Gabriel well knew why she was losing sleep.

"Tired?" Aaron rolled a cue stick across the green felt of the billiards table. "Miss Hunt looks like Miss Hunt to me."

"And what does your wife look like to you these days?" Gabriel turned his back to his brother, taking a good long while to poke up the fire. The room was warm enough, but the question wasn't exactly casual.

"My dear lady wife looks like... a little bit of heaven, dangled right before my crossed eyes. Your injury doesn't appear to be paining you."

Gabriel straightened, which resulted in not so much as a twinge from his back.

"It isn't." Something about Aaron's words tickled Gabriel's memory, where he usually ruminated on the various challenges in his life. "Since taking nigh a week to purely rest, my back is doing better. Then too, I'm trying to keep it limber."

"You didn't before?"

"Hadn't the time to indulge the occasional game of billiards. I was warned in Spain the damned thing would take years to heal, and it has."

But then too, making love seemed to help, at least most of the positions he'd tried with Polonaise did, and her hands kneading his muscles, and grabbing hard at his—

A knock on the door interrupted his thoughts, which was fortunate for his dignity, because Aaron missed little.

"My lords," a footman said, "you have a visitor."

Aaron set his drink down. "It's damned near dark. Are we expecting anyone?"

"A Mr. Tremaine St. Michael," the footman supplied. "He's in the family parlor, and Lady Marjorie is being located that she might receive him."

"Send along a substantial tea tray," Gabriel said. "Aaron, you'll accompany me?"

"You know this fellow?"

"He's Miss Hunt's man of business. I wasn't aware we were to be graced with his presence." Gabriel would have bet his horse Polonaise hadn't summoned the man, either.

"His name is familiar." Aaron started rolling down the cuffs he'd turned back in anticipation of a predinner game.

"You know him as the Sheep Count," Gabriel suggested. "He's something of a market force in the Midlands wool industry. Or perhaps you saw his name on Miss Hunt's contracts."

"I did. You know him in other capacities?"

"There's a family connection between him and the new owners of Three Springs," Gabriel said, which was a truth. As they made their way to the family parlor, he suspected Aaron sensed it was a half-truth.

"So you didn't send for him?" Aaron asked.

"What makes you think I would?"

"You don't seem surprised by this. I recall something in the contracts about his needing to confer with his client from time to time, provided his visits do not interfere with progress on the present project, and so forth."

Gabriel stopped outside the family parlor. "That's the language. Nearly word for word, and you haven't seen those documents in weeks, at least."

"I can usually recall what I've seen, if I was paying attention when I read it. Shall we greet our guest?"

Our guest. That, at least, was encouraging.

They exchanged cordial bows with St. Michael, who had apparently been warned that Mr. North, late of Three Springs, would bear a close resemblance to Gabriel Wendover. The conversation wandered to civilities about the roads, the weather, and the good health of mutual acquaintances at Three Springs.

"There's something else you should know," St. Michael said, setting down an empty teacup. "It might strain your hospitality a bit."

Gabriel refrained from pointing out that keeping his fists to himself was proving a strain on his manners, and not only because St. Michael was the helpful fellow who'd made Polly's eventual departure from Hesketh not merely lucrative, but contractually imperative.

Then too, the man was tall, dark, handsome, well

spoken, and as far as Gabriel knew—and thanks to a few shared soaks in the hot springs, he *did* know—free of disfiguring scars. Worse, he sported that half-French, half-Scot hint of an accent, and he'd known Polly for years.

"How could one so charming strain our hospitality?" Gabriel said, pouring their guest more tea. Where was Lady Marjorie, and more to the point, where in blazes was Polonaise?

"I myself will be no imposition, I assure you," St. Michael replied. "But we had occasion to stop by your stables before coming to the house, and there reacquainted ourselves with Soldier, because he was a familiar face, so to speak, and because the grooms were the soul of attentiveness, I made my way in advance—"

"Mr. North!"

A human meteor came hurtling at Gabriel where he stood near the hearth. Allie pelted toward him from the door at a dead run, braids flying, a smile as wide as heaven on her rosy cheeks. "Mr. North, it *is* you. It *is*. Uncle said only that we were going to have a surprise, and I am surprised to *pieces*."

Gabriel had knelt, mostly to block her from ending up plastered to the hearth, and then his arms were full of little girl, and Allie had his neck in an exuberant choke hold.

"I am so glad to see you, and looking very well, too," she declared. "Aunt must be feeding you properly, but Hildegard has been pining for you and Aunt both. The scraps bucket isn't the same since Aunt left, but Papa says Hildy is lonesome for Mr. Wilson's boar hog. Spring is so far off, and she pines. I pined too, for you and for Aunt, but then Uncle said travel can lift the spirits, and so we're here."

She beamed at him, and Gabriel couldn't help but beam

back as he stood with her perched on his hip. She still fit there, as she had for two long years. He hadn't realized how much he missed her, missed her chatter, her unflinchingly honest emotions, her joy in the smallest of life's miracles.

And if she called Beckman Haddonfield papa, well, that was for the best.

"St. Michael." Gabriel spared him a nod. "Well done. Now, Allemande, I take it you lingered in the stables to greet your old friend Soldier?" Gabriel addressed the child as he settled her in a chair. "What confidences did he share with you?"

"He's very hairy," Allie reported in all seriousness. "Papa says after the past few winters, all the animals are fuzzing up in anticipation of much snow and cold. There were flurries on the way here."

She might have pattered on, but the ladies chose that moment to join them. Because Allie was dwarfed by the back of the chair, her presence wasn't obvious at first, and Gabriel had to stand by and watch as St. Michael not only kissed Polly's cheek but slid a proprietary arm around her waist.

Gabriel leaned over the chair back to whisper in Allie's ear, "Greet your aunt, child."

"You think she'll be pleased to see me?"

"Don't be a hen-wit. She can barely paint for missing you."

Allie shot him a dubious look, then pushed out of the chair and came around to stand beside Gabriel, tucking her hand in his. "Hello, Aunt."

The words were shy, barely audible, and not at all consistent with the greeting the child had offered Gabriel.

"Allie?" Polly was on her knees, arms spread wide in an instant. "My Allie? Oh, my dear, dear child…" She enveloped the girl in a tight hug, not even letting the child go to snatch Gabriel's handkerchief when he dangled it before her. "I am so glad to see you, Allemande. So glad."

"I wasn't sure you would be," Allie whispered. "Mr. North says you missed me."

"I've missed you terribly," Polly assured her, rising but keeping Allie's hand in hers. "Would the company find it terribly rude if I showed my niece to the studio?"

"We would not," Gabriel answered. "Provided both of you ladies join us for dinner in"—he glanced at Marjorie—"two hours?"

"That will suit," Marjorie concurred, though it doubtless meant having the kitchen move the meal up by at least an hour. "And it will allow me to show Miss Hunt where our guests will be staying."

"May Allie have a trundle in my room?" Polly asked then peered at the child. "If you wouldn't mind?"

"I won't mind." Allie grinned hugely, while Gabriel felt a stab of consternation. If the child were there of a night, he most certainly would *not* be. He wiped away his scowl when he caught St. Michael smiling at him.

Nasty bastard, though Gabriel had to allow the man had traveled a distance with a small child, which showed dedication to the cause at least. Polly and Allie took their leave, followed by Marjorie, who was off to negotiate with the cook.

"Shall we switch to something more fortifying than tea?" Aaron posed the question, glancing between Gabriel and St. Michael. "Or do we get down the pistols and swords now, so you two can start in strutting and pawing over the lady?"

"Now, Aaron," Gabriel chided. "Just because you are up to your neck in wooing your wife doesn't mean the rest of us must resort to animal displays. And I must concede to our guest that bringing the child was a brilliant stroke. Polonaise was immediately in tears at your generosity."

St. Michael's mouth lifted at one corner. "Tears of joy. Bringing Allemande along wasn't my idea."

"It wasn't?" Gabriel paused in examining his sleeve buttons, because St. Michael's admission did not support Gabriel's desire to toss the fellow right out the window.

"Would any sane man willingly choose to travel in winter with a human chatterbox? One who wiggles as much as she talks, as much as she needs to stop at every posting inn from here to the South Downs?" St. Michael settled into a chair and let out a weary sigh.

"It would certainly give me pause," Aaron volunteered. "She's a lively child."

"She's the way to Miss Hunt's heart," Gabriel said softly.

St. Michael leaned his head back. "If she is, I can't see why Miss Hunt would have lined up three years' worth of commissions all over the Home Counties."

Because the oversized, accented, good-looking idiot was blind. "Well, if it wasn't your idea to bring Allemande to her aunt's side, whose idea was it?"

"Beckman's." St. Michael accepted a drink obligingly provided by Gabriel's brother. "And Sara's. They said you needed reinforcements."

A slow warmth suffused Gabriel's chest. "I did need reinforcments. I do. I most assuredly do, and I am relieved you perceive whose interests my Allemande is campaigning for."

❧

Polly heard a soft tap on the door and opened it only a crack, because Allie was sleeping on a trundle bed at the foot of the four-poster. Tremaine's hand shot out and encircled her wrist even as he put a finger to his lips, gesturing for silence. He towed her along in the cold gloom of the corridor until they were several doors down.

"Allie's asleep?"

"Of course. Traveling, seeing North... Gabriel again, joining the adults at table. She's had a very exciting day."

"And she saw you again." Tremaine studied her for a moment by the light of a mirrored sconce, then shrugged out of his jacket and draped it around her shoulders. "We need to talk, Polly, and this is not the place to do it."

No, they did not need to talk, but Tremaine apparently needed to jabber at her. "Where are we going?"

"My room," he said, taking her by the wrist. "It's warm and private, and not far from yours should Allie take a notion to wander."

"She won't wander, Tremaine, and you can just... *stop*." She shook her hand free of his and glared at him. "I will not be dragged about like this, and we're not going to your room at this hour." At *any* hour.

He crossed his arms, looking as implacable as a Highland warrior and as imperious as a French king. "Then where?"

"The library. It's almost as warm as the kitchens." Also full of fortifying memories.

He winged his arm at her, and Polly accepted the more decorous version of escort.

"You look tired, Polly Hunt, but you're painting brilliantly."

"My subjects are wonderful, when they hold still."

He patted her hand, and damn the man, in this frigid corridor, his hands were warm. "They're not just pretty people though, are they?"

"Not to me. A portrait is not a still life with human, or it shouldn't be."

"It isn't meant to be," Tremaine agreed, ushering her into the library. "Or it isn't any longer. This was a good first project, though, if you're finding the work enjoyable."

"I am," Polly said, though something in even those two words had Tremaine eyeing her closely.

"What?"

"The work is going well." Polly went to the hearth and spread her hands out toward the fire. The blaze was roaring, as if in preparation for the master of the house to take a late-night nap on the long sofa. "It's hard too."

"What's hard?"

"Being away from home." Tremaine was Reynard's surviving brother, and he knew exactly who was related to whom and how, so Polly offered the more honest sentiment. "Being away from Allie and Sara."

"I saw the miniature of that cat in your room." Tremaine stood beside her, looking at her hands. "Allie did it?"

"She did, and don't you start getting ideas about that child, Tremaine. She needs time to grow up and make her own choices regarding her art."

"She might not get those choices. She's now the stepdaughter of an heir to an earldom, Polly, and if you thought she'd be raised in bucolic obscurity, you're wrong." His words were hard, though his tone was uncharacteristically gentle.

"She's already been raised in some bucolic obscurity." Polly gathered her night robe more closely around her middle, though the fire gave off a marvelous heat, and the library smelled comfortingly of old books. "And she loves it. She's counting the days until Beck and Sara let her have a pony, and she's safe, Tremaine. Safe from all the Reynards in the world, safe from what acknowledging me as her mother would cost her."

"For now. But how old were you when Reynard came across you and so casually destroyed your whole existence?"

Not her whole existence—she still had her art—but Reynard had destroyed her innocence. Also her chance for a lifetime at Gabriel Wendover's side.

"We need not rehash this now." Polly turned to sit on the raised hearth, the fire crackling at her back. "You came to see how I fared with my work. I'm doing well enough, so you can go and find me another commission."

"When this one is complete, I shall." He lowered himself directly beside her. "Have you considered my proposal at any greater length?"

He and Gabriel shared a certain tenacity. On Gabriel, the quality was dear; not so, Tremaine. "No, I have not. I am busy here, Tremaine, and your proposal isn't what's occupying my mind."

She hadn't, in fact, given it a thought since waking in Gabriel's portrait gallery several weeks ago.

"It should be," Tremaine replied, slipping an arm around her waist. "I can see the way you regard your marquess, Polly, and he seems to return the sentiment, but you won't let yourself have him, and we both know it. You'd be honor bound to disclose that Allemande is your daughter, and you won't shatter his illusions like that. The kind thing would be to tell him now that he's wasting his time courting you."

"I've tried," Polly said miserably. "Tremaine, I've told him to his face there is no future for us, but he's just finding his balance here at Hesketh, and I'm familiar, and we were friends of a sort."

"Do you believe what is coming out of your mouth?"

His arm felt like a weight across her shoulders, like a yoke of lies and despair. "No." She studied her slippers, where she'd thought of painting an image of Gabriel's smile. "Well, yes, a little."

"He is familiar to you," Tremaine said. "You've pined for him at length. Now you can get him out of your system, and it's harder than you thought."

"Must you be so honest?" And presuming and bold and bothersome.

He smiled at her, a crooked, genuine smile that some other woman might find charming and Polly found sad. "You're too hardheaded to accept anything but honesty from a friend, Polly Hunt." He drew her against him again and kissed her forehead. "You must do what makes you happy, but as you weigh and measure and sort your options, please recall that I would never knowingly make you unhappy."

"And there's the difficulty," Polly murmured. "You won't make me unhappy, but you can't make me happy, either." Not that her happiness was anybody's responsibility but her own.

Tremaine let her go. "I will settle for making you rich, famous, and content. Were you happy to see Allie?"

"Not subtle, Tremaine."

"Answer the question."

"I was devastated to see Allie, and overjoyed. She thought I wouldn't be pleased to see her." Which was awful, the exact opposite of the truth, and possibly a good thing.

"She worried, as children will, and now she's reassured. You are too, I think."

Polly merely nodded. Perhaps she'd paint Hildegard's image on her slippers, another female held captive by maternal responsibilities.

"So you'd have me depart for Three Springs tomorrow?" Tremaine fired the question with exquisite casualness.

"You know I want all the time with Allie I can get, but the sooner you go, the easier it will be on her and me both."

Tremaine got up and left Polly sitting alone on the hearth. "The sooner I go, the sooner I leave the field clear for North—or Hesketh—to break your heart."

"I suppose you'd best be on your way, then. Except he won't be breaking my heart, Tremaine, though I very much fear I will be breaking his."

"You owe him the truth, Polly." Tremaine paused at the library door. "He might surprise you."

"By offering me pity instead of judgment?"

"He's not a bad sort." Tremaine appeared to study the molding, which was a pattern of strawberry leaves and pearls. "Though why I should argue on behalf of my rival is beyond me. I doubt he'd do the same."

"He's a very good sort," Polly said, rising lest she be tempted to remain in the library alone. "Better even than he knows, and he deserves a wife who can give him children, and whose past will stand the closest scrutiny. I would fail him, eventually, and that would break my heart."

"So you'll break his heart instead," Tremaine said, his tone jaunty. "He won't mind that in the least. Let me escort you back to bed, and all that nobility of spirit you're tormenting yourself with can keep you warm the livelong night."

Polly kept her silence, lest her honest and somewhat violent sentiments provoke Tremaine to more great good cheer at her expense.

The door closed, and on the reading balcony above, where a pair of brothers had tippled their papa's brandy and stolen looks at his "scholarly" edition of a certain work of Hindu erotica, Gabriel sat forward and scrubbed a hand over his face. Tremaine St. Michael had risen a few grudging points in his estimation by proving as honorable as he was shrewd.

But as for Polonaise… Her words had confirmed Gabriel's earliest, long forgotten hunches regarding the relationships between the Hunt womenfolk, and redoubled his determination to ensure Polly at least had somebody to share her secret burden with.

If she allowed it. Polonaise was further gone in her determination to leave than Gabriel had realized, self-sufficiency having become a habitual penance with her. The situation would soon grow desperate, particularly when the woman he loved had barricaded herself of a night in her bedroom tower.

Fortunately, Gabriel's most loyal vassal was barricaded in there with her.

❧

"You always tell me the truth."

"This is so," Gabriel allowed, but with Allie up before him on Soldier, he couldn't see her face, and it was easier to parse truth when one could observe the speaker's expressions.

"I want you to tell me the truth now," Allie said, and she did twist around to enforce her words with a glare. "Nobody else will."

"If I know the truth, I will share it with you. I may not know it."

"You do." Allie heaved a sigh the size of all England. "Everyone knows it but me, and nobody talks about it. Mama and Papa are going to have a baby."

"I don't think that's a secret," Gabriel said, but he knew this child, and though she was a child, she was also a Hunt female and winding up to something. "A baby often follows the vows. How do you feel about this development?"

"I don't know. I'm supposed to be happy to have a little brother or sister."

"But?"

"Mama could die. It's one of the things nobody talks about."

"Sara is in good health, and she will receive the best care." Platitudes the child would no doubt resent. "Why do you think she might die?"

"Ladies do. They aren't like Hildegard. Do you know, if Hildy is five years old, she already has hundreds of pigs in her family, and that's just the babies?"

"You are not a piglet," Gabriel said, mentally starting on the math, because Hildy invariably had at least twenty offspring each year, and about half of those were female.

"She has sisters too, and they have babies, and that means she has thousands in her family. Thousands, and they're all related, but I get only a mama and a papa who aren't my mama and papa."

The air in Gabriel's lungs seized, because in all his tossing and turning the previous night, it hadn't occurred to him that Allie herself shared Polonaise's secret.

But she did. She *was* the secret and a keeper of the secret both, and that was… not fair. Not fair to her, not fair to the mother who loved her.

"And this baby of Sara and Beck's will not be your true brother or sister, but rather, a cousin."

"Nobody admits that," Allie said, anger creeping into her voice. "A cousin is not a brother or a sister, but I'm supposed to act like it is. Babies cry and soil their nappies

and spit up, and as if that isn't bad enough, I'm supposed
to pretend this is my brother or sister. I don't like lying."

"Lies make for a great deal of confusion," Gabriel said,
also a great deal of sorrow and loneliness and possibly some
good art. "Lies can be meant kindly."

"My mother, my real mother," Allies said flatly, "doesn't
love me. Or not enough. I thought she did, but then she
comes here, where it's very grand, and she spends all her
time painting, and her letters are dumb."

"Tell me about her letters."

"They sound like Lady Warne's. Like I'm supposed to
care how much Lady Marjorie likes horses, when I don't
even know Lady Marjorie."

Oh, my poor Polonaise. My poor Allemande. "And what do
your letters say in return?"

"They're dumb too. Aunt doesn't care about Hermione
and Boo-Boo and Heifer. She left us, you see, just when
Mr. Haddonfield came along to look after my other
mama—Sara—and we could have gone off together and
been painters."

"Gone off together?"

"Yes." Allie reached forward to pet Soldier's sturdy
neck. "We all looked after one another, don't you remember? You and Mama and Aunt and me? But you had to
leave, and Mama fell in love with Mr. Haddonfield, and he's
nice, but he's not my papa. Aunt and I should be looking
after each other."

And was Beckman also more problem than solution for
the child? "Why do you call him Papa?"

"I don't want to hurt his feelings and he calls me Princess
and he's very nice. But he's *not* my papa, though he's married to Mama."

"Who is not your mama," Gabriel added, seeing the child's dilemma more clearly than he wanted to.

"I know what a bastard is," Allie said, her tone waxing forlorn. "I am a bastard. My real papa was not married to Aunt when he made me with her. I cannot join the best gentlemen's clubs."

"Were you planning on White's or Brooks's?"

"I was planning on running away," Allie informed him. "To you. But I didn't know where you were."

Sweet, holy, bellowing infant Jesus in His celestial nappies. "What would running away solve, Allemande?"

He'd run away any number of times as a child and made it off Hesketh land exactly twice, and only in his later attempts, because the weather had been fair and the groom trailing him particularly indulgent.

"If I ran away, I could be myself," Allie said. "I wouldn't have to pretend I'm happy about a baby cousin, I wouldn't be at Three Springs so Aunt could come home, and I was going to try to find you, because Papa—Mr. Haddonfield—you know who I mean—said you would let us know where you landed."

"You thought about leaving Three Springs with your aunt," Gabriel reminded her. "You've discarded that plan?"

"I thought we'd go…" Allie's voice became small and hurt. "Mr. Haddonfield is looking after Mama and giving her a baby, and looking after all the animals, except Heifer, who is *mine*."

"And always will be." As a part of Gabriel's heart would be.

"But Aunt left me there, and now Uncle Tremaine looks after her, and I'm supposed to just… lie."

What did one say to a brokenhearted child? What did one say that was honest?

"You miss your aunt. That's to be expected, and she misses you."

"She said she missed me." Allie twiddled a lock of Soldier's coarse, dark mane. "She called me her dear, dear child, right in front of everybody, but then last night when we were brushing each other's hair, she asked me what I was going to paint when I got home. She's not coming home, I know it."

The child fell silent, a miserable stretch of heartache during which Gabriel knew not what to say. While he mentally fumbled for something comforting and honest, both, Allie resumed her lament.

"When I was very little, my real mama and my mama took me for a lemon ice and explained that I must always call my mama Aunt when we reached England. They explained that bastard business, and they said we would always be together, me, my real mama, and my mama. We would love one another, and that was what mattered."

"So you're angry at her? At your real mama?" The very mama who was sacrificing her own chances at happiness so her daughter could resent her endlessly.

"I am *furious*. I can't be angry out loud, though, or she'll never come back even to visit when that baby shows up."

The baby, who would be lucky to survive infancy, based on Allemande's tone. "How would you like your life to be, child?"

"Heifer and I would live here with you and Aunt. I'd call her Mama, and you Papa. I'd have a pony and paint and write letters to Hildy. I wouldn't have to lie. I wouldn't *be* a lie."

Her unhesitating answer said she'd thought at length about this question and her dreams were... absolutely reasonable, also contrary to her entire family's vision of how her life should unfold.

And she wanted to call him, Gabriel Wendover, *papa*.

"May I think about this for a few minutes?"

"You want to talk to Hildy about it." Allie fell silent while she afforded him the courtesy of time to think up an answer for what had no answer, not as far as a lonely child was concerned. Gabriel was still thinking when they got to the stable yard and he lifted her from the saddle.

He was about to hand off the reins to a groom when he changed his mind.

"Let's put Soldier up," he suggested. "Unless you're too cold?"

"The stables are always cozy." Allie skipped into the barn ahead of him, leaving Gabriel to cast one glance at the cold, pewter sky and follow her in. He waved off the grooms, because certain discussions demanded privacy. Allie assembled brushes and fell into a routine they'd perfected over two years of caring for the horse.

And each other.

He passed her the bridle. She dipped the bit in water, rinsed it off, and tied up the bridle for hanging on a peg.

"I want you to know something," Gabriel said as he attached the cross ties to the halter. "Something you will never, ever have to lie about. Not to anyone. Nor would I lie about it."

"I'm listening." She was too small to heft the saddle onto a rack, but she could dip and wipe off the girth, and did so as Gabriel stowed the saddle, then crouched down to her eye level.

"I am your friend," he said. "You were my first real friend, and I will always be your friend. No matter who

your mama or papa or aunt or artist friends are, no matter
that you love your idiot cat best in the whole world, no
matter that you will love your pony as much as that cat.
I am your friend, and you must never run away, because
then I would not know where you were. I always want to
know where you are, Allemande, and that you're safe, even
if you're not precisely happy."

She looked confused, then her lip quivered, and Gabriel
felt something twang in his chest, hard, painfully hard. He
scooped her into his lap and settled with her on a bench,
while Soldier eyed them placidly and cocked a hip a few
feet away.

"It's like this." He kept his arms around her while she
leaked tears onto his chest. "When you love somebody, you
don't care what the labels are. You don't care who is their
mama or their aunt. I'm Hesketh, right?"

She nodded emphatically, damn near knocking his chin
with her crown.

"You don't care about that title. You never even knew
I had a title. Your steppapa could end up with a title, and
you don't care about that either, do you?"

Head wag this time.

"The words don't matter, Allemande, not as much as
the feelings."

"Then w-why don't I feel like anybody w-wants me?"

She howled the question, all the hurt and confusion in
her finally finding a voice. She bawled at length, loudly,
soaking his lapels and clutching wrinkles in his cravat.

"They have me, but they want that stupid b-baby more,
and think up names for it all the time," Allie went on.
"Aunt wants to paint, and Uncle brags that he can keep her
busy for *years and years*, and then I might n-never see her

again. And you wouldn't say where you'd gone, and I hate it all… I just, I hate it *to death*."

He let her cry until he wanted to cry himself, because she was so lost and despairing, so far from home.

From an adult perspective, Allemande Hunt had been afforded legitimacy by her mother's and her aunt's sacrifices, and legitimacy should have been a treasured gift.

From an adult perspective, she'd acquired a wealthy, respected, loving stepfather, one whose connections in the greater world assured her security and likely her pick of husband as well.

From an adult perspective, her wealthy uncle had taken an interest in her future too, and what doors her stepfather couldn't open, her uncle could, and not just in England.

She was a very fortunate and very heartbroken little girl, and she could turn to nobody except Gabriel to put right what was wrong.

Fourteen

POLLY WATCHED HER DAUGHTER SLEEP, SOMETHING she'd taken for granted when they lived at Three Springs. Allie's appearance hadn't changed noticeably since Polly had left weeks ago, but on the inside, where only a mother might see, the child was changing.

Guilt tore at Polly, not that Allie had given her anything to feel guilty about. Allie was polite, pleasant, and entirely without the mischievous spirit Polly had always treasured. Something was afoot, but perhaps it was only suppressed anger at a mother who'd abdicated from the job God assigned her.

And tomorrow, Tremaine would mount up and ride away, taking Allie with him. The thought was unbearable, as unbearable as if he were riding to war with Allie or departing across wide oceans, perhaps never to be seen again.

And the worst, worst part was that Gabriel would think he understood the ache in Polly's heart and would offer her comfort, support, and understanding, though in truth, he wouldn't understand anything at all.

She dreaded the lie she'd allowed to grow between them, dreaded more that Allie was expected to support the lie and live it. In two years of eating at the same table, tending to the same animals, and living under the same roof, Gabriel had never questioned who was Mother, and who was Aunt to the child. He'd worked, hard and incessantly; he'd been kind to Allie, and often more tolerant of her than her own family was.

But he'd not been taken into their confidence, and it was too late now.

Polly brushed a hand over Allie's forehead and pressed a kiss to the child's brow. She recited a mother's prayers for her child's safety and happiness, and never thought to add a word or two regarding her own.

Gabriel's back wasn't hurting, so much, but it was threatening to hurt and had him up and about well before dawn. He'd lost the habit of leaving the kitchen to the help and had thought nothing of repairing there to start his day with a cup of tea rather than wait about in his rooms for the breakfast buffet to be set up.

"What are you doing, prowling about down here?" Polly punched a wad of bread dough hard, folded it, and punched again in a familiar rhythm.

"I might ask you the same thing. Guests are not usually expected to make their own meals here at Hesketh." Though he'd given orders *this* guest was to enjoy free rein in the kitchens at any hour. He pinched off a bit of dough and swung the pot over the open hearth. "One gathers you've had trouble sleeping."

"Does one?"

Punch, fold, punch, fold.

Gabriel made a strategic retreat into the pantry and

assembled the tea fixings on a tray, which he brought to the worktable. A sketch pad lay open, images of Allie covering the page.

"How have you found Allemande?"

"She's… coping," Polly replied as she pounded the dough within an inch of its floury life. "She says she's looking forward to having a younger sibling, because she knows all about being a big sister, courtesy of Hildy and Hermione."

"I suppose the basics are the same across species," Gabriel offered, studying a sketch of Allie drawing her cat. "At least, at first. You keep one end fed, the other clean, and try to figure out which end is in distress when the creatures cries."

"There's a great deal more to it than that." She left off punishing the dough and shaped it into two loaves. "I was going to make sweet rolls."

"Don't let me interfere with your culinary creativity." He took the boiling pot off the hearth and poured the water into the teapot.

"I don't feel like sweet rolls anymore." Polly swiped at her eyes with the back of her hand. "Must you drink that here?"

"Yes." Gabriel got down two mugs. "The fires aren't built up elsewhere in the house, and you're here."

"I don't want to be here." She leaned her back against the counter, wrapping her arms around her middle. Gabriel studied the line of her spine, the determination and misery in it, and set the mugs on the tray.

"Come." He grasped her wrist, because her hands were floury, and pulled her to the back hallway. "Look at the ground, Polonaise."

Polly shot him a scowl, but did as he bid, which meant he could show her a thick blanket of white covering everything—trees, lawns, benches, buildings.

"It started about three in the morning," Gabriel said. "My back was warning me, and it further warns me that this won't let up for a while. You won't have to say goodbye to the child today."

She pressed her forehead to the glass, and her shoulders slumped, in relief, he hoped, then he heard her breath hitch.

He slipped an arm around her shoulders. "It's cold back here, and there's a pot of tea waiting for you." She went without protesting, which suggested more about how upset she was than even her posture had. He passed her his handkerchief and sat her at the table.

"I have to wash my hands."

"Later," he admonished as he poured her tea, added cream and sugar, and pushed the mug into her hands. "You sit and drink, and I will make sweet rolls."

He knew how only because she'd showed him the first winter they'd been at Three Springs. He and Allie had learned on the same magically snowy day, and had occasionally exercised the skill when Polly allowed them the privilege.

"How did you know?"

"Know what?" Gabriel asked as he assembled spices and sugar. "That you'd be down here reverting to old habits?"

"That I was fretting over Allie's leave-taking?"

"I know you, Polonaise," he said, and he nearly added: What mother wouldn't be fretting? Instead, he busied himself with melting butter on the stove. "You might fix a fellow a cup of tea, you know."

"I might, except I have to wash my hands or I'll get flour all over your mug."

"Heaven forfend." Gabriel mixed dark sugar, cinnamon and nutmeg—no cloves—into the melted butter. "Where are the confounded nuts in this kitchen?"

"Over the sink. Walnuts would do."

"Nicely," Gabriel agreed, for walnuts had been all they could afford at Three Springs. "I've asked St. Michael to stay on a bit, which you would know, were you not holed up with that child like a fox with a fall cub."

"You could have told me, though I could have asked, you're right. I'm just too..."

"Upset." Gabriel rolled one of the loaves of dough out into a rectangle and poured half the sweet, buttery syrup over it, then sprinkled nuts over the lot. "If you are upset, Polonaise, you have only to apply to me, and I will deal with it."

"You can't fix everything with a wave of your hand, Gabriel. That's a lot of nuts."

"I like nuts. Allemande likes nuts."

"She does." This was said so miserably that Gabriel dusted his hands and sat beside Polly on her bench at the table. He took time to fix himself a cup of tea but then didn't take a sip.

"You love that child. Why must you take yourself from her?"

"It's time I did," Polly said, resting against him. "There will never be a good time, but Beck and Sara deserve privacy, and I wasn't needed there any longer."

"Have you asked Allemande what she needs of you?"

"Children aren't to be burdened with adult decisions. Hold me."

"I can do better than that." He rose and led her by the wrist to the pantry, closing the door behind them.

"Gabriel, it's pitch dark, and the servants—"

"Know you are to have absolute dominion over the kitchen when you choose," he finished. "And yes, it's dark, so you'll have to go by touch, won't you?"

"Go?"

He hiked her up onto a counter that seemed about the right height. "You've been avoiding me, Polonaise. This is cruel to us both, also pointless." He rucked her skirts up around her waist, and it took a little searching in the dark, but Gabriel soon had her hands planted on his chest.

"Where are your clothes, Gabriel Wendover?"

"I'm naked from the waist up." He assured her of this by moving her hands over his chest. "You will not get flour on anything that matters. Kiss me."

He didn't give her time to protest, but found her mouth with his by virtue of framing her face with his hands and settling his lips over hers.

"Gabriel... we can't." But she didn't pull away; in fact, she hooked one leg around his waist and cinched him closer.

"You're in need of comfort, and pleasure can be a comfort."

"But it can also—"

He kissed her again, and he'd not only removed his shirt in the pitch darkness, he'd also unbuttoned his falls. He let her feel that too.

"God, Gabriel." She hooked the second leg around him and arched closer. "I want—"

"You want my hand on your breast, and my paws are not covered with flour, so you may have what you want." He palmed one breast and applied gentle pressure.

"More," she murmured against his mouth. "And I want you. Inside me."

"Here?" He nudged at her and formed an actual thought as she went still: of all the ways they'd coupled, fast hadn't been among them; nor had he taken her standing up. She was wonderfully open to him, and her hands roamed his back with such possession he couldn't form another thought for all the need clawing at him.

"Gabriel." She tried to lunge her hips at him, but he maneuvered away.

"Promise me, Polonaise." He teased her again with the tip of his cock and a glancing caress to her breast.

She yanked him closer with her legs. "Promise you what?"

"You'll tell me when something troubles you," he growled, nipping at her earlobe. "Give me your word, Polonaise."

"You want too much." She slid her hands around his buttocks, then gave a frustrated growl of her own and slipped her fingers beneath his breeches, whereupon she got her claws into his arse. "Come here."

"Promise." He gave her two slow inches. "Or there won't be any coming, here or otherwise."

"Damn you."

"Please, Polonaise." He went still, except for the hand he smoothed over her hair. "I need you to promise."

"I promise. I will tell you if I'm troubled. Now, I *beg* you, Gabriel, love me, please."

He sank into her, in gratitude and relief, and it was some moments before he was able to reason that simply asking her for what he needed might be a tactic worth considering in the future.

❧

Tremaine, damn his industrious half-French, half-Scottish hide, was already up and about, and likely eluding Polly on purpose. She'd wanted to ask him if the snow was truly reason enough to delay his departure, because if it wasn't...

She'd been up half the night, sketching her sleeping

daughter, pacing, dreading the next day's parting, and longing for Gabriel's arms around her.

Gabriel, who wouldn't understand even if she found the courage to tell him.

Gabriel, who'd extracted a terrible promise, one she couldn't keep even as she'd learned how to beg in the darkness of the pantry.

She made a mental decision to find Tremaine before the day was out and to accept his proposal of marriage, really accept it. As a traveling artist, Polly could not have her daughter with her, but as the girl's aunt, and married to Allie's wealthy uncle, there would be enough of a connection to guarantee she could see Allie very often.

And with Tremaine, there wouldn't be any lies and untruths; there would be mutual consideration and friendship.

He would also expect to bed her.

"I can't think about that." Polly tied her painting smock on. She couldn't work on Aaron's portrait, because the light wasn't going to accommodate them on such a gloomy day, but she couldn't not paint, either.

Not today, not with her emotions in such an uproar.

In the heated darkness of the pantry, something had come clear to her.

She didn't simply care for Gabriel, she wasn't merely fond of him, or sexually infatuated—not *just* sexually infatuated, that is. She didn't even *just* love him.

She'd gone and fallen *in* love with him, head over heels, irrevocably, absolutely. He'd known, he'd *known* easily, without a word from her, what had her so upset, and he'd offered her what comfort he could. The comfort he offered was terribly tempting, and because she did love him, she had to stop matters from going any further. He'd hate her for leaving him, but he'd hate her worse did she allow them to become further entangled.

And Tremaine's proposal was the perfect cudgel with which to beat Gabriel's untoward affection for her into oblivion. Gabriel was pragmatic and deliberate. He'd comprehend the message clearly enough when she announced her engagement, and Tremaine would get them a special license, did she ask it of him.

She'd ask. She'd demand.

If that didn't work, she'd beg. She was getting good at it.

❧

Aaron poked his head into the library, then came into the room, closing the door behind him. "We're off."

"Gone to inspect fences?" Gabriel tossed down his pen and regarded his brother's disgustingly cheerful countenance.

"The sleigh is hitched," Aaron said. "St. Michael is coming with us because his niece batted her pretty dark eyes at him, and Marjorie is joining us, lest her mother use the snow as an excuse to come calling."

Gabriel decided not to ruin his brother's mood entirely. "Enjoy your outing, then. But, Aaron?"

"Yes?"

"I've asked Kettering to travel here at his convenience."

"Kettering?" Aaron grimaced. "Rather like asking Old Scratch over for Yuletide, isn't it?"

Beelzebub, at least. "I've had a few thoughts I need to run by him, but I'm not willing to go back up to Town to do it. For all the coin we pay him, he can take a little country air." While Gabriel kept an eye on Polonaise, Allemande, dear Uncle Tremaine, Lady Hartle, and various others among the *dramatis personae*.

"I'll not have Kettering interrogating Marjorie. I expect your support on that."

"You have it," Gabriel said, leaving his desk to build up the fire. "I don't think it will come to that, in any case, but Kettering will respect your wishes."

"See that he does." Aaron took his leave, though as he attempted to shut the door behind him, Allie skipped into the room.

"Are you coming?"

"Coming where?" Gabriel straightened and saw the anticipation and glee on the child's face. She should look like that more often. *Her mother should look like that.*

"We're going out in the sleigh," Allie announced. "I've been in a sleigh before, when we were in Vienna and I was little, but I don't remember."

"It's great fun, though your cheeks can get very cold."

"Not mine. Uncle will bundle me up."

"You're not taking your aunt?"

"She's painting," Allie said, her joy dimming visibly. "Not just sketching or doing a study. I offered to stay with her, but she said I should go and have fun."

Which meant Allemande still had not confronted her mother. "Will you have fun without her?"

"Without you both," Allie countered. "Aunt was working on something special, and I know how that goes. You forget even what time it is when that happens."

She was trying to put a brave face on being rejected again by her mother, and Gabriel wanted to break things, pretty, delicate things that would make an unpretty, loud noise as they shattered.

"You could stay and keep me company," he offered, knowing it was foolish. He and Allie weren't playmates.

She'd simply been lonely at Three Springs, and fond of animals. He was often around the animals…

"No thank you. You made those sweet rolls, didn't you?"

"How do you know it was I?"

"Because you like nuts as much as I do. When we get back, may we have some sweet rolls together?"

A compromise, suggesting he wasn't entirely outside her good graces. "We'll do that, and put some nutmeg on our chocolate."

Allie grinned. "And whipped cream. You promise?"

"I promise."

"Then 'bye." She grabbed him around the waist in a brief, tight hug, then skipped off, leaving a deafening silence in her wake.

What could Polonaise be working on that she'd deny herself time to enjoy her daughter?

He glanced at the clock, glanced at the pile of correspondence on his desk, and decided he'd go for two damned hours without bothering the woman. As thickly as the snow was falling, she'd be back in the kitchen, baking up some infernally delicious concoction before too much longer. He'd track her down there and force her to confess why she'd been crying when he'd come upon her first thing in the day.

On second thought, an hour ought to be long enough with his correspondence, then, if he had to, he'd lock her in the pantry, and himself too.

❧

The image coming to life on the canvas was a study Polly had done before, in smaller versions, sketches, and even watercolors: Gabriel paused in the middle of tacking a shoe onto Soldier's right front hoof. The horse nuzzled his master's pocket for treats, while Gabriel, an affectionate smile tugging at his lips, scratched the beast's neck.

In this version, Gabriel's shirt gaped open, revealing a chest and abdomen rippling with muscle. His cuffs were turned back to the elbow, showing strongly muscled forearms dusted with soft, dark hair. The smile wasn't coy or self-conscious, but rather, it was that sweet, almost-tender smile Polly had seen more of while here at Hesketh.

His hand on the horse's neck communicated the same genuine regard for the animal, and in his other hand, he held a farrier's hammer. The fingers curved around the handle conveyed strength and competence; those threaded through the horse's mane spoke of kindness and an abiding respect for the animal.

Tears clogged Polly's throat as she tried to get the highlights in Gabriel's hair just right. He'd once said their lovemaking had something transcendent about it, but this image of him, one depicting a moment Polly had caught early in their association, had something transcendent in it too. Allie had seen it and tried to copy the work from a slightly different angle.

But Allie had never seen the real image. When Polly had come upon Gabriel one summer morning in this unguarded pose, Polly had seen for the first time that Gabriel North—for all his growling and taciturn manners, for all his slavish devotion to work, for all his silences and mysteries—was lonely.

And that he loved.

She'd been helplessly attracted from that moment, jealous of the way he touched his horse, jealous of the patience he unfailingly showed Allie, jealous of the hot springs to which he surrendered his tired, healing body.

This was the moment I opened myself to heartbreak. She surveyed the canvas from a few feet back and realized she was crying.

Again. God help her.

"You may not sell that work to anyone but me, Polonaise." Gabriel had stopped right inside the door, as if he knew he intruded on sacred, if sad, ground.

"You've taken to putting the footmen out of work?" She tried to wipe her cheeks surreptitiously, which was a wasted effort, of course. Gabriel set a tea tray down and passed her his handkerchief.

"Is it the subject that makes you cry, or the futility of trying to make it appealing? You make my horse look like an imp."

"He is an imp, at least he is around you. You have the ability to make sensible beings toss common sense right out the window."

"People who have had neither breakfast nor luncheon might be expected to part with their sense. Come eat, love. I can't tarry with you here."

"Eat." She frowned at her work one last time then uncrossed her arms. "I can manage that."

Gabriel took the tray to the seating area set up by the hearth. "It's bloody cold up here, Polonaise. Might we not eat elsewhere?"

She wasn't hungry and didn't care where they ate. "The library?"

"Always toasty. You chose it for that reason?"

"And your work is there, not mine."

He gestured toward the painting. "I'm serious about that. I want it, and you will not deny me."

Of course she would not. "Why won't I?"

"You did not seek the permission of the models. Or perhaps Soldier consented—his honor can be swayed with carrots—but mine cannot. Come along, else our tea will be cold."

❦

Gabriel could see Polonaise did not want to leave the chilly comfort of her studio, so he moved around behind her.

"This thing." He studied the back of her smock. "It's a puzzle in itself. How long have you had it?" And did she realize she was allowing him to undress her?

"Years." The smock tied in the front, but the sashes came from around back, so Gabriel reached around her to untie it.

"And your hair." He drew the apron away carefully, because it had a few fresh spatters of paint on it. "Is this your painting coiffure?"

Her hair was in a single, thick braid down her back.

"It is not. I was in a hurry this morning and didn't pin it up tightly enough, and once I start to paint, I grow heedless."

He came around the front of her, seeing a woman who was anything but heedless.

"You cried this morning, Polonaise, after we were together. Was I heedless of you?"

She shook her head and turned her back to him, only to have him slip his arms around her.

"You found pleasure." And tears. He hated that she'd cried.

"I always do, with you."

"But then the tears." He buried his nose in her hair. "This is an alarming pattern, my love. It threatens my confidence." She sank against him, eyes closed, her head against his shoulder. "Tell me, Polonaise."

"You asked…" She turned in his arms and looped her hands behind his neck. "You said please."

"And my attack of politesse moves you to tears?" He rested his chin against her temple and felt her giving up tension as he held her. Would she also give up the truth?

"It did." She tilted her head up to smile at him. "Under the circumstances, manners from you are surpassingly rare."

The smile was bright, beautiful, and utterly false. He had to kiss her lest he roar out his disappointment.

The way Polonaise kissed him back was not bright. It was dark, desperate, and utterly genuine, and Gabriel was soon gripping her tightly around her derriere and pulling her up against a burgeoning erection.

"You promised, Polonaise." He growled this reminder into her ear, only to find her hand had tangled in his hair, angling his head, the better for her to kiss him senseless.

"Now, Gabriel." She hooked a leg around his thigh and pulled. "I want you now and here and please…"

He raised his head and saw nothing approximating a bed, but there were chairs by the hearth, where it would be a little less chilly. He tugged her to the door, locked it, then led her to the hearth, unwilling to lose contact with her for even an instant.

"Your damned dress…" Her old-fashioned smock had no buttons or laces; it merely dropped over her head. If he took it off of her, she'd be shivering in no time.

He turned her and let her feel his erection against her backside.

"This isn't elegant," he whispered, "but it's the best I can do on short notice." He covered her breasts with both hands and felt the bolt of arousal go through her as she arched her backside against his cock and her breasts into his hands.

"I want you," she panted. "Inside me. Don't just…"

"You have me." He bent forward and put her hands on either arm of a chair so he was covering her from behind. "Too many goddamned clothes…"

For all his voice was rough, his hands were careful as they lifted her skirts and tugged down her drawers. No wonder she could tolerate this freezing studio, she had Continental fashions to keep her warm. "Step," he ordered, and she was left bare from the waist down, save for stockings and slippers. "Hold still."

Something was wrong with his voice, a catch in his throat at the thought of such raw erotic pleasure with a woman he'd seen only by the light of dying late-night fires. He undid his falls, nearly ripping the buttons off; then he was over her again. He glided a hand up her leg, and with his fingers, found her intimate flesh.

Wet, warm, and though she went still, he could feel the need quivering through her. Need for *him*.

"Easy," he whispered. "I'm right here." His fingers traced her folds as he felt her sag against her arms. She made soft, low sounds of wanting as he stroked and teased, raising his own arousal as surely as he did hers.

"Not soon, Gabriel. Now, please now."

"Now," he agreed. She tried to move her hips, to find him, but he stilled her with his hands, bending his body over hers to graze his teeth against her nape. "Now and forever."

He sank home in one slow, sweet glide. To be enveloped in her heat, to cover her and penetrate her, and feel her body rejoicing at their joining was… bliss.

"Move," she pleaded, pushing back into him. "I need you to move."

"And I need to move." He straightened, widening his

stance and steadying her hips between his hands. He went slowly at first, slowly and gloriously, wonderfully deep. He felt her come in the same rhythm, the contractions slow, tight, and endlessly pleasurable to him.

"Better?" He stroked a hand over her buttocks.

"More."

"Always." He gripped her hips and plunged in a single, powerfully hard thrust, then went still. While he let the shock of that pleasure reverberate through her, he bent over her and slid his hands along her belly, until they settled over her breasts. He began pulsing against her in the same tempo as he plied her nipples, and felt her body gathering toward another peak.

How often he brought her to fulfillment he could not have said, and for her part, Polonaise was not saying much of anything other than his name, and "Please." While the tea grew cold and the fire burned down, she begged him to come with her.

He complied with her request—he always complied with her requests—and was left panting over her like a spent stallion, his face pressed to her hair even as his fingers stroked soothingly over her belly.

"Polonaise." He found one of her hands and brought it to where their bodies joined. "Please, because I cannot be trusted to touch you again."

She was to undo them—he always left that to her—but she hesitated and laced her fingers through his where he cupped her sex. He had the terrible thought that she believed this was the last time they'd be close like this, and of all places he'd chosen to join with her where she created her art.

"If we remain like this much longer, I'll take you again, and I've already used you too well for that."

"You don't use me," Polly said as she slipped them apart. "You please me, Gabriel. Always."

GABRIEL   309

He stayed over her, drew her skirts back down over her legs, and wrapped both arms around her middle. "I want that painting."

"You shall have it. My gift to you."

Gabriel kissed her neck. "St. Michael will howl." And Gabriel would too, because it was a parting gift. He was sure of it.

"No, he will not." Polly straightened, and he let her go, but only long enough for him to fish his handkerchief out of his pocket.

"Put your foot up on the chair."

She complied, apparently trusting him in at least these most intimate logistics. He draped her skirt over her thigh and tucked the linen against her sex. "Hold that," he directed, putting her hand over the handkerchief. He retrieved her drawers and folded them over the back of the chair. "You'll need a soaking bath this afternoon."

"I will." She watched him, sorrow behind the languor in her eyes. "I'm surprised you didn't go on the outing in the sleigh."

"I'm awaiting my steward and my solicitor." He busied himself, fussing with the fire, mostly so he would not have to stare at her in such a frankly sensual pose.

"You're convinced George has a hand in your troubles?"

"No." He crossed the room to unlock the door. That she could think of such matters now, now when his seed was still in her body, made him want to destroy the canvas she'd just completed. "Not in the sense you mean. Why didn't you go have fun with Allie and the others?"

"I had to paint." Polly's gaze went to the fresh portrait. "She needs to learn to enjoy people other than her family."

She took the cloth away, refolded it, and pressed it to her again.

"I need to hold you," Gabriel said, lingering a few feet away. "The door is unlocked though."

"And the tea has grown cold."

He stepped close and put his arms around her. "Do you recall your promise this morning, Polonaise?"

"To tell you my troubles?"

"I did not adequately addle your wits, if you can recall it so easily, but yes, that promise. Will you keep it?"

"Easily." She let her skirts fall, closing her legs to trap the cloth next to her. "You are my trouble, Gabriel, and I've found a solution."

"You're marrying me?"

She tucked her face into his throat and held him tightly. "Aaron's portrait will soon be done. You should know Tremaine has offered me marriage."

"As have I."

"I'm considering his proposal, Gabriel."

"Coward." He put affection in the word, trying to suggest he didn't believe her. "I'll not give you up without a fight. St. Michael is a decent man, but he isn't me."

"Precisely."

He fell silent, and despite the now roaring fire, the heat of his recent exertions, and the warmth of the woman in his embrace, Gabriel felt a chill pierce him to the quick.

Fifteen

"WE'RE BACK!" ALLIE BURST INTO THE LIBRARY, CHEEKS rosy, the scent of snow clinging to her layers of warm clothing. "You were right. My cheeks are frozen." She pressed one against the back of Gabriel's hand to demonstrate. "It was like flying. The sleigh moves more smoothly than if it's on wheels. We didn't hitch up Soldier. We hitched up Andromeda, and put sleigh bells on her and everything."

"And I missed it all." Gabriel hoisted her onto his lap. "I've already ordered our chocolate, and gotten a great deal of work done in your absence." Two letters was a great deal, sometimes.

"Do you think Aunt wants some chocolate?"

"I took her a pot of tea not long ago. She was in the middle of cleaning her brushes when I left her."

"She does that to think." Allie tossed her mittens on the low table. "She tidies her work table, folds her rags, and does other silly things to think."

"I talk to pigs when I want to think."

"Do you have pigs here?"

"At the home farm."

"Do you go visit them?"

"I haven't yet." He wondered why, because he'd developed an affection for the beasts in recent years. "I am remiss."

"You are," Allie agreed, pulling off her woolen leggings. "We can go see your pigs tomorrow, unless it starts snowing again."

"You want more snow?" The leaden sky beyond the window suggested the weather might oblige her.

"I don't want to go back to Three Springs."

Gabriel put his arms around her and cuddled her against his chest, because he didn't want to let her go, either. "Why not? Are you on the outs with Hildy?"

"Never." Allie relaxed against him, a rare trust, because she'd soon be too grown-up for this nonsense. "I don't want to hear about that baby ever again. Everybody talks about the blessed event, and the interesting condition, and the family way, and being on the nest—it's stupid. It's just a baby, and everybody was one. I was a baby."

"No doubt the most beautiful baby ever born," Gabriel said, wishing he'd been around to assure her of that when it might have helped.

Allie closed her eyes on a sigh. "Babies are not beautiful. They are bald-headed, squally, and untidy."

She was wrong: to their parents, babies were unfailingly beautiful, but to make such a remark to this child would be unkind.

Also stupid.

"Allemande?" He drew a hand down her braid, which had become untidy in the course of her day's adventures.

"Hmm?"

She was showing every sign of drifting off on him, so Gabriel tugged her braid gently. "You must talk to your mother about the way you feel."

"My mother-mother?"

"The mother who birthed you, whom I know as Polonaise. She loves you, loves you until her eyes are crossed and she can't think straight, but you haven't been honest with her."

"I'm not supposed to be honest." Allie straightened, perhaps sensing defection by one of her few allies. "I'm supposed to pretend, which is the polite way to say I'm to lie."

"Not about your feelings, you're not." Gabriel let a little sternness creep into his tone. "Not to her, not to yourself, and never to me."

Allie frowned at him, looking so much like Polonaise he had to hug her lest the dawning anger in her eyes undo him.

"She wants me to go back to Three Springs and keep pretending. She does."

"She needs to know how you feel," Gabriel said again. "You have to be honest, Allie. For the whole rest of the world, you can pretend, but with the people who love you, you have to tell the truth."

"You aren't a bastard." She thumped down against his chest, all pointy little bones and indignation. "You don't know how they wince and shudder when you try to say the real truth."

"Yes, my dear, I do. That tap on the door is likely our chocolate."

She hopped off his lap, and he wanted to snatch her back, to protect her from all the pretending adults and the lies and the confusion.

"It's the chocolate," she reported, holding the door for the footman.

"Aren't you going to join me?"

Allie remained right at the door. "I'm not hungry, and I never really liked nutmeg on mine anyway."

She was out the door, nose in the air, before Gabriel could muster an argument.

He did like nutmeg on his chocolate, and whipped cream, and a dash of cinnamon. But he did not like having to consume his treat in solitude. When St. Michael came sauntering in, Gabriel offered him the contents of the tray.

St. Michael sniffed at the pot. "You're wandering off now, with all these goodies to tide us over until tea?"

"I am. I've a need to introduce myself to some pigs."

"And they will be better company than I?"

"Precisely."

❦

Gabriel had to hunt Polly down in her studio, where she was cleaning brushes and folding rags, and Aaron nowhere to be seen. This was contrary to Gabriel's agreement with Aaron, but circumstances were extenuating. "I gather your subject is playing truant."

"He got a dispatch from Town," Polly said. "He lit out for the village with his wife in tow."

"Trying to get some air before the next dump of snow, then," Gabriel concluded, though having read the contents of the dispatch, he knew their outing entailed a bit more than winter restlessness. "St. Michael claims we're to have more foul weather this afternoon."

"What does your back claim?"

"That I miss you." As did his front, his middle, his bottom, and his top.

"One learns to cope with not having every piece of candy one craves." She set down the jar of linseed oil she'd been wiping off. "I'm sorry," she said, back to him. "You don't deserve the sharp edge of my tongue."

"Your menses approach, unless they already plague you?"

She shook her head, and he slipped his arms around her from behind.

"The door—"

"I locked it when I came in, and told the footman to wave off intruders. What's amiss, Polonaise?"

"I'll be done here soon," she said, her hands wrapping around his wrists where they locked at her waist. "Leaving."

"If you must." He kissed her temple then desisted, because the sadness radiating from her was palpable. "I'd rather you didn't. Distance makes marriage a tad challenging."

"I will not be married." She closed her eyes and leaned her head back against his shoulder. "Not to you, in any case."

"Right." He nuzzled her jaw. "You'll be the Sheep Countess, and deliriously content. I've been warned."

"I will be Mrs. Tremaine St. Michael, if he'll still have me."

"What?" Gabriel dropped his arms by force of will. "It's permissible to be a French I–don't–use–the–title countess, but not an English marchioness?"

"He doesn't use the title."

"The hell he doesn't." Gabriel turned abruptly to add logs to the fire, because nowhere in his own blessed, benighted, blighted home could he get warm. "You will catch your death in here, Polonaise, letting the fire burn down like this. What can you be thinking?"

He rose from the hearth and studied her, going on in muttered oaths.

"But you can't think for the loss you face, can you? Your heart is so heavy, and you will let none comfort you. Your every breath makes you ache, but you will cling to your hurts as if they succored you."

"Stop babbling at me!" She whirled off and stood clutching her middle, the portrait of Gabriel and his horse at her back.

"I tell you the truth," Gabriel said. "It's a difficult pill, but often has curative powers. Good day, *Countess*."

~

"I'll marry you."

Polly found Tremaine in the family parlor, a smallish room that was easy to heat. She made her declaration as soon as she spotted him, lest she lose her nerve.

"That is good news." He peered down at her, and Polly realized the man was almost as tall as Gabriel, maybe *as* tall, for Tremaine was in his stocking feet. He had Gabriel's overlong dark hair and something of his patrician features, though Tremaine's eyes were the wrong color.

But one couldn't discern eye color in the dark of night.

"What has provoked this capitulation?"

"You made a number of convincing arguments." Polly sidled away from him to stand by the hearth, because after too many hours in her too cold studio, she couldn't seem to get warm. "We would suit, it will simplify our business arrangements, we have family in common, and you are… passably attractive in the right light."

"Such flattery." Tremaine moved to stand beside her, only to watch her as Polly flitted off to stare out the window.

"More damned snow."

"It's December," Tremaine reminded her as he shifted to regard the scenery with her. "Nigh Yuletide. Most people think the snow a prettier alternative to sleet and rain and mud."

"It all turns to mud," Polly said, striding across the room to pour herself a drink. "Shall we toast the occasion?"

"By all means." He stood where he was, which meant Polly had to cross back to him—an inordinately challenging traverse of ten entire feet of carpet.

"So when shall we do this delightful deed?" Tremaine took the drink from her hand. When his fingers slid over hers, Polly repressed a flinch. "A special license will spare us having to cry banns."

"A special license will be fine." Polly took a hefty swallow of spirits then dissolved into a fit of coughing. Tremaine was immediately at her side, taking the drink from her hand and patting her back.

"I'm fine. It just went down the wrong way." A special license was fine, Polly was fine, everything was just… fine.

"Right." Tremaine moved away, and she could breathe more easily. "You'll want your family in attendance?"

"Our family." Polly tried to meet his gaze and couldn't. They were discussing their *wedding*. "Maybe it would be simpler to find a vicar and have done with it."

"Whatever you wish, my love."

"Don't call me that."

He regarded her in a frowning silence, and Polly tried another sip of her drink so she wouldn't start hurling fragile objects at the hearth.

"Why not spend the holidays at my house in Oxfordshire?" he suggested. "I'm on good terms with the local vicar, so we can take care of the ceremony at some point. You can enjoy a break between commissions, consummate our union, and then I'll escort you out to Kent."

Must he be so accommodating? "Kent?"

"Your next commission is the Haddonfield harem,"

Tremaine reminded her. "The new earl has taken it into his head to immortalize his womenfolk in one fell swoop. It will be a challenge, but they're rumored to all be quite attractive."

"Bellefonte is Beck's older brother. Why did you accept work from family?"

"How could I turn family down? The earl is a very persuasive man where his ladies are concerned. Seven is an easy number to group, and they are well respected. The commission will be prestigious, as this one is."

This was how it would be with them. Marital consummation and portrait commissions in the same discussion, all horridly sensible and civil. "I suppose."

"Polly?"

"Hmm?"

"I want you to understand something." He set his drink aside and prowled toward her, as if he were stalking her, like a great, dark cat in the jungle might stalk something small and injured. No compassion, no quarter, no mercy.

"I'm listening."

"We *shall* consummate this marriage." His voice was as dark as his eyes, smoky with inchoate desire and sheer male dominion.

"Of course." She closed her eyes to spare herself the sight of that possessiveness. The idea of a white marriage had passed through her mind, but Tremaine deserved better than that, and he wasn't exactly unappealing.

Except he was—*vastly* unappealing. The idea of him touching her the way Gabriel did, joining with her, seeing her body and having the right to do as he pleased with her, made her physically ill.

The idea of explaining to Gabriel exactly why she'd accept Tremaine's proposal made her worse than ill. It made her want oblivion from her own life, permanent relief from the heartache that started the day she and Sara had first traded roles.

Tremaine's hand settled on her arm. He was so near Polly felt the heat of him. "A kiss to seal our betrothal?"

She nodded but couldn't turn her face up to his. Could not.

So he took her in his arms and dipped his head to kiss her temple, then her cheek. He nuzzled her into turning by kissing her jaw, until he could get to the corner of her mouth, and then, by degrees, to her lips. When he settled his mouth over hers, Polly had to admit he was skilled and patient, and she ought to be relieved. A lifetime of inept pawing and slobbering…

Would be preferable to this stealthy, silky seduction. He took his time, bringing her gradually closer and closer to his body. He was tall, muscular, and he bore a scent of roses about his person that was oddly appropriate to the man.

But he was not appropriate to *her*.

"Kiss me, Polly. It's just a kiss."

But the kisser was wrong, the feel of him was wrong, the scent was wrong. Wrong, wrong, wrong.

His tongue seamed her lips gently, teasingly, and when he gathered her closer, she was too stunned to resist. He would soon become aroused, and she knew that was what this kiss was about. He sought a blunt acknowledgment that theirs would be a physically intimate marriage.

God help her. She found the resolve to put her hands on his chest and push. She didn't shove him away, she just signaled… a halt.

His embrace changed, from that of a man bent on seduction to something tamer and almost protective. They stayed like that for several moments, the only sound the soft crackle and hiss of the fire.

"You're sure this is what you want?" He kissed her temple and tucked her face against his shoulder. "I've had more enthusiastic responses from complete strangers, Polly Hunt."

"I'm just…" She heaved out a big, weary, defeated sigh.

"I suggest you think this through a little longer." He stroked a hand over her hair. "Why marry if exercising one's conjugal rights is worse than a chore?"

"Many women do." The words were out before Polly could assess the way they'd sound.

Tremaine set her away from him but kept his hands on her shoulders. "I know women do, for the roof over their heads or respectability, or simply to get away from Mama and Papa. But I have none of those motivations."

"You?"

He nodded slowly, a sardonic smile curving the mouth that had been kissing her moments before. "I will expect you to meet me halfway in the bedchamber. If you can't do that, then this won't work."

"It will work."

He planted another kiss on her mouth—as she flinched back.

"It needs to work in this lifetime," he said, dropping his hands. "For both of us. I will not entertain further discussion of this topic until you've put the associations here at Hesketh behind you and are thinking more clearly."

She nodded, unable to do more, then left before she tackled him in a desperately determined display of her ability to meet him halfway. For if Tremaine wouldn't have her, what on earth was she supposed to do?

"I need to talk to you."

Gabriel hid a smile at Allie's truculent tone, so much like her mother's.

"Shall we talk over a cup of tea, or have you taken tea into dislike along with nutmeg?"

"What? Oh." Allie scrambled onto the worktable, to sit on it while Gabriel assembled the tea tray. "I don't really dislike nutmeg, not on hot chocolate anyway. I said that only because I was mad."

"Angry," Gabriel corrected her. "I gather your temper has yet to dissipate?"

She cocked her head in consternation.

"Are you still angry?"

"I'm *furious*. Mama was kissing Uncle. I saw them through the window."

"Does your steppapa know about this?"

"Not that Mama." Allie heaved a martyred sigh. "My real mama, in the small parlor. Just now."

Gabriel leaned over and bussed the child's cheek. "Now you're even."

She glared certain death at him. "This is *serious*. It wasn't a friendly kiss. It was a... grown-up kiss."

Tremaine St. Michael's notions of mature behavior left much to be desired. "Have you told your mother yet how you feel about all these changes in your life?"

"When am I supposed to do that?" Allie shot back. "She's always painting Lord Aaron, or there are footmen standing around looking like they can't hear when they hear every word."

"So perhaps tonight would be a good time," Gabriel suggested, pouring Allie a cup of weak tea and adding cream and sugar. "You ladies repair to your tower and have all the privacy in the world."

"She talks, about that baby and the animals. She doesn't listen."

"You have to make her listen." Gabriel let his tea steep a while longer. "If *you* can't make her listen, then it isn't humanly possible, because my own efforts have been unavailing."

"What's unveiling?"

"I failed," he translated, the words sounding all too final.

"You should kiss her," Allie advised, swilling her tea noisily. "Have we any cakes to go with our tea?"

"You've spent too much time with Hildy's offspring." Gabriel rose and passed a hand over Allie's head. "I'm sure we can find some crumpets or scones." He disappeared into the memorable gloom of the pantry, emerging with a selection of sweets as George came thumping and stomping into the back hallway.

"Shut the blessed door, George." Gabriel set the tray down beside Allie and helped the older man remove his coat. "I do believe it's getting colder out."

"Going to damned snow again," George said, unwinding a scarf from his neck. "And our accursed neighbor has not cleared the bracken from her infernal ha-ha."

"And this troubles you?"

"Her ha-ha—when free of debris—keeps drifts off the lane to the west pastures," George reminded him. "We've stock there needing some fodder, and now we'll have to clear the entire bedamned lane... Oh. Pardon my language, young lady."

Mid-rant, he'd apparently caught sight of Allie munching on a scone.

"You can use bad language in front of me. It means you owe me a favor."

"How about I fetch some butter for that scone? Will that do?"

"I like mine plain."

"I'll fetch the benighted butter," Gabriel volunteered. "Pour yourself some tea, why don't you?"

"Do you kiss ladies?" Allie asked.

"Not often enough," George replied. "I do kiss my horse, though. Might I have some tea, little miss?"

"I'm Allemande Hunt." Allie hopped off the table and flopped a curtsy.

"George Wendover." He bowed, poured himself a steaming mug, then drew a flask out of his vest pocket and tipped a dollop into his tea. "Purely to ward off the chill." He winked at Allie then added some to Gabriel's tea as well.

Allie reached out to take a sip of Gabriel's tea, just as Gabriel moved the cup away.

"George? What did you put in my tea while I was in the pantry?" And while an innocent child watched?

"A medicinal tot." George took a swallow of his tea. "You forgot the butter."

Gabriel held out a hand. "The flask, George. What's in it?"

"The flask?" George withdrew the flask from his pocket and passed it over to Gabriel, then went to fetch the butter from the counter. "It's peach brandy. I get it from a fellow up in Surrey. Peaches haven't quite caught on here yet. Too delicate. They need a winter, but not too much winter. Have we a knife for this butter?"

Gabriel opened the flask and sniffed. "In the first drawer."

"May I smell?" Allie tilted his hand to catch a whiff. "It's fruity, but not like the brandy at Three Springs."

"You're young to be a connoisseur," George said. "So was I, once upon a time. Are you going to finish your tea, Gabriel? One doesn't want to let the goods go to waste."

"You spiked my tea when I was ill," Gabriel said, putting the cap back on the flask and returning it to its owner.

"And you recovered handily." George slapped butter onto a scone. "Try it, it grows on you."

"Not my cup of tea, as it were." Gabriel passed over the spiked cup. "Do you suppose you might have told me what you were about, George?"

George paused, butter knife poised over the crock. "You can't tell when your tea is spiked?"

Gabriel took a bite of Allie's scone and munched thoughtfully. "I can't always tell *why* my tea is spiked."

"You make no sense." George bit into a hunk of butter with some scone hidden beneath. "Damn, this is good."

"That's two favors," Allie said, retrieving her scone from Gabriel.

"I have a favor to ask of you, George." Gabriel started on a fresh scone.

"You owe me a bite." From Allie.

"What favor?"

"Tomorrow, will you please bring Lady Hartle to tea?"

"Harry? Here? For tea?"

Gabriel nodded as he passed his scone to Allie, who took a prodigiously large bite.

And while Allie's mouth was occupied with scone, Gabriel went on. "We've more to discuss with her ladyship than bracken in her ha-ha."

"Bracken in the ditches, wasted time, and that rapscallion Pillington stealing her blind," George muttered around a mouthful of sustenance. "The girl isn't thinking straight."

"She's hardly a girl."

"She's hardly an old woman," George countered. "Yes, I can dragoon her to tea tomorrow, and it will be my pleasure."

"I'll send an invitation, and we'll have high tea, so dress accordingly."

"I'll bring my flask accordingly. High tea, indeed. Are you sure those brigands didn't use a cudgel on your head in addition to a saber on your back?"

Gabriel took a slow, slow sip of Allie's tea. "Perhaps they did both."

"You owe me a sip of tea."

"I owe you a visit to my pigs," Gabriel said to the girl. "Will now suit?"

"Yes. I'm still mad at Uncle and Aunt. You have to fix it."

Gabriel rose and hefted Allie to her feet. "Cases such as these require the wisest counsel we can find."

"Aaron said your solicitor will be joining the household directly." George started on a second scone. "Can't get any wiser than a Town-bred man of the law."

"Yes, we can," Allie replied. "We're going to talk to the pigs."

Sixteen

GABRIEL AND ALLIE DUBBED THE HESKETH BOAR HOG
Bellefonte, because like Beck's older brother Nicholas, he
was a splendidly grand, handsome fellow who passionately
adored his ladies. Allie wondered if himself might be trained
to pull a cart, and Gabriel allowed as how the Earl of
Bellefonte was now enjoying double harness, and stranger
things might happen.

They headed back to the house amid a shower of snow
flurries, stopping by the stables to offer Soldier a carrot.

When they emerged, Worth Kettering was handing a
groom the reins of a big, black gelding.

"The errant solicitor." Gabriel greeted the man with an
outstretched hand. "Just in time to bring us more snow.
How typically considerate."

"Considerate is summoning a man away from home
and hearth in the beastly dead of winter merely to
listen to you fret and carp about your brother's marital
mishaps. But we are remiss, Hesketh. Who is your
charming companion?"

"Beg pardon." Gabriel swept Allie onto his hip. "Miss
Allemande Hunt, may I make known to you the nominally

honorable Mr. Worth Kettering, late of London. Watch him closely, my dear, for he's of a legal bent."

"One doesn't use the honorable," Kettering muttered, bowing over Allie's mitten. "Enchanted and charmed. Have I the pleasure of knowing your aunt, Miss Polonaise Hunt?"

Allie shot Gabriel a look, one he interpreted to mean: *See? One must lie and lie and lie.*

"You do," Gabriel answered for her before she blurted out her sentiments. "And Miss Hunt the elder awaits us at the house, as does, for you at least, a hot bath and some victuals."

"Both would be welcome. I trust Lord Aaron received my dispatch?"

"He did." Gabriel gave Kettering an adult glance over Allie's head. "Most appreciated, your dispatch. Lady Marjorie in particular expressed her thanks. Once you've seen to your comfort, can you spare me your attention in the library?"

"Of course."

Gabriel left him in Marjorie's gracious care and tucked Allie up in the studio with Polly, who was finishing the details of Aaron's portrait. She didn't hear them come in, and so they stood, Allie's hand in Gabriel's, and watched the artist at work.

I want to remember her this way. Absorbed in her work, distracted from all that pains her.

Because that thought assumed she would leave, he pushed it aside and slipped away to give mother and child some privacy. He found his solicitor in the library an hour later, bathed, fed, and sipping cognac by the blazing fire.

Kettering regarded him lazily over his drink. "Why the dramatic summons, and what do you mean by bringing the child here?"

"I didn't bring her." Gabriel took the chair nearest the fire. "Tremaine St. Michael did, and because he must have been the one to share Polonaise's confidences with you, he can answer for his actions. I honestly believe he was well intended, and Sara and Beckman Haddonfield were complicit in his decisions, if not driving them. But that, my dear man, is none of your affair."

Kettering's eyes, which some might describe as an icy blue, narrowed. "If it starts defamatory talk about my client, it damned well will be my affair."

"Take it up with St. Michael. You and I and the entire world can see that Polonaise and Allemande are as alike as two peas in a pod. Allemande knows it, too, but Polonaise is not seeing so clearly as an artist might be expected to."

"She looks with her heart, perhaps."

"A sentimental solicitor." Gabriel rose and went to the sideboard. "How novel, but then, I forget you have a niece close to Allemande in age. May I refresh your drink?"

"You may." Kettering held out his glass, and Gabriel knew the man was maintaining a diplomatic silence. It was Kettering, after all, who'd drafted the codicil tacked onto Gabriel's will before the debacle in Spain.

Gabriel resumed his chair, and like every other seat in the house, it was not quite comfortable enough. "Turn your attention, please, to the matter of Aaron's marriage, and listen closely, because I do not want to repeat myself. I've been reading the betrothal contracts and have questions requiring your expert legal opinion."

"Closely is the only way I do listen, and my every legal opinion is expert."

Gabriel allowed him to flourish his verbal saber, because

the man had spoken only the unvarnished truth, and for a solicitor, that was remarkable enough.

⁂

"I come in peace." Gabriel nudged the door closed behind him with his hip because, as seemed to be his frequent fate of late, he had a tea tray in his hands. "You ladies dodged dinner, leaving Marjorie to contend with the lot of us. Not very sporting."

He directed the last at Polly, who couldn't decide if she was glad to see him once again in her bedroom or miserable.

Or both.

"Is that chocolate?" Allie rose from a rug before the hearth, her hair in fresh braids, her nightgown billowing around her.

"I've brought chamomile tea and a scone or two. Where shall I set it?"

Chamomile tea. He hated it, as Polly well knew from trying to get him to drink it when he was threatening to come down with a cold.

"Polonaise, will you pour?"

"Of course." She joined them on the hearth rug and tucked Allie's braids back. "This was considerate of you. We were about to douse our candles."

"I missed you at dinner," Gabriel said, glancing from one lady to the other. "Kettering was hoping to have your company as well."

"He was hoping to join forces with Tremaine regarding my commissions." Polly poured three cups and saw Gabriel grimace.

"Why would they join forces against you, Aunt?" Allie reached for a scone, then withdrew her hand at Polly's chiding glance.

"Because they think that passes for being protective."

"Who do you need to be protected from?"

"From whom."

"Sometimes," Gabriel said, "we need to be protected from ourselves."

Polly passed him his tea, purposely neglecting to add honey. "Like when we're very young and don't know any better."

"I used to be very young." Allie handed Gabriel the honey pot. "I'm almost grown-up now."

Gabriel used the whisk to liberally dose his tea with honey. "I can say the same thing. So what do you ladies find to do when you're closeted up here of an evening?"

"Aunt talks." Allie's temper flared briefly in her eyes, a rare spark of spirit, however ill-timed. "She tells me I must paint, but I can't just now."

"Won't," Polly murmured as she appropriated the honey pot. "Scone, anybody?"

Allie snatched one from the basket.

Gabriel met Polly's eyes over the rim of his teacup. "A little butter on mine, if you please?"

Polly wasn't sure what the request really meant, and spread butter on his, then passed it to him, hand to hand. His fingers brushed hers and captured them, taking her hand to his mouth as he took a bite of pastry.

"My thanks," he said, letting her hand go. "It's perfect. Will you have one?"

"I'm not hungry."

"Aunt has been sketching," Allie interjected around a mouthful of scone. "And she wrote to Mama at Three Springs. They write a lot."

"And have you written to Mama at Three Springs?"

"I have not," Allie replied with a hint of truculence. "We're going home soon, Uncle and I."

"Yes, you are." And somehow, Polly would bear that. "You should still write, because your mama worries about you, as does your papa."

A small silence ensued, during which Polly prayed Allie would not choose now to reveal family matters that should not be aired before a marquess, even when he came bearing scones and tea.

Allie put the uneaten half of her scone down on the tray. "I'm tired now, and I will go to bed."

Gabriel spoke up. "You should rest if you are fatigued, but say your prayers first, young lady."

This bit of paternalistic nonsense had Polly smiling, because Allie's prayers involved a lengthy recitation of animals who must be remembered to their Creator, and at the end of the list, Lord Bellefonte the Boar Hog received honorable mention.

While Allie prattled on to God, Gabriel appeared to be listening to the child as he dutifully swilled the detested chamomile tea. When Allie was finished, she hopped under her covers and ordered the room at large, "Tuck me in."

Gabriel rose from the hearth, tucked the covers in snugly all around, and pressed a kiss to Allie's forehead.

"Now go to sleep and dream of ponies and piglets. Tomorrow will be here soon enough."

"Will you stay until I fall asleep?"

Wretched, dear child.

"Of course." Gabriel smoothed a hand over her brow, then leaned closer to whisper something Polly could not quite make out. Allie frowned at him, then nodded and curled over on her side while Gabriel took up a rocker by the hearth.

Polly couldn't help it. She scooted across the rug and laid her cheek on Gabriel's knee. Of all his tactics—kissing, making love, lecturing, and stern silence—this one cut the deepest. They might have been a family, a real family, ending the day in companionable comfort.

"I heard your every word," Polly said, keeping her voice low.

"My words matter little," Gabriel replied, stroking her cheek with a finger. "It's Allemande who should have your attention now."

Polly said nothing and closed her eyes. When she awoke, she was tucked into her bed, the fire banked, the room in darkness, and she was without the man she loved.

❧

"The sleigh is coming up the lane," Aaron said. "Shall we assemble in the library?"

"The green formal parlor," Gabriel replied. "I've had the fires built up, and tea will be served in there."

Aaron let the drapes fall back before the library window. "Marjorie's nervous, while you seem calm."

Gabriel rose from his desk, the betrothal contracts in his hand. "Is this seeming calm not a skill you found handy when sporting the title?"

Aaron grinned. "Handy? No. It was downright necessary. Shall we?" He gestured for Gabriel to precede him, and they were soon met in the formal parlor by Kettering and Lady Marjorie.

"I wanted Polly here too," Marjorie said as she went to Aaron's side. "She said she had to pack up her studio."

"She's done with both portraits then?" Seeming calm abruptly became a difficult farce to support.

"They're... beyond excellent," Aaron replied. "More of a piece than if we'd been in the same frame."

"Like a good marriage." Kettering observed from the window. "Is the gentleman with Lady Hartle your cousin George?"

"Third or fourth cousin," Gabriel said. "The countess does not look happy to have his escort."

"Mama seldom looks happy these days," Marjorie volunteered. "Dantry is most vocal about it, as are the younger children."

George ushered Lady Hartle in a few minutes later, and Marjorie got her guests settled by the hearth. Tea was passed around, and sandwiches, cakes, fruit, and cheese. All the while, the ladies made small talk, with Kettering providing a surprisingly charming counterpoint, though Aaron, George, and Gabriel said little.

Lady Hartle set her empty teacup down during an opportune lull in the conversation. "I assume you did not drag me out on this one's elbow"—she cast a glare at George—"to share tea and crumpets."

"We did not," Gabriel replied. "I asked you here to save you substantial expense and embarrassment."

Lady Hartle scooted to the edge of a green brocade sofa. "If you're going to harass me regarding enforcement of Marjorie's legal rights, you will be gentleman enough to desist until my solicitor is present."

"You can afford to have him down from Town, then?" Gabriel sipped his tea, letting the question linger in the air. Over this fireplace hung a portrait of the first marquess, a properly stern fellow, considering the gravity of the proceedings. "Perhaps I can save you the expense. My own man is here to answer a few informal questions."

"And I can't stop you under your own roof from interrogating your own solicitor," Lady Hartle said. "Marjorie, you must know all I do, I do with your best interests in mind."

"Lady Hartle"—Gabriel's voice became lethally soft—"you will not suggest your actions are motivated by motherly love, not when your own daughter, of age and more than sufficiently articulate, has asked you to desist."

"She's only trying to be agreeable to you Wendovers," Lady Hartle retorted, eyes glittering. "She's a good girl, and she deserves—"

Gabriel held up a hand. "Kettering, attend me. I've lost patience with this farce and would see matters set to rights." And then he would find Polonaise and assure himself she had not fled the premises entirely.

"Farce, indeed." Lady Hartle started out of her seat, only to be tugged back down to the sofa by George Wendover's hand on her wrist. "Marjorie was betrothed to Gabriel Wendover, who is not and never has been dead."

"Marjorie was betrothed to me, true," Gabriel said, regarding the young lady who sat tucked right next to his brother. "I recall the occasion when the contracts were signed. She brought her doll downstairs to join us for tea, then proceeded to gallop around the parlor while the adults congratulated each other and I tried not to fidget."

"I cantered," Marjorie said, "in deference to the solemnity of the occasion."

Gabriel toasted her with his teacup. "In any case, Marjorie has since attained her majority, rather splendidly, one might say." Particularly now that Polonaise Hunt had revealed the charming young lady lurking behind a girl's insecurities.

"What has this to do with anything?" Lady Hartle spat. "As Marjorie's only surviving parent—"

George gently slid a hand over Lady Hartle's mouth. "Hush, Harry." Likely sheer surprise achieved his aim, for when he withdrew his hand, Lady Hartle remained silent.

"Realizing that my brother's wife is now of age," Gabriel said, "I took the liberty of procuring a special license, which license I put at my brother's disposal. Aaron, I trust congratulations are in order?"

"I have the lines right here," Aaron said, withdrawing a folded paper from an inside pocket. "Vicar assured us it isn't bigamy if the same people marry each other again, though he did account us a sentimental pair."

"A family trait," Gabriel said. "So you see, Lady Hartle, if the marriage was fraudulent before—which notion, I find ridiculous—it's valid now. More valid than ever. I trust you will call off your lawyers accordingly."

"That is preposterous." Lady Hartle seethed. "George, for God's sake, say something. You cannot allow this... You know I was supposed to be the marchioness." Her gaze slewed around, coming to rest on the portrait of the late marquess. "I was to be the marchioness's *mother*. Tell them, and be quick about it, as this grows tedious."

Gabriel held out his teacup, a civilized gesture that compelled Marjorie to look at him rather than at her mother, but it was to the older woman Gabriel addressed his words. "Lady Hartle, if maternal devotion does not compel you to withdraw your petition, then may I suggest you consider doing so before your pet weasel bankrupts you with a frivolous suit."

Lady Hartle's mouth and eyebrows moved in a disjointed symphony of outrage, while Kettering stepped figuratively into the breach.

"He has the right of it, legally, my lady," Kettering said. "Though your own solicitor must of course advise you, the matter was so simple I missed it, until Hesketh started asking very particular questions. The courts do not look favorably on frivolous suits, and you do not want to end up paying my bills in addition to Mr. Erskine's."

"But Erskine said…" She rose, then sank down again slowly, her expression pinched. She turned to George, seated at her left. "This is your fault. You might have reasoned with these two, and now you've ruined everything."

"I'm preventing you from ruining things," George shot back. "Again, Harry."

"We did not suit!" Lady Hartle fumbled for her handkerchief, only to have George thrust his into her hand. "We would never have suited."

"We suited well enough that that girl could well be my daughter," George replied. "And if you weren't going to see to her happiness, I was. Yes, I had Gabriel detained in Spain so Marjorie could spend time with Aaron while he recuperated, and yes, they ended up married, which is how it was meant to be."

"Meant to be?" Lady Hartle reared back, ready to fire all seventy-four cannon, but George trapped her hand in his.

"Harry, please, please cut line." George's tone gentled. "You meant well, you always mean well, but Marjorie has always preferred Aaron, and even if you couldn't have the man of your choice, your daughter should have some happiness on this earth."

"You speak utter foolishness. Marjorie, tell them you support my petition. It's your future we're trying to protect. I'm sure we can have this latest little ceremony annulled."

Marjorie reached for Aaron's hand. "Mama, I love you for trying to fight this battle on my behalf, but I do not support your means or your ends. I love Aaron and I hope

I am carrying his child. If the union wasn't valid before, I assure you, it is valid and consummated now."

"Consum—consum—?" Lady Hartle put her face in her hands and crumpled over against George, who obligingly put his arm around her and patted her back.

"Come, Mama." Marjorie rose. "I'd like to show you my plans for the nursery."

Lady Hartle looked up, dry-eyed, a hound catching a fresh scent. "There's to be a child? But I thought Aaron was being difficult and there wasn't—"

"Aaron could never be difficult. Come with me, Mama. I've expressed my disapproval of your schemes, and I think no more need be said on the matter. Perhaps you've some ideas for names?"

"Names?" Lady Hartle blew out a breath.

"Come along, Harry." George rose and drew the lady to her feet. "You always were knowledgeable about the family archives, and I'm sure you'll have lots of ideas."

"George." Gabriel's voice cut through the clucking and fussing directed at Lady Hartle. "You will leave the ladies to their errand and have a seat, please."

George complied, though nobody said a word until the ladies were gone.

Aaron spoke first. "That woman implied Marjorie was *carrying Gabriel's child* when she was carping at me to marry. That's how she forced my hand, George, but you allowed it, likely knowing it couldn't be true."

"Carrying Gabriel's child?" George looked nonplussed. "I knew Harry was determined, but that tops just about everything."

"Not everything," Gabriel said. "It doesn't top having me *detained* in Spain, George."

"Yes, well..." George ran a finger around his collar and produced his flask from a vest pocket. "As to that..."

"You wanted to see Marjorie married to Aaron," Gabriel supplied, "so you had assassins set on me, with predictable results. And do not try to dissemble here, George, because nobody in England knew I was injured with a saber thrust. As far as all my English connections knew—Aaron included—I took a knife to the back—a lethal knife."

"Not assassins, and not lethal," George said, rising and pacing. "I merely wanted you kept in Spain for a bit, so Marjorie could get her hooks into Aaron. She'd always preferred him, and I didn't want to see Marjorie stumble down the same path her mother had."

Kettering obliged with the necessary question. "What path would that be?"

"Putting duty and station before all else," George said. "I wasn't exaggerating when I said Marjorie could be my own daughter. Harry was determined to marry your papa, who'd already lost two wives. His lordship got wind I harbored a *tendresse* for Harry and told her he wouldn't poach on my preserves. Decent of him, because I was only a poor relation and she was mad to have his title."

"She must have been mad to get her hands on something of yours," Gabriel pointed out dryly.

"Only the once, because she fancied me in some way." George's wistful expression suggested the fancy had been mutual—or perhaps still was. "A week later, Hartle came sniffing about, waving his papa's earldom under Harry's nose—I didn't stand a chance. The banns were cried posthaste, and Marjorie showed up eight months later."

"And this justified killing me?"

"It did not!" George took a pull on his flask and tucked

the thing away. "I only wanted you *detained*, and thought I paid enough coin to have my directions followed. *Detained*, you know? Your horse put out of commission, your papers reviewed at length, your passage held up for a few weeks, your coin taken. Detained, only detained."

Aaron's expression became considering. "How much did you pay for these well-intended troubles?"

George named a ridiculously generous sum.

Aaron shook his head. "In Spain, where the war has left little in the economy functional, nobody would believe you were paying that much for mere nuisance tactics."

"I know that now." George took his flask out again, then stuffed it back in his pocket. "Goddamn it, don't you think I know that? I miscalculated and damned near got my own cousin killed. When I heard no one had seen the body, I began to hope, and then I started listening at tap rooms and asking around, and my hope grew."

"You hoped," Gabriel said levelly, "while I could barely walk and suspected Aaron of the most heinous crime imaginable."

"And I," Aaron interjected, "suspected Marjorie had gotten rid of Gabriel's child to save me the embarrassment of raising my brother's posthumous offspring."

Gabriel looked at his brother in consternation. "Holy Infant Jesus in His celestial nightgown."

Aaron nodded once, angrily. "I resented Marjorie bitterly for that, and hated you, and hated myself for leaving you in Spain, and all along, I should have been hating George."

"It's worse than that," George said wearily. "You're a damned fine hand with the land, Aaron, better than I ever was. You've a genius for it, and that's the God's honest truth."

"So you kept inflicting nuisances on him too," Gabriel

surmised. "Driving the cows into the pond, wetting the hay, and so forth, on the off chance I'd get wind of it and come home to investigate."

"It worked," George said. "Aaron married my Marjorie, and you came home. In the end, it worked."

Aaron's expression suggested both sadness and amusement. "And here I thought it was all my wild living that brought him home."

"The duels?" Gabriel guessed.

"Over nothing," Aaron said. "My fellow officers were complicit with my request for the usual show of drama, but nobody fired anywhere except into the clouds. I had hoped to gain my wife's notice, while she was in London buying frocks she did not want and trying to gain mine."

Had it happened in another family, Gabriel might have found the situation humorous. "What a lot of bother."

"I'll sign a confession," George said. "I'll do whatever you want. I'll swing for it, though I don't like to think of Marjorie having a felon for a father."

"Are you her father?" That from Kettering.

"Stubble it, Kettering," Gabriel said. "It matters not whose daughter she is. Aaron married her very properly here in the village."

"It matters," Kettering said. "It could invalidate the betrothal contracts."

George grasped both lapels, like an actor preparing for his great soliloquy. "My daughter might be a woods filly, but I'll not see her or Harry disgraced for my lapses."

"Continue with this line of inquiry, Mr. Kettering," Aaron added, "and I won't be firing into the clouds."

"Very well." Kettering straightened the crease of his trousers. "Where does that leave us? I doubt George can be

convicted of a crime, because he lacked the requisite intent, but there is all manner of civil liability and a significant breach of his duty to Hesketh."

"I had a duty to my daughter," George said. "A parent can't know how their best efforts will come to naught, or worse than naught, but as long as Marjorie is happy, I'm content."

"Your sentiment does you credit," Gabriel said, finding a faint resemblance between George and the old marquess about the chin, "and you are family, but a punishment must be devised."

"I've a suggestion," Aaron said. "You offer for Lady Hartle. Put right what went wrong two decades ago, George. Take Tamarack in hand and show Dantry how to go on."

"Marry Harry?"

"I think she'll have you. Particularly if she wants to see her daughter and grandchild with any sort of frequency. You've looked after Marjorie in some backhanded sense, now you can look after Harriette, hopefully with better results."

"I like it," Gabriel said. "Particularly because your tenure as steward here has to end."

"It does," George agreed. "I made a proper hash of things."

"Not entirely." Though George's honesty did him credit. "You put another duty before your duty to Hesketh. I don't fault you for that, but your methods…"

"He'll pay," Kettering said. "If he's to put Tamarack to rights, he'll need considerable coin, and it will be hard work. Erskine says Lady Hartle is all but pockets to let."

"Thanks to Pillington," George muttered. "Little shite needs to be hounded from the shire. And I have the coin."

"You will transfer half your Hesketh acreage to Aaron's keeping," Gabriel said. "Perhaps he'll hold some of it in trust for his firstborn, but that's a matter I leave to him and Marjorie. Kettering, you'll see to the deeds?"

"Of course. Are we done here?"

"Not quite." George rose, bringing Aaron and Gabriel to their feet. "It remains for me to apologize. My plans went awry, and I'm sorry for that. I'm not sorry to see Marjorie get the man she wanted."

He extended a hand. Gabriel considered a moment, then offered his own. "Forgiven, George, but it will not be forgotten."

"I understand. You'll give me some time?"

"As long as you need. Lady Hartle will require some wooing, if she runs true to form."

Aaron shook George's hand. "Give her the words, George. Grovel and flirt and tease and tell her."

"It didn't work twenty-some years ago, but she's older and wiser now, and I've considerably more wealth than she suspects."

"So be about it." Gabriel gestured to the door, and George strode off in the direction of the stairs, reaching for his flask as he went.

"What on earth was in that flask?" Kettering asked.

"Courage," Gabriel said. "Aaron, you really thought I got Marjorie with child then left her?"

"How was I to know Lady Hartle would lie about such a thing?"

"How did you figure it out?"

Aaron gave him a look of humor blended with incredulity: *I swived my wife.*

Who, Gabriel realized, would have been a virgin, and Aaron was savvy enough to comprehend that.

"We've both had near misses," Gabriel said. "Don't suppose you'd like to take on the stewarding of all of Hesketh?"

"Don't suppose you'd like going up to Town every time Parliament farts, and dealing with the likes of old Kettering here on a daily basis?"

"I'd rather do that than confer with old Danner on whether horse shite or cow shite makes the turnips grow."

"Horse shite," Aaron said decisively, then grinned. "I'd best go rescue my wife from her mother."

"Aaron?" Gabriel rejoiced to see snow once again coming down outside, heavily enough to deter Polonaise from any spontaneous inclinations to travel. "My thanks, for everything."

"Right." Aaron's grin softened to a smile. "All's well?"

"Well enough." He left, and Gabriel settled back into his chair, while Kettering looked handsome and pensive in his comfortable seat. "What?"

"He tried to have you killed," Kettering observed.

"He tried to ensure his daughter's happiness. I cannot fault him for that."

"Most would."

"Yes, well… I do too, but not enough to censor him publicly."

"So you're happy with this outcome?"

"For Aaron, yes." And even for George and Lady Hartle.

"What about for you?"

Gabriel was silent for a moment. One's lawyers were bound to hold client admissions in confidence. "You recall what I said about the greatest of my challenges?"

"Winning the fair maid. Who is packing to leave as we speak, I believe."

"She is." Gabriel rose, because the snow could stop at any moment. "And hell-bent on marrying St. Michael, who isn't a bad sort, but I'll have to kill him if he goes through with it."

"Pity. He's a good client."

"He's a good man." Gabriel headed for the door. "Polonaise is stubborn, tired, scared, and not thinking clearly. Parents bent on protecting a child can seldom see clearly what is right in front of their faces. You'll excuse me?"

"Don't do anything stupid." Kettering reached for a sandwich. "She's a valuable client, and I wouldn't fire into the clouds either, Gabriel."

"Understood." Gabriel didn't smile, and neither did Kettering.

Gabriel meant to find Polonaise, to tell her to unpack whatever she had packed, for now that lawsuits and death threats were dealt with, he fully intended to deal with her.

"Guests, my lord." The footman looked a little panicked, and Gabriel had to work to school his features to something less than a murderous glower.

"Guests?"

"A Mr. Haddonfield and his lady, from West Pershing," the footman said. "We're alerting Lady Marjorie, but because the formal parlor was in use, and there was a fire in the library, we put them there."

About damned time the rest of the reinforcements arrived. "The library will do nicely. Send along the tea tray."

"Of course, my lord."

He hadn't foreseen this, but it was fitting that the Hunt ladies gather under one roof, because much remained unresolved between them. Gabriel's steps took him to the third floor, where he meant to accost Polly in her studio. Instead, he was nearly knocked off his pins by a small female fury coming out of Polly's room.

"I saw them," Allie bellowed. "I saw them coming up from the stables, and you can't make me go back with them."

He hunkered and took her by her shoulders. "What are you thundering about, Allemande?"

"Mama and Step-papa are here to take me back to Three Springs, and *I don't want to go!*"

"You are not having this tantrum in the corridor for all of creation to hear." He'd used his most stern tones, the ones his own father had used to cow two rambunctious boys, but Allie was in a taking and not to be out-thundered.

"I can so have it here." She jammed her fists onto her narrow hips. "I can have a tantrum wherever I please, and whenever I please, and *put me down!*"

He'd picked her up and carried her bodily into Polly's room, kicking the door shut behind them, then settling into a chair with the child still bellowing her intentions in his ear.

"Allemande, if you do not hush this instant, I will tell Hildy on you."

She blinked, mouth open, then shut her mouth and smiled.

"Hildy would be on my side. She doesn't leave her piglets until they're nearly grown-up."

"I'm on your side," Gabriel insisted. "You must believe I did not know Beck and Sara were coming to call. Your mother is in a delicate condition..." He caught her wounded glare. "*Sara* is in a delicate condition, it's snowing, and I cannot think what possessed your... Beckman."

"Mama wrote to them," Allie declared. "She wrote that she was thinking of marrying Uncle Tremaine, and I read the letter as it was drying, and she started crying."

"It's hard when she cries. Did you tell her you don't like to be at Three Springs without her?"

"I like to be at Three Springs. I don't like lying about who I am."

"You're Allemande Hunt."

She gave him a very adult, very disappointed look. "I'm Polonaise Hunt's daughter and Reynard St. Michael's daughter. Sara Haddonfield is my aunt, and she is married to Beckman Haddonfield."

"Is that what you want to say to your mother?"

"No." She subsided against his chest, and Gabriel allowed her time to think. *He* certainly needed some—time they did not have.

"I want to ask something," Allie said, "not tell."

"What do you want to ask?"

"I want to ask my mama." And there was no mistaking which lady she considered worthy of that appellation.

"Now?"

"Yes, now." Allie sat up again. "If I don't ask now, she'll leave with Uncle, I'll go back to Three Springs, and she'll be gone forever, painting."

"I begin to fear you have the right of it. I'm sorry."

"It isn't your fault."

That was all the absolution she had to grant, but Gabriel still lingered for a moment in the chair, idly stroking Allie's bony little back. "She makes the choices she does to try to protect you, you know."

Allie hopped off his lap. "She makes them because they're what she wants. She's trying to be a good girl, and she's being dumb. I've had a talk with Hildy about this."

"Apparently so." Gabriel rose. His heart was not easy, not when this confrontation was coming at a terrible time for Polonaise. Though he'd pushed and pushed for it indirectly, now he wanted to protect both mother and daughter from what might be said in anger and hurt.

"You'll stay with me?"

How he wished he could. "Some things are private, Allemande."

"But when I try to talk to her, she changes the subject and starts moving around, like she's too busy to listen."

"She's too scared," Gabriel said. "I'll stay for a time, but you'll do the talking."

Seventeen

THE TWO PORTRAITS WERE CURING ON EASELS AWAY from both direct sunlight and the heat of the fire, and they'd turned out well, if Polly did say so herself. Marjorie had posed seated, gazing off to her right, while Aaron was standing, gazing down and to his left. Together, the portraits were an ensemble, the figures appearing to communicate with each other across their frames. Both parties wore expressions of tender regard, and the effect was impressive.

"Polonaise." Gabriel dropped Allie's hand to inspect the paintings. "You amaze me. These are wonderful."

"Wonderful?" The simple sound of his voice was wonderful.

"No other word will do."

"They're very good," Allie agreed. "Where did you get the idea to make two paintings?"

"From the duet I played with your mother before I left Three Springs," Polly said. "Two instruments, each with its own voice, but in harmony."

Allie glanced at Gabriel as the words "your mother" were spoken.

Polly caught the glance and felt foreboding well up, engulfing even the sadness she'd carried to be parting again from her daughter and from Gabriel. These two people whom she loved more than life looked set on cornering her, and she hadn't the strength to elude them. She was going to disappoint them, and how she'd bear their contempt she did not know.

Polly tossed another log on the fire before Gabriel could tend to it, and watched as a flurry of sparks went up the flue.

"Your daughter has something to ask you." Gabriel spoke quietly from immediately beside her. "Please try to answer honestly."

"What did you want to ask me?" Polly shifted to face Allie, who was looking at her so solemnly. "Or perhaps we should sit. This looks like serious business."

And then it hit her: *Your daughter, your daughter, your daughter...* Polly could not so much as dare a glance at Gabriel.

Allie took a cushioned chair and scooted into its depths, looking small, determined, and scared. Polly took the other chair, Gabriel hovering at her side, which was just as well, because she didn't want to see his expression as she shattered both her daughter's heart and her own.

She smiled at Allie "Ask. I'll answer the best I can."

Allie traded another of those glances with Gabriel, while he merely stood by Polly's chair and kept his peace.

"Why...?" Allie's shoulders shuddered as she took a breath. She hitched back in the chair and fixed her gaze on her half boots.

"Why what, sweetie?"

"Why... don't... you want to be my mother?"

Allie's whole face contorted with her grief. She closed her eyes, and tears leaked down her cheeks as she hunched up in a ball and tucked herself into a corner of the chair. "I know you have to p-paint, because you didn't, for a long time, and it will m-make you rich. But why can't you be my mother too?"

Polly felt a hand, warm and reassuring on her shoulder, but before her eyes, her only child was dissolving into tears.

"I *am* your mother," Polly said, closing the distance and reaching for her daughter. "I will always be your mother. You know that."

"Mothers don't go away," Allie howled. "You can paint and be my mother, but not if you're far away. You can't. It isn't right, and I *hate* it."

"Sara is the one who raised you," Polly tried, but her own eyes had filled with tears. "Sara loves you too, and so does Beckman."

"*I want my mother! You are my mother.* We have the same hair, and we love animals, and we paint, and I help you bake things, and we love *him*. Why can't you stay with me? I'll be good, and I won't bring in the mud when I visit with Hildy, and I won't argue, and *why don't you want to be with me?*" She trailed off into brokenhearted sobbing, only to be lifted into her mother's arms and held fast.

"Hush," Polly crooned. "Just hush, you mustn't take on so. I didn't want to leave, Allie, I didn't."

Polly looked up, expecting to see Gabriel's brooding frown, but he'd left. He'd heard enough, and he'd left.

Polly rocked her daughter and saved the grief of destroying Gabriel's regard for her for another time. She was going to lose him anyway, and right now, her daughter needed her.

"We must talk about this," she said, holding her handkerchief to Allie's nose.

"That's what I tried to tell you." Allie shuddered out a sigh and cuddled up. "You wouldn't listen."

"I'm listening now, but it's complicated."

"It is not." Allie blew her hair out of her eyes. "You're my mother. You should be with me."

"Maybe I should." Of course she should. "We're not the only people who have to be considered, though. I have obligations, Allie, paintings that will keep me busy for at least the next year."

"You can paint later," Allie said. "For now, can't you just be my mother?"

⁓

Gabriel left the studio as quietly as he could, praying every merciful angel in heaven would stay with Polly and Allie and see them through what needed to be said. Those tears, though, so heartbroken and sincere… they'd been more than he could stand without scooping mother and daughter into his arms.

"You're in a tearing hurry." St. Michael's peculiarly accented drawl cut through the fog of emotion and left Gabriel wanting to put his fist right through the man's toothy smile.

"I thought you were packing to leave?"

"I was, but have you seen the weather?"

"Don't let a blizzard stop you," Gabriel growled. "If you're looking for Polonaise and Allemande, they're in the studio, though they need some privacy."

"They paint together sometimes, with interesting results."

"I know that."

He knew what they painted and how their styles differed minutely and how much each enjoyed the other's critical input. He knew the exact tilt of their heads when they studied a work of art, and the particular rhythm with which they kneaded bread dough. He knew they both liked whipped cream on their hot chocolate, and they were both ticklish around the ribs.

He knew so much, except how to win them for his own.

"Something else you should know." St. Michael's pretense of lazy disinterest fell away. "I've withdrawn my proposal of marriage."

"She turned you down." Gabriel could not believe the man would cede the field for any other reason.

"She did not. She will not, but she deserves better, and as to that, she's more likely to paint well married to you— assuming you won't exert your atavistic streak and confine her to your bedroom?"

"I should be so lucky," Gabriel snapped back, "as to be confined with her, but she isn't having me either, so fear not."

"She isn't?" St. Michael's frown became speculative. "I thought you'd cleared up the business with the death threats and the lawsuits, and were now in a better position to offer."

"My offer will stand. It will stand until hell freezes over and pigs fly, but she won't have me."

"Why not?"

The question, Gabriel saw, was genuine.

"I am damned at this point to fathom her mind. I thought it had to do with my station or her past, but now, I'm not sure."

"Give it time. There's a blizzard going on, and nobody can go anywhere at present."

"Somebody did go somewhere," Gabriel said. "Beck and Sara are warming their idiot toes in the library."

"He let her go out in this mess?"

"It wasn't snowing early this morning," Gabriel reminded

him. "Come. They'll want to see you, and there are issues to sort out before I lose my bloody goddamned mind."

"Wouldn't want that. Things are dodgy enough when you're in possession of your few and feeble wits."

Gabriel marched him to the library, exchanged greetings with his guests, and built up the fire.

"Your back must be better," Beckman said. "You're tossing around firewood with veritable grace."

Gabriel rose and dusted off his hands. "I'll toss some right at your fool head. Coming all this way under threatening skies with your lady wife in tow. But now that you're here, I'm of a mind to fetch Polonaise to join us. You lot need to resolve a few little miseries that have come to my attention while she's been here at Hesketh."

When Beck gave a terse nod, Gabriel left the library, hoping Polonaise hadn't bolted while he'd rounded up the other principals. He tossed up a prayer that Allemande also would not have decamped for parts unknown before they were done, but had to track his ladies down in the kitchen, where they were preparing to enjoy a cup of hot chocolate with George.

"You." Gabriel picked Allie up under the arms and thrust her at George. "Keep your eye on him, child, or he'll have you tippling that god-awful peach hog swill."

"You." He grabbed Polly by the wrist. "You are coming with me, and not one word out of either of you."

He towed her along to the library, relieved to see when they got there that Beck and Sara were on the sofa, while St. Michael, the varlet, looked bored and relaxed at Gabriel's own desk.

Gabriel took up a stance by the window, unwilling to look at Polonaise as he began to speak.

"This assemblage will, perhaps for the first time, turn its attention to the well-being of one small child whose heretofore chaotic style of existence must come to an end. Half truths and patchwork efforts will no longer suffice, or she will make each of us come to regret it. Polonaise, you know what it means to be a young girl shuffled aside, casually allowed to believe you matter less than the others in your household. You know this, and you can ensure your daughter does not make the same mistakes you did based on such an upbringing.

"You will therefore turn your thoughts to what your daughter needs to be happy and safe in this life, and you will start, I beg you to start, by telling us what you need to be happy, because the child cannot be happy if you are not."

He turned in time to see Polly dip her head and cover her face with her hands, and still he did not go to her. From where he stood at the chilly window, he silently willed her to feel his faith in her. She was brave, she was strong, and she was going to do this for her daughter.

Also for herself.

"I need…" She took a breath and swiveled her gaze to her sister. "I need to be a mother to my daughter."

Silence, while Sara and Beck exchanged some intuitive communication, and then Sara was on her knees before Polly.

"I am so sorry," she said. "I've never said how sorry I was, how sorry I am, that I brought that conniving, scurrilous man into your life. I ruined your life, Polly, and you never once blamed me. And then I took your daughter… I am so sorry."

"You didn't—" Polly looked up as the protest died on her lips. Gabriel met her eyes with as much steadiness and courage as a human gaze could communicate.

"I hated you," Polly said wearily. "I hated you and Reynard and myself, but I never hated my daughter. I let you take her, and I'm grateful to you, but, Sara, I need her too. I thought I could finish the giving away and she'd be better for it, but I can't… I just cannot."

Sara extended a hand toward her sister. Polly closed her fingers around Sara's, and the tears started. The men reached for handkerchiefs, swallowed a few times, and carefully avoided one another's eyes, while Sara shifted to get her arms around Polly.

They held tightly to each other, until Polly began to speak again, slowly, finding the words to say the hard, true things. Sara listened, and spoke, and slowly, carefully, they began to tackle the problem like the mothers they were. Before they were done, Gabriel slipped away, because of all the people in that room, he was the one without any right to be there.

❦

Polly didn't know whether to be relieved or frustrated, but the snow made it impossible for anybody to journey on from Hesketh. Lady Marjorie had had dinner served the night before on trays in people's rooms, and Allie had dragged Polly off to bed at an early hour, emotionally exhausted by the day.

The next morning, the skies were still leaden, with the occasional flurry drifting down through brutally frigid air. Sara found Polly in the studio, where she'd gone to make one final assessment of her first commissions.

"Are you all right?"

"I am." Polly gestured to Lady Marjorie's image. "Did I make her too diffident?"

"No. She's reserved by nature but warm too, just as you've caught her. She can't help but like this painting."

"She likes it." Polly liked it too. "Her husband likes it, but I've yet to hear Lady Hartle's opinion. She's too preoccupied with impending grandmotherhood."

"Has she named the baby yet?"

Babies, everywhere babies. Other people's babies. "That is a detail. Given the way Marjorie and Aaron look at each other, there's bound to be one soon."

"And then Hesketh will have its heir, assuming you and Gabriel don't see to the matter."

"That isn't possible, much less likely." Polly hunkered to stack a log on the fire, then changed her mind. She was leaving Hesketh, and Gabriel was not likely to set foot in the studio again before she left. "The marquess hasn't found it needful to even address me directly since learning just how fallen I am. I don't think it's Allie's bastardy bothering him, or even my youthful lapse of judgment, but rather, my inability to be honest with him until now."

"The secret wasn't exclusively yours to tell," Sara said, studying Lord Aaron's portrait. "If you haven't spoken with the man, how can you know what he's thinking?"

"His silence speaks loudly enough, and Gabriel values honesty above all."

Sara took the chair nearest the hearth, the very chair Polly had braced herself against the last time she and Gabriel had been intimate.

"You owe him, Polly," Sara said. "We all do—you, me, Allie, even Beck and Tremaine. We weren't going on as well as we should have, not where Allie was concerned. And he cares for that child. You must admit that."

She would go to her grave admitting it. "He does, and

he would not hurt her by publicly scorning me, but you're also right that I owe him my thanks."

"Allie said he was going out to visit his horse."

"She did?"

"She was intent on learning how to cheat at cards from Beckman, abetted by Tremaine."

"A pair of bad influences, though it's a useful skill if Allie's to have younger cousins."

"I never learned," Sara said, rising. "I'll go supervise Allie's first taste of corruption."

"I'll want a full report."

"Polly?" Sara paused at the door. "You said Gabriel values honesty, and I think he does, but he deceived us too, when he had every reason to trust us."

"He told me some of his situation eventually," Polly said. "He was trying to keep us safe."

"We were trying to keep Allie safe. I don't think Gabriel would judge you harshly for that."

Polly said nothing, and heard the door close quietly when her sister left.

She considered the paintings again, the palpable love reflected between two people who'd not been able to be honest with each other for almost two years, the same two years she and Gabriel had been living side by side at Three Springs.

Honesty was hard, but Sara was right: Polly owed Gabriel her thanks, and if he would hear her out, her apology. Her mind and her heart might settle if she could say goodbye to a man who'd been as much lover as friend, and certainly a friend to her daughter as well.

Polly put on two cloaks, a scarf, and mittens, and made her way along the shoveled paths to the stables. Once Polly was inside the barn, Gabriel was easy to spot, for there was little other activity save the horses munching hay contentedly in their stalls. Soldier sported a freshly groomed coat and was lipping at Gabriel's pockets for a bite of carrot or lump of sugar.

"How is your beast?"

"Enjoying an excuse to stay tucked up in his stall. Why aren't you tucked up in my nice, cozy library?" He gave the horse a final scratch on the chest then led him down to his stall.

"Your library has been turned into a gaming hell," Polly said, trying to match his casual tone, despite the memories she had of that library. "Beck and Tremaine are teaching Allie to cheat at cards, and Sara is cadging a lesson as well."

"A little vice never hurt on a snowy day. You've come out in the cold to find me, Polonaise. What can I do for you?"

So reserved now. Not her imperious, affectionate Gabriel, but instead, Hesketh, escaping to the company of his horse rather than attending his own impromptu house party. When he'd put the horse in its loose box, he came sauntering up the barn aisle, gaze unreadable.

"I need a little of your time." And she needed so much more than that, too.

"If you've come to take your leave of me, we needn't belabor the matter."

"I know that." He was North again, as he'd been two years ago. Silent, self-contained, needing no one, despite shadows in his eyes and fatigue around his mouth. "That wasn't exactly what I wanted to discuss."

He gestured toward the end of the aisle. "The saddle room is warmer, and we can sit. I trust this won't take long?"

"It will not."

He closed the door to the saddle room behind them and ushered Polly to a bench set along an inside wall. The room was cozy, because the grooms had brought in braziers, and the air was richly scented with clean leather, hay, and horse.

"Might I sit as well?" Gabriel asked. "The cold has my back twinging."

"Of course." She twitched her skirts out of the way, and he lowered himself beside her, making the bench creak. Her mittens went next, so she could stall a little longer by warming her hands over the brazier.

"Polonaise?"

"I'm gathering my thoughts."

"Take as long as you please." His hands were bare and a bit less than pristine for having groomed his horse. She loved those hands, loved the ways they touched her hair, her body, her heart. Loved the competence and elegance and strength of them.

"I want to explain. You might not want to hear this, but I need to say it."

"I will listen until you have spoken your piece, and then you will listen to me." His voice was stern, forbidding even. He wanted what was fair, and she owed him at least that.

"What I want to say is…" She bowed her head as the words formed a lump in her throat.

"Take your time, Polonaise," Gabriel said, his voice taking on the soft, purring quality she'd not thought to hear again. "You needn't speak if it's too painful. These days have been difficult, I know."

"Difficult, yes, but necessary, Gabriel, and for that I thank you."

"You thank me?"

"For giving me my daughter." She wrapped her arms

around her middle. "For seeing what was before our eyes, for listening to Allie when I wouldn't, and Sara and Beck couldn't. We are in your debt. We will always be in your debt."

"You most assuredly will not." Gabriel sounded testy, angry almost. "Friends speak the truth to each other, in the general case. You would do the same for me."

"But I didn't." Polly managed only a fleeting glance in his general direction. "I didn't tell you the truth, and I should have."

He was silent, and Polly felt her heart physically aching. He was too kind to rail at her, too much a gentleman to berate her for her deceptions now. But she wished he would, because it might give her some sense of atoning for mistrust of him and her pride.

"Are you finished, Polonaise?"

She had nothing else to say. *Thank you and I'm sorry*. The most useless, necessary words in the language.

"I've said my piece." She reached for her mittens, but he stopped her, closing his fingers around hers.

"My turn."

She nodded, expecting him to turn loose of her fingers, except he laced his through hers and set her hand on his thigh.

"I will tell you a few more truths now," he said, studying their hands. "And I will thank you to do me the courtesy of listening, not simply staring at those dying embers until I cease speaking."

She internally braced herself, ready for her verbal thrashing.

Gabriel closed his fingers around hers more snugly. "First, you let the world believe Sara was Allie's mother out of love for your child. You were right to protect her that way, Polonaise, and you never tried to deceive the child herself. I cannot judge you for this, other than to conclude you are among the most loving, devoted mothers I will ever encounter."

He paused, and Polly hunched in on herself, because his words hurt as much as they healed. To hear this from him—and he would not lie to her, would not offer false flattery—was balm to a weary and heartsore soul. But to know he'd give her credit for her motivation even as they parted was ripping that same soul to shreds.

"There are more truths I would tell you," he went on, but as he spoke he eased his fingers from hers and settled his hand—warm, steady, and comforting—on Polly's nape. That he could yet touch her in such a manner soothed the pain of their separation, and she went still lest he withdraw the contact.

"Only Aaron and Kettering are privy to this next truth." Gabriel's voice dropped further. "I have a daughter, Polonaise. Well, I don't really have her. She's being raised in another's household. Her mother had provided her titled spouse with an heir and two spares, and thus she was permitted her freedom. Her husband sincerely thanked me for getting him a daughter. He'd wanted one, and he genuinely dotes on the child, but she has no idea who I am, nor will she ever. I've seen her though, and she has my eyes."

He fell silent again, and Polly saw those eyes were closed, and his expression one of old pain.

Gabriel had a daughter, one he could not acknowledge. It explained his affection for Allie, and so much more.

"I am not proud of my indiscretion," he went on, "though I am very proud of the child herself, for she is… Well, none of that. Her father corresponds quarterly, and you can read his letters, for I save them."

He went quiet again, and Polly had to wonder why he'd share something so painful and personal with her now. These were not words of parting, but what they were, she could not divine. She sat under the weight of his single hand, and waited.

And hoped.

"I had begun to wonder if a consolation hadn't come my way in the form of someone else's daughter." Gabriel's thumb swept over the soft hairs at the back of Polly's neck. "I met a dear young lady, who wanted loving and cherishing, whose mother could use the loving and cherishing just as much, if not more. I was not called upon to make a choice for my daughter; you were, and when faced with an impossible decision, you made the only one you could: you chose out of love, and this is why you must allow me the same privilege, Polonaise."

His hand moved over her hair, the merest hint of a caress, as tears spilled down Polly's cheeks.

"I can't have babies."

"You can have me and Allie and a future. We'll be Aunt and Uncle to Marjorie and Aaron's children, and that will be enough."

"I've deceived you over and over. I've lied to you. I am not chaste. I cannot be your marchioness."

"Then I'll tell Aaron to keep the title," Gabriel said, drawing her against his side. "Nothing would make Lady Hartle happier. I can remain your true North."

"You'd do that? Give up all...?"

"I've had nothing, and I've had nothing but you and your family to love. It saved me, when all of Hesketh's wealth and prestige meant nothing but duty and a possible threat to my life. The choice was simple, and had I to do it over again, I would have made you mine sooner."

"I am yours." Polly pressed her face to his shoulder. "I am yours, Gabriel." No other words could get past the soaring, joyous feelings taking wing inside her. She was flooded with gratitude and a fat, leavening portion of sheer relief, because going on without him would have blighted her soul.

"And our Allemande?" Gabriel rumbled the words near her ear, bringing his scent comfortingly close as well.

"She wants us all to stay here and celebrate the holidays with you," Polly said. "It was going to break my heart when you declined to extend us that much hospitality."

"I most assuredly do decline." Gabriel pressed a kiss to her temple. "You must celebrate not merely Christmas, but every day with me. If your relations will stay for the holidays, then there's time for a wedding as well, beloved."

"There's no hurry."

"Polonaise."

"There isn't." Polly leaned into him, feeling curiously light, and yet still she cried. "I cannot bear your child, and there will be much to work out with Tremaine if I'm not to get him embroiled in breach-of-contract suits."

"We will deal with your illustrious career and your avaricious, untitled man of business later," Gabriel said. "You haven't gotten your courses though, have you?"

Polly straightened but did not leave his embrace. "I'm only a few days late."

"Thus begins every interesting condition," Gabriel reminded her. "And unless you are content to spend the afternoon on this chilly bench, I would like to take you up to the house and turn you loose in my kitchens."

"I should like that as well." Polly rose and his arm slipped around her waist. She wished she were with child, wished she could look forward to parenting all over again, but this time doing it properly, with a partner who loved her and their child as much as she loved him and their baby.

That was greed talking, she admonished herself as Gabriel escorted her to the house. She had Gabriel and Allie, and that was more, so much more than she'd thought to have.

"What did you resolve with Beckman and Sara regarding Allemande?"

"We didn't really get down to details," Polly said. "We agreed she needs us all, including Tremaine, and Beck suggested we sleep on it."

"He wanted to run ideas past his wife, no doubt, or give us time to come to our senses."

"Us?" Beautiful word, though not accurate. "I was the one who didn't think you'd have me."

He passed her a handkerchief she'd embroidered for him months ago. "And I was the one who knew in my bones that with your daughter and your art, your life would be far too complete to take on an uncheerful fellow with a bad back, much less his title and his ring, particularly when that fellow hadn't quite put his sentiments before you. I was a coward and feared very much to lose my prizes."

"Can Aaron keep the title?" She wasn't going to dignify the rest of it with a response, but she treasured his honesty nonetheless, and his courage.

"I wish he could, but he cannot. Prinny is issuing another letter patent as we speak, confirming the title and honors and my entitlement to them. Aaron is so relieved, he's agreed to take on George's job, and leave the voting, paperwork, and commercial business to me."

"So you really are asking me to be your marchioness?" She spoke slowly, dumbstruck by the very notion.

"My marchioness?" Gabriel stopped and took her handkerchief from her, using it to wipe the last of the tears from her cheeks. "That matters little, but be mine to love and to cherish, and I will be the happiest man on earth."

"I wish you could stay."

Polly handed her sister another folded-up nightgown—if such a skimpy, lacy garment qualified as a nightgown—and saw it packed away in Sara's trunk.

"If the Earl of Bellefonte and his entire entourage are to descend on us," Sara said, "I must be back to Three Springs to ready the house."

"Nicholas isn't worried about his countess traveling in such a delicate condition?"

"His traveling coach is larger than a coal barge, and Nicholas will see to every comfort his ladies could want."

"You're nervous?"

"A little." Sara sat on the bed, and Polly settled beside her. "Beck's older brother is imposing, and though I met all the Haddonfields at the wedding, they are…"

"Overwhelming. Allie is looking forward to it, though she hasn't met them."

"You haven't either, but Nicholas will insist on fussing over Allie and congratulating you on your nuptials."

"I'd rather meet them and do a portrait at Three Springs than go up to Town with Gabriel and deal with all that parliamentary nonsense."

"You'll miss him."

"Terribly. I realize we'll have the rest of our lives together, and many married couples cannot dwell consistently under the same roof, but yes. I will miss him. He says we need our time at Three Springs, for Allie, but also for you and me. He'll come down as often as he can, and said he might escort Lady Warne if he can pry her away from Town."

"She will enjoy seeing what Beck has done with the property. How is Tremaine coping with all this?"

"He's gloating," Polly mused. "It was his idea to have Kettering put language in the contracts that all sittings shall be at the location deemed appropriate by the artist. Kettering is confident that allows me to do the work at a studio in Town, and Tremaine says he'll have an appropriate space fitted out by this spring."

"So your menfolk have the situation in hand. How does all this sit with you, though?"

Sara was not merely a sister, but an older sister with maternal tendencies getting stronger by the week, meaning there was no avoiding the question.

"I'm… adjusting." Some days; other days, she reeled. Could a marchioness reel? "We've never had menfolk, Sara, not in any meaningful sense, and you've never been without Allie. You'll miss her."

"But the change is for the better," Sara said then eyed her sister closely. "You are worried about something, Polly Wendover. Spill, or I'll tell Gabriel to forbid you the use of the kitchens."

"I'm not worried, precisely." Polly reached for another lacy confection and began to fold it. "I'm at sixes and sevens."

"I am your sister," Sara said in tones that presaged a sororal lecture on the topic of people who were too stubborn to share their troubles with those who loved them.

This nightgown had rabbits embroidered on the hem. "Were you ever late?"

"Many times," Sara said. "But… Oh, you mean *late*?"

She bit her lip, her gaze focusing on the bunnies cavorting across Polly's lap. "I was not, not until this situation got under way." She gestured to her middle. "Are you late?"

Polly buried her face in the folded nightgown, breathing in the homey scent of lavender. "I've never been late before, Sara."

Sara put an arm around her and pushed Polly's head to her shoulder. "You're carrying, then?"

"I can't be," Polly said miserably. "I heard what the midwife said all those years ago."

"The midwife?" Sara took the nightgown from her sister's hands before the thing could get mangled in Polly's desperate grip. "That midwife. What did you hear?"

"She told you and Reynard quite sternly that I wasn't to be having more children, and conception was very unlikely, because I wasn't built for it, and my labor had been long and difficult."

"You heard that?"

"Every word. Gabriel should have an heir, and I had to tell him."

Sara tossed the bunnies to the foot of the bed. "Oh, my dear. I owe you yet another apology. The midwife divined very clearly who was the father of your child and that you were used ill by your own brother-in-law. She offered that sermon to put Reynard in his place and hopefully to spare you from his further attentions. It worked, I think, but maybe a little too well. You are as capable of conception as anybody."

Polly's insides went reeling, again, and the sensation should have been familiar, but it wasn't. Not in any particular. "What about my labor being too long and difficult? It took me forever to recover."

"First babies are the hardest, or so Nicholas's countess has told me." Sara took Polly's hand. "Your recovery was difficult because of the circumstances, and because the entire time you were carrying, we were haring all over the Continent, making do in drafty inns with damp sheets and questionable rations. Our situation was little better once Allie appeared, and you were so... upset."

"I was," Polly said. "I was very, very upset." She was quiet a minute, trying to grasp the ramifications. "So I could be... carrying?"

"You very likely are, if you took no precautions. Are you happy?"

"I am... you can't know how pleased I am, to be able to give Gabriel children. We will never take our children for granted, Sara. Never." She was quiet a moment, joy expanding in a crescendo that came to a grand pause. "Good lord, what will I tell Allie?"

"Nothing for the present, because it's early days. If you tell Gabriel, he might forbid you to travel, as Beck tried to do with me."

"Beck has his reasons to be overly protective of you, but a baby. Oh, Sara... A baby and a husband and my daughter and a studio of my own and a niece or a nephew..."

"Go ahead and cry." Sara handed her back the night-gown to use as a handkerchief. "Gabriel will see your tears and demand an explanation."

"And I will give him one," Polly said, rising and passing the abused nightgown to her sister. "Right now." She paused to hug her sister hard then left the room on winged feet.

She found her husband ruining his supper with spice muffins and a pot of tea at the kitchen counter, and had to stand for a moment in the doorway, loving the sight of him.

"Come, Polonaise." He extended a hand to her. "You should have some sustenance. Your sister leaves tomorrow, and you will need to keep up your strength."

"I will," she agreed, tucking herself against his side. "If it weren't for Allie on guard in my room all night, you'd no doubt have me worn to a shadow."

Gabriel kissed her cheek. "Fortunately for me, there are libraries and saddle rooms and other locations where one can make love with one's wife, though after that little session this morning, I'd best inspect your backside for splinters."

"Eat your muffin. You may inspect at length, when Tremaine takes Allie riding this afternoon."

"He has his uses. Now, why have you been crying, beloved? I won't have it, you know. You're my wife, and crying—other than for lack of me—is not permitted."

"May I cry over good tidings?"

Gabriel set his muffin down. "This depends on the nature of the tidings. I do not necessarily consider another three years of commissions the best of tidings, selfish brute that I am."

"You don't?" Polly felt nonplussed until she caught the devilment in his eyes.

"I do not. Unless you've decided to accept a commission from a certain newly minted marquess, who wants you to paint him in the nude, and, my dear, a miniature of that subject will most assuredly *not do*."

"Well, as to that, I have accepted yet another commission, though this one will not directly involve paints, at least not for a while."

Gabriel considered her, his smile nowhere in evidence.

"You tease me, Polonaise. I do not enjoy this kind of teasing, when the limited charms of the pantry are the only ones close at hand."

She pressed her cheek to his chest. "Gabriel, I'm carrying."

His hand went still mid-slide around her waist, then detoured lower, over her womb. "Carrying?"

"Your child." Then, more softly, "Our child."

His closed his arms around her, the most tender and cherishing embrace Polonaise Hunt Wendover could recall them sharing, and then began to speak in a torrent of low whispers right to her ear.

He told her he loved her, told her he'd take unceasing care of her and of their child—of all their children, for they would have many. He told her she must endure his doting, must learn to bear up under the strain of his clumsy efforts to care for her, and give him at least fifty years to perfect his efforts in that regard.

He told her again that he loved her, and again, and again, and again.

Five days later, five years later, five decades later, Gabriel was still prone to frequent and lavish lectures along these selfsame lines, and his marchioness, his love, his wife, and the mother of his eight children, was prone to listening to every word, and believing each one.

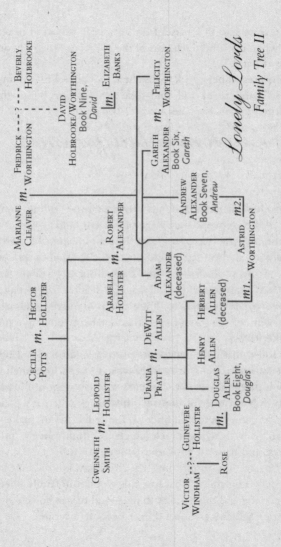

Lonely Lords
Family Tree II

Acknowledgments

A reader characterized my upbringing—"riding horses and reading novels"—as a bit of heaven, and it was. I am indebted to my late godparents, Bob and Jeanne McCarthy, for adding me to their brood of six as a shirttail cousin, and for making room for my first horse, Buck, on their farm. Bob was a professor of food science; Jeanne had a master's degree in dairy science. They made a move, midcareer, from our college town to a 138-acre farm twenty-five miles up the valley.

I loved that farm, in part because on a farm, everybody's contribution is valued. A three-year-old can help shell the peas; a thirteen-year-old can stack the hay wagon. I learned how truly wonderful corn on the cob is when it's picked only an hour before dinner. I learned how to make ice cream, can peaches, pluck chickens, mind sheep, mend fences, and have an enormous amount of fun.

If I have any insight into the "country squire" aspect of Regency England, it's because this wonderful family opened their home and their hearts to me—and to my horse!—long before I had any notion I'd ever become a writer.

About the Author

New York Times and *USA Today* bestselling author Grace Burrowes hit the bestseller lists with her debut, *The Heir*, followed by *The Soldier* and *Lady Maggie's Secret Scandal*. *The Heir* was a *Publishers Weekly* Best Book of 2010, *The Soldier* was a *Publishers Weekly* Best Spring Romance of 2011, *Lady Sophie's Christmas Wish* won Best Historical Romance of the Year in 2011 from RT Reviewers' Choice Awards, *Lady Louisa's Christmas Knight* was a *Library Journal* Best Book of 2012, and *The Bridegroom Wore Plaid,* the first in her trilogy of Scotland-set Victorian romances, was a *Publishers Weekly* Best Book of 2012. All her Regency romances have received extensive praise, including several starred reviews from *Publishers Weekly* and *Booklist*.

Grace is a practicing family law attorney and lives in rural Maryland. She loves to hear from her readers and can be reached through her website at graceburrowes.com.

New York Times and *USA Today* bestselling author

Darius

by Grace Burrowes

— ❧ —

A story that breaks all the rules…

Darius is a gripping and remarkable tale of desperation, devotion, and redemption from award-winning New York Times *and* USA Today *bestselling author Grace Burrowes. Her gorgeous writing and lush Regency world will stay with you long after you turn the final page…*

With his beloved sister tainted by scandal, his widowed brother shattered by grief, and his funds cut off, Darius Lindsey sees no option but to sell himself—body and soul. Until the day he encounters lovely, beguiling Lady Vivian Longstreet, whose tenderness and understanding wrap his soul in a grace he knows he'll never deserve…

— ❧ —

For more Grace Burrowes, visit:

sourcebooks.com

New York Times and USA Today bestselling author

Lady Jenny's Christmas Portrait

by Grace Burrowes

They share a dream…

Elijah Harrison is working on the commission that could
finally gain him a place at the Royal Academy of Artists
when he meets Jenny Windham. She is both a talented artist
and an inspiring muse, but if Elijah supports Jenny's career at
the cost of his own, he could lose her forever.

…but can only one achieve it?

Jenny is thrilled to assist Elijah with his portraits for a holiday
open house. Working with an artist of Elijah's stature is her
greatest desire…until chemistry develops between them and
other desires begin to burn. Jenny isn't sure which path her
life should take, but Christmas with Elijah might be just the
thing to light the way.

Praise for Grace Burrowes:

*"Burrowes brings to life a deeply moving
romance that's sure to be remembered and
treasured."* —RT Book Reviews

For more Grace Burrowes, visit:

sourcebooks.com

Also by Grace Burrowes

The Duke's Disaster

The Windhams

The Heir

The Soldier

The Virtuoso

Lady Sophie's Christmas Wish

Lady Maggie's Secret Scandal

Lady Louisa's Christmas Knight

Lady Eve's Indiscretion

Lady Jenny's Christmas Portrait

The Courtship (novella)

The Duke and His Duchess (novella)

Morgan and Archer (novella)

Jonathan and Amy (novella)

The MacGregors

The Bridegroom Wore Plaid

Once Upon a Tartan

The MacGregor's Lady

What a Lady Needs for Christmas

Mary Fran and Matthew (novella)

The Lonely Lords

Darius

Nicholas

Ethan

Beckman

Gabriel

Gareth

Andrew

Douglas

David

Captive Hearts

The Captive

The Traitor

The Laird

Sweetest Kisses

A Kiss for Luck (novella)

A Single Kiss

The First Kiss

Kiss Me Hello

True Gentlemen

Tremaine's True Love

Daniel's True Desire

Will's True Wish